Chasing the Dream

Never Give Up : Book Two

by

Suzie Peters

GWL

PUBLISHING

First Published in 2021
by GWL Publishing
an imprint of Great War Literature Publishing LLP

Produced in United Kingdom

ISBN 978-1-910603-90-1 Paperback Edition

GWL Publishing
2 Little Breach
Chichester
PO19 5TX

www.gwlpublishing.co.uk

Dedication

For S.

Chapter One

Eva

"Is this your first time in St. Thomas?" The flight attendant looks down at me with a friendly smile on her face as she gathers up plastic beakers and stray wrappers, reminding passengers to put their trays back into place before we land.

"It's my first time in the Caribbean," I reply, and her smile widens.

"Well, I'm sure you'll have a lovely vacation."

She moves on, making platitudes with the next passenger, not giving me time to point out that I'm not on vacation. I'm not even on holiday. My trip is for business, through and through. And I'm dreading it.

Even so, looking out of the window at the lush greenery of the island below, I can't help but feel relieved that at least my journey is almost over. I've been travelling since before six this morning, and it's nearly three in the afternoon now. Which could explain why I'm exhausted.

I can't wait to get to the hotel complex, have a shower, something to eat, and fall into bed. Because I know the next four weeks are going to be ludicrously busy, and incredibly stressful, and I want to make the most of this one evening by myself, before it all goes downhill.

I look down the aircraft at the backs of other people's heads… most of them going on holiday, I guess… not travelling on business, like me. That makes sense, really, considering the island of St. Thomas in the Caribbean is a popular holiday destination. And that's why the company I work for is building a brand new hotel down there. They have one already – the one I'm going to be staying at, which is in a place called Point Knoll – but the new one is going to be something else. It's going to be very sophisticated, featuring everything the discerning holidaymaker could wish for. And that's not the Crawford Hotels sales brochure talking. That's me. Because I helped to design it. Well… I helped to design the interior, anyway. Actually, I'm probably doing myself an injustice. I *did* design the interior. It was the first job I took on when Bree Crawford – who owns the company, together with her two brothers, Max and Chase – first brought me out to the States last June… just four short months ago. She 'discovered' me, for want of a better word, last autumn. That was during a competition I'd been persuaded to take part in, by my brother Ronan, which was being organised by a charity in conjunction with the university where I was studying interior design. Being naturally quite shy and unsure of myself, I'd been reluctant to put my work forward. But Ronan convinced me I had nothing to lose… and he was right. Because, as it turned out, Bree Crawford was one of the judges, and she liked my designs so much she offered me a job. There and then. On the spot.

I can still remember standing, staring at her, with my mouth open, and the smile that formed on her incredibly beautiful face, while she waited for me to come back to my senses and reply.

"I'm still at university," I said eventually, my voice quiet, as usual.

"I know." She nodded her head, her dark curls bouncing. "But I'm willing to wait for you."

That shocked me even more than her job offer, I think.

"I—I won't finish my course until next summer. You do realise that, don't you?"

"Yes."

"And you want me to come and work for you? In America?"

"Yes. Our head office is in Boston, and don't worry about any of the red tape… you know, the employment regulations?" I hadn't realised there was any red tape, and I knew nothing about employment regulations, but I nodded my head, pretending I understood exactly what she was talking about. "I'll take care of it all," she said.

"Where will I live?" I asked her. Back then, I was living in a rented flat close to the university campus, in south-west London. But Ronan had arranged that for me. I had no idea how to go about finding a property... especially not in America.

"Don't worry about that either," she said, brushing away my concern with a wave of her hand. "It'll be easier if I just find you an apartment and make it part of your package."

"You... you mean I won't have to pay rent?"

She grinned. "No. You won't have to pay rent."

I felt like I'd be a fool to turn down such an opportunity, so I said, "Yes." And then I spent the next eight months wondering if I'd imagined the whole thing. Obviously I knew I hadn't, because Bree kept in touch, via e-mail. She sent me through my contract of employment, and then details of the apartment she'd found for me, which made my jaw drop, in terms of its luxury. It was certainly a lot more palatial than the little studio flat I'd been living in for the last couple of years. And when I arrived in Boston in June, having graduated with a First in my course, I found the apartment – and Boston itself – to be even nicer than I'd expected.

My flat is in a red-brick building about a ten-minute walk from the Crawford Hotels offices, and it has a large foyer downstairs, with a gym in the basement. Not that I've ever used that. I'm afraid I'm too shy to venture down there. My flat itself is absolutely beautiful, though. The colour palette is neutral, with each room having a feature wall. In the living area, it's a deep grey, while the furniture is paler, with bright purple accents. My bedroom is a kind of duck-egg blue, although everything else in there, even down to the curtains, is white. And the guest room is navy. The kitchen, which is slotted into one corner of the living space, is incredibly modern, although it is a little on the small side. But Bree explained that a lot of people eat out over here, which I guess makes sense of not needing much space to cook. I haven't eaten out myself. I haven't wanted to. It's not that I'm worried about eating on my own. It's just that I wouldn't know where to go... and the kitchen is more than big enough for me.

I love the fact that I can walk to work, even if everyone at the office thinks I'm crazy for doing so, especially Bree's bodyguard, Dana. But why would I want to do anything else? Like I say, it's only ten minutes away, so it hardly seems worth catching a bus or taking a taxi. And I enjoy the fresh air. Plus the walk gives me some exercise… being as I'm too shy – or is it too scared – to go to the gym.

I glance out of the window again as we come in to land, the tarmac runway coming up to meet us, and then the wheels bumping slightly as the plane touches down. There seems to be a collective sigh of relief, which I don't really understand. It's as though the passengers in the plane were holding their breath, and now they've let it out. Still, I smile to myself, because I think I probably did the same thing on my first flight… which was only when I came over to America to start work.

Since then, in the ensuing four months, I've travelled a fair amount, I suppose. At least I have compared to the previous twenty-one years of my life, when I remained firmly settled in England… either at home in Oxford, or at university in London.

But since June, I've been to both Chicago and Houston. I didn't see very much of either city though, because I had to spend my time at the Crawford hotels in each place, working on refurbishing the bedrooms and main public spaces.

That was a task which had been given to Bree – and, therefore, to me – by her brother, Max, who kind of runs the company. Bree and her other brother Chase definitely have an equal share, but Max is the one they defer to. Not that I blame them. He's quite a commanding character. At least, he's very tall, if that counts as commanding. He's friendly enough, though… and has always been very pleasant to me, so I'm not complaining. Although other people had been… not about Max, but about the decor in some of the Crawford hotels, which was why he'd asked Bree to upgrade them. A lot of them. The list was extensive, and when he first gave it to her, I could tell she was a little overwhelmed. We were already really busy, and given her kindness to me, it felt like the least I could do to help out. So, I made us a schedule, working out which hotels were most in need of attention, and then we got on with it. And I think that, because I was so organised – or at least

I came across that way – Bree asked me to oversee the first of the refits, in Chicago, back in August.

And I hated it.

I hated every moment of it.

Bree must've been pleased with my work, though, because she sent me to Houston to do the same job there. But that doesn't mean I enjoyed the process, in either case.

I was given a team of people to work with, and they were obviously used to each other's company… and to working with Bree. She has the family name, and a lot more personality than me. And it didn't seem to matter to them that I'd been tasked with taking charge of the refits. They rode roughshod over everything I said. They undermined me at every turn, until I wondered if I should just jump on the next flight home… to London, that is. And by the end of each project, I felt so out of my depth, it seemed as though I was drowning.

I haven't told Bree any of that, because I don't want to appear weak, or incompetent. I know that handling the refits themselves is part of my job, and I'm not much use to her if I can't do it. And maybe one day I'll grow a backbone and it'll get better.

The thing is, though, if I'm going to do that, I need to do it soon. Because most of the people I worked with in Chicago and Houston are going to be joining me here in St. Thomas… which could explain why I'm so nervous. And why I'm looking forward to spending tonight by myself, before I have to face them all again.

As I exit the airport building, I'm hit by an oppressive wall of heat and humidity. I pull my sunglasses down from on top of my head, just as a taxi driver leaps from his car and comes over to me.

"Here, let me help you with that, miss," he says, taking my suitcase and grinning broadly.

I have to smile back, because he's like a ray of sunshine in his bright green t-shirt and red baseball cap.

"Thank you." I watch while he loads my case into the boot of his saloon car, and then opens the rear passenger door, waiting while I climb in. I nod my head in thanks and he smiles again before getting back behind the wheel.

"Where to, miss?" he says, turning around to look at me.

"The Crawford Hotel, Point Knoll," I tell him, and he nods his head.

"Ahh… you're on vacation," he says, selecting 'drive' and pulling out of the taxi rank. "From England, I'm guessing. In which case, you'll like the fact that we drive on the left over here. It'll make you feel at home."

Somehow I doubt that, but I give him a smile, anyway. "I'm not on vacation, I'm afraid. Although I am originally from England. I'm here on business to oversee the interior design work on the new Crawford hotel at the Mermaid's Chair?" I give my answer as a question, because I'm still not entirely sure about the place names.

He nods his head, pulling the car out of the airport complex. "I know it," he says. "My brother is one of the electricians working up there. He tells me they've been having a few problems… getting hold of supplies, I think."

"Oh… I don't know anything about that." I'm lying. I know exactly what he's talking about. Bree told me earlier in the autumn, when we first started planning this trip, that her brother Chase had informed her of some issues with the construction. She reassured me at the time that everything had been smoothed out. But then, just before I left, Bree said there were still some delays, and that Chase had flown down here a couple of weeks ago to iron them out. It's not ideal, but these things happen. And the least said about it, the better. I'm sure no-one at Crawford Hotels wants any adverse publicity when we're so close to having the new site completed.

The driver doesn't respond for a few minutes as he drives us through Charlotte Amalie. It looks lovely, with little pastel-coloured buildings, leading down the harbour.

"That's where the main part of the town is," the driver says, pointing to a turning, as we whizz on past. "That's where you'll find the market and all the restaurants and cafés… and obviously Fort Christian."

Obviously. I nod my head, taking a look down the road, even though I can't see anything. Not that it matters. I won't be visiting the local sights, anyway.

Within minutes, we've left the town behind and are on a winding single-lane road, with just the odd cluster of ref-roofed cottages, and the occasional sea view to break up the greenery. I settle back in my seat and wind the window down, letting the breeze play through my long blonde hair, smiling to myself as I think about how different my life is to anything I'd ever imagined.

I certainly never expected to be working in America, or taking on big design projects, single-handed in the Caribbean, that's for certain. It's so far out of my comfort zone that anyone who knows me would probably wonder at my sanity. I often do myself, actually.

But that's because my childhood was so sheltered and quiet. Which probably explains why I'm the same... unobtrusive to the point of going unnoticed. That's what most people say about me... "Oh, I'd forgotten you were here," or words to that effect. And I don't mind that in the slightest. I've never wanted to be the centre of attention. Not once.

I suppose that stems from my very early childhood, that abiding feeling of never really belonging. It was nobody's fault I felt like that. It was just the way things turned out.

My parents died before I was even aware of their existence, in a car accident, when I was eighteen months old. As a result, my brother Ronan and I were taken in by our paternal grandmother, who was the only parent I've ever known. She was a lovely lady, but she was quite old when our parents died. So, she sent us both off to boarding school at the first opportunity, partly because it was easier for her, and partly because it was traditional in her family. Our father had gone, and that meant we were going too. And in Ronan's case, because he's eight years older than me, he was snatched from me just a few short weeks after our parents' deaths, at the start of the next term.

Because of his absence, I spent a lot of my early youth by myself, and I think that's why I'm so shy. I just got used to living in a silent world, being quite content with my own company.

It's also the reason I found it hard to mix with other children when I finally went off to school. I didn't form any friendships, and I relished the school holidays, when I could go home and see Ronan. That is, until our grandmother died. I was twelve at the time, and he moved me into his flat in Oxford because I had nowhere else to go. I saw my chance then, and I asked him if I could go to the local school, rather than having to spend so much time away from him. He agreed. No questions asked. And life became a lot better.

It might seem odd that I'm as attached as I am to a brother who's so much older than me, but he's always been there for me. The only constant. My best friend and my only confidant. I suppose you could say he's been like a guardian angel. He remains that to this day, even though he's now back at work in Oxford, his summer having been spent on an archeological dig in Greece.

I smile to myself as a gust of wind catches my hair, because I can still remember how surprised he was when I telephoned him last autumn and told him I'd accepted a job in America. I told him it was his fault, too, because he'd persuaded me to enter the competition in the first place. He laughed and congratulated me. Then he came down to London to see me the following weekend and helped me through the process of applying for a passport, because I didn't even possess one. I was in a bit of a panic about it, even though I had months to go until I was due to start working in the States. But, as ever, Ronan was there for me. And while we worked everything out, he told me he'd come and see me in Boston… and we even set the date, there and then. We decided November would be a good time. It would give me some time to settle in, and Ronan was scheduled to undertake a dig in South America, and he thought he might be able to squeeze in a brief visit before it started. And now his visit is only a few weeks away, I can't wait to see him again.

The driver pulls up outside the canopied entrance to the hotel complex and I look up at the bright blue and white painted building. It's not quite what I expected, having been to two other Crawford hotels, and found them to be modern, quite sterile places – at least before we'd completed the make-overs we'd been tasked with. But then, we are in the Caribbean. And this isn't really a hotel. It's an apartment building, with a few beach-side cabins, and lots of on-site facilities, such as two restaurants, a bar, a café, a pool, and a gym, as well as a beauty salon, I believe. And, in any case, the Crawfords didn't build this place. According to Bree, this is one of Max's acquisitions, which he made a couple of years ago as a first step into the Caribbean. From what I can gather, he always meant to build further hotels down here, but it's taken him a long time to find the right plot of land, and then to get all the permissions in place… and then for Chase to design it, of course.

I check the meter and then climb out of the taxi, as the driver fetches my suitcase, and I take it from him. I make sure to tip him generously, because he's been welcoming and informative, and then I stand back as a porter, dressed in a quite unprepossessing uniform of beige trousers and shirt, bustles in to remove my case from my hand.

"Welcome to the Crawford Point Knoll," he says, with a wide-toothed grin, giving the driver a bit of a glare at the same time, which I regard as something of a facial accomplishment.

"Thank you," I reply, although I'm not really sure which one of them I'm addressing, and the driver gives me a kind of half salute before he climbs back into his cab and pulls away.

"This way, miss," the porter says, and I follow him through the wide double doors, into the reception area, which is wonderfully cool. Everything in here is very tropical, from the brightly coloured sofas, to the potted palms and ferns that are dotted around. And I have to say, the overall impression is a bit over-the-top.

The porter leads me to a desk on the far side of the room, where the receptionist, who's wearing a bright red blouse, turns her pearly white smile on me.

"Welcome to the Crawford Point Knoll," she says, repeating the porter's greeting, with an astounding lack of originality.

"Thank you. I'm booked into one of the cabins," I explain. "My name is Eva Schofield."

"Ah, yes… Miss Schofield." The receptionist smiles even more broadly. "We've been expecting you."

That doesn't surprise me in the slightest, and neither does the warmth of the greeting. I worked out during my previous two stays at Crawford hotels, in Chicago and Houston, that a visit from someone at head office warrants special attention. And while I don't feel worthy of such notice, I'd rather be greeted with smiles than misery.

She opens a drawer and selects a card – like a credit card, but with nothing printed on it, other than a bar code – which she hands to the porter, rather than to me.

"Gregory will show you to your cabin," she says, with a nod of her head.

"Thank you." I nod in reply, and turn to the porter, who waves his arm, indicating a door at the rear of the reception, which leads out onto the pool area.

"This way, miss," he says, repeating himself, while opening the door, and I pass through, waiting for him on the other side, as I don't know which way to go. The pool is quite large, and is surrounded by loungers, about half of which are currently occupied. A few of the sunbathers look up, some of them bothering to lower their sunglasses and assess me, I presume, as we pass by, around the side of a low hedge that encloses the pool to either side. Their gaze follows us and I'm happy to admit I'm quite relieved once we're beyond their view.

In front of me now is a wide expanse of beach, with white sand, and deep blue water… and a row of maybe ten log cabins, stretching off around the shoreline.

The porter takes off at a pace, and I struggle to keep up, eventually stopping to remove my shoes. They're only making it harder to walk through the sand… and I wonder why there's no path, maybe behind the cabins, to make this journey easier. It would certainly be more sensible. And it might be worthy of suggesting…

"Which one am I in?" I ask the porter, when I catch up to him.

"The last one," he replies, pointing to the final cabin in the row. I want to roll my eyes, because I'm not looking forward to making this trek every day… twice a day. Perhaps if you're here on holiday, and can take this walk at a slower pace, wandering along the sand, hand in hand with someone you love, then it wouldn't be such a trial. But when you're here to work, it's a nuisance.

"There should be a car ordered for me, for tomorrow morning?" I say to the porter, as he swipes the card against a reader beside the door, and the light at the top flashes green.

"There is a car, miss… yes."

I nod my head, relieved that my transport to the new hotel site is organised. Me not driving hasn't been an issue since my arrival in America, because – as I said – I can walk to work, and when I went to Houston and Chicago, I was staying on site. But here, I knew it would be a problem, and I asked Bree what I should do. She told me to have a car pick me up and bring me back here each morning and evening. Of course, being me, and not having a clue, I had to ask exactly how I would go about organising that… but Bree was as kind and helpful as ever, and said she'd do it for me. And, thank goodness, it seems she has.

The porter waits for me to enter the cabin, and I step inside, letting him follow, and take in my surroundings.

The room before me is larger than I would have expected, especially as the cabin didn't look that big on the outside. Directly to my left is a small kitchen, with a breakfast bar which separates it from the main living area, where there are two long sofas, either side of a low coffee table, and beyond those, a rectangular dining table, with six chairs surrounding it. The whole of the left-hand wall, on the other side of the kitchen, is made of glass, bi-folding doors, leading out onto an area of decking, furnished with a corner sofa and table, and what appears to be a patio heater, although why you'd need one of those here, I've got no idea. The colour scheme is, essentially, yellow. But it's not the kind of yellow that makes your eyes bleed, and is actually quite cheering.

I can live with this, I muse to myself, admiring the neatly arranged flowers on the breakfast bar as I turn and see that the porter has made his way towards one of the three doors on the right. I let my handbag drop from my shoulder onto the floor by the sofa and walk over to him.

"This is the bedroom," he says, opening the first door, and I follow him inside, where he puts my suitcase on the end of the bed, and I smile to myself. The bed is simply enormous. It's made up with white bed linen, but otherwise, there's no furniture in here, although there's a large window, which overlooks the sea, to the front of the property.

Waking up to that view every day for the next month isn't going to hurt, and I tip the porter, taking the key card from him and returning his smile as he leaves. And then I hear the front door close and know that I'm alone, and I feel the relief wash over me, as I flop down onto the mattress and lie back, looking up at the still ceiling fan above my head.

"Gosh, this is nice," I say aloud to myself, and get up again, finding the switch for the fan, which is near the door, given away by the small 'fan' symbol printed on it, in red. I watch, kind of mesmerised, as it starts to spin. I'm not sure how to adjust it though, so I make do with the rather gentle speed with which it's rotating, and open my suitcase, looking around the room, and wondering where on earth I'm supposed to put my clothes, being as there is literally no furniture in here.

"How bizarre."

There's a door in the corner of the room, and I open it... and all becomes clear, as I discover a tiny dressing area, made out of a corridor really, which contains some hanging space behind a sliding mirrored door, and a narrow chest of drawers, set into an alcove, leading on to a small shower room beyond. It may not be the most roomy of wardrobes... if it even qualifies as a wardrobe, but I can make do with it. And I don't mind. It means the bedroom is completely clutter-free. And I like that. It feels very calming.

I set about unpacking, and make quick work of it, being as I've mainly brought shorts, t-shirts, sleeveless blouses, and the odd vest top, because those are going to be the most practical for working. And I've packed a few sundresses too, to wear in the evenings. I won't be going anywhere, of course, but I do like to shower and change my clothes when I've finished work.

I find some space in the dressing area for my suitcase, storing it on end in the bottom of the wardrobe. Then I go into the shower room to unpack my toiletries, putting them where I need them, before I get undressed, leaving my clothes on the floor, and step straight into the walk-in-shower.

The water is beautifully cool, and I tip my head back, relishing the feeling of it cascading over my body. The hotel has provided some body-wash, but I use my own for now. It's citrus scented, and I wash off the grime of the journey, feeling invigorated, as I step out and wrap a towel around me, fastening it under my arms.

I pad back through to the bedroom, my feet leaving prints on the tiled floor, and I stop dead…

"There's no getting away from it. I'm gonna have to speak to Trent… again." The male voice rings out loud.

"Yeah, looks like you are."

Oh, God… there are two of them. Two men. Both American. And they're here… in my cabin.

They continue to talk, although their voices have become mere background noise as I look around the room in a state of panic. There's no telephone in here… mainly because there's nowhere to put one. And my mobile is in my handbag, out in the living room, where I left it.

What shall I do?

I can't stay in here and do nothing, especially not as the bedroom door is ajar and one or both of them could walk in here at any moment… so I think it's best if I take the bull by the horns, and go out there. Because this is my cabin after all, and whatever it is they think they're doing, they can just go and do it somewhere else…

Chase

I open my eyes to searing bright sunlight and promptly snap them closed again.

Hell… I must've forgotten to close the drapes last night. But that's not surprising. I don't really remember very much at all about last night… except that I drank far too much. I was probably letting my hair down – metaphorically – because I'm finally finished here in Atlanta. At least I am for the time being, and having been here for what feels like forever, I'm keen to move on. There's nothing wrong with Atlanta, and I kinda like this hotel, but I could really do with going home. I won't be doing that, of course… because I've gotta head down to St. Thomas again, which is probably the other reason I got drunk last night… to try and forget that I've got yet more trouble-shooting to do. And, if there's one thing I hate, more than all this damn traveling around, it's clearing up other people's shit.

This job in St. Thomas has been nothing but trouble from beginning to end. First there was the land, which cost a damn fortune, thanks to the greed of the original owner. Then there were all the permissions we needed to build our hotel there, which my brother Max dealt with, thank God, because I don't have the patience for all that crap. And once that was all signed and sealed, and I stepped in and designed the hotel building, it's just been one thing after another… mainly revolving around supplies, and getting them onto the island in the right order, at the right time. I suppose I should've guessed that constructing our first hotel in the Caribbean wouldn't run as smoothly as building one in the States, but I never expected this level of crazy.

Which is why I really need to get my eyes open, regardless of the bright sunlight that seems to want to burn them to smithereens. Then I need to get showered and packed, and get to the airport… because the sooner I do that, the sooner I can wrap things up down there, then move on to our hotel in Denver… and then – finally – get home for a few weeks' well earned R&R. And I mean well earned. I've been traveling around the country for months now, and I could do with a break. But first I need to deal with whatever the hell it is that's gone wrong in St. Thomas. And I know something's gone wrong, because I've had our site manager, Trent Anderson, on the phone, telling me we're never gonna open in time. And that's not something I'm willing to accept.

Apart from anything else, I promised Max I'd get this job done… and my little sister Bree has arranged for her new assistant, Eva something-or-other, to bring her team down to St. Thomas in just a couple of weeks' time to start on the interiors… so we kinda need some interiors for her to work on. Or it's all gonna be a colossal waste of time. And money. And I'm gonna be the one who gets it in the neck, because it's my team working down there, so it's my responsibility.

I let out a sigh and pluck up my courage, opening my eyes again, more gingerly this time. Then I turn over to my left, away from the two large windows that fill the wall, a smile spreading across my lips as I come up against the soft female form lying beside me. Her copper colored hair is spread out across the pillow, and her slender body exposed, where she's pushed the sheet down, letting it twist around her ankles. She's got her back to me, but her ass is so shapely, my body responds quite naturally to the sight of her.

I have to say, this isn't an unusual state of affairs. I often wake up beside one woman or another, and it's a fairly common occurrence – as in this instance – that I have absolutely no recollection of who she might be. If I ever knew in the first place. But for now, I don't care about any of that. I'm simply giving thanks that all our hotels come with emperor sized beds, so I've been able to sleep in peace. And clearly so has she. Neither of us aware of the other's presence.

Even so, that doesn't mean I can't take advantage now that I am aware, and I shift across from my place in the center of the bed, getting closer to her, and slipping my right hand between her slightly parted legs. She moans in her sleep and I smile as she instinctively parts them wider, allowing me access to her smooth, shaved pussy, letting me slide my fingers between her wet folds, to give her clit a gentle rub with my middle finger. She grinds her hips, even though I'm damn sure she's still asleep, and I slip my finger inside her, gathering up her juices before returning my attentions to her hardened nub, which makes her sigh gently and part her legs again.

I palm my cock with my other hand, stroking it while I play with her and trying desperately to remember what I might have done with her last night… not that anything is coming to mind right now.

"Do you want any help with that?" I jump out of my skin, my hand dropping from my dick, as the whispered voice behind me interrupts the moment, and I turn my head to see a cute brunette with baby blue eyes smiling at me from the other side of the bed.

Well, well, well… How the hell could I have forgotten this?

I give her a smile, but before she can do anything, I turn onto my back and switch hands, using my left on Red's now dripping pussy, while my right goes to work on Blue Eyes. I kinda wish I could remember their names, or that I'd maybe written them in marker pen across their foreheads, or something, because I feel slightly disadvantaged at this moment. But then, I'm not sure these two will remember who I am, either… and it doesn't really matter. We won't be seeing each other again. Not after today.

Blue Eyes moans loudly as I dip a couple of fingers inside her, and I can sense that Red is close to coming, just from the way she's now grinding her hips into the mattress. And I've gotta say, bringing off two women at the same time is kinda gratifying, especially when one of them still seems to be asleep. They start to sigh and groan, almost in unison, while I try desperately to focus my mind on last night… on how this rather fantastic state of affairs came about in the first place… and whether their names might be somewhere in the depths of my memory.

I recall being at the bar, with a couple of women… presumably these two. I can even vaguely remember coming back here to my room, with one of them on each arm. Eli – my bodyguard – was walking behind, with a tiny blonde beside him, and he gave me a wink as he went into his room, which is opposite mine. But the rest of the evening is a blur. I've got no names, that's for sure… and no matter how hard I try, all I'm getting is a hazy fog of writhing bodies.

"Oh… yeah. Right there… right there…" Blue Eyes starts to shake beside me, her body bucking off the bed, and then she lets out a loud howl, her orgasm claiming her, as my fingers work their magic over her clit.

Red startles, presumably at the noise, and she comes hard, thrashing against me and screaming something incoherent.

I smile to myself as they slowly regain their breath and Red turns to face me, the two of them leaning over, and I raise my hands, crossing them over and holding my fingers up.

"Taste," I whisper, and their eyes widen as they both grab at my hands and lick my fingers of each other's juices... and my cock almost explodes, just watching them. *Fuck, that's hot.*

Once they're satisfied, they look at each other with a kind of deep hunger and lean closer, their tongues meeting before their lips do, in the most erotic of French kisses, right before my eyes. I lie back and watch them until they break apart, and slowly move down the bed, coming face-to-face with my straining cock, and I suck in a breath as they join together in an ecstasy of lips and tongues, to my sole benefit.

I close my eyes, relishing the sensation of their diligent attention, the crazy feeling of being sucked by one pair of generous lips, while having the base of my cock, and my balls kissed and licked, all at the same time. It's kinda mind blowing, in the best possible way. But just as I'm getting used to it, they stop, and I open my eyes in time to see Red kneeling up and crawling across the bed, reaching over to the nightstand for a condom. She brings it back, tearing into the foil packet with her teeth, before she unrolls it over my cock and straddles me, lowering herself down. Her head rocks back, she lets out a low moan of pleasure, and I smile as Blue Eyes, who's kneeling beside me, leans in, circling her fingertips over and around Red's clit.

"Oh, yeah... Dani, yeah... make me come," Red moans, leaning forward and kissing her friend.

Dani? Okay... so I've got one name. Blue Eyes must be called Dani. Or Danielle. Or Daniela. Who cares. Dani works for me, especially when she's doing such a good job of bringing the woman who's riding my cock to orgasm. Red grinds down onto me, circling her hips, and then reaches up, pulling at her nipples with the forefingers and thumbs of each hand as she tips over the edge, the word, "Yes," leaving her lips over and over, until she slumps forward, completely spent.

Dani raises her friend's face and they kiss, very tenderly, their tongues touching and dancing without their lips even making contact... and a memory flits into my head. It's hazy, but it's there, nonetheless. I recall lying on the bed last night, propped up on the pillows and feeling kinda worn out. I'm not sure what we'd been doing, but whatever it was, it had obviously taken its toll and I clearly needed some recovery time. The girls didn't, though. They needed more, and they weren't willing to wait for me… so they'd gotten on with things themselves, and while I took my time and watched the show, they got into each other, fondling, caressing, kissing and licking… And once they'd brought each other off, very loudly, I was sufficiently recovered to join in again… I think. Well, I can't imagine I wouldn't have been, because just the thought of that is enough to make me wanna come…

Dani breaks the kiss with Red and looks down at me with a hungry expression on her face. And while I'd love to lie here and let her take me, I'm in the mood for something more… pro-active. So, as Red climbs off of me and lies back on the bed, exhausted, I kneel up and lift Dani into my arms before I lower her onto my cock. She lets out a sigh, wrapping her legs around me and using her arms around my shoulders as leverage to ride me hard.

"You have an amazing cock," she whispers, grinding her hips into me. "Has anyone ever told you that?"

"Once or twice, yeah." I can't lie. And why would I?

"He's good, isn't he?" Red's voice rings out and I glance over Dani's shoulder, realizing that Red's clearly not as tired as I'd thought she was, because she's parted her legs and is gently rubbing her clit, while she watches us, her eyes fixed on the point where our bodies are joined. And I have to admit, I'm kinda mesmerized by what she's doing. I want a closer look. Much closer. And with that in mind, I lower Dani down onto the bed, taking care to lie her directly between Red's parted legs, her head resting at the very top of Red's thighs.

Red surprises me then by moving her hand away, and slowly licking her own fingers while she avidly watches me fuck her friend.

I'm disappointed that Red has stopped the show, but then I love the whole concept of making two women come at the same time, and although I've already done it once today, once is never enough for me. So, balancing on one arm for a moment, I move Dani's hair out of the way with my free hand and then lean down, running my tongue along the length of Red's exposed pussy, from her soaking entrance, to her swollen clit. She gasps and parts her legs even further before she brings her hand down on the back of my head.

She's dripping… literally. And I lap up her juices, swallowing them down as I let my tongue flick over her.

Beneath me, Dani's writhing and bucking as I up the pace and pound into her pussy, while I suck and lick Red's clit. And between the two of them, their moans and sighs fill the room.

"Fuck her harder. Make her come." Red's voice is breathless, urgent, and I oblige, sensing that Red is close to coming herself… as am I. Dani's head is right beside mine in the valley of Red's thighs, and I'm aware of a building crescendo of noise coming from her, which matches the one that's coming from Red. Dani tightens around my dick at the same time as Red's hand forces my face even further into her pussy… and they both come in unison. And that's all it takes for me to explode… deep and long, and hard.

We all kinda slump at the same time, and I pull out of Dani and roll to one side, catching my breath, a smile settling on lips…

Wow… what a way to start the day.

By the time I've showered, dressed and have poured myself a coffee, the two of them are on their way. They smile contentedly and give me a cute wave as they leave… and that's exactly how I like my women. Happy, satisfied and preferably closing the door behind them after a good night's fucking.

We said our goodbyes with smiles, not kisses. We didn't exchange numbers and I've still got no idea what Red's real name is. And I don't care. We all had a good time. And that's all any of us wanted.

I'm not into anything else. I'm certainly not into commitment, or ties. And I'm definitely not interested in settling down. I know people do it all the time. Hell, my little sister has just got together with my brother Max's bodyguard. And although they're happy, they went through hell to get there. I know they'd say it was worth it, and maybe it was. For them. But that's not the life I want. It never has been.

I guess that might have something to do with our dad. He was something of a tyrant when we were growing up, and if that sounds a little melodramatic, all I can say is, you had to be there.

He planned out our lives, including what we'd study at college and where we'd work, before we were even old enough to understand what we might want for ourselves. For Bree, it was laid down that she'd study interior design and go straight onto the board of the company who did all the work on our hotels. For me, he decreed I should study construction engineering, and be employed by the firm who undertook all the design and construction of our new hotels. And as for Max, he got the top prize. He was to become CEO of Crawford Hotels itself, and sit at Dad's right hand. We all knew our places, although Max kinda spoiled Dad's rigorous planning by enlisting in the military straight out of high school. Dad got his way in the end though, and after Max was injured in the line of duty, he left the army and joined the family firm – just as Dad had always intended – and that was when Max married his high school sweetheart, Eden.

I can remember standing at their wedding, watching them together, and wondering why anyone would want to do that. Everyone there said they were the happiest couple they'd ever seen, and although I still didn't really understand the concept, I guess I couldn't argue with that. It was like they were meant to be together. They both wanted the same things, were both serious about their careers. And they were so in love it was sickening.

They'd been that way ever since they'd first met, when they were both seventeen years old, after Eden's family had moved to Boston from Portland. Max was absolutely besotted with her, right from day one. He was like a dog with his tongue hanging out, following her around, like he had nothing better to do with his life. And she was the same, from what I could see. I thought it was kinda pathetic, but then I was only a kid at the time and hadn't really worked out what girls were for. Even when I did work it out, though, I still couldn't see the point in limiting myself to only one of them at a time. That just felt like a waste to me. It still does.

But it wasn't that way for Max and Eden. So, when he joined the military, they waited for each other. And when he came home again, after he'd been injured really badly and had nearly died, she sat by his bedside, weeping and willing him to get better. He did. Obviously. And then he proposed to her, only waiting until he was able to get down on one knee without breaking something.

And she accepted. Naturally.

I can still hear Dad's voice even now, as we waved them off on their honeymoon…

"So, Chase… when are you gonna find yourself a good woman and settle down?"

I was still at college at the time, and was having a blast. Settling down – with any kind of woman, good or otherwise – wasn't part of my plan. I told my dad that and he just huffed at me and walked away.

And then a few days later, he dropped another hint… and another… and another, until in the end I snapped, and yelled at him…

"I'll work my ass off for you, Dad. In case you haven't noticed, I already have. And I'll continue to do so. I'll study hard and I'll learn whatever has to be learned. But I won't sacrifice my entire life for you. And I'm sure as hell not gonna settle down. Ever. I'm not your puppet, and you don't own me…"

I kinda ran out of puff at that point and he glared at me and then said, in a very quiet whisper, "You were always destined to be a disappointment. I knew it the moment you were born."

That cut deeper than I would ever let him see.

I'd already sacrificed a lot at the altar of his ambitions. And yet, it wasn't enough. I wasn't enough. And even though Max had defied him and gone into the military, against Dad's wishes, he was still being held up as the golden boy.

And that was how it continued. Even once I'd graduated and gone to work for the company Dad had selected, he still kept telling me how Max was so great at this, and so fabulous at that… and how happy he and Eden were.

Of course, Bree had taken a little of the heat off of me, when she'd gone to college herself, a couple of years behind me, and promptly married the first guy she met. He turned out to be a complete loser by the name of Grady Sharp. At the time, of course, Bree didn't know how miserable he was gonna make her and she seemed happy enough. Dad wasn't, and he threatened to write her out of his will altogether. It was an idle threat that he never saw through, although he gave her a really hard time. And even though I thought she'd been hasty, and probably a bit dumb in marrying the guy – as did Max – I was grateful to her, because at least I wasn't the only disappointment in the family anymore.

She had the good fortune to be living away from home, and as for myself, I did my best to ignore our father, and not to take his rejection too personally, especially where my relationship with Max was concerned. After all, it wasn't Max's fault, any more than it was mine. But Dad continued to drive the wedge between us, forcing us to compete for everything… most especially his time and attention.

That all came to an end when our father died. I was on the west coast when Max called to say Dad had suffered a massive heart attack, and I only just made it back to Boston in time. I did though, and we stood around his bed, a family united at last, and watched him pass. What Max and Bree were thinking at the time is anyone's guess. I don't know, because I've never asked them. I know the only thought that was going through my head was that it was such a waste. He had three children who'd have given anything for a few minutes of his time, and an ounce of his love. And yet he couldn't even give us that. And I vowed then that I'd never have children of my own. I mean, it's not a viable prospect anyway, given the way I live my life. But the thought of my own children looking down at me on my deathbed and feeling nothing was enough for me to make the decision. In a heartbeat.

After Dad died, of course, we inherited a fortune each, and our share of the company. Then Max brought Bree and myself into the family firm, allowing us to set up our own departments and run things how we wanted. I finally felt like I had the freedom in my professional life to match the freedom I'd always maintained in my personal one. Things were working out.

Of course, working with Max gave me constant reminders of how I'd 'disappointed' our father by not settling down myself. But I solved that problem by avoiding the office as much as possible. Instead, I traveled around the country, getting laid at every opportunity, and only returning home when either work or exhaustion got the better of me.

In the meantime, he and Eden continued to be blissfully happy… or at least that was what it felt like… until that afternoon a few years ago, when I was driving through the center of town and saw Eden getting out of a cab in the company of another man. That wasn't anything to write home about. But as I pulled up at the lights and waved out the window to attract her attention, my hand froze in mid-air… because the guy she was with leaned in and kissed her. And I'm not talking about an innocent peck on the cheek. I'm talking about a full-on kiss, in which I had little doubt there would have been tongues involved. She dropped her briefcase on the ground and returned the kiss, letting her hands wander up his arms and onto his shoulders, making it clear to anyone who happened to be watching – like her brother-in-law – that there was something going on between the two of them.

I drove away, in a state of confusion, my initial instinct being to go straight back to our offices – even though I'd only just left them – to tell Max what was going on. I didn't want to gloat. I didn't want to crow that his marriage wasn't what he, or anyone else, thought it was. I just felt he had a right to know. But what if I'd been mistaken? How much trouble would I be causing if I'd misunderstood the situation? I didn't really see how that was possible, given what I'd witnessed, but even so, I decided in the end that the best course of action was to confront Eden instead. Doing nothing wasn't an option. I couldn't just pretend it hadn't happened. Max was my brother and although we still weren't that close, I didn't like the idea of him being played.

So I went around to Eden's office the next morning. She was surprised to see me there, and completely floored when I told her what I'd seen. She didn't deny it, though. In fact, she admitted she'd been having an affair with the guy – who, it transpired, was her boss – for a little over a year. That shocked the hell out of me, and I couldn't stop myself from asking her why.

"You and Max have always seemed so happy," I reasoned, when she didn't answer me straight away. "He loves you."

"I know," she replied, staring at her desk and not at me. "But I've never been with anyone else, Chase." She sounded truly pathetic. "I guess curiosity got the better of me."

"Curiosity?" I shook my head at her. "That's bullshit, Eden. Curiosity is a one-night stand, to find out what it's like to fuck another guy. It's not having an affair for over a year. There's a big difference between the two things."

She looked up and narrowed her eyes at me then. "What the hell would you know? You've never done anything except have one-night stands."

"I know. But we're not talking about me." I stood up then and leaned over her desk. I'm not as tall as Max, but at six foot two I'm still quite intimidating, and it showed on her face. "You know Max has never been with anyone else either, don't you? You were his first, and he's been faithful to you... all the way through."

"I know," she whispered, looking down at her hands.

"Then how would you feel if it was the other way around?" I raised my voice. "How would you feel if he cheated on you?"

She paled then, and I straightened up, feeling angry and disappointed in her.

"Are... are you gonna tell him?" she said, fear written all over her face.

"No." Her relief was obvious and sickening. She sat back then, looking just a little smug, until I added, "You are."

Her mouth dropped open. "I—I can't. He'll leave me."

I shook my head. "That's a chance you're gonna have to take. I won't keep your secret, Eden. He deserves better than this. He deserves better than you." She blinked a few times then, and I wondered if she was gonna cry. She didn't. Not that I'd have cared either way. "I'll give you twenty-four hours to tell him... or I will."

I left her sitting there at her desk, staring at me, like she didn't believe I'd actually go through with it. I would have done... but in the end, I didn't need to. Because Eden came clean. She must've gone home from work that evening and told him. I know that because Max moved out of their house in Lexington, and into one of our hotels later that day. I felt guilty and responsible, even though I wasn't the one who'd been cheating, and I tried to call him, but he'd turned his phone off, making it clear he wasn't in the mood for talking, and I know Max well enough to know when to leave him alone.

A few days later, though, he moved back into the house. I half expected to hear that Eden had moved out, but that never happened, and instead Max took some time out of work. Unfortunately, I had to go away just a couple of days later, so I didn't get to ask him what was going on. I was gone for a few months, visiting different locations... and when I came back, I was surprised to find out that Eden was pregnant. Tia was born around five months later.

He's never talked to me about what happened, and I've never raised the subject with him either. It seemed to me like they'd got their lives back on track, and although Eden would occasionally shoot me a glance, I kept my mouth shut and made out like nothing had happened. I figured that, if Max could forgive her, then it had nothing to do with me. But I knew then that, in his shoes, I'd never be able to do the same thing. I'd never be able to forgive that kind of deception or betrayal. Not that anyone ever gets close enough... but there's no way I'd give anyone that kind of chance. Not ever.

Of course, what no-one saw coming was that, just a couple of months after Tia was born, Eden would become the target of a kidnapper, who picked her up outside the gym she'd just joined, and held her hostage... or that the police would screw up so badly, resulting in her death.

Max was there when it happened, and he watched her die. And because I've never known love, I can't imagine what that felt like. And I never want to. He fell apart. Not that he shared any of it with me, or with Bree. He turned to Colt, his old army buddy. And I tried hard not to take that personally. It was another situation where the rift between us was too great to bridge, and I guess he felt closer to Colt than to either of us. I wish it hadn't been that way. But it was.

And even now, although he never talks about it, the pain is visible in his face...

And that's why, every time I look at my brother, I'm reminded of why it doesn't pay to get involved...

Because love hurts.

Besides, why would I want to go through any of that when I'm having so much fun? Obviously, I don't get to wake up quite like this all the time. It's happened twice before… once after a party in Boston, when I was approached by a couple of women. And once when I was at one of our hotels on the West Coast. I can't deny the pleasure I get from having two women at the same time… and if they're willing, my attitude is, why not?

In this instance, although my memories are still a bit of a blur, even after a shower and two cups of coffee, I do recall talking to them at the bar, sharing a few drinks – or maybe more than a few – and thinking to myself at the time that I'd have trouble choosing between them. They both had attributes I enjoy. Dani – as I now know her to be called – was stacked. And I mean seriously stacked. And Red… well, she had an ass to die for. As it turned out, of course, I didn't need to choose, because they were willing to share. And there's more than enough of me to go around…

There's a single tap on my door and then it opens and Eli comes in, pocketing his own copy of my key card. He smiles across at me.

"Good night?" he asks.

I smile back. "Not bad. What about you?"

"About the same. I take it they've gone?"

"Yeah."

He nods his head and then checks his watch. "Do you want me to order up some breakfast? We've got time before the flight."

"Sounds good."

He picks up the phone, while I pack my clothes, ready for our departure.

It would be easy to resent the intrusion of having a bodyguard, but I don't. And that's entirely down to Eli, and the way he manages things between us. The need for a bodyguard only arose after Eden's death, when Max became paranoid about the rest of us, and our safety. I don't blame him for that, even though I was kinda shocked when he first told me his plan to have his old army buddy Colt Nelson provide guards for himself, Tia, our sister Bree and our mom… and me. I didn't baulk at the idea in itself, but I do often wonder what Max and Colt would say if they knew that, while Eli does his job perfectly well, he's also partaking of whatever is on offer… just like me.

Eli and I are two of a kind, really. But then maybe Colt knew that, and that's why he assigned Eli to guard me in the first place. Because on the face of it, Eli and I shouldn't get along, simply because he's ex-military, just like Colt and Max. Except that's where the similarities end, because he's nowhere near as uptight as they are. He gives me all the latitude I need to have a good time, while letting me know he's there when I need him.

"They'll bring it up in fifteen minutes," Eli says, hanging up the phone and turning around to face me. "That should just about give you time to clear up this mess."

"It's not a mess. I know where everything is," I reason. "Vaguely."

He chuckles and walks over to the window, sitting down on the couch. "How long are we gonna be down in St. Thomas?" he asks. This trip has been kinda thrown in at the last minute, so all the arrangements are a little disorganized compared to normal.

"Two weeks," I tell him. "I've gotta be in Denver by then."

"And we're gonna need the whole two weeks, are we?"

"I've got no idea, until I get down there and see how bad things are. Why? Have you got somewhere else you need to be?"

He smiles. "No. But I'm thinking about sub-letting my apartment. I'm never there anymore."

I shake my head. "I know the feeling. Still, the sooner we get there, the sooner we can leave again… speaking of which, if you wanna help me pack…"

He laughs and sits back on the couch, getting comfortable. "I'm your bodyguard, not your maid…"

"Yeah, but you'd look great in the outfit."

He picks up a cushion from behind him and throws it at me. I catch it and throw it back, and get on with my packing… because unfortunately it's gotta be done.

***

Our time in St. Thomas has been nothing short of hell.

We've been here for two weeks already and we ought to have been on our way to Denver today. That's not gonna happen, though, and I've had to call ahead and delay my arrival there by a week. I can't leave it any longer than that, because if I don't make it there by then, that project is gonna fall too far behind... and then Max will be really mad with me.

As it is, I've kept him in the dark about the problems down here, but whether I can continue to do that now, I'm not so sure. Because it looks to me like the problems begin and end with Trent Anderson.

And that's unfortunate.

Trent was one of the first people Max employed when he became CEO of Crawford Hotels, after our father died. He was a good choice. Trent's background in the construction business helped Max to pave the way for the new direction he wanted to take the company. We stopped just running hotels, buying up new ones and modernizing them... and started to construct our own. I'd been involved in the modernization side of things too, but only from a distance. And I didn't work exclusively for Crawfords, unlike Bree, who did, when she started working for Taylor & Sutton on the interior designs.

Even though Max brought us both in-house, I think he was concerned about my lack of experience in the hotel construction field, and Trent was a good fit for helping me out. I'm not going to deny that. And for the most part, things have worked out okay. It's my name on the door, and it's my department. But there have been times over the last few years when I've had to remind Trent of those two minor facts. There have also been times when Trent has made a point of reminding me he's got nearly twenty years of experience... and that I'm a mere novice by comparison. And that's true. He's been around a lot longer than I have, and he understands the business better than I do.

Except this time around, Trent isn't firing on all cylinders. That much is obvious. We're short of supplies, just when we need them most. There are problems with the labor force that he should have, and could have, resolved without my intervention. And he's letting the schedules run away with him. As for the budgets… I'm not gonna think about them right now.

I've tried talking to him before now, because it's been clear to me for a while that things aren't right down here, and every time, he's found someone else to blame. But now I'm here again, and can see how he's running the site first-hand, it's obvious he's making excuses. I'm just not sure why. And whenever I raise the subject, he finds some way to dodge the issue… or to 'pull rank' and remind me he knows better than I do.

I'm getting kinda sick of being spoken to like an errant schoolboy, especially by someone who actually works for me. And although I know some of this is probably down to me, for letting things slide for too long – and because man management has never been my strongest suit – I'm damned if I'm gonna let this project fail. That said, I'm not sure quite what I am gonna do. Calling Max is out of the question, because although I know he'd help me out, he'd also ball me out for not telling him about the problem sooner.

"You're looking kinda frayed around the edges," Eli says to me as we walk along the beach to our cabin.

"I'm feeling frayed around the fucking edges." I don't look up at him, but shake my head. "To be honest, I'm sick of yelling at people. It's not who I am."

He lets out a sigh. "Try and forget about it for tonight. We'll grab a shower and head out to the restaurant, shall we? Who knows, we might get lucky…" He lets his voice fade and I try hard not to think about the fact that I haven't gotten lucky since that night – and the following morning – back in Atlanta with Red and the other girl, whose name has escaped me. Again. God, that was good… but it feels like a dim and distant memory now.

"Yeah, maybe you're right." I turn and look at him now. He's grinning, and I smile back. "But don't let me drink too much."

"Why the hell not?" He frowns.

"Because that assistant of Bree's is arriving today… sometime… and my sister sent me a message earlier saying, as we're still here, could we give this Eva Whatever-her-name-is a ride to work in the morning. I agreed, obviously, but the last thing I'm gonna need is a hangover, while I try to explain to her that half the hotel is still a construction site."

He chuckles and says, "Okay… I'll track her down later and make the arrangements for the morning. And I'll make sure you're sober."

"And I really need to deal with things at the site," I remind him, before we both get carried away with the idea of an evening of relaxation… and sex.

He opens the cabin door, using the key card. "I know," he says, his voice quietly resigned, as I walk inside ahead of him.

"There's no getting away from it. I'm gonna have to speak to Trent… again."

"Yeah, looks like you are."

He closes the door, throwing the key card into the bowl on the breakfast bar.

"Do you want a beer?" I ask him, going over to the refrigerator in the small kitchen area.

"Yeah… why not?"

I open the door and pull out a bottle, taking off the top and handing it to him, before grabbing another for myself as he makes his way over to the couch.

"We'll drink these and then shower and head on out, shall we?" I suggest and he gives me a knowing smile, raising the bottle to his lips, just as the first door on the right of the living room opens, and we both stand there, our mouths dropping open at the sight before us.

Chapter Two

Eva

Oh, my goodness…

I'd realised that there were two men out here, obviously. What I hadn't expected was that they'd look like this.

The one standing right in front of me, by the sofa, is tall, with blond hair, a deep tan and a confused expression on his handsome face. He's wearing smart navy blue linen shorts and a white, short-sleeved shirt, and is holding a beer bottle just a few inches from his lips, just staring at me. I'll admit I'm staring back, because he's the sort of man that women would stare at. At least until the sound of someone coughing distracts me and my attention is drawn to the far side of the room, and my mouth dries as I observe the other person out here, who isn't a man at all. He's a walking god, who happens to be moving around the breakfast bar, vaguely in my direction. He's roughly the same height as the first man, at around six foot two, I'd say, and is dressed in the same kind of clothes, although his shorts are a mid-grey. But there the similarities end, because this man has thick dark hair, a few strands of which have fallen across his forehead. His jaw is square and stubbled and, even from here, I can see that his eyes are a completely crazy shade of blue. And that they're currently roaming over me.

And as I contemplate that thought, I remember that I'm only wearing a bath towel. And that I'm not even really 'wearing' it, when

I come to think about it, because it's only tucked loosely under my arms, just above my breasts, and I'm feeling very exposed under the man's intense gaze.

"Oh, God," I yelp, and without another word, I duck back into my room and slam the door closed behind me, leaning back against it and taking a deep breath, just to try and calm my nerves.

I know I'm blushing, but I'm also in a state of utter confusion.

What on earth are those two men – those two very handsome men – doing in my cabin? And why did they look so at home here?

There's got to be some kind of mistake, and the only way I'm going to resolve it is to go out there and talk to them. Because I won't get anywhere hiding in here, no matter how much I want to.

The thing is though, if I'm going to talk to them, or even berate them for letting themselves into my cabin and helping themselves to my beer, then I need to put some clothes on. So, I step away from the door, heading into the tiny dressing area, where I grab some knickers from the top drawer, pulling them on, and then reach into the wardrobe for my white sundress. It's the quickest thing I can think of to put on, being as I don't wear a bra with this, and all I have to do is quickly do up the zip at the side.

I brush my hair, leaving it hanging damply over my shoulders, because that's the best I can do at the moment, and taking yet another deep breath, I go back to the door and open it for the second time.

The two men are sitting now, on one of the sofas, although they both jump to their feet the moment they notice me. The blond-haired man gives me a smile, showing his perfect white teeth – which somehow doesn't surprise me. But the dark-haired one has a very intense, sort of bewildered look on his face, and as my eyes lock with his, he takes a half step forward and I feel a strange heat building inside me.

God, I wish I didn't feel so nervous.

Because that's what that heat must be, mustn't it?

I square my shoulders and step forward. "Excuse me, but what are you doing here?" I ask, surprised by how small my voice sounds. I know I'm naturally shy, but I sound positively pathetic.

The dark-haired man stops, hesitates and then eventually steps forward again. He even manages a smile, which makes his eyes sparkle, and that funny heated sensation, which is right at the pit of my stomach now, seems to intensify.

"I was gonna ask you the same question," he replies, with a lovely, deep American voice. "But hearing your accent, I'm gonna take a guess that you're Bree's assistant, Eva?"

"Yes, I am."

He moves closer still, offering me his hand, which I take, marvelling at the firmness of his grip . "Chase Crawford," he says and while I feel relieved that at least these men aren't strangers – not in the literal sense, anyway – I'm still confused.

"You're Chase Crawford?" It's the only thing I can think of saying, considering that he wasn't supposed to be here; on St. Thomas, let alone here in my cabin.

"Yes. And this is Eli Brooks. My bodyguard." The blond man steps forward now and shakes my hand too, before moving back again. "We've been staying here for two weeks," Chase continues, looking down at me, and I assume he thinks that gives him seniority over the accommodation. It probably does. But then he owns the company, so he has seniority anyway.

"I—I wasn't treading on anyone's toes," I try to explain. "The lady at the reception gave me the card for this room, and the porter brought me here."

Chase holds up his hands as I start to ramble. "Don't stress," he says, smiling again. "I'll work it out." He goes over to the telephone, which is on a side table at the end of the sofa, nearest the doors that lead out onto the terrace, and presses a single digit, which I'm guessing will put him through to the reception desk. "Hi, this is Chase Crawford here," he says into the receiver. "There seems to be have been a mixup…"

"Can I get you something to drink?" The voice in my ear makes me jump, and I turn to see the other man – Eli, I think his name was – standing right beside me.

"Um… yes, please."

He smiles and nods in the direction of the kitchen. "Come with me," he says, and although I still feel a little uneasy, I follow him. "We've got just about everything you could want," he adds, going around the other side of the breakfast bar, and opening the refrigerator. "There's white wine, vodka, gin, beers…"

"I don't drink alcohol," I point out and he turns, raising an eyebrow.

"Orange juice? Soda?" he suggests.

"Orange juice would be fine, thank you."

He grabs a glass from the cupboard above his head, adds a few cubes of ice from the freezer and pours me an orange juice, which he hands to me across the breakfast bar.

"Thank you," I repeat, and he smiles.

"It's not rocket science," Chase yells from behind me, and I jump, yet again, turning to see him standing by the side table, the phone clasped to his ear and a dark expression on his face. "I own the fucking hotel. Or have you forgotten?"

And with that, he slams the phone down into its cradle, taking a breath and running his fingers back through his hair.

He turns and notices me, shaking his head, just once.

"God. I'm sorry," he says, with a much quieter voice now. "I didn't mean to swear."

"Yeah, you did," Eli says from behind me, and we all laugh, which is a good thing, because it breaks the awkward atmosphere.

"Can I assume there's a problem?" I ask as Eli comes back around the breakfast bar and indicates, with a slight wave of his hand, that we should rejoin Chase in the main living area. I follow him again, and the three of us stand looking at each other.

"Yeah, you can," Chase replies, picking up his bottled beer from the table between us and taking a long sip.

"Did the receptionist make a mistake?"

"Yes… and no."

"Well, that's about as clear as mud," I mutter under my breath, and then remember who I'm talking to. "I'm sorry," I say a little louder, although I can feel myself blushing. "I didn't mean to say that out loud."

I look up and see that Chase is smiling at me, looking confused again. "Don't worry about it," he says. "I'm the one who should be apologising."

"Why?"

He shrugs. "Because this cabin was originally assigned to you," he explains. "Eli and I should have been out of here by now… and we should have been on our way to Denver."

"I know. Your sister mentioned that was where you were going."

"And I would have been, if things had gone to plan," he says, shaking his head, as though he's thinking about something.

"But they haven't?" I guess.

"Hell, no."

I smile at the way he says that, and he tilts his head, looking even more puzzled now. "Sorry," I say again. "I just liked the way you said that. It was very American."

He chuckles. "Well, I guess that's because I am… American, that is."

I stare at him for a moment. He stares back. And I bite my bottom lip, wondering what he's thinking. I know what I'm thinking; I'm thinking that he's probably the most gorgeous man I've ever seen in my life. And that I'm in the way.

"I—I'll go and pack my things," I say, putting my glass down on the table and backing up towards my bedroom door. "I can be out of your hair in half an hour. I'm sure they can put me in another cabin, or an apartment."

"No, they can't," he says, and I stop in my tracks.

"Why not?"

"Because there isn't one available. This place is slammed. There are a lot of tourists, obviously. But we've also booked out quite a few of the apartments ourselves, for contractors, and your team."

I know the five members of my team arrived here yesterday evening and I contemplate suggesting that I could stay with them. Not that I want to, after my experiences with them in Houston and Chicago, but I can hardly stay here either.

"I could…"

He holds up his hand. "Moving in with them isn't an option," he says, as though he's read my mind. "The three girls on your team are already in an apartment which is only really meant for two people. And they're complaining long and loud about it, evidently. So that's not an option." He must have asked the receptionist, though, or he wouldn't know any of that. "The point is," he continues, before I can properly process any of that, "the guys here should have told me there wasn't anywhere else available for you. And that's the reason I just yelled at the receptionist. Because if they'd bothered to tell me that, then I could have contacted Bree and delayed you coming down here."

"Even though my team are already here, waiting to start work?"

"Yeah." He sucks in a breath and closes his eyes, just for a second or two. "To be honest, it wouldn't have mattered if you'd arrived a week later. I have to be outta here by then anyway, but we're so far behind schedule, I've got no idea what you're gonna be able to do for the next few days. Your team could've just sat by the pool for a week. It wouldn't have made much difference."

He sounds really fed up.

"I'm sure there will be things we can make a start on," I say, doing my best to sound optimistic.

"Then I admire your confidence."

He sits down heavily on the sofa, his head falling into his hands, as though he's got the weight of the world on his shoulders. And with that one movement, my heart goes out to him. Despite my built-in shyness, I surprise myself and decide to see what I can do to help.

"How much of the hotel is actually ready?" I ask, moving between the opposite sofa and the coffee table, and sitting down myself, looking across at him.

"The main restaurant, and the bedrooms in the west wing are complete," he replies. "It's the kitchens, the bar, the cafeteria, the lobby and the rest of the bedrooms are that proving to be problematical."

I nod my head. "Okay then. So I'm not going to be sitting around twiddling my thumbs. I can do something?"

He manages a half laugh. "Yeah. I guess."

"As long as you don't mind sharing this place with the two of us for a week," Eli says from behind me, and I turn to look at him, thinking how unobtrusive he is. I'd forgotten he was here until he just spoke.

However, in my attempt to be of assistance, I'd also forgotten all about the sleeping arrangements, and I look around now, feeling somewhat nervous.

"We've all got our own bedrooms." Eli moves a little closer as he speaks, so he's standing at the end of the two sofas between Chase and me.

"Yes," I whisper, biting my bottom lip again.

"And bathrooms," he adds, which I suppose is true. There won't be any need to wander around the cabin half-naked. We can all stay shut away until we're decent.

"We'll respect your space," he continues, when neither Chase, nor I respond. "And your privacy. And we were gonna be driving you to the hotel site anyway, so this just makes things easier."

I hadn't realised that my lift to work was going to be in the form of Bree's brother, but Eli's right, this does simplify matters. I turn back to Chase again, wondering at his silence, and see that he's glaring at Eli, which I take to mean he's not best pleased with his bodyguard's attempts to make the situation work for all of us.

"It doesn't really make sense for me to fly back to Boston when there's work I can do here," I point out, and Chase seems to startle and focus on me again.

"No," he says suddenly and gets to his feet. "I'm sure it'll be fine. You… you should stay."

It's hardly a ringing endorsement, but what choice do I have?

"Okay," I whisper, looking up at him. He stares again, just for a moment, and then seems to come to his senses, shaking his head.

"I—I'm gonna go grab a shower," he mutters, and without another word, he turns and leaves the room, going into the bedroom along from mine and closing the door behind him.

I turn to Eli, wondering if I should offer to leave again. Not that I know where I'll go. But he's smiling, and I relax again. This is the best idea, after all, even if Chase doesn't seem very comfortable with it.

"Don't worry about him," he says. "He's really stressed right now."

"I noticed."

And it looks like having me here isn't helping.

Chase

I'd already decided I was gonna take a shower.

I decided that when I was walking along the beach with Eli, because I needed to wash off the remnants of another terrible day. It was all set out in my head; have a beer, chill for a while, then shower, change, and go over to the restaurant. And do my very best to find someone who I could bring back to bed with me. I haven't done that since we've been here, mainly because I've been too busy. Tonight, though, it felt right. It even felt necessary.

But now, although I'm standing in the shower, exactly as I expected to be, nothing feels right. Not even the raging hard-on I've been struggling to conceal for the last twenty minutes, which I can guarantee isn't gonna go away anytime soon.

And the reason for that is sitting right next door.

In the form of Eva Whatshername.

I've never been struck dumb by the sight of a woman before, but I swear, when she opened that door earlier on, I honestly thought I was looking at a goddess. I know the lighting had a lot to do with that, because the sun was behind her, and with the water glistening on her body, she seemed to glow. Her blonde hair was still wet from her shower and was dripping onto her shoulders, the droplets gliding down over her barely covered breasts, which despite the towel she'd wrapped loosely around her, I could see were rounded to perfection and really full, just how I like them. The towel hung, touching her slim hips, but it gaped slightly, revealing a hint of smooth, toned thigh. And all of that was enough to make me hard in an instant. Not surprisingly.

And that had nothing to do with the fact that I'd been thinking about going out and getting laid tonight. Or even with the fact that it's been a while, at least by my standards. It was just because she was so beautiful.

I think she was also embarrassed when she caught sight of Eli and me, because she shot back inside her bedroom and slammed the door, leaving the two of us staring at each other.

"Who the fuck was that?" Eli whispered.

"No idea."

"Well, I wouldn't say 'no'," he mused, sitting down on the couch, keeping his voice low. "In fact, I might even see if I can get her to say 'yes', preferably while I'm buried…"

And at that moment, the weirdest thing happened, and I turned to him, a strange feeling welling up inside me. "Leave her alone," I said, trying hard not to shout.

He looked up at me, frowning. "Hey, man. Calm down. If you're interested, I'll back off."

"I didn't say I was interested."

He shook his head. "You didn't have to."

I sat down opposite him. "I'm not. But we've got no idea who she is."

"And? Since when has that stopped either of us? Hell, you don't even remember the names of most of the women you fuck."

I could hardly argue with that, and yet… "That's not the point. I'm just…"

He held up his hands. "I know. I get it. You're not interested." He sat back and added, "Much," in a quiet whisper, at which point the door to the woman's bedroom opened again and we both tried to act as normal as possible, getting to our feet, like the gentlemen we both occasionally pretend to be, and looking across at her.

She'd changed into a stunning white sundress, her hair hanging long and loose around her shoulders, exposing her pale neck, and with the sun behind her still, it was easy to see her shapely legs through that sheer skirt.

And in that moment, I honestly thought I was gonna die if I didn't just take her. I thought about striding up to her, walking her back into her room, closing the door, kissing her really hard, and then pushing her back against the wall and burying myself deep inside her, making her mine; making her scream my name and beg for more.

Over and over and over.

I've never reacted to any woman like that before. I've never wanted to stake a claim, or to just take possession, without words getting in the way. But I did then.

I think I might have done it too. I'd even taken a half step forward, because the thought of her being with Eli, or with any other man, made something snap in my head, and the need in me was so great, I'd kinda lost control of my body.

She was gonna be mine, and no-one else's. I'd decided.

And then she spoke.

She asked what we were doing there, in a voice that was so quiet and delicate, I had to strain to hear her, and I knew then that she was all wrong for me. Even though she was so damn right.

I also knew exactly who she was. Her accent gave her away.

This was Bree's assistant, Eva. Of course, I couldn't remember her last name. And to be honest my poor memory was the least of my problems, because I knew, even as we were shaking hands, that she was gonna haunt my dreams. Probably for the rest of my life.

Because I knew I couldn't stake a claim or take possession. There was an innocence about her; a purity that meant I couldn't make her scream or beg. I couldn't be me. Not with her.

And yet, she was so beautiful. Too beautiful.

It was quite amazing how quickly my brain worked. In just a few minutes, while I was introducing her to Eli, and she was panicking about the mixup with the rooms, I realized that my only hope for survival was to get her out of the cabin. If she stayed, I was doomed. I wouldn't stand a chance. I knew that much.

So I told her I'd work it all out.

And I fully intended to do just that.

Except someone, somewhere, clearly hates me. Or maybe this is karma. Maybe this is all the women I've screwed over the years, finally getting their own back, and sending the one, perfect woman to torment me.

Either way, although I fought so damn hard to get Eva moved – even down to asking if she could be squeezed in with the female element of her team, in their cramped apartment, just for a week – it seems it's not to be.

Eli didn't help. He had a sly smile on his face when he kept pointing out how simple it would be for the three of us to share this place... and I knew what he was doing. He was trying to set things up between us. Ordinarily, I wouldn't be complaining, but in this instance, I was seriously contemplating how far down I'd have to bury him to ensure his body could never be found.

It's partly my fault, I guess. If I'd thought to check with the reservations desk, instead of leaving it to the hotel staff to let me know there was a problem, then I could have called Bree back in Boston, and delayed Eva's arrival.

I turn around in the shower and let the cool water wash over me, turning the temperature down a little further, because I'm getting nowhere right now. My cock is still rock hard, and it's clouding my concentration. I can't even think straight. And that's not like me.

The problem is... the problem is... if I'd delayed Eva's arrival, then I'd never have met her. Is that a problem? Yeah, it is. Because who'd wanna go through life, not meeting the woman of their dreams.

Someone who can't have the woman of their dreams? Maybe?

I let out a long sigh, wishing I could work out what's wrong with me. I'm not normally so confused by women. In fact, I'm never confused by women. Period. But that's because I don't normally give them this much thought.

And, in any case, I'm wrong.

Because I'd still have met her, even if I'd delayed her arrival down here. She works for the company, after all. We'd have been bound to meet at some point in time.

But it wouldn't have been like this. It wouldn't have been here, in a tropical paradise, with deep blue seas, white sandy beaches and beautiful sunsets. It wouldn't have been romantic.

"Romantic?" I say out loud. Since when do I do romantic?

I slam the temperature control around to 'cold', and shudder into the ice cold darts of water, staring down at my still swollen cock and wondering if I'm gonna have to wait for it to turn blue and fall off before I can actually count myself as 'in control' again.

To hell with it. The cold water is nearly killing me, and it's not achieving anything. There are other ways. I flick the water back to a warmer heat, and lean back against the tiles, closing my eyes and letting the image of Eva in that towel drift through my mind as I palm my cock. I slowly stroke along the length of my shaft as, in my mind's eye, she lets the towel drop, revealing a perfect hourglass figure, and she lets her hands roam across her skin.

"Fuck, yeah…"

I climax without warning. Hard and fast, trying not to groan too loudly as my body tenses and come spurts up the tiled wall opposite in great long streams.

I struggle to regain my breath, letting my head roll forward, spasms still rocking through me, until eventually I get back some control, and stand upright again. My legs feel kinda unstable, and I take a moment, before I grab the soap and quickly wash, making sure I've cleaned down the wall at the same time, and then I shut off the water and get out, wrapping a towel around my hips.

I wander back out into my bedroom, and pull on some clean shorts and a shirt, then sit on the bed and grab my phone, quickly checking back through my messages until I find the one I'm looking for. It's from Bree and it tells me Eva's last name is Schofield, and while I feel like I should have known that, I have been kinda busy lately.

The sound of Eli's laughter filters in from the other room, breaking into my thoughts and, for a moment, I get that same feeling I had earlier; the one that made me tell him to back off when he said he was gonna go after Eva. I'm not sure what that is. It's like a protective, jealous urge. And while I want to fight it – because it's so not me – I know I can't. There wouldn't be any point. It's like something I have no control over. Like that warm feeling I've got in the pit of my stomach right now, and that surge of excitement that's washing through my body.

And why do I feel like that?

Pathetic as it sounds, it's because I know Eva is right outside my door. And I'm gonna see her again in just a few minutes. And as hard as I try to ignore those thoughts and the feelings they seem to inspire, there's nothing doing.

I've lost control.

Completely.

I open the door and step outside again, stopping dead when I see Eva on the couch. She's laughing now at something Eli's just said, and as she turns to look at me, her laughter dies, although her pale blue eyes are still twinkling right at me.

And just looking at her, I'm hard again already.

And I know I'm screwed. I'm so fucking screwed.

Chapter Three

Eva

I turn as the door opens, stopping mid-laugh as I see Chase standing in the doorway. God, he looks good. He's changed, although his clothes are similar to those he was wearing earlier; namely linen shorts and a loose fitting, short-sleeved shirt. His hair is damp and messy, as though he's forgotten to comb it, but it looks really sexy like that. Or maybe the sexiness has nothing to do with his hair. Maybe it's because of the way his eyes are fixed on mine, darkening as he comes into the room.

"I thought you were gonna take a shower," he says, finally turning to Eli.

"Yeah, I was, wasn't I?" Eli gets to his feet and wanders towards the third bedroom, right at the back of the cabin. "I was just enjoying myself talking with Eva, and I completely lost track of time."

"I'll just bet you did," Chase murmurs under his breath, although I can still hear him.

They exchange a glance, and I feel myself blush. I'm not sure what that was about, but before I can pay it too much attention, Eli's gone into his room.

He was quite right. The last twenty minutes or so have been fun. He asked me about growing up in England, and although I normally don't enjoy talking about myself, he made it easy. I didn't go into any detail, because I don't know him, but it was nice to talk.

"Can I get you another drink?" Chase asks, moving closer. "I—I can open some wine, if you'd like."

"I don't drink alcohol," I explain, remembering that he was on the phone earlier, when I told Eli.

"Oh. Well, would you like another orange juice then?"

"Okay."

He picks up my glass and takes it over to the kitchen, returning a few moments later, with a refill, and a glass of white wine for himself, putting them both on the table, before sitting down opposite me, in the place the Eli has just vacated.

"I'm really sorry about the mixup with the rooms," he says, leaning back and staring at me.

"Don't worry about it. I'm sure we'll manage. It's only for a week, after all. And we've got more than enough to keep us busy, don't you think?"

"Yeah… we sure have." He sounds fed up again, and lets his head rock back onto the cushion behind him.

"I've heard there have been quite a few problems." I wonder if he needs to talk.

"You have?" He sits forward, suddenly alert. "Where have you heard that from?"

"Bree told me," I explain. "Wasn't she supposed to?"

"Oh, I see. No, that's okay."

"But if you're worried about rumours, I should probably tell you there are a few circulating around the office in Boston."

"What are people saying?" He frowns, his eyes narrowing slightly.

"Just that this build isn't going very well." They're actually using words like 'disaster' and 'fiasco', but I don't think it'll help if I tell him that.

He lowers his head now, into his upturned hands, shaking it at the same time. "Max won't like that," he mumbles. "It'll look bad for the business."

"I'm not sure Max knows yet."

He raises his head again.

"Well, if we can get everything completed by the end of this week, he'll never have to find out... but if I can't get to Denver on time, then I'll have no choice other than to tell him, because I can't be in two places at once."

I shake my own head now, because this is all sounding so disorganised. "What's been happening down here?" I ask. "Why is everything so far behind schedule?"

"It's not that far behind," he says, sitting back again, and taking his wine with him, sipping it as he puts his arm out along the back of the sofa. "But schedules are always tight, so even being out by a few days can be a problem... and we're out by a little more than that."

"I noticed," I say, smiling across at him, in the hope he might chill a little.

He gives me a half smile back and takes a breath. "It's the plumbing," he says, out of the blue. "And the electrics."

"Anything else?" I ask, because those two problems sound quite major.

"No. And in themselves, even those two things aren't a big deal, as long as you keep on top of them."

"And you're not?"

He frowns again. "I am. But I haven't been here all the time. I've got a hundred other places to be."

"I wasn't meaning you personally, but you in terms of... well, whoever's in charge in your absence."

"Yeah..." He rolls his eyes. "That would be Trent."

"And who's Trent?"

"He's the site manager. At least he's meant to be."

"And he's not... managing?"

"No." He shakes his head again. "He's not keeping it together this time."

"Is there a reason for that?"

Chase shrugs his shoulders. "I've got no idea."

"Have you tried asking him?" I suggest.

"I've tried talking to him, if that's what you mean." He takes a slightly larger sip of wine, looking like he needs it.

"And what does he say?"

"He blames everyone else. And that just pisses me off. If he's got some kind of issue, then he needs to own up to it, not point fingers. I hate that kind of attitude. If you screw up, the very least you should do, is admit it."

"I agree. But that wasn't exactly what I meant. I—I was wondering if he might be unwell, or something."

"He could be. But I'm not a mind reader, so if he's got health problems, then – again – he needs to tell me."

"Hmm… men are great at that, aren't they?"

He pauses and then smiles. "Not really, no." He takes another sip of wine. A smaller one this time. "I'm sorry. I shouldn't be bothering you with my problems."

"You're not. I asked the question. And while I know I'm quite new to all of this, I'm happy to help, if I can."

He gazes at me for what seems like quite a long moment, and then says, "Thanks," although his voice is a bit strangled. I wonder if there's something else that's wrong; something he's not told me. But I can hardly keep asking.

At that moment, Eli comes out of his bedroom, and I smile to myself, wondering if the two of them have matching wardrobes. And an endless supply of linen shorts and shirts, being as that's what Eli is wearing. Again.

Before Eli has even crossed the room, though, Chase gets to his feet and puts down his wine in one fluid movement.

"Shall we all head out then?" he says.

"Where to?" I ask, looking up at him.

"The restaurant." He gives his answer in a way that makes me feel like my question was rather stupid, but I didn't have any plans to go anywhere, regardless of whatever they might have decided on doing with their evening.

"You go ahead," I mumble. "I'm just going to order something in."

Chase glances at Eli, and then turns and looks down at me. "Is everything okay?" he asks, frowning.

"Everything's just fine. I'm tired, that's all." It isn't 'all'. But I'm hardly going to explain to either of them that I'd rather not eat in the restaurant, especially now I know that the people who made my life fairly miserable while I was in Houston and Chicago, are not only staying here, but are also unhappy with their accommodation, and are no doubt blaming me. The last thing I need is a confrontation with them, especially as I didn't make the arrangements for this trip. I also doubt it would help my situation if I became the subject of office gossip for fraternising with the boss. They already think of me as an unwelcome outsider; being seen socialising with Chase and his bodyguard would be the final nail in my professional coffin.

I don't look up at either of them, but I'm aware of something wavering between them, and then Chase says, "Okay, why don't we all eat here?"

I look up now. "You don't have to do that. We might be sharing accommodation, but we're not really staying here together, are we? I'll be perfectly alright by myself." My argument sounds quite reasonable to me, and yet, even as I'm saying the words, Eli is already wandering to the kitchen, and turns back a moment later, with a menu in his hand.

Neither of them replies, but they both come and sit down opposite me again, which I guess is the only response they feel they need to give me. Even so, I feel guilty now for spoiling their evening, although they're not really giving me much of a choice in the matter, and I feel tears pricking at the back of my eyes for some inexplicable reason. What's wrong with me? I know I'm tired after the journey, and I'm worried about starting work here tomorrow, with a team I know don't like, or respect me, at all. But there's no need for me to start weeping, just because two men have been kind to me.

"Do you wanna have a look?" Eli suggests, handing me the menu, which I take from him, keeping my head down.

"Thanks," I murmur, and open it. There seems to be so much to choose from, I don't know where to start, but I can feel them both watching me, and it's making me even more self-conscious.

"I know," Chase says, after a few minutes. "Why don't we just order the Seafood Platter? Then we can sit and pick at whatever we like."

I scan the menu as quickly as I can, searching for the Seafood Platter, and eventually find it.

"But it's two hundred dollars." I can't help the shock in my voice.

"I know it is," he replies, smiling. "But I own the hotel, remember? The price doesn't matter."

I feel myself blush, for the umpteenth time this evening, and hand him back the menu, nodding my acceptance. Then I watch him as he gets up and phones through the order, while Eli smiles at me with a sympathetic and understanding expression on his face.

And I wish they'd just leave me alone…

∞

Chase

Our food arrived about ten minutes ago, and we laid it out on the table, along with some wine and mineral water, although only Eli and I are really eating anything. In front of us, there's a dish of lobster, crab, langoustines, oysters, green lipped mussels, and giant shrimp, and so far all Eva has done is to look at it. She's picked, but not eaten, and I'm damned if I can understand why.

Her reaction to my suggestion that we should head out to the restaurant together was kinda weird, especially when we'd been having quite a comfortable conversation while Eli was in the shower. Okay, so neither of us had been laughing, like the two of them had been, and it was all about work, but at least I didn't make an ass of myself. Well, I don't think I did. But did I believe she was too tired to come out and eat with us? No, I didn't. She's shown no great signs of tiredness since she got here. And besides, there was something about the look on her face when she said that, which made me think there was more to her excuse than jet lag, or fatigue. Especially when Eli handed her the menu, and she seemed reluctant to order anything. She wouldn't even look at us, for heaven's sake. And as for her thinking the food was expensive…

I stop for a moment, and study her, watching as she nibbles on a shrimp, and remember that not everyone was brought up the same way as Max, Bree and myself. And that I had the same issues with Eli, when he first started working with me. Not that I consider it to have been an 'issue'. But I remember how he used to order the cheapest item on the menu, or have water rather than wine, whenever we were out together, and how I had to explain to him he didn't need to do that. Not while I was around. I could appreciate his caution, and I think seeing him like that helped me. It made me more aware of other people and their situations, probably for the first time in my life. It wasn't something I'd ever had to think about before, having been raised with no appreciation for money, or what it can buy. And, more importantly, what it can't.

None of that explains Eva's reluctance to eat with us in the first place, but I guess it makes sense of her slowness in ordering and I study her lips, as she takes a bite of her shrimp, wondering why things have to be so complicated. Because right now, that's how they're feeling. At least, they are in my head. She's doing crazy things to my body, and my mind. But I know, deep down, she's not for me. Or, to be more precise, I'm not for her.

She's the kind of woman who'd expect a guy to notice things… like how she's feeling; when she's not happy; when she needs something from him. And I'm not a noticing kind of guy. She's the kind of woman who'd want love and romance, and forever. And I don't understand love and romance. And as for forever? It's not something I even wanna think about.

I shudder against the thought, wishing now that we'd listened to her in the first place and gone out to the restaurant. I know it would have meant leaving her here by herself, but she seemed quite happy with that idea. And at least we wouldn't be sitting in such an awkward atmosphere. Eli and I could have been having some fun.

I sit back, realizing that I've finally hit upon the problem. I need to get out of here. Or, more to the point, I need to get laid. I may have jerked off earlier, in the shower, but that's not enough. That urge hasn't gone anywhere, and sitting here looking at Eva isn't helping one bit. I may not be able to fuck her, but that doesn't mean I can't do the next best thing, and fuck someone else. And once I've done that, I'll be fine. I'll feel more like myself again, that's for sure.

I finish up, my appetite waning – at least my appetite for food, anyway – and I turn to Eli.

"Shall we go and get that drink at the bar?" I suggest, like we'd made plans. Which we hadn't.

"Um… okay." He just about manages not to frown, and blow the whole thing, although he does look confused. "I guess we should just clear away first."

"Don't worry," Eva says, getting to her feet. "I'll deal with all this."

Eli won't hear of it though and, between the two of them, they stack the dishes into the kitchen.

I could help. I know I could. But that would mean getting close to Eva. And that's the last thing I need right now. Because my mind is definitely elsewhere.

Once everything is piled into the sink, ready for housekeeping to deal with in the morning, Eli turns to me.

"Ready?" I say, trying my best not to sound impatient, even though I am.

"Sure."

He looks back at Eva. "Are you gonna be okay here by yourself?" he asks, and she smiles at him.

"I'll be fine. I'm going straight to bed, and I imagine I'll be asleep within about ten minutes." She turns her gaze on me, and I try hard not to think about her lying across that enormous bed, hopefully naked, the moonlight playing across her skin. "You guys go and have some fun," she adds, and for some reason, my skin prickles. Does she think I need her permission to have fun? I'm a free agent. I can do whatever I want. And I practically invented the concept of having fun…

I don't bother to reply, but head for the door instead, and Eli follows, grabbing the key card from the bowl on the breakfast bar.

Outside, it's getting on for dusk, although the beach is well lit, and we make our way back to the main building.

"Wanna tell me about it?" Eli says once we've been walking for about five minutes.

I turn to look at him, but he's studying the sand in front of him. "Tell you about what?"

"Whatever the fuck it is that's eating at you?"

"Nothing's eating at me."

"Yeah… right." He's not convinced. But then, neither am I.

"Okay. If you must know, *she's* eating at me."

"Who? Eva?" He turns to face me now, and even in the dim light, I can see the surprise on his face.

"Yeah. Eva."

"Why? She's sexy, and cute, and easy to talk to."

"You think?"

"What? You don't think she's sexy?"

Is he insane? "Yeah, of course I think she's sexy. She's perfect."

"And that's why we're leaving her behind by herself and going to the bar, is it?" He sounds as confused as he looks.

"Yeah. Because if I stay around her for too much longer, I'm gonna go crazy."

"Well, if you want my opinion, which I know you don't, I already think you're crazy."

"And how do you work that out?"

"Because we established earlier on tonight that you're interested in her. And even if we hadn't, it's written all over your face every time you look at her. And yet, we're heading to the bar… presumably so you can act like a dumb prick."

I stop and grab his arm, pulling him back and staring at him. "*I'm* the dumb prick?"

"Yeah, you are." He points towards the cabin. "There's a beautiful woman back there… one who's actually worth spending some time with, for once. And you're gonna blow it… for what?"

"For the sake of my sanity. I already explained. And if you're so keen on her, you go fuck her!" I turn away, marching toward the bar, trying to ignore Eli's words, which are ringing in my ears. Because it doesn't matter if I'm interested in Eva. She's not for me.

I wander over to the bar, which is pleasingly busy and noisy, and attract the attention of the barman, ordering two beers, because I know Eli well enough to know he'll still be doing his job, regardless of how rude I am to him. And sure enough, within a couple of minutes, he saunters up and takes a seat beside me.

Neither of us says a word, but we both take a drink from our bottles, and I glance around the room. There are plenty of couples in here tonight, which isn't surprising. It's annoying, but not surprising. And there's a group of six or seven older women, who look like they've come away together to escape their lives, or maybe just their husbands... and get drunk, judging from the amount of noise they're making. I'm just wondering if we should move to a quieter part of the bar, when my eyes settle on a brunette, who's staring at me from the other side of the room. She's sitting facing a blonde, and although they're talking, the brunette keeps looking over in my direction, which makes me wonder whether I might be the topic of their conversation. And whether I might be in luck. Again.

It's gotta be worth a chance, anyway.

I clink my bottle against Eli's. "Don't wait up," I murmur and he frowns, as I nod my head toward the two women. He rolls his eyes and lets out a sigh, and while he doesn't normally show any signs of disapproval, I choose to ignore him and get down from my seat, wandering over to the two women. The brunette sits up slightly as I approach, which is a good sign, and then she smiles, and I smile back.

"Hi," I say, when I get to their table. "I'm Chase."

The brunette looks up, directly into my eyes. "I'm Rachel." She nods toward her friend. "And this is Sara."

I glance down at the blonde and give her a smile, too. "Hi Sara."

She bites her bottom lip. "Do you wanna join us?" she asks.

"I'd love to."

I grab a chair and sit at their table, attracting the attention of a waitress and ordering us some drinks, which she brings back really quickly, considering how busy this place is.

"I was wondering if you'd come over," Rachel says, once the waitress has departed.

"You were?"

"Yeah." She smiles. "I noticed you when you walked in."

"Well, I noticed you too." That's not strictly true, but it sounds good, and they both smile in appreciation.

"We're… um… we're going home first thing tomorrow morning," Sara says, and I turn to face her.

"Oh, that's a shame, when we've just become acquainted." It's not a shame at all. It's perfect. I can fuck them for a few hours and then walk away, on the grounds that they'll need to get up early.

"I know," Rachel replies. "But we've just been saying…" her voice fades and I lean a little closer.

"Saying what?"

"That if we're gonna go, we might as well go with a bang."

I can't help the grin that forms on my lips. "You sound like my kinda girls." I move my hands under the table and place one on each of their legs.

"Well, you look like our kinda guy," Sara says, sucking in a breath as I move my hands a little higher.

"Wanna get outta here?" I suggest, and they both nod their heads enthusiastically before we all get to our feet, abandoning our drinks, and head for the door.

"We're staying here, in the apartment block," Sara says, leading the way, and I follow, with Rachel bringing up the rear as we make our way around the deserted pool and into the main entrance, taking the elevator up to the third floor. They both keep looking up at me expectantly, while we walk along the hallway, with one of them on either arm, but I'm in no hurry to get started. They're not leaving until tomorrow, and I'm so wired right now, I could fuck all night.

We're about halfway along the corridor when a door on the left suddenly opens, and a woman comes out. She's facing into the room, talking to someone inside still, and almost backs into us, before she turns and apologizes.

"I'm sorry," she says, and then makes eye contact with me, and I want to curse out loud as I recognize the familiar features of Alyssa… one of Eva's team of workers. She's pretty enough, I guess, but there's something about her I've never liked. Maybe it's that she tries so hard. "Why... Chase..." Her voice is like sandpaper across my skin and I wish for a moment that I'd stayed downstairs. Or better still, back at the cabin, with Eva.

"Alyssa," I mumble, as she eyes the two women on either side of me.

"I didn't realize you were still here," she says, once it's become clear I'm not going to make the introductions she so obviously expected.

"Yeah. I'll be here for another week," I reply, without bothering to tell her why, because it's none of her damn business.

"Oh. And are you staying here, in the apartment block?"

"No, I'm in one of the cabins," I reply, and then wish I'd kept my mouth shut, as a slight smile curls at the corners of her lips.

"Oh," she says softly. "I see. Well, I think we're due to start working with you tomorrow, so I'm sure we'll catch up then."

Not if I can help it.

I give her a slight nod of my head and pull Rachel and Sara away. Because I'm damned if I'm gonna stand around being judged by someone who works for me.

Rachel and Sara's room is right at the end of the hallway, and we stop outside while they find their key, seeming a little uncertain which one of them has it. I glance back, but Alyssa is nowhere to be seen, thank God, and I put her out of my mind as Rachel finally opens the door and positively drags me inside.

Their room is kinda basic, although I'm pleased to note that, in common with all other Crawford hotels, it has an emperor sized bed, and being as there's nowhere else to sleep in here, it looks like they've been sharing... which makes me wonder if my luck might really be in.

As the door closes behind us, on an automatic spring, they turn to face me and it becomes clear they want to get straight down to business, as Sara leans up, her lips locking with mine in a deep kiss, while Rachel kneels, her fingers making quick work of the button and zipper on my shorts, which drop to the floor.

I'm not wearing any underwear, and my dick springs forth, making Rachel gasp, right before she clasps it around the base and strokes slowly along my length.

"Look, Sara," she whispers, her voice a little husky now. "I told you he'd be huge."

I can't help smiling, even as Sara breaks the kiss and looks down at my cock, her eyes widening.

"Oh my God," she breathes, and joins her friend, kneeling at my feet, and while Rachel continues to stroke me, Sara takes me in her mouth and I close my eyes, just as my brain does the weirdest thing; something it's never done before.

It shuts down.

In spite of the fact that, when I open my eyes again, I can see two gorgeous women devoting their very best attentions to my needs, and even though I'm aware of Rachel's hands and Sara's lips and tongue, I can't actually feel a thing. Even when Rachel stands and removes her top, revealing her firm, rounded breasts, it's like I'm not really here, and this isn't really happening.

I close my eyes again, hoping I can somehow regain the moment. But all I can see is Eva's face, shrouded with disappointment, her eyes sad and bewildered. And then the unthinkable happens. My cock shrinks. Oh, Jesus. This is so embarrassing.

I'm trying to work out what to do to get myself out of here, when Sara stops sucking me and stands. I'm not sure whether she's noticed my uninspired reaction, or whether she just feels like a change of scenery, but either way, she takes her top off too, and turns to Rachel, kissing her. Their hands roam over each other's bodies, and for a moment, I wonder about taking a seat and watching for a while, to see if I can get motivated again.

But then I realize that's not going to work. Because I don't belong here.

"I'm sorry," I mutter, and they break their kiss and look over, their eyes clouded with lust. "I'm not feeling well."

They both pout and turn to face me, Rachel letting her hands rest on my chest. "You can stay for a while if you like," she purrs. "I'm sure you'll like what you see."

I smile, even though I've never felt sicker in my life. "Sorry," I repeat. "I really need to go."

I pull up my shorts, fastening them as I speak, and then I turn and open the door, bolting through before I pull it closed, and lean against the wall outside, dragging air into my lungs.

I've got no idea what's going on here, but whatever it is, I need to work it out… before that happens again.

I make my way back downstairs, going straight outside and around the pool, figuring I may as well head back to the cabin, being as tonight has turned into a raging disaster.

"That was quick." I flip around at the sound of Eli's voice and see him lying on one of the loungers at the poolside, his beer bottle in his hand.

I wander over and take a seat beside him, letting my elbows rest on my knees as I shake my head.

"What happened?" he asks.

I contemplate lying, but what would be the point? "I couldn't get it up," I say, lowering my head.

"What?" I can hear the shock in his voice.

"I know you heard me, Eli, and I'm not repeating myself." I look up at him to find he's staring at me, perplexed. "There were two of them," I continue, a bit unnecessarily. "*Two.* And I couldn't…" I let my voice fade.

"Man, you have got it bad," he says.

"What are you talking about?"

"Eva."

"This has nothing to do with her."

"Yeah it does. You like her. A lot."

"No, I don't."

He sits up, twisting around, and puts down his beer bottle on the ground before standing. "Okay, I'll go fuck her then, shall I? Like you suggested."

He moves away, but I'm on my feet in an instant, right in his face. "You go near her and I'll break you," I growl. "And then I'll fire you."

He smiles at me, taking a half step backwards, while holding up his hands in surrender. "I'd like to see you break me. But I get the message. I got it the first time, when you told me to back off. And even if you can't see it – or you're just choosing not to – you've got it bad. Whether you like it or not."

I sit back down on the lounger, my head in my hands.

"What the hell am I gonna do?" I say, almost to myself. "I've never been in this position before."

"What position would that be?" I'm aware of Eli sitting opposite me again, and I look up at him, scowling.

"You know what I'm talking about."

He shrugs, doing his best to look innocent, having clearly decided he's gonna make this hard for me. "No," he says, shaking his head. "You tell me."

I suck in a breath, letting it out slowly as I lean back. "I want her," I say simply, because it's the truth.

Eli smiles. "I know. That much is fucking obvious."

"Okay… but this is different. *She's* different. I don't just want her. I *want* her."

He grins. "To quote Eva, that's about as clear as mud."

I shake my head at him. "You've seen her. You've spoken to her. She's not gonna respond well to a guy like me."

He tilts his head to the left, and then the right, like he's thinking and then says, "Okay then, don't be you."

"What?" That doesn't make sense. "How can I be someone I'm not?"

"Has it ever occurred to you that maybe the guy you're being now isn't really you. And that maybe the man you could be with Eva is exactly who were always supposed to be?"

"If I understood what that meant, I might be able to agree with it."

"I'm just saying, you've never tried being different. But if you did, you might find you actually like it."

"Different?" I echo, giving the matter some serious thought.

"Yeah. You know? Romantic, committed, monogamous…"

"Jesus! Stop talking right now. You're scaring me." I get to my feet and he laughs out loud. "What you're suggesting… it's impossible. I've spent all my adult life avoiding it. Where would I even start? I mean, I wouldn't know how," I mutter and he stands too.

"So you'd rather carry on as you are now, would you?" he says, shaking his head and looking at me like the pitiful wreck I am.

"No."

"Then why not give things a chance with Eva?"

"And how exactly am I supposed to do that?"

"Well, there is this really old-fashioned concept called dating. You could start there."

"I've never dated anyone before in my life," I admit.

He shakes his head and comes to stand beside me, putting his arm around my shoulder. "There's a first time for everything, my friend," he says, and releases me, chuckling as he wanders off toward the beach.

Chapter Four

Eva

I've slept really well.

But then the bed here is absolutely enormous, and judging from the mess I've made of the sheets, I think I've used up most of it during the night, because I seem to have completely trashed it. Still, I think someone comes in and makes up the beds every day, and tidies the cabin too, so hopefully they'll be able to make sense of the tangled web I've left on the mattress. Because I need to get a move on.

I've slightly overslept, and I dash through the shower, braiding my damp hair for speed, and putting on a pair of shorts and a sleeveless blouse, before opening my bedroom door for the first time today, to see Chase already sitting at the dining table, studying his phone. He still looks gorgeous, and very relaxed, and that warm feeling I had in the pit of my stomach yesterday seems to be back again. And I struggle not to blush as he glances up when I come out into the main room.

"Good morning," he says, smiling over at me. "I wasn't sure what you wanted for breakfast, so I ordered a selection."

I look down at the table, and only now notice that it's loaded with food. There's fresh fruit, muffins, bagels with smoked salmon, pastries, and stacked pancakes with a jug of maple syrup on the side, and it all looks delicious. My stomach grumbles, reminding me I didn't eat very much last night, because I was too wound up and nervous by the time the food arrived to consume any of it.

"Thank you." I smile back and take a seat at the table opposite him, helping myself to a lemon muffin and taking a small bite. He puts down his phone and picks up a piece of mango, popping it into his mouth, and my eyes are drawn to his generous lips. For a brief second, my mind drifts and I wonder what it would be like to be kissed by him, to be held in his strong arms, against that hard, muscular chest, to lie...

"Eva?" His voice brings me out of my daydream, and I feel my cheeks flush, knowing what I was just thinking about.

"Yes?" I struggle to regain some composure.

"I just asked if you'd like some coffee?"

"Oh. Yes please."

I take another bite of my muffin and look around the room. "Where's Eli?"

"He's up in the main building," he explains, pouring me a coffee and pushing the cup in my direction. "There's some kind of issue with their security system, and he's gone to look at it for them. It's not really his job, but he's into security – kind of – so he said he'd see what he could do."

"Oh. I see."

Chase tops up his own coffee and takes a sip, looking at me over the rim of his cup "I'm gonna have to call Max later on, I think, and talk to him about maybe putting in some new management down here."

"They don't seem very efficient, do they? Although I'm no expert."

"You're not?" He looks surprised. "You work for Crawford Hotels, but you're not an expert?"

I chuckle. "In hotels? No. I'm an interior designer, remember? And before I came to America, I'd never even stayed in a hotel before."

"You're kidding me," he says, frowning.

"No." I shake my head, and sip my coffee. "I had a really, really sheltered upbringing."

"How sheltered?" he asks, helping himself to some pancakes and putting them on the plate before him, adding a handful of blueberries.

"Very." I pause for a moment, because while I want to explain myself to him, it's always hard getting through the first part of my story. Not that I reveal it to many people. I didn't tell Eli last night, for example... but somehow Chase is different. And I want to tell him. Everything. "My parents died when I was a baby," I begin, keeping my eyes fixed on the coffee pot. "So my brother and I moved in with our grandmother. She was quite elderly when she took us on. Lovely, kind... but quite elderly. She couldn't really cope with both of us, so she sent us to boarding school as soon as we were old enough. My brother didn't mind so much, but I hated it... I found it a very lonely existence. Except the school holidays, when I could be with Ronan again..."

"Who's Ronan?"

I glance up to find Chase staring at me. "Oh, sorry... he's my brother."

He nods his head. "Go on," he says with an encouraging smile.

"Our grandmother died when I was twelve," I continue, "and that's when I moved into Ronan's flat. We agreed I could go to the local school, and well... he's looked after me ever since."

"Do you see much of him?" Chase asks.

"Not as much as I'd like. He's an archeology lecturer, which sounds very stuffy, even though he isn't. But it means he's either cooped up in Oxford, or on a dig somewhere. H—He's coming to visit me next month, though." I can't disguise the excitement in my voice and Chase clearly picks up on it, because he smiles again, and this time, his eyes sparkle.

"If he's a lecturer, shouldn't he be teaching in November, rather than visiting his sister?" he asks.

"Hmm... probably. I'm not entirely sure what's going on with him at the moment. He's got a dig scheduled, in Peru, I think. But we haven't been able to talk about it. So I don't really know why he's got so much free time in the middle of the semester."

"As long as he hasn't been fired," Chase says, clearly joking.

"I hope not. He wouldn't be able to fly around to all these different dig sites – or come and see me – if that were the case."

"You're looking forward to his visit," he says, and although it's not a question, I nod my head.

"Yes. I am. He makes me feel safe." God... why on earth did I say that out loud?

"Safe?" he queries, sitting forward slightly.

"Yes. I've always been a bit insecure. But I probably shouldn't have said that."

"Why not?" He frowns slightly, although the expression doesn't diminish the perfection of his face.

"Well, because it's… it's personal."

"Yes, it is. But that's no reason not to say it," he replies, and the corners of his lips twitch upwards. Which, oddly enough, means that mine do the same.

Once we've finished eating, Chase calls Eli to find out where he is, and how long he's going to be, and when he puts down his phone, informs me that Eli is just on his way back, and that we should probably get ready to leave for the other side of the island.

"How long does it take to get there?" I ask him, getting up from the table.

"About twenty minutes."

"Okay. I'll just grab my things. I won't be long."

I head back into my room, where I pick up my laptop and the roll of plans I brought with me, which are in a long cardboard tube, and I carry them both out into the main room.

"Do you need any help?" Chase asks, taking a last sip of his coffee.

"No, thanks. That's everything I need to take." I put my things down on the sofa and turn to him. "I meant to ask, did you have a nice time last night?" He chokes, putting his cup down, coughing hard, and I hurry over, patting him on the back. "Are you okay?"

He nods his head and finally regains control. "Yeah. Sorry."

"Don't be."

I move away from him, just as the door to the cabin opens and Eli steps inside.

"Good morning," he says, all bright and breezy.

"Hello." I smile across at him.

"Are we ready to go?" He looks from me to Chase, who nods his head.

"Yeah, I guess," Chase replies, pocketing his phone before he goes over to the sofa and picks up my things, handing the tube to Eli and putting my laptop under his arm.

"I can carry those," I say, but he shakes his head.

"Don't worry about it."

Eli grins and picks up the car keys from the bowl on the breakfast bar, and grabbing my handbag from the floor, we all head out.

They walk on either side of me, and before we've gone too far, I turn to Chase. "I was thinking yesterday, when I got here, that it would be so much easier if there was a pathway that led behind the cabins, rather than having to traipse along the beach."

He looks down at me. "Yeah, it would, wouldn't it?" His eyes dart over my head to Eli. "Why didn't you think of that?" he says.

"It's above my pay grade," Eli replies, and we all laugh.

"I'll suggest it to Max the next time I speak to him," Chase says. "But apart from having to clear out some of the foliage behind the cabins, I can't see why it wouldn't work… and make life a lot easier."

I smile up at him. "Well, you might want to see what other people think first, before you put it to Max. I'm probably not the best judge of these things. And I'm sure a lot of people think it's very romantic to walk along the beach. But…"

"Is it?" he says, looking down at me, a confused expression on his face. "Is it romantic?"

It's almost as if he doesn't know and is looking for the answer, but then I know little of romance myself. "Well, I guess it is, if you've got nothing better to do. But when I arrived here yesterday evening, all I wanted was to have a shower and fall into bed. I didn't particularly want to trek along half a mile of sand first. Maybe if I'd had someone to trek along the sand with, I'd have felt differently… but as it was…" I let my voice fade, aware that Chase is still staring at me. "Is something the matter?"

"No," he says quickly. "Not at all."

The drive to the Mermaid's Chair doesn't take too long. Chase sits up front in the Jeep with Eli, who drives with confidence, like he knows the roads well. For myself, as the journey progresses, I become more and more anxious, and by the time we arrive and I take in the building site before me, I'm almost shaking with fear and I can barely control my nerves as Chase helps me out of the car.

"Are you okay?" he asks, looking into my face.

"Yes, thanks," I lie, attempting a smile.

"I know it's a train wreck," he says, turning and looking at the building behind him.

He's not kidding. Although I can see the structure, which is complete, and the aim he obviously had in mind when he designed this place – and how spectacular it will be when it's finished – I can't deny it still needs a lot more work than I'd expected.

There are a huge number of people milling about, but Chase leads us through them and into the lobby, where I'm greeted by my worst nightmare… my team, all standing in a huddle, waiting for me.

There are five of them: Shannon, Stacy, Alyssa, Brett and Martin. Joanna, who was also with us in Chicago and Houston, isn't here. She's in Minneapolis – or she will be by the end of this week – because Bree decided she could take over supervising some of the refits, having gone through two of them with me. They're all fairly similar and Bree felt it was a waste of my time to undertake all of them. I was quite relieved when she said that. I didn't relish the idea of going around all the hotels – not with that team, anyway. And Joanna had never been particularly friendly; just like the rest of the team, really.

"I'll be back in a minute," Chase says, putting down my laptop, beside the tube of plans that Eli has already deposited against the wall, and before I can answer, he disappears, and I feel abandoned, as Eli goes with him, leaving me by myself.

As though sensing my insecurity, Alyssa turns and sees me, and the rest of them follow suit, staring in my direction and waiting for me to make the first move. Which I do, walking over to them, with my hands in my pockets and a fake smile plastered on my face.

"Hello, everyone," I say, trying to sound positive, and pleased to see them.

They mumble their 'hellos' in return, although Brett manages a smile, which seems genuine enough.

"Did you all travel down yesterday?" I ask, to make conversation.

"Yes," Shannon replies, being as monosyllabic as possible.

"And you're settled into the hotel okay?"

"If you call being squashed into two tiny apartments 'settled', then yeah, I guess so." Alyssa glares at me, her dark eyes shining. She's very attractive, with almost black hair, and olive skin, and as much as I want to like her, she seems to hate me. "But I guess we're not as important as some people, who get a cabin, all to themselves."

I want to correct her and tell her I don't have a cabin to myself, but I think better of it. She could do a lot more damage with the knowledge that I'm sharing a cabin with Chase and Eli.

"Well, I'm sorry if you're uncomfortable, but the hotel's really busy, and it's not like we're going to be here for very long."

"I'm not sure why we're here at all," Stacy says, looking around the lobby, her light brown pony tail swishing from side to side.

"Yeah," Alyssa joins in, before I can reply. "This place is a dump."

"It's not a dump," I correct her. "It's a building site. But by the time we're finished with it, it's going to be beautiful; just like Chase Crawford always knew it could be."

"Well, there's a ringing endorsement." I turn and blush, seeing Chase standing just a few feet away. He obviously overheard what I said and is smiling down at me, as is Eli, who's just behind him. "And I admire your confidence, Miss Schofield." He raises his eyebrows, his smile broadening, and I have to smile back. "Now, let me show you whereabouts in this *dump* you're gonna be working." He gives Alyssa a hard stare as he speaks, and then turns away, and I follow, leaving everyone else to bring up the rear.

We make our way through a connecting walkway with glass walls that's filled with ladders and workmen, wires dangling from the unfinished ceiling.

"This part of the hotel actually is a dump," Chase mutters as I catch up to him, and I have to chuckle. He smiles back and we turn through a wide doorway that's lacking in any doors at present, into a vast expanse of a room. "This," he says, waving his arm around, "is the main restaurant. Or at least it will be by the time you've finished with it."

"Like you said before, I admire your confidence, Mr Crawford."

He grins, his eyes twinkling and for a moment, we just stare at each other, until we're joined by the others, who stand around, looking at the enormous space.

"So, what are we doing in here?" Alyssa asks, like she's all about the business, which she's not.

"Oh... I left my plans in the lobby." I suddenly feel flustered for forgetting them, until Eli steps forward and hands them to me, together with my laptop and a smile. "Thank you," I say, smiling back, and step over towards the floor-to-ceiling windows that dominate one complete wall of the room, where there are some tables set out. "My plans are in here," I say, opening the cardboard tube, and tipping it up, cursing under my breath as the contents fall out onto the floor.

"Do you want some help?" Chase says from behind me.

"No, it's fine, thank you." I'd actually quite like him to leave, so I can humiliate myself in private, but although he's moved away just a little, he's still leaning against the wall, within my line of sight, and isn't showing any signs of going.

I find the drawings for the restaurant, laying them out flat on the table as everyone stands around. "What about the instructions?" Stacy says, folding her arms.

"I e-mailed everyone a copy, so you should already have your own lists of what to do." She knows that's how I work. It's what we did in Houston, and in Chicago.

"We do," Brett says, being helpful, unlike the others.

"Your supplies have all arrived," Chase says from behind us and I turn as he pushes himself off the wall. "We stored them away in this closet over here." He nods towards the other end of the room and starts walking in that direction. I follow him and he unlocks the door, revealing a large room, filled with piles of fabric, tins of paint and rolls of wallpaper, from floor to ceiling. To me, this is like a treasure trove and I step inside, my hands clasped together, a smile etched on my face.

"You look like a kid in a candy store," he says, and I glance up.

"I feel like one."

He smiles and shakes his head, like he's humouring me, and we leave the room again, closing the door behind us, and going back to the team, who are still standing at the table.

"I'm gonna show Miss Schofield around the rest of the hotel," Chase says, taking charge, before I can even say anything. "I suggest you guys make a start?"

They all nod their heads, making appropriately positive noises and, feeling relieved that I can get away from them for a short while, I quickly check that everyone is okay with their instructions, and then follow him from the room.

Chase

I'm standing by the doorway waiting for Eva, while she just runs through a couple of things with her team, when I notice Alyssa staring at me. She's got a weird expression on her face, which I can't read, but then Stacy says something to her and she turns away.

Alyssa is trouble with a capital 'T'. She always has been, and I've never been sure why Bree keeps her on. But it's Bree's department and not mine, and ordinarily, I don't have to work with her, or the rest of the team. I'm usually long gone by the time they start on the interiors. I've met Alyssa in passing, though, at the office, and she's always struck me as someone who's best kept at arm's length.

And that's exactly what I intend doing with her now. It wouldn't surprise me if she took what she saw last night as an opportunity to try something with me. She's that kind of person. But I'm not interested.

I'm not interested in anyone, except Eva. And although that thought is more than a little alien to me, I'm trying to go with it. At least for now…

I am kinda relieved, however, to see that Eva and Alyssa don't seem to be that friendly. That's partly because I'm not sure I like the idea of Eva being friends with someone like Alyssa, but also because their lack of 'sisterhood' makes it a lot less likely that Alyssa's gonna spill the beans on what she witnessed last night. They don't seem to have that kind of relationship, from what I've seen, and while I know there's nothing going on between Eva and myself – yet – I'd really like there to be. And I doubt she'd think very highly of me if she knew what I'd been thinking of doing last night.

Eva joins me and this time, instead of turning left and going back the way we came, we turn right into what should be the second connecting walkway, except that before we enter it, we have to step outside.

"This is the worst part," I say, looking back at Eva as I offer a hand to help her step over the gap where there's a fairly wide channel that's been dug out for some cabling.

"I can see what you mean." She takes my hand and steps across toward me, surprising me by not immediately letting go, but turning around and looking back at the incomplete structure, my hand still clasped in hers. "What's happened here?" she asks.

"It probably looks worse than it is," I point out, aware of the contact between us, and looking down at our hands as I speak. "The… um… there was a problem with the wiring for the lights in both of the walkways," I explain, once I've got my voice to work properly. "The other side is just about done, as you saw when we arrived, and this one should be ready in the next day or so."

She turns to look at me. "Really?"

"Yeah. Don't be fooled by the lack of walls. They're made of glass panels, and only take about an hour to put in."

"Oh. I see." She smiles and nods her head.

"We need to go this way," I say, leading her over to the west wing of the building. "We'll go around the other side and come back in through what will be the staff entrance. It's marginally less dangerous… just watch your footing," I warn, taking advantage of the fact that the ground is uneven to keep hold of her for a little longer.

Her hand feels small and delicate in mine, her skin soft, with a kind of fragile purity to it, and I'm reminded – again – of last night and of the fact that I came so close to doing something I know I would have regretted, if my body had been able to go through with it. Looking at Eva now, touching her – even if we're only holding hands – I can't believe I thought that fucking someone else could even come close to how good it feels, just to be breathing the same air as her.

We go around the side of the building, into the shade, and I let out an involuntary shiver. I know that's not because it's cold, though. And it's not because my thoughts are taking me to places I've never been before either. It's because I'm with Eva. She has that effect on me.

"Here's the door," I say, when we reach the staff entrance around the back of the hotel, and unfortunately I have to release her hand to let her go through ahead of me.

She steps inside and waits while I close the door behind us.

"You lead the way," she says, smiling up at me. "I don't know where we're going."

I nod my head, smiling back at her, and set off down the maze of hallways that eventually bring us back to the front of the hotel, close to the walkway we've just taken such a detour to avoid. We start up the wide stairway, which is actually complete, and turn to our right at the top.

"You know there are two different types of bedroom, right?" I say, turning to face her.

"Yes. I've done designs for both." She nods her head as we by-pass some opened doors leading off of the hallway.

"Great. All the rooms on this floor are the superior type, and the luxury ones are on the floor above. It's the same on the other side of the hotel, but the electrics haven't been completed over there yet." I stop by one of the doorways and let her enter. She does, walking into the room and looking around, before going over to the window, which looks out onto the pool below.

"It's beautiful," she says, on a soft breath.

"Nowhere near as beautiful as the luxury rooms," I point out. "I'll show you one of those in a minute."

"There's an en-suite, isn't there?" she asks, and I step back so she can go into the private bathroom, which is just to my right. She looks around in there as well, and then comes back out, staring up into my face.

"You certainly know how to design a hotel," she says, and coming from her, that feels like praise indeed.

"Well… it's nice to find someone who can see through the construction site, and imagine the end result."

"Oh, I can imagine it alright," she replies, with a dreamy note to her voice, as she wanders back over to the window.

I'm just about to follow her when my phone rings and I pull it from my back pocket. Trent's name appears on the screen, and I know that means trouble.

"Sorry," I say to Eva. "I'm gonna have to take this." She nods her head, and I connect the call. "Chase Crawford…"

"Hi, it's me. Where are you?"

"Up in the west wing, showing the interior designer around. Why?"

"Because there's a problem in the kitchen."

"Which you can't deal with?" I don't know why not. It's what he's paid for, after all.

"I probably can, but they've just delivered the refrigeration units, and they don't seem to be the ones we ordered…" His voice fades.

"For fuck's sake," I mutter under my breath. "Okay. I'll be right there."

Eva turns as I hang up my call. "Is there a problem?" she asks, as though she doesn't already know the answer to that question.

"Yeah. Isn't there always? I'm really sorry, but I'm gonna have to go. Can you find your own way back to the restaurant?"

She smiles. "Of course. You go and do whatever it is you have to do."

I wish I could stay. But I can't. Unfortunately, as much as I'm enjoying being with her – and I am – I've still got a job to do. So, with great reluctance, I step back out into the hallway, where I find Eli waiting for me.

I hadn't even been aware he was following us, but that's how good he is at doing his job. He's so unobtrusive, he's sometimes invisible.

"Trouble?" he asks, obviously noting my expression.

"Looks like it. I'm needed in the kitchen."

He nods his head and falls into step beside me as we make our way back along the hallway to the top of the stairs. "How's it going?" he asks.

"How's what going?" I decide to play innocent, and he smiles.

"You know exactly what I'm talking about." He shakes his head at me, and I reach the conclusion that I'm clearly not very good at playing innocent. Not surprisingly.

"It's going okay. I think. Breakfast was good, once I'd managed to control my reactions to how fantastic she looked when she came out of her bedroom. And my urge to take her straight back in there." He chuckles. "And it certainly made me glad I'd told you to have breakfast in the main building." I felt guilty for lying to Eva about Eli's absence, for fabricating an excuse for him not being there this morning. But I wanted some time alone with her, and I don't think that kind of lie counts… not really.

"Why? What did you end up doing to her?" he asks, grinning now.

"Nothing… you ass. We just talked, that's all. She told me a little about her childhood… about growing up without her parents."

He turns to look at me, holding open the door that leads into the corridor that will eventually take us to the kitchens. "She told you about her childhood?"

"Yeah. Not in any great detail, or anything. Why?"

"No reason. It's just that when I was talking to her yesterday evening, while you were in the shower, I was asking her about what it was like to grow up in England, and she kept it very general. She just talked about the food, and the education system, and things like that. I got nothing personal out of her."

"Good." I narrow my eyes at him, although I can't help smiling, because I like the fact that she shared things with me that she didn't share with him. I'm not gonna claim that I understood everything she was talking about, like that moment when she revealed her insecurity. I've got no idea what that feels like. But it felt good that she wanted to tell me about it. It made me want to protect her, and although that was almost as weird as having breakfast with her in the first place, I liked it. I liked it nearly as much as when I overheard her just now, singing my praises to her team.

"I'm not sure why you're so pleased with yourself," Eli says, interrupting my train of thought, and I glance at him.

"Why?"

"Because I saw the looks Alyssa was giving you earlier. What's going on there?"

"Nothing's going on." I defend myself, because for once I'm actually innocent.

"Then why did she keep staring at you?"

"Because she saw me last night, with those two women," I explain, keeping my voice low.

"Oh." He looks down at me and frowns. "Is that gonna be a problem?"

"I don't think so. You saw the way she was with Eva. They're not exactly friends. I doubt they even exchange a 'good morning' unless they really have to."

He shakes his head. "I wasn't talking about Eva, even though you clearly can't think about anyone else. I was talking about Max; about the company."

I stop, being as we're right outside the kitchen doors. "Why would it be a problem for Max? He knows what I'm like. Or what I was like." I stop talking and tilt my head. "Whichever way it is." He smiles at me, like he understands how confused I am right now. "And as for the company, I don't see what Alyssa can do. Those two women were with me of their own free will. In fact, it was their suggestion that we went to their room… where, if you remember, nothing actually happened."

"No, I suppose not," he says, with a shrug of his shoulders.

"And besides, they've already left. They told me they were leaving first thing this morning. So, even if she wanted to cook up some kind of trouble for me, it's too late."

He nods his head now, seemingly relieved, and then pushes the door open so I can pass through ahead of him.

Inside the kitchens, I'm faced with two delivery guys, dressed in black coveralls with red baseball caps, one of whom is arguing with Trent, while the other is leaning against the back wall, looking like he doesn't have a care in the world.

"What's going on?" I raise my voice above the noise Trent and the other guy are making, and they both turn to face me, giving me the chance to notice that Trent looks kinda stressed. He's a little older than me, being much nearer to forty than thirty, with graying hair at his temples. But today, rather than having his usual tanned and relaxed appearance, he looks tense and pale. Still infuriatingly handsome, but tense and pale, nonetheless.

"Ahh… Chase," he says, sounding relieved to see me as he walks over in my direction, holding a piece of paper. "They've fucked up the delivery of th—"

"We haven't fucked up anything." The guy next to him glowers and follows Trent. "We've delivered exactly what you guys ordered."

"No, you haven't." Trent comes to stand beside me, showing me the piece of paper and pointing to the items listed. "We ordered the G1270K," he says, quoting the stock number at me, like I'm supposed to remember it.

"Right. And?"

"And they've delivered the G1270LS."

"Yeah. Because that's replaced the G1270K," says the delivery guy, shaking his head slowly. "I already explained this."

"I know," Trent says through gritted teeth. "But what you haven't explained – at least not to my boss – is that the G1270LS is fourteen hundred dollars more than the G1270K."

I think that's the first time he's ever referred to me as his boss, and I'm almost inclined to remark on the momentous event. Except he and the delivery guy look like they're about to start tearing chunks out of each other. So, I hold up my hands to try and calm both of them. "Are we actually getting charged the extra fourteen hundred?" I ask.

The delivery guy shrugs his shoulders. "How the fuck do I know?" he replies. "I'm just told where to deliver the units. The sales team handle the costings."

I turn to Trent. "Have you checked?"

He shakes his head, and I let out a sigh, pulling my phone from my back pocket and dialing the number at the top of the piece of paper in my hand. Once I'm connected, I request to be put through to the company's sales department, and ask the question.

The woman on the other end listens and then replies, "We sent out an email about this over two weeks ago," sounding kinda tetchy. "The G1270K had to be taken out of production because of safety issues. It's been replaced with the G1270LS."

"Okay. I can understand that. But the point is, who's paying the extra fourteen hundred? Us, or you?"

"That was what the email was about. The alternative model has several additional features that weren't available on the older one. So, we gave customers the option to pay the extra for the new one, or to have the G1270L instead. It's a more basic model than the LS, or the K, but comes in a little cheaper than either of them. So you could choose whether to spend a little more, or get a refund on the difference."

"And you say you sent us an email about this?" I ask.

"Yeah… hold on a second." The line goes quiet, although I can hear her tapping away on a keyboard, and then she comes back again. "The message was sent out on the third of this month, to someone called Trent Anderson. He replied the same day and said you'd take the LS and pay the extra."

"Oh, okay." I feel like an idiot now. "Thanks. I'm sorry to have troubled you."

She tells me it's fine, but I can hear the insincerity in her voice as we both hang up, and I turn to face Trent and the two delivery guys, folding the piece of paper I'm still holding in my hand. I look up, trying to control my patience. "Everything's fine. It was just a mixup."

The delivery guy glares at me, but I glare back, letting him know it's not something worth arguing over, and I sign the documentation required to get him and his buddy out of our hair.

Once they've gone, and we're alone, I look over at Trent. "She told me you'd approved the switch from one model to the other, two weeks ago," I tell him.

"I did?"

"Yeah. By email."

He scratches his head. "I don't remember doing that."

"You don't remember? Christ, Trent. How many other things don't you remember?"

He sucks in a breath. "I'm sorry, man. I'm just not…"

"No, you're not, are you?"

I slam the piece of paper down on the countertop beside me and leave the room, before I end up saying something I imagine we'll both regret.

Outside, Eli catches up with me and we walk in silence for a few minutes, in the vague direction of the restaurant. "Say it," I mutter under my breath.

"Say what?"

"You were gonna tell me I could've been more understanding."

"No. I was gonna ask if you think he's got some kind of problem. Like maybe he's drinking too much or something."

I stop and turn to him. "Drinking too much?"

"Yeah. Since when does someone forget something like that? Not to mention all the other fuck-ups he's made lately."

"Yeah, but… drinking?"

He shrugs his shoulders. "Okay, maybe he's not drinking. But it's kinda weird, isn't it? To arrange something, then forget all about it, and then lay into the delivery guy? I mean, I get that we all lose track of things, especially when we're busy. But when someone turns up, delivering something that you've actually approved by email, that would normally trigger the memory. At least it would for most people."

"Yeah. It would."

I start walking again, wondering what I'm gonna do. I can hardly ask Trent outright, but at the same time, I need to know if he's got a problem. And if it is alcohol related, I need to get him off of this site, because having him here if he's not in control of himself could be really dangerous.

"This is just what I need…" I mutter under my breath.

"Where are we going now?" Eli asks.

"Back to the restaurant."

"And why would we be going there?" He's smiling, and I know why. *Asshole.*

"Because I wanna make sure Eva got back there okay. I kinda abandoned her upstairs."

"And you don't think she's capable of finding her way around? Or asking someone, if she got lost?"

"No. But…" He shakes his head. "I know, I know… I've got it bad. You don't have to say anything."

He chuckles and steps forward to open the door to the restaurant, just as a female voice rings out from inside.

"She's such a bitch." I recognize that as Stacy talking.

"I know." That's definitely Alyssa, and probably because of what happened last night, and the way I saw her interacting with Eva this morning, I put my hand on Eli's arm, stopping him from opening the door any further. I want to hear what they've got to say…

"You should have been made Bree's assistant, and we all know it," Stacy says.

"Wasn't Joanna more likely to get a promotion, out of all of us?" That's a male voice, and although I'm not certain, I think it's Martin. "She's been with Crawfords the longest, hasn't she?"

"Yes, but she didn't want the promotion," Stacy replies. "I think even she knows she's better at organizing than she is at design. Bree needed someone with design capability, which means she should have gone for Alyssa. Instead of which, she went outside the company, and we're having to prop up a talentless hack, who doesn't have a clue how to do anything."

"Tell me about it." Alyssa has a very slight southern drawl, which is accentuated by her bitchiness. "I mean… whoever told her it was okay to put gray and yellow together?"

They both laugh, and I feel my blood boil beneath the surface.

"Especially in the Caribbean," Stacy adds. "Gray just isn't a Caribbean color. Doesn't she know anything?"

I grab the door handle, pulling at it, but Eli yanks me back.

"Don't," he whispers, although his voice is loud in my ear. "You'll only make things worse."

"How?" I turn to face him. "How can anything I do possibly make things worse for Eva, when she's gotta work with people like that?"

He sighs and pushes his fingers back through his hair, looking at me like he feels sorry for me. "Because if they even begin to suspect there's something going on between the two of you, not only will Alyssa take great pleasure in telling Eva what she saw last night, but they'll assume she only got her job because she's sleeping with the boss… even though she isn't. Yet."

I can see his point. It might suck, but I can see it, and I let out a long breath. "Okay. But that doesn't mean I can't help her out." Eli shakes his head at me, smiling at the same time. "Oh… be quiet, will you?"

He holds up his hands. "I didn't say a word."

"You didn't need to. It seems that pretty much everything I say and do at the moment is a huge giveaway to how much I want her."

"Pretty much," he says, grinning, and to avoid the topic of conversation, I pull the door open and march into the restaurant.

"Where's Miss Schofield?" I ask, speaking loud enough that everyone present will hear me.

"Here." I spin around at the sound of Eva's voice, coming from the doorway behind me, where she's now standing beside a smiling Eli, and I feel my blood freeze. Did she just hear me admit I want her? Hell, I hope not. I mean, I didn't name any names, but… oh hell! "Did you want me?" she asks, and I actually choke.

"Yes. I mean, no. That is…" Fuck it. Why won't my mouth work? I take a breath, moving back over to her so I can try again. "I just came to make sure you found your way back here, that's all."

She smiles up at me. "I managed it in the end," she says, and then adds, "I met the site manager just now… Trent, is it?"

"Yeah, it is." I feel something stirring inside me; something unpleasant.

She nods her head. "He was outside, pacing around, and seemed a bit put out about something, but he was nice enough."

"I'm sure he was," I mutter under my breath, knowing that Trent was probably put out by me yelling at him, and also that my site manager's reputation with women isn't a great deal better than mine. "You need to watch Trent," I say out loud, and am surprised when Eva's smile widens.

"He is a bit of a flirt, isn't he?" she says, shaking her head, like she's remembering something – presumably their conversation – and that unpleasant stirring swells. "But it's okay." She leans in, lowering her voice. "He's not my type."

I stare down at her, wondering what her type is, and whether I might fall into that category. But then Eli coughs gently, reminding me I'm not supposed to be giving myself away. Not in front of Eva's team, anyway.

I step back and Eva looks up at me, inquiringly. "So, were you looking for me?" she asks.

"Not especially, but now I'm here, do you think I could take a look at your drawings? I haven't seen them yet."

She grins. "No, I don't suppose you have, but they're all over here." She indicates the benches on the far side of the room, and moves forward, leading the way over there, to where Alyssa and Stacy are standing, poring over them; or at least pretending to, while Martin is studying something on Eva's laptop. The other two members of the team appear to be in the closet where the supplies are, if the voices coming from there are anything to go by.

"It's one of the hazards of never going into the office," I remark, making conversation. "I'm always one step behind the curve."

Eva pushes a few of the drawings aside, under the glare of her assistants, and nudges one toward me. "That's the one for the restaurant," she says, biting her bottom lip nervously.

I pick it up and look at her, smiling, because she's so damn cute and I can't help myself. But then I gaze back at the image before me, and I have to stop myself from gasping out loud. It's a strange thing, but whenever I design a building, I always have an end product in mind, even though I know I won't get to create the final look and feel of any of the rooms. That's down to the interior designers, and not to the likes of me. But in this instance, it's as though I'm looking at the reflection of my dream. Eva couldn't have designed something any closer to my image of this place, if she'd climbed inside my head, sat down, and drawn it from my own imagination.

"This… this is incredible," I breathe. "It's perfect. I love that it's so understated. And the gray and yellow really work well."

"You think so?" she says, sounding doubtful as she comes to stand beside me, gazing down at the drawing I'm still holding onto.

"Yeah."

"I'm so pleased," she says. "I experimented with it for ages, trying brighter colors instead, because I know they're more traditional in the Caribbean. But I wasn't happy with it, and I talked it through with Bree, and she said I didn't have to stick with tradition…" Her voice fades and I smile down at her, loving the way she talks about her work, the unbridled enthusiasm in her voice.

"You definitely don't need to stick with tradition," I say, shaking my head at her. "It's seriously overrated."

She chuckles and I'm so tempted to kiss her I have to take a step back, just to stop myself.

"I—I should probably leave you to get on," I stutter, knowing that if I don't get out of here soon, I'm gonna give myself away.

"Hmm… there is quite a lot to do," she replies, looking around the room, and I put down the drawing and, giving her a last smile, I make my way back over to the door.

"We're going to see Trent," I say the moment Eli and I are outside, but he grabs my arm, pulling me back and over into a corner, away from the restaurant.

"What for?" he asks.

"To tell him to back off of Eva."

He shakes his head. "That would be a huge mistake. By all means, have a word with him about whatever his problems are, but leave Eva out of it."

"But you heard what she said; he was flirting with her."

"Yeah. And I heard her say he's not her type as well. You need to chill. For her sake, more than yours, you need to keep whatever is going on between you to yourself. And, most important of all, you need to trust her."

"I do," I reply. "I do trust her. But I don't trust Trent. He might not be firing on all cylinders at the moment, but the guy doesn't care who he fucks. He never has done…" I stop talking, realizing that I'm describing myself, as well as Trent, and Eli raises his eyebrows at me. "I can't let it go," I say, after a moment or two.

"If you don't, you'll regret it," he replies. "You need to play it cool."

I stare up at him. "And what makes you such a goddamn expert on women all of a sudden? You, me, Trent… we're all the same."

"Yeah, except I wasn't always like this," he says quietly, lowering his eyes. "I was engaged once."

"You were?" That's a shock. A big one.

"Yeah. It was a long time ago, and I fucked it up. So before you do likewise, take some advice from a guy who failed miserably at doing the right thing, and focus on Eva. Not Trent. Forget about him. And everyone else for that matter."

His eyes betray a deep sorrow which I've never seen in him before, and I decide to take him at his word. "Focus on Eva?" I repeat.

"Yeah."

"How?"

He rolls his eyes. "You remember last night, when we talked, and I suggested you could try dating her?"

"Yeah…"

"Well, stop prevaricating and try it."

"You mean, I should ask her to have dinner with me?" I'm so out of my depth here, I'm drowning. And it shows.

"You could do," he says. "Except she had dinner with us last night, so I'm not sure…"

"I wasn't suggesting we'd both be there."

He nods his head. "I guess I'll be having dinner by myself tonight then, will I?"

"Yeah. But I doubt you'll be by yourself for very long."

He smiles, although I notice that the sorrow in his eyes is still there.

Chapter Five

Eva

By the end of the day, I'm exhausted. And I'm fed up. And I really wish I hadn't let Bree persuade me I was ready for this. Because I'm not. I might be able to design. Bree thinks so, and so does Max, and even Chase. Evidently. But what I can't handle, it seems, is actually getting the job done.

So, nothing important then.

My team aren't the only people who work under me. In reality, there's an entire army of painters, decorators, carpenters, seamstresses and other workers, who create the final touches for the hotel. It ought to run like clockwork, because while I'm in overall charge, each of the people directly beneath me is supposed to take responsibility for an individual element of the work, which has been allocated, agreed and scoped in advance. And that would be just fine, if they'd remember to stick to their brief and not keep interfering in each other's problems, or getting involved in petty arguments that don't concern them. But they do. I'd like to say it's worse because the hotel isn't finished and, sometimes, they're not actually able to do the jobs I assigned to them. But I know that's not true, because I had exactly the same problems in Houston and Chicago. Except here, everything seems more complicated. And as a result I feel like I've spent most of my day man managing, rather than doing my job.

I've also spent it firefighting, defending myself and my decisions, and trying really hard not to break down and cry in front of everyone.

And somehow, I've made it to six o'clock.

Somehow. But God knows how.

"Hey…" I actually let out a sigh at the sound of Chase's voice and turn to see him standing in the doorway of the restaurant. He looks up at the main wall, opposite the windows and raises his eyebrows, because what was once plain plaster is now a beautiful pale grey. "That's impressive," he says, nodding his head.

"Thanks. We've made a start on the superior bedrooms as well." I don't want him to think this is the only thing we've done all day. And besides, I know how worried he is about the schedules, so I want to help out, if I can.

"Great."

A few strands of hair have come loose from my braid, and I tuck them behind my ears. "Well, we need to try and get ahead, so we can move into the newly completed parts of the hotel, as soon as the construction crews vacate," I explain and he nods his head, staring at me.

"Couldn't agree more," he murmurs. "But I think you've done enough for one day, don't you?"

"Definitely. I need a shower."

His eyes widen slightly, and he smiles. "Can I assume that means you're ready to go?"

"Yes… please." I can't keep the tiredness out of my voice.

He steps closer, looking right at me. "Are you okay?" he asks.

"Yes."

He frowns. "Sure?"

I glance up to where Alyssa and Stacy are standing on the other side of the room, staring at me and feel myself shudder.

"I'm fine. Honestly. Just take me home."

He frowns and puts his hand on my elbow, steering me towards the door, just as Martin comes through it. "You guys have transport back to Point Knoll, right?" Chase says to him.

"Yeah. The company laid on a car for us."

Chase nods his head. "Okay then. See you all tomorrow."

He doesn't give me a chance to say anything, but guides me out through the door, turning us to our left and into the walkway, which is now completed, with not a ladder or hanging wire in sight.

I'm too tired and too fed up for conversation, so we make our way in silence to the front of the hotel, where Eli's standing by the car waiting for us. He smiles and opens the back door, and I climb inside, trying not to register my surprise when Chase gets in beside me. I'd expected him to ride in the front with Eli, like he did this morning, but for some reason, he's back here... with me.

"You wanna tell me what's wrong?" he asks, once Eli's started the car.

"Is it that obvious?" I turn to face him and can't help smiling, because he looks so worried.

"Yes."

I shake my head. "It's nothing, Chase. Really. And it's certainly not your problem. You've got enough on your plate as it is."

"Is it to do with your team?" he asks, like he's read my mind. "I know some of those guys can be kinda hard to handle."

"I—I thought it was me," I mumble. "I thought it was something I'd done wrong; that they didn't like me."

"No," he says. "It's them. They'd bitch about you, whoever you were, and however good you were at your job. Don't let them get to you."

I huff out a half-laugh. "That's easy for you to say. You own the company. They can't argue with you."

He chuckles. "That doesn't stop them from trying. They seem to enjoy arguing with just about everyone from what I've seen. But you need to remember, Bree hired you for a reason."

"Yes, to be her assistant."

He smiles. "Yeah. But what I mean is, she could have promoted one of them, and she chose not to. She chose you. And even though I'd never say this to her face, my sister's damn good at her job, so if she thought you were better than those guys, she was right." I stare at him for a moment, blinking, and a little stunned, until he moves across the seat, getting closer. "Look, why don't we forget all about them, and go out to the restaurant tonight?"

I stare up into his eyes, and while I like the idea of spending some more time with him, I can't. Not at the restaurant, anyway. I shake my head and struggle not to react to the disappointment that clouds his eyes. "Sorry," I whisper. "I'm really not in the mood. But you two can go, if you want."

"Without you?" he says, frowning. "Hell, no. We'll order in."

I turn to face him, twisting in my seat. "I don't want to stop you from going out."

"You're not," he replies simply, and turns to face the front again.

Because it seems that's all there is to be said on the matter.

We get back and start our trek along the shore, my legs and back aching, and I wish more than ever that there was a simpler, faster route to the cabin, because I'm dying for a shower. I'm also looking forward to having dinner, now I know we're not going out. I couldn't have faced doing anything else tonight. For the very simple reason that my day has been spectacularly awful.

Actually, it's been worse than that. And that's the main reason I don't want to go out to the restaurant with Chase and Eli tonight. Because after what happened with Alyssa this afternoon, I'm not sure I can face her again. Not yet, anyway.

I ought to feel reassured by what Chase said, that the team can be hard to handle, and that they can be difficult with him sometimes too. But I don't. Because Alyssa was beyond hard to handle. She criticised both me and my designs in front of the entire workforce, and even some of the construction workers, who happened to be there at the time. She seemed to enjoy laughing at my drawings and talking over me, cracking jokes at my expense, when I was trying to give everyone a briefing after lunch. And I didn't react well. I know I didn't. Where I should have been strong, and put her in her place, I ended up getting flustered and dropped my plans, coming over all tongue-tied and embarrassed. I saw pity on some of the faces in front of me, but on others, I just saw contempt. And that hurt.

"I'm going to take a shower," I announce the moment we get inside the cabin. Chase looks at me, and although I can tell he's dying to say something, he doesn't argue, and I head into my bedroom, closing the door behind me, peeling off my clothes, leaving them trailing behind me, as I walk through to the shower, turn on the water, and stand beneath it, the warm cascade washing the day away...

It's remarkably soothing, just standing here, and I tip my head back, luxuriating in the sensation of actually feeling relaxed, for the first time since Chase and I left here this morning... which reminds me, we're supposed to be having dinner. So, I probably shouldn't stay in here for too much longer. I should have a wash and get dressed before he and Eli go ahead without me.

When I come out, wearing my pale blue sundress, with my hair re-braided, I'm surprised to find that Chase has opened up the bi-folding doors that lead out onto the decking, and that he's also evidently showered, being as his hair is damp still.

"Can I get you a drink?" he offers, getting up from the sofa as I pull my bedroom door closed behind me.

"I'll have a mineral water, if that's okay."

He smiles and nods his head, going into the kitchen and returning a few moments later with a bottle of beer in one hand, and a tall glass containing ice and sparkling water in the other. "Shall we sit outside?" he suggests, nodding towards the terrace.

"Okay."

I let him lead the way outside. "Oh, this is pretty." I look around at the open decking which lies to one side of the house. It offers a view of the ocean and is furnished with a large soft, pale yellow corner sofa, and a low table. There are a few potted ferns and a railing around the edge of the deck, and although it's not very private, it gives the impression of being secluded, simply because we're the last cabin in the row, and it seems unlikely that anyone would walk down here if they didn't have to. I mean, frankly, who would be bothered?

Chase puts our drinks down and I take a seat on the longer part of the sofa, facing out towards the sea, sitting back and getting comfortable. He sits beside me, and leans forward, picking up the menu from the table and handing it to me, already open, and unlike yesterday, I take my time going through the options on offer.

"I'm going to try the black mussel linguine," I announce at last, handing the menu back to him and picking up my drink. He smiles and puts the menu down again. Not bothering to look at it. "Aren't you going to choose?" I ask. "Or are you waiting for Eli?" I feel slightly embarrassed that I've only just noticed he's not here. But then Eli can be very inconspicuous when he wants to be.

"I already know what I want," Chase says, staring at me, as he pulls his phone from his back pocket and dials a number, placing our order, and telling the person on the other end that he wants the grilled salmon, in addition to my pasta dish, before he ends the call and puts his phone down, his eyes still fixed on mine.

"What about Eli?" I ask him.

"Eli's not gonna be dining with us."

"He's not?"

"No." He moves a little closer. "I—I... um... I wanted to spend some time with you."

"Oh, God... has someone said something about work today? Look, I'm..." He holds up his hands and I stop talking.

"This has nothing to do with work," he says softly. "I just wanted to be alone with you."

"You did? What on earth for?"

He smiles. "Isn't it obvious?"

"No." I shake my head and he moves closer still, so we're almost touching, and I feel that flicker of heat deep inside me again, as I gaze into his piercing blue eyes... and I finally understand, just as he leans in and lets his lips brush against mine. I gasp at the gentle contact and then feel his tongue dart into my mouth, which makes me moan, even though I didn't mean to. His hands come up and cup my face and I sigh into him, that heat inside me fanning into flames now, as he tilts his head and deepens the kiss, and I struggle to breathe, raising my own hands to touch his arms, and feeling his muscles tighten beneath my fingers.

He pulls back, looking down into my eyes. "Is it obvious now?" he asks, and I notice that his voice has deepened.

"I suppose," I whisper.

He smiles. "You only suppose?" He shakes his head, like he doesn't understand. "Eva, I think you're the most beautiful woman I've ever seen in my life, and I've never wanted anyone as much as I want you..." His voice fades, and I lean away from him.

"W—What did you say?"

"I said, I want you," he murmurs, his eyes still fixed on mine.

He wants me. He's said it twice now, so he must mean it. And I won't say I'm not tempted. Because I am. But how can I just jump into bed with him? Assuming that's what he means, of course. Is that what he means when he says he wants me? I've got no idea. But if it is, how can I? After all, I've never done anything like that before in my life. And besides, I don't know him...

Chase

This isn't going quite as I'd planned.

Parts of it are going well. Eva's kisses are. They're like nothing else. They're filled with innocence and fire, which is a weird but very enticing combination that I've never experienced before, but which has got my body craving her even more than it already was. Except that's not helping, because, like I say, this isn't going as I'd planned. I'd hoped to have Eva naked and underneath me by now, begging me to take her, but in reality, she's actually staring into my eyes, looking all doubtful, and despite the fire in her kisses, that isn't promising at all, being as I've just said I want her. Twice.

"What's wrong?" I ask her outright. Something clearly is and I'm too wired for playing games.

"I need to ask you a question, only I don't know how," she whispers.

"Just ask," I tell her. "Whatever it is, it can't be that bad."

She frowns. "You think?" Okay, so now I'm feeling doubtful too. She takes a deep breath, like she's plucking up the courage, and then she says, "What do you mean, exactly, when you say you want me?"

I can't stop the smile from tweaking at my lips, because I'm so relieved that at least she only wants an explanation. I was getting scared that she was gonna ask who the hell I thought I was…

"I mean I want to make love to you." I put it as clearly as I can, although I'm kind of surprised she doesn't get it herself.

"That's what I thought," she says, and then adds, "But I—I can't…" She leaves her sentence hanging, and my smile fades as I really struggle to hide my disappointment.

"Why not?"

"I don't know you."

Is that all? For a moment then, the thought crossed my mind that maybe she already had a boyfriend, or that she found me physically repellent. Admittedly, either of those answers would have made the fire in that kiss of hers even more weird. Except they're not true, so it doesn't matter. "But that's the whole point," I say out loud. "We can get to know each other."

She looks down at the space between us, biting her bottom lip. She doesn't reply. Instead, she looks really unsure – even more than she did before – like she doesn't know what to say, or how to say it.

"Are you trying to tell me you're not interested in me?" I ask, because it's starting to feel that way.

Her face shoots up, and her eyes meet mine, right before she leaps from her seat and jumps on me. Wow! I wish I'd tried that earlier. She straddles my lap, holding my face between her hands, and stares into my eyes.

"No," she says, shaking her head. "God, no. That's not what I meant at all."

I smile because I can't help it. And because she's so beautiful, and cute. And adorable.

"Are you saying you wanna take it slow?" I ask, even though that's not a question that's ever left my lips before.

She hesitates for a moment, and my smile widens, because that brief pause tells me everything I need to know. She may have doubts, but she's not entirely sure about taking it slow either… any more than I am.

"I—I don't know," she says, confirming my thoughts. "I—I've never been in a situation like this before."

"Neither have I." That's the truth, although she looks confused by my statement. But the reality is, I've never waited before. I've never even hesitated before. I've always just gone for whatever I've wanted. Until now. I might be on a tight schedule, being as I've gotta be in Denver on Monday, but I'm willing to try… anything.

"Why don't we just spend some time together?" I suggest. "And see where it takes us…"

She stares into my eyes although I'm not sure what she's expecting to see there, other than my complete and absolute need for her. And then, after a moment or two, she nods her head. I clasp my hand around the back of her neck and drag her closer, kissing her hard and deep, and she groans into me, her tongue clashing with mine. She lets her hands rest on my shoulders, her breasts crushed against my chest. And even through the fabric of her dress and my shirt, I can feel her nipples hardening as she grinds her hips. I'm not sure she knows what she's doing – other than driving me insane – but she wants this. I know she does. It's all I can do not to flex my hips upwards, to let her feel how turned on I am by her. But I manage to control myself. Although I let my hands wander a little, up and down her back, and over her gorgeous rounded ass, which makes her moan even louder. If we could just lose our clothes, I swear to God, this would be the best sex ever, because this perfect woman would be riding my dick right now, in a slow, sensuous fuck. But as it is, I'll make do with what she says she's ready for, and let my imagination do the rest.

We have to stop kissing when the food arrives, although we spend the entire meal staring at each other while we eat, which is something I've never done before. It's actually really erotic though. I'd never realized that eating could be such an arousing pastime. But it is. Or it is when Eva does it, anyway. Especially as her lips are swollen from my kisses, and her eyes are kinda glazed… and when we're finished, we leave the plates on the table, and sit back on the couch, looking out at the setting sun. I turn and lean in, kissing her again, simply because she's here, and she's irresistible, and she twists around to face me, her body molding into mine as I pull her closer.

I've never really made out with anyone in my life. I've always been more interested in the main event than any of the preludes. But with Eva, it feels different. I'm not sure what that 'different' means though, because while I know I ought to be thinking of the many ways I can get her naked and into bed. I'm not. I'm just thinking how incredible she is, and how I don't want this to end.

It does end though, when Eva pulls back from me, gazing around at the shrouding darkness.

"Oh," she says, sounding kinda sad. "I didn't realize it was so late."

"No. Neither did I."

She sits up, looking down at me, and I can't help smiling. "What's wrong?" she asks, seemingly puzzled by my reaction.

"You. You look…" I want to say 'just fucked', but that's wrong, because she isn't. "Disheveled," I say instead.

"Do I?" She starts to straighten her clothes, but I grab her hands, holding them still between us.

"Don't. I like you all messed up. Especially when I'm the one who made you that way."

She bites her bottom lip and smiles the sweetest of smiles, and I get up, pulling her to her feet and into the cabin.

"Is it bedtime?" she says, in the most innocent voice I've ever heard from a grown woman, and I turn to look at her.

"Yes."

It takes all my strength to lead her to her own bedroom door, and not stop at mine, and when we get there, I turn to face her, looking down into her eyes, which are shining and kind of expectant. I'm pretty sure if I suggested taking things further, she wouldn't say 'no', but at the same time, I also feel like that wouldn't be getting to know each other, or taking it slow. And I'm so torn as to what to do, that I don't do anything.

"Is this goodnight?" she asks eventually, when the silence has stretched to ludicrous proportions.

"I guess. If you want it to be goodnight." I put the ball in her court and she frowns in a very cute way.

"I don't know what I want, Chase."

I smile at her. "Well, that sounds kinda promising."

She smiles back. "Like I said, I've never been in a situation like this before."

I run my fingertips down her cheek and push her back against the wall next to the door, before I lean over and open it.

"I know," I say, my body pressed hard against hers as I let our lips meet and feel her relax into my kiss. "And that's why I'm gonna say goodnight."

She breathes out a soft sigh as I pull back, taking a step away from her, despite the fact that my body is crying out for her. "Goodnight," she whispers, and with a gentle smile, she walks into her bedroom and slowly closes the door behind her.

I stand for a moment, wondering if I'm completely insane. She practically offered me the chance, and I turned it down.

Yeah... I must be mad.

I've slept better than I thought I would, considering my state of mind when I went to bed last night, and this morning, I feel refreshed and optimistic, and kinda hopeful. I might even say, happy. Those aren't emotions I'm used to experiencing, not all at once. But none of this is familiar to me, and at the moment, I'm just going with it, in the hope I'll get somewhere that I recognize sometime soon. Preferably before I go completely insane.

Eli's already sitting in the main room when I come out, and he smiles up at me.

"Good night?" he asks, looking behind me, like he expects to see Eva.

"Yeah, thanks." I shut the door and he frowns.

"So… not a good night." He lowers his voice.

"No, it was. Honestly."

"But—" He stops talking as Eva's door opens and she comes into the room. She's dressed like she was yesterday, in cut-off shorts, but this time she's wearing a vest-style top, with her hair tied up in a ponytail rather than braided.

She looks stunning and I can't stop staring, as she smiles and says, "Good morning," to me.

"Hi," I say, finding my voice, even if it is a bit strangled by the way she makes me feel.

She turns to Eli and they exchange a nodded greeting, although Eva blushes slightly, and then Eli gets up, checking his watch. "Shall I order breakfast?" he says. "It's nearly seven."

"God, is it?" Eva shakes her head. "I must've overslept." She looks worried and I go over to her, taking her hands in mine, ignoring Eli's presence.

"Don't look so scared. No-one's gonna fire you for being late. I'm the boss, remember?" She frowns, a shadow passing across her face, and she tries to pull away. Like I'm gonna let her do that. "What's wrong?" I ask.

"Nothing," she whispers, blushing again.

Without letting her go, I turn to Eli. "Can you go outside for a minute, please? Order us some pancakes for breakfast… with coffee?"

He doesn't say a word, but nods his head and disappears out onto the terrace as I turn to Eva.

"Now, what's wrong?"

"Nothing," she repeats, and I shake my head, stepping closer to her.

"Is this because I just called myself 'the boss'?" I ask.

She sighs, her shoulders slumping slightly. "Well, it is a bit of a cliché, isn't it? Sleeping with your boss…" Her voice fades and she lets her head fall.

I place my finger beneath her chin, exerting just the slightest upward pressure to raise her face again. "Except you haven't slept with me, have you?"

"Well, no. But…"

"But what? If you're worried about what people are gonna think, then don't. Eli's trained not to notice, and—"

"It's not Eli," she says sharply. "I just don't want anyone to think I'm taking advantage. That I'm furthering my career by…" Her voice fades and I notice her eyes are glistening.

"Hey…" I take a half step closer, so my body's pressed against hers. "No-one in their right mind could think that. Not about you. And, if you wanted to take advantage, you'd have slept with me already. I suggested it last night, if you remember?"

"I remember," she whispers, taking a deep breath.

"Good." I smile down at her and then move my hand, cupping her face. "We both know this has nothing to do with your career. And, frankly, I don't care what anyone else thinks, because it's none of their damn business." She sighs as I caress her cheek with the side of my thumb. "This is between us, Eva. You and me. Okay?"

She stares into my eyes and nods her head, and then leans up, brushing her lips across mine. And with a low, throaty moan, I claim her in a deep kiss, which I only end when a knocking on the door announces the arrival of our breakfast.

"What was this morning all about?" Eli asks, once we're alone, walking through the carnage that's meant to be a hotel by now.

I turn to him. "Which part?"

He smiles. "Well, I gathered you didn't spend the night together…"

"No. We're getting to know each other… taking it slow. I think. It's what Eva wanted."

"And you're okay with that?"

"Yeah. I'm trying to be different, like you suggested."

His smile broadens. "And how's that going for you? Alien territory, I imagine."

"Yeah. But, so far, it's surprisingly good."

"That's because some things are worth waiting for, man," he says, with a kind of faraway tone to his voice, that makes me study him a bit more closely. He's not giving anything away, though. He never does.

And I'm not going to ask.

The second connecting walkway is almost finished, I'm pleased to say, with just the last bits of wiring to complete, and now the kitchens are almost ready too, I'm actually feeling like we're on top of things here, for the first time. Part of me wonders whether my optimism is because of the advances we're making, or whether that's just Eva's influence, but either way, everything feels a lot better today, and at lunchtime, I decide to go and find her, to tell her about the progress we've made.

It takes me a while to track her down, but eventually, I come across her in one of the luxury bedrooms in the west wing, standing by the window, gazing out at the sea view.

"Hey," I say, going into the room and leaving Eli out in the hallway.

She doesn't turn, and I walk up behind her, putting my arms around her waist, pulling her back onto me and kissing her shoulder. She sighs, but then she makes a stuttering sound, and I realize she's crying and spin her around, looking down at her tear-stained cheeks, her eyes overflowing, and at that same moment, I notice a sharp pain in my chest…

"What's wrong?" I cup her face in my hands. "Tell me…"

She shakes her head and I get ready to be told 'nothing' again, which I'm damned if I'm gonna take from her. "I've just had a bad morning," she says, surprising me.

"In what way? Is this something to do with your team again?" I'd hoped my little pep talk in the car last night might have helped with the situation. And I wasn't making any of that up either. Yeah, I wanted to make Eva feel better, but what I told her was true. Bree might never have explained her motives for not promoting from within her own team, either to me, or to Max, but when she came back from London and told us about discovering Eva in that contest she'd been asked to judge, it was obvious she'd found someone special. Which she had.

She'd found someone really special.

Eva gazes up into my eyes, tilting her head slightly. "How did you know?"

"Because I know them." *And I think I'm getting to know you too.* "What's happened?"

"Oh, it's nothing, really. Nothing that different to yesterday, and the time I was in Houston, and Chicago with them. I just need to grow a thicker skin, that's all…"

"No, you don't. I like your skin exactly as it is." She manages a smile, and I brush my fingertips down her cheek. She closes her eyes and shudders, and I add, "Your skin's perfect," as she opens her eyes again, gazing at me with a mix of desire and vulnerability that cuts right through me. "Tell me what they did," I whisper, desperate to protect her. "I'll deal with it."

"No!" she says sharply, grabbing at my arms, and I know I've spoiled a moment that had the potential to be something special between us. "That'll only make things worse. If they think something's going on between us."

"Something is going on between us, isn't it?" Surely she's not gonna deny that. Not after last night, and this morning.

"Yes," she says, and I heave out a sigh of relief. "But I don't want them to know. Can't you see?"

I suppose I can, especially when I remember Eli's words, about how her team would judge her, if they knew about us. And Eva's own fears from this morning ring loud in my ears too.

"What do you need me to do?" I say, rather than answering her directly.

"I don't need you to do anything… except…"

"Except what?"

She looks up at me. "Could you hold me?"

"Of course I can hold you," I reply, pulling her close. She sighs into me as I stroke her hair, resting her head against my chest, and I notice that pain I felt earlier has gone, and all I can feel now is a strange floating sensation, like I've never felt before. I'm not sure what it is, but I guess it's gotta be related to Eva, being as she's in my arms, and it feels so good to hold her.

She pulls back after a while, which is a shame, and looks up at me. "Thank you," she whispers, and I push a stray hair away from her face.

"You don't have to thank me."

"Yes, I do. I needed that… and it felt good."

"Yeah, it did." I lean down and kiss her lips, far too briefly. "Have dinner with me again tonight?"

"At the cabin?"

"No. I thought…"

"I can't go to the restaurant," she interrupts. "I can't…"

"I'm not asking you to. I'll find us somewhere to go… away from the hotel."

"You will?"

I smile at her. "Of course. If that makes you more comfortable."

She lets her head rest on my chest again, and although she hasn't actually said 'yes' to my suggestion, I somehow know that's what she means.

It was Eli who actually found the restaurant in the end, in Charlotte Amalie, and although he's had to come with us, he's sitting in the background on the other side of the room, unobtrusive as ever.

Our evening so far has been fabulous. I knew it would be, from the moment Eva opened her bedroom door and stepped outside. She was wearing a yellow sundress, with her hair up, revealing her long neck. And when I saw her, I just wanted to walk her back inside her room and kiss her. Hard.

I didn't. Because we're getting to know each other, and taking it slow… or trying to. And that means talking. Which is what we've been doing ever since we got here.

"So," she says, once our appetizers have been brought and we've started to eat, "tell me about your childhood. I've told you about mine…"

"You've told me *something* about yours," I clarify. "I'm sure there's still more to tell."

"There is," she replies. "But it's your turn now."

I smile, taking a sip of wine. "What do you wanna know?"

"Tell me about your parents," she says, tipping her head to one side.

"My parents?"

"Yes. I don't have any. I'm always interested in hearing about other people's."

I guess that makes sense. "Well, my dad was a control freak," I say simply, because it's the truth, and I watch as her face falls. "I'm sorry, but if you were hoping for tales of a happy, loving family, you've come to the wrong place."

"You weren't happy, as a child?" She sounds so sad, it's heartbreaking.

"I wasn't unhappy. But I don't remember being particularly happy, no. I don't think any of us were."

"And your parents didn't notice?" She seems surprised by that, but I think she's got a rose-tinted view of the world, or at least of families, anyway.

"My father was too wrapped up in his business, and himself. And Mom was too wrapped up in trying to please him. Dad was the kind of man who expected to be pleased by the people around him. And failure wasn't an option. He'd mapped out our futures before we were even born, I think. Max was always gonna take over as the head of the company, so he had it worse than Bree and I did…" I stop talking and take a breath, realizing that I've never spoken about my family before, other than to my family. And even we don't talk about ourselves that much.

"What were you going to say?" Eva asks, intrigued by my sudden silence.

"Nothing. I was just thinking… that's the first time I've ever really spoken about my family."

"You're quite a private person, aren't you?" she says.

"Yeah. I don't let people get too close." I don't let them get close at all, actually.

She lowers her head. "If you'd rather not talk, we can…"

I put down my fork and reach out, taking her hand in mine. "It's fine. It's okay. At least it's okay with you." I've got no idea where that came from, but it is okay. I want to talk to her.

"We can change the subject, if you'd rather," she says, looking up again.

"No." I shake my head and she smiles. "I was telling you about Max, wasn't I?"

"Sort of," she replies. "You were saying he had it harder than you and Bree."

"Yeah. He did. That's probably why he joined the military."

"Bree told me he'd served in Afghanistan, with Colt. Is that right?"

"Yes, it is. They did three tours. Max was injured right at the end of their third tour. Colt saved his life…" I let my voice fade, because no matter how much Colt and I don't really get along, I can't deny the fact that we owe him. And that it's the kind of debt we can never repay.

"Is that why they're so close?"

"No, not really. They were close before. They've known each other since high school."

"And Colt is Max's bodyguard now?" she asks, clearly intrigued by the setup, which isn't that surprising.

"He is. He started his security company when he left the army, and then, when Eden was killed, Max turned to him for help."

"Eden was Max's wife, right?"

"Yeah…"

"Bree told me something about that."

"It was horrendous," I whisper, in a gross understatement of the facts. "She was shot. Max was… it was just…" I find I can't talk as I stare into her eyes, and I have to look away. That's never happened to me before. In the past, on the rare occasions when the subject of Eden's death has come up, I've always just stated the facts of the matter. But for the first time, I've realized something of what Max must have gone through, and even contemplating that kind of loss really hurts. Deep inside.

"Are you alright?" Eva asks, and I look back at her.

"Yeah. Sorry."

"Don't be sorry. It must have been an awful time."

"It was." I shrug my shoulders. "It still is, for Max."

"He's got a daughter, hasn't he?"

"Yeah. Tia. She was only a couple of months old when Eden died. Max dotes on her. Obviously." I roll my eyes.

"Why do you say it like that? Don't you like children?" she says, and then snaps her mouth closed and blushes, pulling her hand from mine. "You don't have to answer that."

"Yeah. I think I do."

"No. I shouldn't have asked such a personal question."

"Why not? We're getting to know each other, aren't we?" I reach right over and grab her hand again. "I don't think there should be anything we can't ask each other, do you?"

"No," she whispers, and although this feels scarily like a long-term question – the kind people ask when they're actually in a relationship – I know I have to tell her.

"I decided on the day my dad died that I don't want to have children." Her face falls slightly, and I wonder if I should've taken the option not to answer, when she gave it, or maybe just lied, or fudged the issue. Except it doesn't feel right to lie to her. "Standing there in the hospital, watching him die," I continue, trying to explain, "I felt nothing. I didn't feel sadness. I didn't feel regret. And I certainly I didn't feel love. I just felt empty, like his role in my life was nothing more than a void. And the thought of having children myself and them feeling the same way about me…" I stop talking and almost shudder at the thought.

"But you're assuming you'd be like your father," she whispers.

"I guess."

"And what if you weren't? Don't you think you'd like to try… to see if you could do a better job?"

"It's a helluva risk to take, on the off chance of maybe getting it right," I say, shaking my head. "I mean… having a child and then getting it wrong, is really messing with someone else's life, isn't it?"

"I suppose," she says, sounding wistful now, and I suddenly feel scared, although I'm not sure why.

"Does my answer bother you?" I ask, and she tilts her head to one side.

"Only from the perspective that you seem to have already made up your mind that you'd be a terrible father. But you're not taking into account that, even though your dad wasn't what you needed him to be, there's absolutely no guarantee you'd be the same. You're not him, Chase, and..." She stops talking.

"And what?"

"And you shouldn't let him control your life, or your choices, anymore," she says, in a rush, and then falls silent.

She has a point, although it's not one I've considered before. I haven't had to. And we sit in silence for a moment, before I ask, "What about you? How do you feel about kids?"

"I don't know," she says, and I wonder if her answer has been influenced by my own, until she adds, "If I'm being honest, I've never really thought that hard about having children myself. I'm only twenty-one and, well... it's not something I've had that much time to contemplate." She pauses for a second and then says, "I suppose it's just tradition that makes us think we ought to have a family, isn't it?"

There's something about her voice that makes me say, "And the fact that you've never had one of your own?"

She shrugs, and whispers, "Maybe. Although I do have Ronan."

"Is having a big brother the same as having parents?" I ask.

"I don't know. You're better qualified to answer that than I am. You've got a big brother, and a mother. And you had a father."

"All as part of a fairly dysfunctional family," I point out, and she smiles a little indulgently.

"I'm sorry your childhood wasn't a happy one. But thank you for being so honest with me. You didn't have to be."

"Yeah. I did," I say. "Isn't that why we're spending time together? So we can find out about each other?" She nods her head. "Exactly. And there wouldn't be much point if we didn't tell the truth, would there?"

"No," she replies. "But I didn't expect you to…"

"You didn't expect me to what?"

"To be so genuine, I suppose."

"Well… you've learned quite a lot about me this evening then, haven't you?" I say, smiling at her. "You know I'm a private person – except where you're concerned; that I had a fairly mixed up childhood; that I probably still let my dad and my feelings about him have too much influence over my life. And that I'm completely honest."

And that with you, I'm in danger… real danger…

Chapter Six

Eva

Last night was so lovely, sitting in the restaurant and talking, that when Chase asks me out for dinner again tonight, I don't even hesitate. Not for one second.

"I'd love to."

I look up into his eyes and smile. And he smiles back.

We're on our way home, both sitting in the back of the car while Eli drives, and although today hasn't been as bad as yesterday, I'm glad it's over.

Yesterday was horrendous, caused mainly by Alyssa showing me up again, in front of everyone, to the point where I felt I had to find myself a quiet space to be alone. I hadn't expected to burst into tears, or for Chase to find me there, or that he'd be so kind. But he was, and as he held me in his arms, I felt like I never wanted that moment to end. I wished he could have just held onto me and made me feel safe forever. Because he did make me feel safe; like no-one else ever has. Not even Ronan.

And then, when he asked me out to dinner, and said he'd take me to a restaurant away from the hotel, I just wanted to cry some more, because he'd realised, without me having to put it into words, that I couldn't be around the people I'm working with. Especially not when I'm with him. They'd make my life even more miserable than they already are. And they're doing a fairly grand job as it is.

But when it came down to it, he found the perfect place; a candlelit French restaurant in the heart of Charlotte Amalie, where we sat together in a quiet corner, and talked... and talked. He told me something of his background, but not much, and I got the feeling that talking isn't something he does very much of. And then I stupidly blurted out that question about him liking – or rather, not liking, children. How could I have done that? It was such a lame, silly thing to do. But he didn't seem to mind. In fact, he said it was all part of getting to know each other. Which I suppose it is. And I suppose it also must mean he's serious about this. Whatever 'this' is. Because I can't see why else he would have told me all of that, about how he felt when his father died. It was all felt very committed and very sincere. And, while I suppose I was surprised that he was so adamant about not wanting children, I had to admit it wasn't something I've ever really thought about myself. I still haven't now, to be fair. It feels too early to be thinking about that kind of thing. So we let it drop and we ended the evening with a really lovely walk around the harbour, after which Eli drove us home and then silently disappeared into his own room.

Chase kissed me goodnight outside my bedroom door then, and as I felt his arms come around me and his lips crush against mine, it seemed as though my heart was floating and fluttering in my chest and I wondered whether I might be falling in love with him.

If such a thing were possible, on so short an acquaintance.

Which it can't be, can it?

Can it?

Except now, when I look up into his eyes, in the bright, late afternoon sunshine, I have to wonder...

"I'll meet you out here in half an hour?" Chase says, when we get back to the cabin.

"Okay."

He kisses me gently on the lips and I open my bedroom door, ducking inside and closing it again before letting out a long sigh.

I'm not entirely sure whether this is love, never having experienced it before, but if it is, I like it. I like it very much indeed. And with a slight giggle, I undress before heading into the shower.

*

When I come out, with my hair loose around my shoulders, and wearing my white sundress again, Chase turns to face me, his eyes lighting up.

"You look beautiful," he says, shaking his head, like he can't quite believe what he's seeing, which is very flattering.

"Thank you," I murmur, although I can feel myself blushing.

Eli is sitting on the couch, reading, and just smiles to himself, without looking up, and then Chase turns away, going over to the kitchen and grabbing what appears to be a picnic hamper, holding out his free hand to me.

"Coming?" he says, tilting his head to one side.

"We're having a picnic?" I can't help smiling.

"Yeah. Is that okay?"

I nod my head. "It sounds lovely."

He leads me towards the open, bi-folding doors, turning back to Eli as we cross the threshold. "We'll be back later," he says.

"I'll be here," Eli replies, looking up from his book. "Keep your phone switched on."

"Yes, Mom," Chase says sarcastically, and I giggle.

"Laugh it up," Eli replies, setting his book aside and getting to his feet before he crosses to the kitchen, his eyes on Chase. "But if I call and you don't answer, I'm gonna come find you."

"There is a reply I could give to that," Chase says, narrowing his eyes.

"Yeah, I know… don't call." Eli shakes his head and Chase pulls me out onto the terrace.

"Can I take it from that conversation that we're not going to be sitting out here?" I ask, as he leads me beyond the decked area and onto the beach.

"You can." He smiles at me, keeping a firm grip on my hand, and we walk along a little further, around a slight headland, until we come to a secluded area of flat sand, where Chase stops and puts down the picnic basket. "This should do," he says, and leans into me, kissing me gently.

I turn and look out over the ocean, the golden sun casting its evening rays onto the still surface of the sea, and I let out a long sigh.

"This is just perfect."

"Yeah, it is, isn't it?"

I turn again, and see that Chase has pulled a blanket from the hamper and laid it out on the sand, and he offers me his hand and lowers me onto it. I kick off my shoes and lie back, leaning on my elbows, enjoying the last of the sun's heat against my skin, as he sits beside me, and checks his phone, putting it down on the blanket.

"You're actually doing as you're told?" I say, teasing him.

He turns to face me, smiling. "Yeah. I may seem quite rebellious sometimes, but with Eli, I generally do what he tells me. He only ever acts my best interests, I know that."

He starts to pull packages from the hamper; cold meats, cheeses, fruit, bread…

"What's it like?" I ask, sitting up and helping him.

"What's what like?"

"Having a bodyguard?"

He thinks for a moment. "It took some getting used to, I guess. And I'm not sure it would have worked with just anyone. But Eli and I get along really well.And I guess we have Colt to thank for that, being as he's the one who assigned him to me."

"And you don't mind him being there, all the time?"

"No. I don't even notice him, to be honest." He stops what he's doing and looks into my eyes. "Why? Does he bother you?"

"No." I shake my head. "That's not what I meant. It's just that I've never known anyone who even needed a bodyguard. Apart from Bree, and your brother, obviously."

"Well, I guess it's still quite new to all of us, really, and we've all adapted in our own ways. Although I think Bree is finding it a lot easier now she's with Colt."

His eyes twinkle mischievously and I have to smile. "I gathered they'd become… um… close."

"That's one way of putting it."

I don't ask what he means by that. Bree is still my boss, after all. "I was surprised when Colt didn't take Dana's place as her bodyguard," I say instead.

"I haven't been home enough to know what's going on," he replies. "But I guess Colt probably wanted to keep things professional. Or maybe Max did. Especially as Bree's the one who struggled the most with the whole bodyguard thing at the beginning."

"Really?"

"Yeah. I know everyone expected me to be the one who'd rebel against it, but it was actually Bree. Her ex-husband was a total loser, and he'd made her life a misery…"

"She told me a little about him," I say, interrupting him. "At least, she told me you'd helped her out."

He looks embarrassed, staring down at his hands for a moment. "I didn't do anything," he mumbles.

"Except help Bree leave her abusive husband, and pay him a quarter of a million dollars, so he'd agree to divorce her."

He frowns. "She told you about that?"

"Yes. I was in her office when she got an e-mail from her ex, and Max was there too. He said he'd deal with the message, and after he'd left, I think Bree felt she owed me an explanation. She didn't, but…"

"She explained it anyway?" he says and I nod my head.

"We'd been talking about families, and she'd been saying that the three of you weren't that close." I look up at him. "After she told me her story, I suggested she might be wrong."

He smiles. "We were brought up to compete with each other. I guess it's taken us a while to adjust to the fact that we're on the same team now."

"I get the feeling Max is definitely in charge though, is that right?"

"Hell, yeah," he says, and I giggle, which makes him chuckle in return. "I wouldn't want Max's life, and neither would Bree."

"Personally, or professionally?"

His smile fades. "Both," he says softly and I know instinctively he's thinking about Max's wife, and I remember how upset he got, talking about her last night, and wonder whether to change the subject. But then, I'm interested. Apart from anything else, I'm intrigued by his reaction. It seemed odd.

"What was his wife like?" I ask, hoping that's a good place to start.

"She was the love of Max's life," he says simply. "At least, that was the way it seemed."

"Seemed? What does that mean?"

He shakes his head, leaning back slightly. "I probably shouldn't have said anything," he murmurs, "but… I don't wanna hide things from you."

He doesn't? That sounds almost as serious and committed as our conversation last night.

"You don't have to tell me anything you don't want to," I say, because he doesn't.

"I know…" I sit and wait, staring at his handsome face, and then he takes a breath and says, "Eden had an affair," quite simply, as though he's talking about the weather, or his latest holiday.

"She did?" I'm shocked, and struggling to hide it. "Bree told me about Eden's death but she didn't mention an affair."

"That's because Bree doesn't know about it," he replies.

"And yet, you do?"

"Yeah, but only because I saw the evidence of it, first hand."

"How?" I lean back slightly, wondering what he's going to say next.

"Don't worry," he says, smiling. "It wasn't like I actually walked in on them together, or anything. I—I just saw her, one day, getting out of a car, with another man. I didn't think anything of it to start with… until they kissed. It was a very intimate kiss."

"Oh, my God… what did you do?"

"I thought about telling Max to start with, but then I decided to talk to Eden instead."

"That had to be awkward."

He shrugs. "Just a little. But at least she didn't deny it. She told me the guy was her boss, and she'd been seeing him behind Max's back for over a year. She said it was because she was curious. She'd never been with anyone else and she wanted to know what it would be like."

"Really?" I want to tell him I think that sounds pathetic, but the woman was his sister-in-law, and she is dead, so I stay quiet.

"Yeah. I told her I thought it was all a crock of shit…" He looks up at me. "Sorry," he says, his lips twitching upwards, as I smile. "And then I gave her an ultimatum. I gave her twenty-four hours to tell Max about the affair… or I would."

I'm stunned. "You told her that?"

"Yeah. And she did it."

"How do you know? Did she tell you?"

"No. Max left her… at least for a few days. But then they got back together again. I've got no idea what went on between them. That was none of my business. Max and I have never talked about it. He doesn't even know I'm aware of Eden's affair, or that I had anything to do with her admission."

"Did you like her?" I ask.

He takes a moment and lets out a breath before he answers, "I did… before she cheated. But afterwards, I couldn't really bring myself to talk to her."

"In that case, can I ask you a question?"

He twists around to face me properly. "Sure."

"Yesterday, when we were talking about Max and Colt, and Eden being shot, you got kind of emotional…"

"Yeah."

"Well, if you didn't like her that much…"

"You wanna know why I reacted like that?"

"Yes."

He takes a breath and shifts the food that's lying between us to the other side of the blanket, moving closer to me. "That would be because I'd just worked out – for the very first time – how tough it had been on Max."

"It hadn't occurred to you before that losing his wife had been hard for him? I mean, I know she cheated, but you said they'd made up, so it had to still be hard… right?"

"I guess. But because I knew what she'd done, I never really thought about it in those terms. I never thought it would hurt him as badly.

Yesterday though, sitting with you, looking at you, and really thinking about what it must be like to lose someone like that, I got a clue what he must've gone through."

"Y—You did?"

I'm not sure what he's saying, and I'm too scared to ask, so I just look at him, until he says, "Yeah, I did. And I realised I hadn't been a very good brother to him."

I reach up and touch his cheek with my fingertips. "I'm sure that's not true."

He pushes me onto my back, and moves on top of me, raising himself up on his arms, before he leans down, kissing me, his tongue finding mine in an instant. I bring my hands up around his neck, my fingers knotting in his hair and he groans into me and flexes his hips so I can feel his arousal pressing against me, but he doesn't make a move, or do anything else, other than kiss me, with a surprising intensity.

The heat within me builds, and I feel like my heart is turning somersaults in my chest.

Is this what love feels like?

Or is this just lust?

How would I even know? It's not like I've ever done anything before, so I can hardly judge. And he's obviously quite experienced... which means this could end badly. Very badly.

After all, he might not be looking for the same thing as me. He might not want a relationship at all. And besides, I might be no good at this. I might be an enormous disappointment to him. And that would be awful... to be with him and find that he didn't want me anymore.

Not when I want him, so very much.

Chase

I lie awake, staring up at the ceiling as dawn breaks.

I haven't slept much; hardly at all, really. My mind has been too full of Eva, and the evening we spent on the beach. The last two nights have been amazing with her. I've talked, like I've never talked before. But then Eva seems to have that effect on me.

She makes me open up without even trying. And although that thought would normally fill me with horror, it doesn't when I'm with her. She makes me want to be completely honest… about everything. Except, I guess, for the fact that I haven't really told her how much I want her. I haven't told her that my body burns for her, whenever we're close to each other, or that I'm struggling not to take her… that I'm finding it harder and harder to be near to her and not act on my feelings.

And with just a couple of days to go until I have to leave for Denver, that struggle is only going to get worse.

The problem is, I've got no idea what I'm going to do about it. And that is really starting to wear me down.

Things are getting so bad, I even thought about talking it over with Eva last night, when we got back here to the cabin. I'd told her earlier on in the evening, how I'd felt about Eden and Max, and what happened between them, and how being with her had changed my perspective of all of that. I'm not sure she completely understood what I meant, but it felt good to tell her. And then as the evening progressed, her kisses, in between snatches of food and conversation, became more and more intense, to the point where I was having to keep repeating the words 'hold back' in my head, over and over, just to stop myself from taking things too far, too fast. Then, I had my arm around her all the way along the beach as she nestled into me, and the feeling of her body against mine made me want to walk her straight into my bedroom and take her. And yet, when we stood outside her door and I looked into her eyes, I still saw that innocence, and that threw me completely. And I felt that making a move, or even talking about it, would be wrong.

If I don't move soon though, I know I'm going to lose it. Because I can't imagine leaving her here like this.

I throw back the covers, trying to ignore my ever-present hard-on and head for the shower, taking my time over jerking off. I've done this every morning since Eva arrived... out of sheer necessity. And even then, I feel as though I'm little more than a bundle of hormonal nerves when I'm around her.

This morning, I close my eyes, stroking along the length of my cock, and I picture her naked beneath me on the sand... essentially in the same position we were in last night, right after she asked me about Eden. Only without our clothes. I imagine running my fingers over her soft skin, licking and kissing her, using my tongue to bring her off, and finally entering her. And at that point, with my imagination unable to take anymore, I explode, letting out a low groan.

I'd like to say I feel satisfied. But I don't. Because there's only one thing that can satisfy me now. And she's asleep next door.

Getting dressed, I go out into the main room and notice that the folding doors are open. I know I locked them last night when Eva and I got back, so I wander over and see Eli sitting out on the deck, already dressed, his sunglasses shielding his eyes from the early morning rays.

"You're up early." I keep my voice quiet, so I don't wake Eva.

He turns and looks up at me. "Yeah." He doesn't elaborate, and I don't ask. I know he sometimes has nightmares about his time out in Afghanistan. Max does from time to time, and I guess Colt might do too. Not that he'd ever tell me.

It's not something any of them would ever share with me. I wasn't there.

I go over and sit on the smaller end of the L-shaped couch, leaning back and crossing my legs.

"You look like you've got the worries of the world on your shoulders," he says, sitting forward. "I thought everything was going okay at the hotel now."

"It is."

"So we'll be leaving on Monday morning, as planned?" he asks.

"Yeah." I can't disguise my disappointment.

"And I'm guessing you're not so keen on that idea now?"

"No, I'm not. Although I'm not convinced hanging around here would be that great either."

He frowns and takes off his sunglasses, putting them down on the table in front of him and gazing at me.

"Why?"

"Because I don't think it would matter how long I stayed here; I'm not sure I'm ever gonna get anywhere with Eva."

He smiles. "You are aware it's only been a couple of days, aren't you?"

"Yeah."

"And that you guys are meant to be taking it slow?"

"Yeah. Of course I'm aware of that. I told you, if you remember. But the problem is, I've never done any of this before. I don't know what I'm supposed to do next. I've taken her to dinner. I've taken her for a romantic picnic. We've kissed. We've talked. But how do I move things to the next level, without scaring her off? I mean, I'm not even sure she's ready for the next level…"

"You're not?" He looks surprised.

"No. Obviously I want her…"

"Yeah, I think we established that already."

"And I think she wants me," I continue, ignoring his interruption. "But I'm leaving on Monday. I'm not sure I have time for the luxury of taking it slow. Not if I actually wanna get anywhere."

He shakes his head at me, resting his elbows on his knees. "You think you're taking it slow? I've seen you guys kissing, and if that's your idea of taking it slow, then you're doing it wrong."

I can't help laughing. "I've never really kissed anyone before. There's a lot more to it than I'd expected. So, taking it slow is proving kinda challenging."

"Yeah, I noticed."

"But that's not really the point, is it?"

He tilts his head to one side. "Then what is?"

"That I'm running out of time here. And I don't even know what she wants yet."

"You need to chill," he says, holding up his hands. "You're worrying about it all, far too much. I've been watching Eva too, and if you want my opinion, she's interested. But if you really wanna know what she wants, you need to get her to do some of the running. Stop chasing after her so much. You could even try playing hard to get for once in your life."

"How?"

"By doing exactly what I just said. Don't make yourself quite so available. Let her come to you. That way, she'll let you know what she wants… because she'll have to."

"Really? Is that how it works?"

"In my experience, yes."

I frown at him. "And where did you get all this experience?"

He leans back again, clasping his hands behind his head and looking up at the sky. "Do you remember I told you I was engaged once?"

"Yeah. And that you fucked it up."

"Precisely. That's where I learned my lesson. The hard way."

"What happened?" I ask and then realize it's personal. "Sorry… you don't have to tell me."

He lets his head rock forward, releasing his hands to his sides, and looks across at me. "No… it's fine. I don't mind." He takes a deep breath and says, "You know I served in the military with Colt and your brother?"

"Yeah."

"Well, I met Sienna between my first and second tours. She was incredible. And I mean the kind of incredible that just blows your mind, and leaves you in pieces, kinda wrecked on the floor."

"Yeah, I know the kind," I whisper, because I understand exactly what he's talking about. At least I do since I met Eva.

"We met at a club," he continues with a slight smile. "A friend of hers, who I knew, introduced us, and we just seemed to hit it off. I invited her back to my place, and she said yes… and didn't leave again until two days later." He looks away, down the beach for a moment, before returning his gaze to me. "They were the best two days of my entire life. But I was due to leave for Afghanistan a couple of days later, and to be honest, although being with her was kinda life altering, I wondered if I'd ever see her, or hear from her, again. We'd exchanged numbers, but I didn't know whether she was interested in being with a guy who wasn't even around that much, so I left it. I suppose I hoped that, if she wanted to be with me, she'd let me know, but I had no expectations. And then, out of the blue, just a few days after we'd got to base camp, I got a message from her. She made it clear she was more than interested. And needless to say, so was I. So I called her. I stupidly forgot the time difference, and called her early in the afternoon, which meant I woke her up at something like four-thirty in the morning. But she didn't care, and she cried down the phone at me, because she was so glad to hear from me. At least that's what she said, anyway. And although we couldn't talk for long, we started writing and sending each other messages all the time. She kept me sane during that tour, which had some really dark moments, I can tell you. And then she blew me away by meeting me at the airport, when I got back, and I think I knew then, when she ran at me and threw herself into my arms, that I'd met the woman I wanted to spend the rest of my life with."

"So you proposed?" I guess.

"Yeah, a few days before I shipped out again. She accepted, and we started making plans for when I got back. I knew Colt and Max were talking about leaving the army after that tour, and having met Sienna, I'd lost my enthusiasm for staying in too. I wanted to settle down, get a proper job, maybe have a few kids... the whole nine yards."

I'm surprised, although I do my best to hide it. I'd never pictured Eli as the settling down type. He's far too much like me...

"I'm guessing something went wrong?"

"Yeah, you could say that." He shakes his head and sighs deeply. "I'd been away for a couple of months, I guess, so I still had a while to go before I was due to come home again, and suddenly Sienna's messages started to get really weird."

"In what way?"

"She was much more distant. Her texts were shorter, and much less affectionate. It was way too noticeable to miss. I'd try calling her and she wouldn't pick up. When I wrote and asked her what was wrong, she just wrote back and said everything was fine, and that I was imagining things. But I knew I wasn't. That went on for ages, and I'm not kidding you, I was going insane over there, not knowing what was going on, but feeling absolutely certain, deep in my gut, that something definitely wasn't right back at home." He sighs, like he's remembering how it felt. "Anyway," he continues, "About a month before I was due to come back home again, I got a message…"

"From Sienna?"

"No, from the friend who'd introduced us. Madison." He scowls, and I know something bad is coming. "She… she told me that Sienna had been sleeping with someone else. Evidently, according to Madison, Sienna had gotten cold feet about the wedding, and had met up with an ex-boyfriend of hers, and didn't know how to tell me. Maddy thought I should know…" His voice fades, and he shakes his head, letting it fall.

I'm not sure what to say to him. Having been in the same situation as his friend Madison, when I found out about Eden's affair, I can sympathize with her predicament. And I know that if Eden hadn't come clean, I would've told Max. But seeing it from the other side – seeing Eli's pain – it puts a different perspective on things.

"What did you do?"

"I didn't do anything to start with," he says, looking up at me. "I wasn't gonna have it out with Sienna by phone, or by text. Or even in a letter. So, I had to wait until I got back home. And when I did, I went straight around to her place and confronted her. She started crying the moment she saw me, and although she denied it, there was something about her; about the way she wouldn't look at me. It just didn't ring true. I told her I'd have respected her more, if she'd been honest, and I stormed outta there, and went and got drunk. Very drunk. And… and then I slept with someone else."

"Not Madison?" I hope not, because that would be too complicated.

"No. She was just a woman I picked up in a bar. I can't even remember her name. And I felt awful afterwards. I regretted every second of it, even if I did feel kinda justified, because Sienna had cheated first. And with her ex. But, I still loved her. So, once I'd sobered up and showered, I went back round to her place, hoping we could talk things through and try to work out a way forward. Sienna wasn't home, but her mom was. And she told me that Sienna was... Sienna was in the hospital." His voice cracks on the last word and he coughs, taking a moment to calm himself. I don't say a word. I just sit and look at the table. Waiting. "I—I panicked," he continues, eventually. "I assumed she'd been in an accident and asked which emergency room she was in. But her mom said she wasn't; she was in the oncology department of Mass General, having treatment for cancer..."

"What the fuck?" I whisper. "She had cancer?"

"Yeah." He looks up at me.

"And you didn't know?"

He shakes his head. "I went into a kind of meltdown at that point, but I managed to drive to the hospital, and I found her, lying on a bed, all wired up to a machine. She burst into tears when she saw me, and so did I. And then she explained that she'd found a lump in her breast not long after I'd shipped out to Afghanistan that last time. She'd had all the tests done, and they'd discovered it was malignant and had removed the lump. They'd caught it early, she said..." His voice fades.

"But she hadn't told you?"

"No. She said she thought she'd be able to have the surgery and the treatment all over and done with by the time I got back, which was why she'd been so upset to see me the night before. That was literally her last course of treatment, and she wanted me to come back and find her all well again. I—I was angry with her for not telling me, and relieved she was okay, and so damn guilty for what I'd thought about her, and what I'd done." He stutters in a breath, and I can tell he's struggling to keep it together. "Sh—She wanted to know where I'd gone the previous evening, when I'd stormed off."

"What did you tell her?" I ask.

He shrugs his shoulders. "I tried lying to her, because I didn't wanna lose her, but she saw right through me. She guessed I'd been with someone else, and I knew from the look in her eyes that we were through. I begged her to forgive me, but she said she couldn't, and I hated myself for what I'd done to her. She blamed herself, for not telling me about the cancer in the first place. But in reality, it was my fault. I should've trusted her. I should've listened to her. And I sure as hell should've believed in her. She handed me back my ring, there and then, in the hospital. She told me she was sorry, and that she still loved me, but that she couldn't be with a man she couldn't trust. And then she told me to leave. I drove around for hours, because I couldn't think what else to do. But when I finally went back home, I found Maddy sitting on my doorstep waiting for me."

"Maddy?"

"Yeah. I knew she'd lied to me about Sienna. And when I confronted her, she admitted she was jealous of what Sienna and I had together. I—I've never actually hit a woman. But I threatened to hit her. It felt like she'd cost me everything, and I wanted to hurt her for that. It took me a long time to see that it wasn't Maddy's fault. Or Sienna's. It was mine."

He gets to his feet, straightening his shorts and steps off of the decking onto the sand.

"I'm gonna go for a walk," he says, over his shoulder. "I'll be back before it's time to leave."

I don't reply, because I can't think of anything to say.

But I reason to myself that maybe he's right. Maybe I should give Eva some space. I've gotten so hooked up on the deadline of Monday, that I've forgotten the bigger picture.

Chapter Seven

Eva

I'm really struggling not to cry and I wish, more than ever, that we didn't have to trek along the beach to get to the cabin. Not that I think Chase would notice the tears in my eyes. Because, let's face it, he's ignored me all day. So why would he notice me now?

It's been the worst day of my life, I think. Probably made more so because last night was so perfect. At least, I thought it was. I even thought Chase was going to suggest taking things further when we got back to the cabin after our picnic. But he just said goodnight. And I'll admit, I was disappointed by that, because we'd had such a lovely time on the beach, I really wanted to try. I wanted to know what we'd be like together.

Except he didn't.

And since then, he's acted like I don't exist. He even sat in the front of the car with Eli on the ride to and from work, and I've hardly seen him all day. He didn't take the time to come and find me at all, which he has done for the last couple of days, even if only briefly.

And I could have done with seeing him too, being as Alyssa was worse than usual. She was so bad, I had to tell her to see me in the site manager's office. Her snide remarks and back-chatting had been really getting to me, and maybe because I was feeling upset about Chase's attitude, I kind of lost it with her. I didn't actually dress her down in front of everyone else. That would have been unprofessional. But I told her to see me in Trent's office, and when we got there, he kindly vacated his room. Then I told Alyssa, in no uncertain terms, that if she stepped out of line one more time, I was going to report her to Chase. I could tell she was dying to say something to me. She had a sly look on her face. But she kept quiet and held herself in check, and then she left. And I took a few minutes to myself, just so I could try to stop my hands from shaking.

Despite my nerves, I felt kind of pleased with how I'd handled the situation. It could have gone a lot worse. So, when I spied Chase talking to Trent as I came out of his office, I went over to tell him what I'd done. Even now, walking along the warm sandy beach, I can still recall the distant look in his eyes when I finished talking.

"Okay," he said, with a bland tone to his voice, and none of the warmth I've grown accustomed to in him. "But you need to remember I'm leaving on Monday morning, so after that you'll either have to handle her yourself, or you'll have to get Bree involved."

I stared at him and tried not to cry in front of Trent. Chase had seemed so supportive before, and now he was saying I was on my own? He was letting me know that telling Alyssa I'd report her to him was pointless, even though he'd offered to help me out? I'd lain beneath him on the beach last night. I'd kissed him as hard as he'd kissed me, felt his arousal and wanted him, like he'd wanted me… and he was shunning me.

What had I done wrong?

I had no idea, but I had to get through the rest of the day.

And I have.

But even now, walking along the beach, he's acting like I'm invisible.

He's two steps ahead of me, instead of being by my side, telling me about his day, or making plans for the evening. Except, he hasn't mentioned doing anything tonight, so I guess he doesn't want to see me.

I feel a tear hit my cheek and wipe it away, grateful that he's ahead and not behind, so he can't see the gesture. Not that I think he'd care.

I just wish I could understand.

Eli lets us into the cabin and steps to one side as I pass.

I think about telling them I'm going for a shower, but why should I? Chase has made it very clear that, whatever was going on between us, is no longer important to him. Just like me. I don't matter. So I may as well just get on with it, regardless of him. I dump my things on the breakfast bar and head straight into my room. Closing the door, I feel my shoulders slump with relief that I'm finally alone and can let my tears fall.

I don't know why he's doing this. He told me he wanted me, repeatedly. He kissed me for hours on end, held my hand and hugged me… and now he can't even bear to look at me.

I take off my clothes and traipse into the shower, just about holding in my emotions, but as I turn on the water, I can't hold back any longer. I let out a sob which echoes off the tiled room. It's followed by another, and another. And as my legs give way beneath me, I huddle myself into the corner of the shower. I wrap my arms around my knees, and I weep for what might have been… and the man I wanted so much.

The man I thought I loved.

Chase

I look up at Eli as the sound of Eva's crying echoes around the cabin.

"I guess the plan didn't work out," he mutters.

"No shit," I reply, shaking my head. "Do me a favor and disappear, will you?"

He nods, and pockets the key card, before heading out the door, and I suck in a breath and then let myself into Eva's room, closing the door behind me.

The room is empty, but I can hear her crying still, and I guess she must be in the shower.

For a moment, I think about sitting out here and waiting for her. Except I'm done waiting. It doesn't seem to work very well for me.

So, I make my way across the room. I have to step over her discarded clothes before making my way through the narrow dressing area and into the bathroom. And then my breath catches in my throat as I see her curled up, naked, in the corner of the shower, sobbing her heart out.

"Don't cry." I keep my voice quiet, but she hears me and startles, looking up.

"What are you doing in here?" she says with a harsh glare, pulling her knees closer to her chest. "Get out!"

"No."

I kick off my shoes and walk into the shower, kneeling down in front of her as the water cascades over me, soaking through my clothes.

"You can't…" Her voice is a whisper now, but the hurt is still visible in her eyes. It cuts through me and I reach out and take her hands in mine.

"Yeah, I can. I'm sorry."

She frowns. "Do you even know what you're apologizing for?"

I nod my head. "I wasn't very kind to you today."

"No, you weren't," she says. "And I don't understand. The last few days have been so wonderful. You've been romantic, and caring, and considerate. But today you were like a different person. You made me feel worthless; like I didn't exist, like I meant nothing to you. If I did something wrong, you only had to…"

"You didn't do anything wrong," I interrupt her. "I did. I ache for you, Eva, and I want you like I've never wanted anyone in my life. But I wasn't sure whether you felt the same way. I wasn't sure if I was moving things too fast for you. So I thought maybe we should slow things down a bit more, give ourselves time to—"

"Time?" She stares up at me, incredulous. "You have remembered you're leaving on Monday?"

"I know."

She gulps down her tears. "I still don't understand why you didn't just come and talk to me, instead of ignoring me."

"I didn't mean to ignore you. I suppose I was trying to wait for you to be ready." I raise my right hand, releasing hers, and I cup her cheek. "Except it seems I'm not very good at waiting."

"Then don't," she whispers, looking up into my eyes, and I swear my heart stops beating. Did I hear that right?

"A—Are you saying what I think you're saying?" I struggle for control of my voice.

"That depends on what you think I'm saying."

"Are you saying you don't wanna wait anymore?" I hold my breath and she nods her head.

"Yes, I am."

I can't talk. My voice won't work. So, I lean in and crush my lips to hers, hearing her soft moan. And then she slowly unfolds, her arms coming around my neck as I stand, raising her to her feet at the same time.

I'm tempted to take her here, in the shower, but that feels wrong for our first time, so I break the kiss and look down into her eyes as I shut off the water.

"You're sure?" I say, surprised by the rasping depth of my voice.

"Yes."

I grab a towel from the shelf by the basin, and wrap it around her, hiding that beautiful naked body, just temporarily, as I lead her into the bedroom, both of us dripping over the wooden floors.

When we reach the bed, I turn her to face me, and lean down, kissing her again, before I lower her onto the soft mattress, unwrapping the towel to reveal her once more.

"You're perfect," I whisper and she blushes, biting her bottom lip, while I let my eyes roam downwards, taking in her generous, firm breasts, her flat stomach and narrow hips, and that neat triangle of trimmed blonde hair at the apex of her thighs, which I part gently, with my hands placed on the insides of her knees, while keeping my eyes locked on hers.

I push her legs up and outwards, and then pull her closer towards me, so her ass is on the edge of the bed. Then I kneel, leaning forward and licking along the length of her folds, finding her hardened nub and letting my tongue gently caress it.

"Oh…" she whispers, like she's surprised by the contact. "Oh, yes." She seems to like what I'm doing, so I carry on. I let my tongue work over and over her, harder and faster, as she raises her hips to meet me, and then brings her hand down, clasping the back of my head, holding me in place. She tastes sweet and exotic. She tastes like paradise. And after a lot less time than I might have expected, her breathing becomes really erratic, and she grinds her hips into me, bucking hard as she comes apart, letting out a long, low wail of pleasure, her orgasm claiming her body.

I wait, lapping up her juices, drinking her down, and letting my tongue linger, until her cries have died down to soft whispers. Then I stand and quickly shrug off my shirt, pulling down my shorts too, and letting my wet clothes fall to the floor, before leaning over her and pulling her up the bed. I kneel between her legs, raising myself above her. Her eyes are slightly misted over still, and I palm my cock, easily finding her soaking entrance and nestling against it for a moment as she sucks in a breath, and I push inside her. She gasps and bites her bottom lip, her eyes locked on mine.

"You're so tight," I whisper, battling for control, and then I freeze. There's something stopping me. A barrier. And as I gaze down at her, I feel as though we're on an island all of our own; like nothing else exists but us. "Y—You're a virgin?" I stutter, unable to hide my shock. Sure, I knew she was innocent. I knew she was inexperienced. But a virgin? This isn't something I've done before, and for a second, I wonder if I should stop, while I still can. I know what I'm like.

"Yes," she murmurs, on a deep sigh, and I know that, no matter what I might have just told myself, I can't stop. Even so, I have to give her the chance. This has to be her decision.

"You're absolutely sure this is what you want?"

She reaches up, touching my cheek with her fingertips, the contact sparking off every nerve ending in my body, so I'm struggling even harder for control.

"Yes," she repeats, and I nod my head.

"In that case, I'll do my best not to hurt you." And as I speak, I lean down and kiss her. Because I've never done this before though, I'm uncertain how to go about my next move, but I decide that, as with most painful things, it's probably best to get is over with, and I push all the way inside her in one swift movement. She cries out, but I swallow her pain with my kiss, my lips brushing gently over hers as I hold still inside her. Waiting. "Does that feel okay?" I ask her eventually.

"It stretches," she says softly.

"In a good way?"

"God… yes." A smile lights up her face and I have to smile too, as I raise myself back up again, and pull out of her, before plunging all the way back inside, and she hisses out a throaty, "Yes," bucking beneath me. God, she's hot. I repeat the movement, keeping it slow at first, letting her get used to the rhythm. But once we're matched, I increase the pace, just slightly, taking her deeper, her body rising to mine with every stroke. I've never been this gentle before, nor this tender, and I balance on one arm, letting my other hand roam over her body, tweaking her hardened nipples between my fingers and thumb, and then holding her waist, clinging to her for a while, until I move my hand down, behind her, cupping her ass and raising her just slightly off the bed.

The change of angle seems to be all it takes, because she suddenly stiffens in my arms. "Oh… Oh, Chase." She cries out my name on an extended breath, and then her body shatters beneath mine, which is too much for me, and as she tightens around me, I groan out my pleasure, and fill her deeply, losing my mind in the process.

I take a few minutes to find my mind again. When I do, though, I discover that I've all but collapsed onto her, so to avoid crushing her completely, I turn us onto our sides, keeping us connected. The very last thing I wanna do right now is end this.

"Are you okay?" I ask, looking into her eyes, noting her flushed cheeks and swollen lips.

"Hmm… yes, thank you," she whispers. God, she's thanking me? She's thanking me for the best sexual experience of my life. I'm not even sure why it was the best. I just know it touched me in ways I've never felt before. And I know I need more.

I hold her tight in my arms and start to move again, my cock still bone hard inside her. She responds, raising her top leg and wrapping it around my hip, while I trace a line of kisses from her neck, along her jawline, and up to her ear.

"I want you," I murmur.

"I want you too." She clings to me, her hips thrusting against mine, confirming her words with her actions. I clasp her ass with one hand, molding her flesh with my fingers as she pants harder and harder, and I know she's close again.

"Come for me, baby," I urge, desperate to feel her climax again. She stares into my eyes, right on the brink, and then she tumbles, throwing her head back, tightening around me once again, her body clenching into her orgasm, and my name a repeated murmur on her lips.

As she calms, she leans back slightly, gazing up at me. "God, that was good," she says, and I have to smile, right before I pull out of her, and flip her over on her front. She yelps in surprise. "What are you doing?" she says, twisting around and looking back up at me over her shoulder.

"You'll see."

I straddle her prone body, keeping her legs closed, and then raise her ass just slightly off the bed before I lean over and enter her dripping pussy, slamming my dick into her. She cries in delight, trying to force herself back into me, but I hold her down, my hands on her waist, and I fuck her... so damn hard.

"Yes!" she screams, bucking against me. But even as she comes again, I keep going. The need in me is overwhelming, like nothing I've ever experienced before. It's urgent. Insatiable. This isn't me. This isn't who I am. I don't put this much of myself into sex. And yet it seems I do. I do with Eva. And even now, it's not enough. I need more.

"Please..." she begs, as I pound into her.

"Please what?" *Don't tell me to stop. I'm begging you. I can't.*

"Give me more..."

She's feeling this too?

Her words ring through my body, echoing my own thoughts, and I lift her higher, kneeling up and hammering into her, so hard that beads of sweat form on my chest and back. I reach around in front of her and find her swollen, drenched clit, circling my fingers around it, and with that she comes apart again, her back arching, her whole body shaking with pleasure, as she screams my name.

I manage not to come, and slow my pace, and once I know she's capable of coherent thought, I pull out of her, very gently.

"Are we stopping?" she says, sounding disappointed, and I smile.

"Hell, no."

She sighs and I move aside, letting her turn over as I kneel beside her. She really does look just fucked now... because she is, and I hold out my hand to her.

"What are we doing now?" she asks, wide eyed.

"We're gonna go shower together."

"But I've already had a shower."

I lean over her. "I know you have. But I guarantee this one will be a lot more fun."

She giggles, and I pull her up into a sitting position, and then shift backwards, bringing her with me to the edge of the bed, where I stand right in front of her.

"Oh my God," she whispers, her eyes darting from my erect dick – which is right in front of her face – up to my eyes, where they lock with mine. "I knew it felt big, but..."

I chuckle and take a step back, raising her to her feet and into my arms.

"It feels just right, when it's inside you, baby," I murmur and she nods her head.

"Yes, it does."

"Now, come with me."

I turn and lead her back into the bathroom, and straight into the shower, turning on the water and pulling her close to me.

"Are you ready for this?" I ask, and she gazes up at me.

"I don't know. I've got no idea what you're going to do."

I stare down at her, the water falling over my shoulders and onto her perfect breasts, and it occurs to me that, maybe, this is why I'm finding her so irresistible. Her innocence is beguiling, and teaching her how to enjoy her body, and mine, is one of the most erotic things I've ever done. Maybe that's why being with her feels so different to normal. Because what else can it be?

"I'm gonna take you," I growl, and she gasps, her eyes widening in anticipation.

"S—Standing up?" she says, wonder filling her voice.

"Yes."

"Oh. What do I have to do?"

God, she's eager. But I like that. She's not predatory, like most of the women I've been with in the past. She just seems to like sex. A lot. And she wants to learn.

And who am I to complain?

"You let me do the work," I explain, bending down and lifting her into my arms, her legs hooked over my elbows.

She yelps and giggles, throwing her head back, and I lean forward and kiss her neck, which makes her sigh, and then moan.

"I like that," she says, clasping my cheeks with her hands as I pull away again.

"I noticed." She smiles and lets go of me. "Hold my shoulders, baby," I tell her, and she grabs hold of me again, as I raise her up and then support her with one arm, using my other hand to guide her onto my waiting cock.

She lets out a long sigh as I impale her, giving her what she seems to want, one slow inch at a time, lowering her down until I'm buried deep inside her.

"Oh… Oh, G—God, Chase," she stutters, clinging on to me. Her lips meet mine and she kisses me with a fire and a hunger that take my breath away as she raises herself up, using her arms for leverage. I help her, my hands clasped on her ass, and within moments, she's riding my cock, so damn hard, I know I can't last.

"Fuck, Eva… yes!" I yell, breaking the kiss and, as she comes around me, her screams echoing off the tiled walls, I explode inside her, at the same time as I get a light, floating sensation in my chest. It's the strangest feeling I've ever known. I don't think it's got anything to do with what we're doing, because – let's face it – I've done this before, on countless occasions. And besides, it's not a painful or disagreeable feeling. On the contrary, it's really warm and comfortable, and even once we're both calmed and our breathing has returned to normal, I keep hold of her in my arms, because I don't want this feeling to end.

And I don't want to let her go.

Chapter Eight

Eva

I wake up and stretch my hands above my head. And I smile, even though I feel utterly exhausted. I think I've had about three hours sleep – certainly no more than that. So I've got no idea how I'm going to function at work today, because even though it's Saturday, there's no such thing as a weekend, when you're working on a job like this. I don't mind that though. I don't mind anything anymore. Not really.

I can't believe an evening that started so badly could have ended so well. And yet it did. I know it did because muscles I didn't even know I had are feeling a little achy this morning. But that's hardly surprising, I suppose, given the amount of exercise – well, sex – I've had over the last twelve hours. I never realised it would be like that. Not that I'd really ever allowed myself to imagine what it could be like. But I'd certainly never pictured the unremitting levels of pleasure that Chase takes me to. Every time. Over and over. It's like he doesn't seem to know when, or how, to stop. And I'm certainly not complaining about that. Because I don't want him to stop either.

I turn over and come face to face with Chase, who's leaning up on one elbow and staring down at me.

"Good morning," he whispers, his lips forming into a perfect smile.

My body tingles, just at the sight of him, and I have to smile back. "Good morning."

"Are you okay?" he asks. "I'm sorry I kept you awake for so much of the night."

"Don't apologise. I enjoyed it."

His smile broadens. "Hmm… I noticed," he says, then adds, "I enjoyed it too," and pushes down the covers, exposing us both. I look up into his eyes, licking my lips, as I move my hand down his muscular chest, over his rippling stomach, and keep going, until I'm touching the base of his erection. I circle it with my fingers, but only just, and then move my hand along his shaft, back and forth, and he sucks in a breath, letting it out slowly.

"Is that okay?" I ask, because I really don't have a clue what I'm doing.

"It's perfect," he breathes, and I pump my hand a little faster. A small drop of clear liquid appears at the tip, and I lean forward and lick it, which makes Chase moan, so I take him in my mouth, wanting to pleasure him, like he does me. This is pure instinct on my part, and although I can't take very much of him, I enjoy the sensation of his soft as silk, and yet hard as nails, arousal against my tongue and lips.

"Oh… fuck, yeah," he murmurs, and I feel him gather up my hair, holding it behind my head. He doesn't force my head down, or raise his hips. He just seems to want to get a better view, which becomes obvious when he says, "I think watching you take my cock in your mouth is one of the most beautiful sights in the world."

I like hearing him say that, and run my tongue around the tip of his arousal, which makes him shudder. I do it again, and he drops my hair, sitting up, and lifting me onto him, pulling me up his body, so we're facing each other.

"Is something wrong?" I ask.

"No. Except I don't wanna come yet, and you were about to make me…"

I smile, feeling kind of satisfied with myself, considering I've never done that before. But I don't have time to dwell, as he moves my legs either side of his and, with his hands on my hips, lowers me slowly onto his arousal. I feel that intense fullness as he stretches me, and I cling to his shoulders, his lips crushing against mine, as he raises me again, moving his hands to my backside, and creating a slow, steady rhythm.

"Oh… G—God, that feels good," I stutter, as he breaks the kiss, staring into my eyes.

"Yeah, it does," he whispers, increasing the pace, which is all it seems to take for my body to respond. Just like last night, I find myself at a peak of pleasure, every nerve inside me tangling into a mist of star-filled wonder, as I fall, shattering against him, crying his name.

I find it hard to catch my breath, but I manage it, just before he tips me backwards onto the mattress, kneeling, and raising himself above me.

"I'm gonna take you so fucking deep." He grinds out the words, still looking straight into my eyes, and my body quivers in anticipation, my skin tingling and my nerves on fire, desperate for his touch.

He kneels back on his haunches, and parts my legs, impaling me with such force that I let out a yelp of surprise as he grabs my ankles, parting them, and exposing me to him, before he lowers his eyes, watching me.

"How can anyone be this beautiful?" he says, almost to himself, taking me harder and deeper with every stroke. I love this so much. I love him so much. The words are on the tip of my tongue, but I hold them back, relishing the feeling of being joined to him, watching as his body films with sweat, his muscles rippling. "Tell me you're close," he growls urgently, but I can't speak, because my body is about to fall again. I look him in the eyes and manage a nod of my head, and he thrusts deep inside me, which makes me scream his name, as I shatter all around him, and he throws his head back, letting out a howl of pleasure that fills the room.

It's so hard to concentrate. The only thing I've been able to think about all morning is Chase, and all the things he's done to me since yesterday evening. I'm sure the people I'm working with must have noticed my pre-occupation. Although I've done my best to be professional, and do my job, and ignore the fact that, even though we've only been apart for a few hours, by body is humming with need for him.

Fortunately, Alyssa and Stacy are working together in the restaurant, and I'm upstairs in the west wing, so at least I haven't had to cope with their prying eyes and snide remarks. I've just come back into one of the superior rooms, having left most of the team working on the luxury ones upstairs for now, while I take a look at the fabrics we're using for the soft furnishings, which are currently spread out on the floor. I kneel down on all fours and move the darker blue material to one side, so I can get a better look at the pale one, which is what we're going to be using in these rooms.

"That's a tempting sight."

I jump and turn, looking over my shoulder at the sound of Chase's voice, to find him standing in the doorway, his arms folded across his magnificent chest, and a smile etched on his lips as he stares at my backside.

"Well, don't just stand there being tempted," I urge, kneeling up, although I've still got my back to him, and he grins, stepping into the room.

"I persuaded Eli to give me a half hour to myself and I was gonna invite you to have lunch with me," he says, his voice dropping to a lower note. "But I can think of a hundred and one things I'd rather do with you."

My body trembles, and a pool of heat gathers at my core. "Care to demonstrate?"

"Gladly."

He kneels behind me, letting his hand wander over my bottom, in gentle, circular caresses, before he brings it around the front, rubbing against me through my shorts. I groan, pushing back against him, needing to feel him.

"You want more?" he whispers.

"Yes. Yes please."

He unfastens the button at the front of my shorts, then unzips them, pulling them down around my thighs, along with my white lace knickers, before he lets his fingers start their work again; this time, flesh against flesh. "Christ, you're wet," he says softly as I squirm into him.

"Because I want you. I've been going crazy all morning."

He chuckles, kissing my neck. "I'm glad it wasn't only me."

"It wasn't only you," I confirm, just as his phone rings.

"Shit," he mutters, and although he doesn't stop circling his fingers around that most sensitive spot between my legs, he answers the call, "Hi, Max," and I have to stifle a giggle.

I wonder whether I should stop him, whether I should turn around, or stand even, and call a halt to this. Except I love being exposed to him. And I love what he's doing. He falls silent, listening, while I struggle not to make a sound, wishing I could part my legs still further, that my shorts weren't restricting me.

"I thought we were just gonna look at extending the public areas," he says eventually, dipping a finger inside me, pushing it inwards, right down to his knuckles, making me sigh.

"What sound?" he says, after a moment. "I didn't hear anything." I bite my lip, because I'm so close to laughing, as he continues, "How many extra rooms do you wanna look at adding?" There's another pause, and then he says. "Okay, e-mail me the details of what you're thinking and I'll see what I can do when I get there." Silence descends once more, before he adds, "Here? Yeah, everything's going really well. So well, I'm not sure I wanna leave. But I guess I'm gonna have to. On Monday morning, unfortunately." There's another brief gap, before I hear him say, "No, it's nothing like that. I'm just gonna miss certain things about this place, that's all. It kinda grows on you."

He moves his fingers back to my swollen nub, and I grind my hips against him as he ends his call and drops his phone. Then, putting his arm around my waist, encircling me, he pulls me close to him, his back against my front, his mouth beside my ear.

"That was you I was talking about, by the way," he whispers.

I turn my head so we can make eye contact. "Do you mean I've grown on you, or you're going to miss me?" I'll settle for either. I'll settle for anything right now.

"Both," he says, smiling, and I feel his hand come between us, and hear the zip on his shorts.

"Chase? Are you up here?"

We both startle at the sound of a man's voice coming from the corridor outside, which I think belongs to Trent, the site manager, and then Chase pulls away, raising my shorts, before doing up his own. We exchange a glance as I re-fasten my clothes, and both struggle not to laugh. Then he checks I'm decent, straightening my top, before he calls out, "Yeah... in here."

"Do I look alright?" I whisper.

He smiles, getting to his feet. "You look fucking amazing."

I can't reply, because at that moment, Trent comes into the room, and I pretend to be busy with the fabrics again.

"I need you to come and sign off on the kitchen," Trent says, and I turn to face him, giving him a smile, which he returns. He doesn't seem to notice anything amiss between Chase and me, or if he does, he doesn't say anything.

"You mean, it's finished?" Chase replies, sounding surprised.

"Yeah. But I don't wanna let the electricians go until you're happy with it."

"Okay. Just give me two minutes, and I'll be down."

Trent nods his head and leaves the room without another comment.

"Two minutes?" I whisper, getting to my feet and letting Chase pull me into his arms. "Can I conclude that our time is up?"

"Yeah." He looks really disappointed. But so am I. "I'm sorry, baby."

I love it when he calls me that, and I can't stop the smile from spreading on my lips. "I'll forgive you, just this once. Although what I'm gonna do with all this pent-up frustration, heaven only knows."

"You're gonna hang onto it until we get back to the cabin tonight. And then I'm gonna show you a really excellent cure."

"For frustration?" I ask, teasing him.

"Yeah."

"And what would that be?"

He leans down and kisses me, just briefly. "That would be telling. But I guarantee it'll be worth the wait."

"I hope so…"

He smiles and kisses me again, staring into my eyes and groaning loudly as he pulls back. "I've gotta go," he says with great reluctance.

"I know."

He sighs. "See you later, baby." I nod my head and he releases me. "I miss you already," he says as he gets to the door.

"Hmm… me too."

If I thought this morning was hard, my afternoon has been torture. The memory of what Chase did to me in that bedroom, how I knelt on the floor and let him touch me, and how good it all felt, has lingered in my mind ever since. And by the time six o'clock comes around, I'm so on edge, I can hardly stand.

"Ready?" Chase says, coming into the restaurant, where I'm admiring the almost finished product. He stops and gazes around. "Wow. This looks amazing."

I want to thank him, or to tell him how well everyone has done, or just accept his praise. But I can't. Because all I can think about is getting back to the cabin and discovering what his cure is. I manage a smile, which he returns, and then he just says, "Let's go," like he understands exactly how I feel, and after I've said goodbye to everyone, I grab my things and join him by the door.

We're careful not to touch, or even look at each other too closely, and he leads me out to the front of the hotel, where Eli is waiting by the car.

Chase helps me into the back, and then joins me, reminding me of how different this is to last night, when he rode in the front with Eli.

"I prefer this," I whisper, leaning over to him.

"Yeah, me too." He turns to look at me, but doesn't move, because we're still visible, and as Eli starts the engine and pulls the car away from the front of the hotel, we just inch our hands across the seat, and let our fingers touch. Even that slight contact is enough to make me gasp, and Chase smiles, his eyes on fire.

I wish we didn't have to wait, but we do, and tonight the car journey seems to take longer than ever. We keep our fingers entwined, but that's all we do, and that restraint builds a kind of tension between us, which quickly becomes unbearable. So by the time we get back to Point Knoll, I'm almost panting with need.

"See you later," Chase says to Eli, who simply nods his head as he's locking the car, and makes his way towards the main hotel building while we head for the beach.

"Where's he going?" I ask Chase.

"Anywhere but the cabin," he replies, looking down and smiling at me. "I spoke to him earlier and asked him to give us some space. We have so little time to be together, and the last thing we need is my bodyguard making his presence felt."

I bite my bottom lip, although a smile is already tweaking at the corners of my mouth. "He doesn't mind?"

"No. I'm sure he'll find some way of amusing himself. And besides, I don't particularly care whether he minds. I want some time alone with you."

I lean into him, resting my head against his shoulder as we walk along the shore, wishing more than ever that we didn't have so far to trek, because I want to be alone with him, too.

The moment we get back to the cabin, Chase slams the door and drags me into his bedroom. His. Not mine. I just about have time to notice that it's identical to my own room, other than that there's a chest of drawers at the end of the bed, and a small wardrobe over in the corner, before he turns me around, kissing me.

"I don't know about you," he says, between kisses, pulling my vest top over my head and undoing my bra, freeing my breasts, "but I'm hungry."

"You're hungry?" Seriously? Is he kidding?

"Yeah."

"You want to eat? Now?"

He smiles and guides me backwards towards the bed, letting me fall across the mattress, and then reaches over and undoes my shorts, pulling them down along with my knickers. He drags me back over towards him, right to the edge of the bed, and parts my legs, gazing down at me. "Yeah… I wanna eat. Right now." He kneels down on the floor and blows soft air against my sensitised skin, right at the tops of my thighs, and I shudder. "You're hot," he murmurs. "You need cooling down." He parts my lips with his fingers, and this time blows across my clitoris.

"Chase… please," I whimper, and then I feel him lick me. I've needed him all day, especially since lunchtime, and I can't help moaning loudly and grinding my hips.

"You taste incredible," he murmurs, looking up at me, our eyes locking.

"I'm… I'm hungry too," I whisper, and he stops what he's doing, leaning back slightly.

"You wanna taste me too?" he asks, making sure.

I nod my head. "Right now, I think I want to do everything."

He chuckles. "Be careful what you wish for, baby." I shudder as he kisses me between my legs and then stands and quickly undresses before he walks around and crawls over me, starting at my head, until I come face to face with his enormous erection.

I place my hand around the base, and then open my mouth, swallowing down the tip and the first inch or so of him.

"Fuck, yeah…" His voice rings out, and then I feel him lean over, parting my legs, his head dipping down and his tongue finding that sweet spot once more. I arch up into him just as he starts to move, taking my mouth. He doesn't force himself too deeply inside, but I love the sensations he's creating. It feels fabulously promiscuous, especially when he's got my legs spread so wide, and I know he's getting a close-up and very intimate view of me. But, with the grunting noises he's making, it feels like he can't get enough of me. And I feel the same.

I'm just feeling that now familiar quiver deep inside me when he parts my legs still further and inserts a finger inside me. I want to cry out, but my mouth is full, and I buck against him, moaning loudly, as my whole body comes apart in the most shattering orgasm yet. Thrashing beneath him, I try to take more of his length down my throat, wanting all of him, as my body surrenders to pleasure like I've never felt before; wave upon wave of it rolling over me, until eventually I can take no more, and I reluctantly turn my head enough to pull his erection from my mouth.

"Stop," I breathe. "Please… I can't."

He does as I've asked and stops, shifting positions, so he's kneeling beside me.

"That felt so good," he murmurs, leaning down and kissing me. I taste of me and, just like yesterday, when he first did this, I find I like the sweet, musky scent, and I bring my arms up around him, clinging to him, craving more. He breaks the kiss eventually though and looks down into my eyes. "Come shower with me," he says, and I know he's not just talking about taking a shower, so I smile my acceptance of his suggestion, and he gets up, holding out his hand, which I take, letting him pull me from the bed.

Once we're in his ensuite, which is a lot bigger than mine, he leads me to the shower area and turns on the water, pulling me close to him, his erection still pressing into me.

"Can I ask you a question?" I say, looking up into his eyes.

"Of course."

"Why didn't you climax just now, in my mouth?" I can feel myself blushing, but I'm intrigued. "Was I doing something wrong?" I add, because that's the only thing I can think of.

He smiles and shakes his head. "No," he replies, moving his hands down so they're resting just above my bottom. "What you just did was sensational. But I didn't wanna come in your mouth."

"Why not?"

He looks at me like he doesn't really understand my question. "Because I wasn't sure you'd want me to. Given what I was doing to you at the time, it would've been hard for me to warn you, and I didn't wanna just come… not if you haven't done that before. You haven't, have you?" He sounds unsure of himself, or of me. It's not clear which.

I rest the palms of my hands against his hard, bare chest.

"Chase… I haven't done anything before. I've lived a very sheltered life. Remember? I was always a bit of a loner."

His smile fades, and he tilts his head to one side. "Was there a reason for that?"

"No, I don't think so. I was quite shy. I still am. I found it hard to mix. It was the same wherever I was, at both of my schools, and at university."

His smile returns, and he runs his fingertips down my cheek. "You think you're shy?" he murmurs.

"With most people, yes. But not with you." It's true. I've never felt timid around him, like I normally do, not even when we first met.

"I was gonna say, if what we've been doing is you being shy, I really wanna see you when you let yourself go."

"I think I've let myself go enough already, don't you?" I lean into him, but he pulls back, clasping my chin in his hand.

"No," he says. "I'm not sure the people in the next cabin along know my name yet. So I think I can push your limits a little further, don't you?" I can't help moaning at that thought, and he smiles. "Now, answer me one question…"

"What's that?"

"The next time you take me in your mouth, do you want me to come?"

"Oh… yes, please." I struggle to hide my enthusiasm, and he chuckles.

"You've got it, babe."

He leans down and kisses me, his hands wandering all over my body as I sigh into him, and lose myself, yet again.

Chase

Since Friday night, I've done nothing but make love to Eva, whenever work and snatches of sleep have allowed, and I can honestly say, it's never felt like this before. There's definitely something different about her and although I've still got no idea what that is, I'm willing to devote some more time to finding out.

Okay, so I don't actually have very much time, because I'm leaving in the morning, but I'll be back in Boston not long after Eva, and I don't see any reason why we can't try to work things out then. Assuming she wants to, of course.

Today has been even harder than yesterday, because I didn't get to see her at all. It was my last day at the hotel site, and there was so much to do, I couldn't even spare five minutes to go and find her. Although even if I had, I imagine we'd have been interrupted, just like we were yesterday, which I've gotta be honest, felt like a conspiracy to keep us apart. And I would have believed that, if it wasn't for the fact that no-one knows we're even together. And I like it that way.

I've signed everything off with Trent, and I guess my only regret is that I haven't got to the bottom of whatever his problems are. That's probably because I've been too wrapped up in Eva to find the time to talk to him. There's definitely something wrong, but I guess it's gonna have to wait for now. We shake hands and he wishes me well in Denver. He's staying on here for now, until the interior work is complete, just in case they run into any problems.

Part of me still wants to warn him off, to tell him Eva is spoken for, but I recall Eli's advice, and stay silent, telling him instead, that if he needs me, I'm only a phone call away. I kind of hope he doesn't though, just because I'd like him to try and manage by himself.

I turn away and find Eli waiting for me further down the hallway. He pushes himself off the wall and walks toward me.

"Are you done?" he asks as we head for the lobby.

"I think so."

"So, we just need to find Eva?"

"Yeah. Speaking of which, do you think you could make yourself scarce when we get back to the cabin? Eva and I have only got tonight, and I'd really like to…"

He holds up his hands, and I stop talking. "I get it," he says. "You don't need to go into details. But I'm only staying out for a couple of hours, and then I'm coming back, because I need to pack, and so do you. So can you try and make sure I don't walk in on anything I can't unsee?"

I smirk. "I'll do my best."

He nods. "Shall I wait by the car?"

"Okay. I'll find Eva and join you out there."

He turns and walks out through the huge glass doors, and I make my way to the restaurant, where I'm hoping Eva will be, because if she isn't, I'm gonna have to wander around the hotel trying to find her. I turn the corner and bump straight into Alyssa, who seems to be struggling with a roll of fabric.

It's the first time I've really seen her to talk to, since that night at the hotel, when she came out of her room and caught me with those two women. And it's definitely the first time we've been alone. And as much as I don't really like her, and I hate the way she behaves around Eva, I can't just let her cope by herself.

"Do you need some help?" I ask her, and she looks up at me, blushing slightly.

"Oh… yes, thanks." She smiles and flutters her eyelashes a little, and alarm bells ring in my head. She's never reacted to me like that before, and I've got no idea why she'd be doing so now. Still, I can hardly withdraw my offer. So, I take the roll of material and tuck it under my arm as she falls into step beside me.

"This is a beautiful hotel," she says, her voice a little breathy. "You've done an incredible job."

She seems to have forgotten that she referred to the place as a 'dump' just a few days ago, but I don't remind her.

"I didn't do it all by myself," I point out instead.

"No, but it's your design, Chase." She leans into me, and I attempt to put some space between us as we approach the restaurant and I hold the door open.

She passes through, looking up at me, and lets her body brush against mine unnecessarily, just as Eva looks up from where she's studying some drawings on the far side of the room.

"Where do you want this?" I ask Alyssa.

"Oh, I'll take it now," she replies and as I hand over the roll of fabric, she rubs her hand up and down my arm.

"Thank you for coming to my rescue," she purrs, and I step away, moving toward Eva, who's staring at me, confusion etched on her face.

"Eli's waiting… are you ready?" I say, taking care to keep my voice soft, but not too soft. I don't wanna give the game away now, but at the same time, she looks like she could do with some reassurance after Alyssa's little performance.

"Yes," she replies, lowering her eyes and packing away her things, gathering up her bag and her laptop, and turning to me once she's ready. She doesn't look at me though, and I know I'm gonna have to do something about that once we get back to the cabin.

She walks slightly ahead of me until we get outside, and then I catch up, although she won't look at me still, and I can't take her hand, or put my arm around her, because I've got no idea who's looking at us. So, I walk beside her, pretending we're nothing more than work colleagues – although we're so much more – until we get to the car, where Eli holds the door open. He glances at Eva and then frowns at me, clearly noting her expression, but I don't say anything. I can't. And instead, I climb into the back seat of the car, sitting beside Eva, who's clutching hold of her laptop and purse, looking away from me, out the window.

Eli gets into the driver's seat, directly in front of me, starts the engine and begins the drive back to Point Knoll, and the moment I know we're out of sight of the hotel, I turn to Eva, and move across the seat.

"Hey," I say, putting my hand on her thigh, skin on skin.

She hesitates and then twists around, facing me, and I see the tears gathering in her eyes, and I know that whatever I need to say to her isn't gonna wait until we get back to the cabin. It's gonna have to be said now, regardless of Eli's presence.

"Baby, what's wrong?" I grab her laptop and purse and move them onto the seat beside me, shifting closer to her.

"What's going on?" she asks, her voice cracking as she blinks rapidly. "What was happening with you and Alyssa?"

"Nothing was happening. She was struggling with the roll of fabric. I offered to help. That's all."

"But why? I—I mean..." she falls silent for a moment, and then turns away.

It feels like she wants more of an explanation, but I don't have one. I don't know why Alyssa was behaving like that, and I've just told Eva what happened. This feels strange to me. I'm not used to justifying myself to anyone, and as I sit here thinking about my own involvement in the situation – or lack of it – I'm not sure I wanna start now. So, I sit back, moving my hand away and letting it rest on my leg, because I know I haven't done anything wrong, despite the tone of her voice. At that moment, I glimpse Eli's face in the rear-view mirror, and he frowns at me, nodding in Eva's direction. I shake my head, but he narrows his eyes and nods toward her again. I get his message. He's telling me to try again, and although I'm not really sure why I should, I turn back to her.

"I think she was flirting with me," I say.

She flips her head around and stares up at me. "Why?" she says and then a smile tweaks at her lips and she puts her hand out, resting it on my arm. "I'm sorry, that came out wrong. You're a very handsome man and it makes sense that women would flirt with you. But I don't understand why she'd do that today, of all days. She's worked with you before, hasn't she?"

"Not directly, but we've known each other for a while, and seen each other at the office fairly often."

"Exactly... that's what I meant. And I'm assuming she's never shown an interest in you?"

"No. She hasn't."

"And, like everyone else, she knows you're going to Denver tomorrow. So what's the point?"

"I've got absolutely no idea, baby," I whisper, pulling her into my arms. "But I didn't flirt back. I don't want her… I want you."

"I know. I didn't mean to sound jealous, or unsure about you. It's just that I'm confused about why she'd do that."

"So am I. But can we just forget about it? I don't want to waste our last night together talking about Alyssa, when there are so many more pleasurable things we could be doing."

Her eyes sparkle, and she bites her bottom lip. I pull it free with my thumb, and she whispers, "Are there?"

"Hell, yeah."

She chuckles, and I lean down and kiss her. Hard. She responds and our tongues clash as she moans into me… and Alyssa is forgotten. Thank God.

When we get back to the cabin, I take Eva inside, kicking the door shut, and then without a word, I lead her out onto the terrace.

"What are we doing out here?" she asks, her voice laced with disappointment.

I turn to her and rest my hands on her waist, looking down into her upturned face. "Why? Were you hoping I'd take you straight into the bedroom?"

"Yes," she says, with disarming honesty, and I have to smile as I unbutton her sleeveless blouse. "Chase? What are you doing?" She clutches at my hand, glancing around, even though there's no-one in sight.

"I'm undressing you."

"Out here?"

"Yeah. Who's gonna see? We're right at the end of the beach, and no-one ever comes down here. They all hang out near the pool."

"I know, but…" She hesitates for a moment, her hand still on mine, and then she releases me. "You're… you're sure it'll be okay?"

"I'm positive."

She sucks in a breath, nodding her head, and I take up where I left off, unfastening her buttons, before I push her blouse off of her shoulders and let it fall to the floor. Her bra follows, and then I kneel and remove her shorts and lace panties, leaning in and kissing the tops of her thighs. I'd like to linger, but I'm impatient, bordering on desperate, and I stand again and quickly shrug off my shirt, letting my shorts drop to the floor beside the pile of Eva's clothes.

"Do you ever wear pants?" she asks, distracting me.

"Pants?" I tip my head to one side. "Sure, I wear them all the time. But it's too hot here. That's why I'm wearing shorts."

She frowns, and then smiles. "No, I didn't mean trousers, I meant pants. You know? Underwear, boxers, or trunks, or whatever you call them."

I smile. "Oh, I see what you mean. Yeah, I do. But I don't wanna waste time wearing them when I'm with you."

"Why's that?" she asks, leaning into me and letting her hands rest on my chest.

"Because I wanna be inside you, that's why."

She sighs, and while I'm tempted to kiss her, I know we're on a schedule tonight, so I sit down on the couch, and then lie out, with my back against the rear of it. She looks at me and I hold up my hand to her, which she takes, and I pull her down.

"Lie beside me," I tell her, and she does, letting me turn her, so her back is to my front, and I hold her close, my hands naturally finding her full breasts, cupping them and giving them a gentle squeeze. Her nipples respond, pebbling in my palms, and I kiss her neck at the same time. She writhes against me, her ass grinding into my stiff cock, and I move my right hand down, parting her legs. She lets me push her left leg downward, so her foot is touching the floor, and then I pull her right leg up, balancing her foot on the back of the couch, behind me. Having her spread wide like this, completely exposed to me, is a huge turn-on – for both of us – and I hear her sigh as I run my forefinger downward from her clit, finding her entrance and delving inside. She's really wet and I don't waste time with foreplay, but move my hand between us, palming my cock and shifting down slightly.

"Please," she murmurs as I sink the tip of my dick into her, and I ram it home in one move. "Oh, yes…" she hisses and turns her head, so we're looking right into each other's eyes.

"Do you like that?" I tease, pulling out again.

"Yes. Give it back," she murmurs, and I oblige, giving her my whole length. She sighs, kissing me, and I take her, letting my fingers strum over her clit, while my other arm stays wrapped around her, my hand cupping her breast. "I want more," she urges, breaking the kiss for a moment, and I oblige, pounding into her until her breathing changes.

"Come for me," I whisper into her ear and she locks her eyes on mine as her body trembles and she tightens onto me, clamping around my cock, a low cry coming from her lips.

"Oh, God. Chase…"

"Yeah, baby." I thrust deep inside her and let go, filling her with everything I've got, not taking my eyes from hers as she grinds against me, moaning out her ecstasy. Her orgasm goes on and on, but eventually she calms, and then she reaches out and runs her fingertips down my cheek and across my lips.

"I—I needed that," she whispers.

"Yeah. I noticed." She giggles, and I lean in and kiss her, swallowing that perfect sound. "Do you want something to eat?" I say, pulling back again.

Her eyes light up and she licks her lips, pushing her ass back into me, and I have to smile because I know exactly what she's got in mind. "Well, if you're offering," she murmurs.

"I meant food," I reply and her face falls. "I've gotta pack, and I'm aware of time running out on us," I explain, and her eyes fill with glistening tears. "Hey… don't get upset. I don't want to spoil our evening. I just wanna enjoy you."

She nods her head. "I know," she murmurs, although I can hear the emotion in her voice.

"Look… if we order something in from room service, we can eat in my bedroom, and then it doesn't matter when Eli comes back. Because he is going to, fairly soon. But if we're shut away, it won't matter. And you can help me pack, and I'm sure we'll find plenty of time to do whatever you want." I lean in and kiss her again. "We've got all night, baby."

"All night?" she echoes and I nod my head.

"Yeah. All. Fucking. Night."

She chuckles, and I kiss her. Like my life depends on it.

I order us in a small seafood platter, which we eat in my bedroom, on my bed, without bothering to get dressed, Although I remembered to bring our clothes in from the terrace.

Eli comes in a little later on, slamming the door, which I'm fairly certain is for our benefit. I'm only vaguely aware of the sound though, because at the time, I'm holding Eva in my arms, upside down. She's got my dick in her mouth. And the only thing I can really think about is not coming. Not yet. It's taking all my concentration to focus on licking her sweet pussy and keeping hold of her. She's got her legs over my shoulders and kind of around my neck and the very last thing I wanna do is to drop her, or collapse and have her head hit the floor.

She takes me deeper, and I groan in pleasure, sucking her clit into my mouth, and she bucks against me, her juices flowing as she moans loudly and comes hard on my tongue. That's all I can take, and I let go down her throat. She stills for a second, and then swallows, and swallows again, milking me dry. My legs buckle, but I remain upright – just – until we're both done. Then I slowly walk us back over to the bed, flipping her the right way up and laying her down. As I sit beside her, I rest my hand gently on her breast and lean over to kiss her.

"You were spectacular," I whisper, and she smiles up at me.

"I enjoyed that," she says.

"Good. I enjoyed it too." She lets out a sigh and stretches her arms above her head. "Are you tired?" I ask her.

"A little."

"Then why don't you rest, while I get on with my packing?"

Her face falls, and I lean down again and brush my lips against hers. "I've gotta go, baby," I reason with her. "There's no getting away from it."

"I know," she whispers, and shifts up the bed, resting her head on the pillow. I take that as my cue, and stand, going over to the small closet, where I stashed my bags, and pull them out, before dumping them on the bed.

"The quicker I get this done, the sooner we can take a shower," I suggest, and she grins at me, her eyes sparkling with enthusiasm. "I've gotta say," I muse out loud, while I open up the drawers and start pulling out my clothes, "for someone who wasn't too sure about sex just a couple of days ago, you've certainly taken a liking to it."

"Are you complaining?" she teases, and I smile at her.

"Hell, no. I'm just remarking on the change in you."

"Well… it's easy to like something when you're being taught so well," she says and I drop my t-shirts into my bag, closing the gap between us, then kneeling up on the bed and putting my hands down on either side of her, so she's pinned beneath me.

"That's good to know." I lower my voice. "But I hope you're not gonna fall into bed with the next guy you meet, just because you've discovered a liking for all this…" My voice fades as I notice tears welling in her eyes. "What's wrong?" I move closer, so we're barely inches apart.

"Don't you know?" she whispers.

"No." *I'm not a mind reader.*

"H—How can you even think I'd do something like that?" She tries to pull away from me, but she can't. I've trapped her. "D—Don't you know me at all?"

I'm tempted to say 'no', because in reality, neither of us knows the other very well. But that's hardly surprising. We've only been together for a few days. And I know that's a lot longer than I've spent with any other woman, but it's still not very long. Yeah, we've talked a little, but I know my main aim in doing that was to get her into bed. I'm not gonna deny that. I'm not a saint, and there's no point in pretending I am. And since then, we've mostly made love, or we've talked about making love, in its various forms. So, no, I don't know her. But I'm fairly sure I've hurt her feelings.

"I'm sorry." I raise my left hand and brush my fingertips down her cheek. How do I tell her I'm scared? How do I admit that I'm terrified she'll find someone else before I get back from Denver? I want to say that I need her to wait for me. I know I don't have the right, but I need her to promise she's mine… even though I've never asked that of any woman in my life. But I can't say any of that. Not out loud. I don't know how. "I shouldn't have said that," I murmur instead, holding her close, hoping she might get the message. Somehow.

We separate after a few minutes, and she lies back down, while I get to my feet and finish my packing, closing up my bags and leaving them by the door, ready for the morning. I'm leaving really early, just eight hours from now, in fact, and I want to spend that time with Eva.

"Do you still wanna shower with me?" I ask, because I feel like we've taken a backward step, thanks to my insensitive comment.

"Of course." She looks up at me, a little surprised, and I hold out my hand to her.

"I really am sorry if I hurt you," I say, pulling her into my arms.

She shakes her head, resting her hands against my chest. "Can we forget about it? You're leaving soon, and I don't want to dwell on negative things."

I lean down and kiss her, and then without another word, I pull her into the shower, turning on the water, and pushing her gently back against the wall. I kiss her again, more slowly this time, my lips dusting over hers, as I raise her left leg over my right arm and enter her. She gasps and then gently bites my bottom lip, her soft moan seeping into me as I start to move. I've never made love to anyone like this, but for the first time in my life, I'm truly tender. I keep my movements slow and considered, our eyes fixed on each other, and although there's no denying the physical pleasure, it feels like something more. So much more.

Eventually, her breathing changes, and she grinds into me, and I know she's close. I wanna watch her come and I change the angle slightly, and take her deeper. And that's all it takes. She's comes apart spectacularly, her body bucking and curling into her orgasm, while I take her weight, holding her up. Her face is a picture of ecstasy and sadness, and something else I can't identify. And as she whispers my name, her voice catches, and then she falls into me, clinging to my shoulders as she sobs.

"Hey, Eva." I hold her close, pulling out of her at the same time, and lowering her leg to the floor. "Baby, don't cry."

She's inconsolable and weeps on me, until I shut off the water and grab a towel, wrapping her up and then lifting her into my arms, her head buried in my chest as I carry her back through to the bedroom and lie her down, kneeling beside her and gazing at her tear-streaked face.

"What's wrong?" She turns to face me and reaches out, her fingertips touching my cheek as she shakes her head. "Do you wanna stop?" I ask.

She pauses for a second and then swallows hard. "W—Would you mind?"

I'm not gonna deny I'm disappointed, but I bury it. "Of course I don't mind. We can just sleep together for tonight, if that's what you want."

She nods her head and whispers, "I'm sorry," through her tears.

"There's nothing to be sorry for." I lean over and kiss her. "Let me get dried off, and I'll be back."

She smiles and as I drip my way back to the bathroom, she sits up on the edge of the bed and uses the towel to pat herself down.

I take just a few minutes to get dry, trying not to think about all the things I'd planned to do with her over the next few hours; trying not to feel disappointed that our last night together for a while isn't going to be quite what I'd expected, and then I go back out into the bedroom, to find she's lying down again. She hasn't bothered to pull up the sheet, and is sprawled, naked, on the mattress, her beautiful body on display, and it takes all of my willpower to walk around to the other side of the bed, quickly set the alarm on my phone, and then climb in beside her, without touching her.

"Do you wanna hug?" I ask, because I'm not sure what she does want anymore. I don't know her well enough to understand her.

She turns, surprise written all over her face. "Of course I do," she says, and I move closer, pulling her into my arms. She nestles against me, her head on my chest, and then brings her arm across too. We're kinda wrapped in each other, and I take a moment to think about that. I've never done anything like this before, not even with Eva. Because over the last couple of nights, we've just slept in snatches, wherever we've fallen, and then woken up twisted in the sheets, but not necessarily in each other. Looking down at her now though, with her arm wrapped around me and our legs entwined, her head nestled against me, I've gotta say, this feels incredible. I've got that same urge to protect her; the one I had on that first night, when she was talking to Eli, and again, when she told me about her past, and her insecurities. But this is different, because in this position, I feel like I *am* protecting her. I'm not sure what I'm protecting her from, but the point is that she was upset, she needed comfort, and she turned to me. And now she's in my arms. Right where she belongs.

I wake to the sound of my alarm, and I have to free myself from Eva to turn it off. I'm surprised to find that we're still wrapped up in each other, but at least my movement doesn't seem to have woken her, although she snuffles slightly, which makes me smile. She looks so beautiful, and I'm tempted to just stay here and watch her for a while. Except I can't. Because I've got a flight to catch.

So instead I get up and shower quickly, dressing in jeans and a button-down shirt, because while it's hot here, the weather in Denver is forecast to be at least ten degrees cooler, and according to the app on my phone, it's evidently raining. Once I'm dressed, I grab my phone from the nightstand and gaze down at Eva. She's still fast asleep, lying on her back, the sheets pulled down far enough that her breasts are exposed, and I'm so damn tempted to wake her. But at the same time, it would just be easier to leave. And I know it.

If I wake her, the goodbye is gonna be hard. And besides, what would I say to her? Would I ask her to wait? No, I don't think I would. Aside from the fact that I don't have the right, I'm not sure what this has been, other than the most sexually fulfilling two days of my life. Obviously. But is there anything else? Anything more? I've got no idea.

We haven't talked about the future. I don't even know if we have one. I'd like us to, I think. But that's not a conversation for right now, when I'm running out the door. That's something to be discussed back in Boston, back in the real world, when we've got time to talk properly, and when we've both had the chance to think about what we want. After all, I've got no idea what this has meant to Eva; if it's meant anything at all. Okay, so she got upset last night when I made that dumb comment about her falling into bed with another man, but that doesn't mean she wants a future with me, does it? It just means she was offended by what I said. And quite rightly. Because she's not that kind of girl. Even I know that. I might not know very much else – like how to say goodbye, or how to tell her I'm gonna miss her – but I do know that.

I make my way over to the door, picking up my bags, before I go out into the main living room, where I see Eli's luggage, already there, by the couch. There's no sign of the man himself, but I can hear movement coming from his bedroom. As I put my bags down beside his, I notice the vase of flowers on the breakfast bar, and I wander over, picking out a deep red rose, taking it with me back into my bedroom.

Eva's still asleep, and I place the rose on the pillow beside her before leaning over and gently kissing her forehead. She snuffles again, just like she did earlier, and I have to smile… as I turn and walk away.

Chapter Nine

Eva

I open my eyes to bright sunshine, streaming in through the floor-to-ceiling window at the foot of the bed, and extend my arms above my head, stretching out the sleep from my body, as I turn over and realise that the bed is empty.

"Chase?" I call out, sitting up sharply. But I'm greeted by a solemn silence, and I know he's gone. I glance back at the pillow, and notice the long-stemmed, red rose lying there, reaching over and picking it up. I hold it to my nose, breathing it in, but then let it fall. It smells slightly stale and sickly, and I shake my head, wishing he'd woken me before he left. Except, I know I would have cried again, and probably begged him to stay, even though I know he couldn't have done. I'd probably have told him I'm in love with him too. And that would have ruined everything. So I guess it's better this way.

It just doesn't feel like it.

Because I miss him.

I get up and return to my own room, closing the door on Chase's, and feeling rather sad, because I know that, by the time I return from work this evening, someone will have come in and cleared it up, and changed the sheets, and wiped away every trace of our time together in here. I suppose I've still got the memories, but somehow, without him, in this stony silence, without even the whisper of a fond 'goodbye', none of it feels the same.

It's as though the last few days never happened.

Except I know they did.

I shower and get dressed, and then make my way out into the living area, wondering what to do with myself. I could order breakfast, but I'm not hungry, and I'm about to reach into the fridge for some orange juice, when I notice a piece of paper, folded in half on the breakfast bar, with my name written on it.

He's left a note!

I'm not sure why he didn't leave it in the bedroom, but at least he wrote. I abandon all thoughts of orange juice and grab the piece of paper, unfolding it and feeling my heart sink as I realise it's not from Chase at all. It's from Eli...

Eva,

Just thought I'd let you know that I've arranged for someone else to drive you over to the Mermaid's Chair site each day, starting this morning. He'll call for you at 7.30. Chase wasn't sure if you could drive, so this seemed like the best solution.

Hope your work goes well and maybe we'll catch up when you get back to the States.

Eli.

'Maybe' we'll catch up? That doesn't sound very promising. I struggle to swallow down the lump in my throat, wishing that Chase had been the one to write, and that Eli hadn't made it sound so uncertain that I'd ever see Chase again. Although I know I will, because I work for his company. But how am I supposed to react to him? Am I supposed to behave like the last week never happened? Like he never made my body sing with pleasure or made my heart yearn for more? Or will he be okay if I tell him how I feel? Maybe drop a hint that I'd be more than happy if he wanted to pick up where we left off? I wish he'd said...

Unless this is his way of saying.

Did he get Eli to write this note, with that less than promising ending, as a way of telling me it was fun while it lasted, but that was all it was, and he'll see me around sometime?

God, I hope not.

We might not have talked about the future, and he might not have mentioned seeing me again, but to let it end like that would be so cruel. And so cowardly.

And although I don't know Chase very well, I don't think he's either of those things.

I put down the note and turn around, feeling more lonely than ever, and am just wondering whether it would look too desperate if I called Chase and asked him why he left me the way he did, and whether he meant for me to feel as used as I do right now, when I realise I don't have his number, and another wave of desolation washes over me. I'm struggling to control my tears, to understand how he could just walk away and leave me like this, when someone knocks at the door. Could it be Chase, come back to tell me he made a mistake? Could he have had second thoughts and decided to stay, after all?

I rush over and pull open the door, feeling my heart crash to my boots when I see Trent standing before me.

"Oh, it's you." I can't stop the words from leaving my lips.

"Yeah." He smiles, but it doesn't touch his eyes, and I wonder if I've hurt his feelings.

"Sorry," I mutter. "I wasn't expecting to see you."

He shakes his head. "Didn't Eli tell you? I'm gonna be driving you to work from now on."

"H—He told me someone would be driving me to work. He didn't mention any names."

"Oh... well, I'm staying in one of the cabins further along the beach, so it makes sense, as we're both going the same way."

"You're staying here?" How can I not have noticed? I guess because I've been too busy with Chase.

"Yeah," he replies. "But I've been keeping myself to myself on this trip..." His voice fades and he looks a little awkward, shuffling from one foot to the other. He's nothing like the slightly flirtatious man I met on my first day at the hotel site, and I wonder what can have happened. "Are you ready to go?" he asks, before I have too much time to think about that, and I nod my head.

"Yes. I just need to grab my things."

He waits while I gather up my bag and laptop and then, retrieving the key card from the bowl on the breakfast bar, I join him outside.

We walk in silence to the main hotel car park and Trent opens the passenger door of a red saloon car. I climb in and he closes it again, before walking around and getting in beside me, letting out a long sigh.

"Is everything okay?" I ask, and he turns his head, looking at me. "Why?"

"You just seem out of sorts." I'm not sure I'm qualified to say that, being as I don't know him. But he seems a bit disheartened about something.

"That would be because I am," he says, starting the engine and pulling out of the parking bay.

"Is something wrong?" I ask, even though I know it's probably none of my business.

He shrugs his shoulders, but his expression tells me everything I need to know. He looks distressed, bordering on tormented, and I turn in my seat, so I'm facing him.

"Trent, I'm happy to listen, if you want to talk. I know we don't know each other, but if something's wrong, I'll do my best to help."

He slows the car and turns to face me. "You really wanna listen?" he says, seemingly surprised.

"If it helps, yes."

He sighs, picking up speed again, and clutching at the steering wheel, like it's a lifeline. "I'm such a fucking failure," he says, and then stops talking, before he adds, "Excuse my language."

"Don't worry about it. But why would you say that?"

"Because it's true. I've screwed up so many times on this job, I'm amazed Chase hasn't fired me. I would've done in his shoes."

"We all have bad days," I reason.

"Do we all have bad months?" he retorts, sounding angry now.

"Yes. Sometimes."

"You don't understand," he continues, like I haven't spoken. "I'm out of my depth here. I've never gone through anything like this before, but I feel like I don't know what I'm doing from one minute to the next; like I'm walking through quick-sand, sinking a little further every day.

And there's nothing I can do about it. I'm trying to cover my ass, but I'm failing miserably." He glances over at me. "I flirted with you the other day, because you'd asked me a question. I can't remember what it was now, but I couldn't remember the goddamn answer, so I turned on the charm instead."

"So? People do that kind of thing all the time."

"Yeah, but do they wake up each morning, covered in sweat, just thinking about going into work? I do. I have panic attacks all the time… and I've started getting chest pains…" His voice fades.

"Trent, you need to talk to someone. Or see a doctor. You can't carry on like this."

He shakes his head. "I know. But who's gonna believe me? It's pathetic, a guy like me having panic attacks over doing his own job."

"No, it's not. I'm terrified most of the time."

He turns again, his eyes fixing on mine. "Yeah, but you're…"

"I'm what?" I interrupt. "If you're about to say that I'm a girl, or that I'm young, then just forget it. I'm still here to do a job, exactly like you. And just because you're a man doesn't mean you can't suffer from anxiety. It happens to all kinds of people. Only most of them aren't brave enough to own up to it."

He huffs out a breath. "I'm not brave, if that's what you're trying to say. I'm being a total pussy over this…" He stops talking again. "Sorry. I shouldn't have said that."

I smile. "Stop apologising. And please, go and see someone. You can talk to me whenever you want, but I'm not a professional. You need to find someone who actually knows how to help you."

He shrugs again. "I'll think about it," he murmurs. "But promise me you won't tell anyone about this."

I'm not sure that's the best idea. I think he needs help, and somehow I don't see him asking for it himself. But I can't betray his confidence, so I just say, "I promise," and resolve to keep an eye on him, at least while I'm here.

He drives for a few minutes in silence, and then he glances over at me again.

"I'm sorry if I embarrassed you the other day, flirting with you like that."

I smile across at him. "You didn't."

"I know I just said I was doing it to get out of an awkward situation, but that wasn't the only reason…" He shifts in his seat slightly, like he's embarrassed, and then says, "You're very beautiful, and while you're here, and I'm here, if you'd…"

I can feel myself blushing, but I know I have to say something.

"I'm sorry, Trent, but I'm afraid I'm spoken for."

He looks even more disheartened now. "Oh, so you've got a boyfriend already?" he says.

"Something like that, yes."

"What does that mean?" He seems confused, but I don't blame him. I'm confused too. "Surely you either have a boyfriend, or you don't."

"I'm not sure 'boyfriend' is the right word, but I'm involved with someone." That seems like the best way of putting it, considering that, until I hear otherwise from Chase, I'm going to consider myself very much involved with him. I'm in love with him, after all.

Trent sucks in a breath and lets it out again.

"Well, I hope the guy appreciates what he's got," he says softly, turning to face me.

I don't know whether Chase does or doesn't appreciate me. I don't know how Chase feels at all, being as he didn't tell me. He didn't say anything to me… not even 'goodbye'.

Trent doesn't flirt with me anymore, and we don't continue our conversation about his anxiety attacks, either. But we get to work, and go our separate ways, after he's said he'll meet me by the car at six. I agree, although I wish I could turn the clock back, and that it could be Chase who was coming to find me at the end of the working day. It would be so much nicer.

My morning goes smoothly, mainly because I'm working by myself in the lobby, which is now ready for decoration. I'm handling this area personally, being as it's the first place that guests will see when they arrive, so it has to be perfect, and I need to make sure the decorators interpret my designs properly. Now that the hotel is completed, other than a few tiny details, my team are scattered around all over the place, and to be honest, that makes my life easier, because we're all busy, and they seem to have less time to gang up on me. And if that makes me sound pathetic, or maybe even paranoid, then unlike Trent, I don't care.

I've just finished a long conversation with the flooring fitters, who've arrived a little earlier than expected, when my phone beeps, letting me know I've got a message. *Could it be Chase? God, I hope so.* I pull it from my back pocket and almost groan in disappointment when I see the text is from Bree and not her brother. I feel abandoned by him, but I click on the message anyway, because I'm here to do a job, and keeping busy is the only thing that's stopping me from crying at the moment.

— Hi Eva. I hope your first week went well. Can we have a quick Zoom call this evening at maybe 7pm? I don't want to interfere with your working day, but I just want to check up and see how things are going. Let me know if that works for you. Bree.

I text back and say that seven o'clock is fine with me. I should be back at the cabin by then, and to be honest, a Zoom call with Bree sounds like a good idea. The distraction will be useful, if nothing else. I've got nothing much to do now that Chase has gone, and maybe I can ask her to give me his number. Heaven knows what excuse I'll come up with for needing it, but I have to find out why he used me like he did.

I settle back on the sofa, with an ice cold glass of mineral water beside me, and wait for the call to connect. When it does, it takes a few moments for the screen to catch up, and then Bree comes into focus. I'm instantly reminded of Chase, although I'm not really sure why, being as they don't look that similar, other than their hair colour I suppose, but when she smiles at me, I can see a definite likeness, and my heart lurches in my chest.

"Hey," she says, lifting a glass of what looks like red wine to her lips. "How's it going?"

"Okay, I think. The restaurant is done, and so are about half of the superior bedrooms in the west wing. I've started on the lobby today, and I've got teams working on the rest of the hotel. So far, we're on schedule."

"Sounds like it," she says, smiling, and I notice Colt Nelson walking behind her, across the screen in what looks like a very nice kitchen.

"I like your apartment," I say, to be friendly.

"We're not at my apartment," she replies. "Colt bought us a house. And he proposed."

"Wow. Congratulations."

"Thanks." She smiles. "How are things with the team?" she adds, returning us to the topic of work.

"Not too bad." I don't want to talk out of turn, so I don't tell her about the difficulties I've been having. And besides, today has been better.

"And the hotel itself? Is it actually finished?"

"Yes. Chase got everything done, so we can push ahead." Damn. I wish I hadn't said that. If I'd thought about it, I could have used a problem at the hotel as a reason for needing to contact Chase.

"How did you get along with my brother?" she says, grinning, and interrupting my train of thought. "This was the first time you'd actually met him, wasn't it?"

"Yes… we got along fine," I say, hoping that my blush doesn't show on the screen.

She takes another sip of wine. "Well, I can't imagine he was too much trouble. Knowing Chase, he'd have been far too busy."

I nod my head. "He certainly seemed to be. From what I could see, he worked really hard."

Colt laughs in the background, and Bree giggles too. "I wasn't talking about work," she says, shaking her head. "I was talking about women. Chase has something of a reputation."

"For what?" I ask, feeling a chill creep across my skin.

"Sleeping with anything that moves," she replies.

"Yeah, right before he abandons them and moves on to his next victim," Colt adds from behind her, and that chill becomes a freeze.

My throat closes over, but I know I have to say something. "Surely you're exaggerating. He can't be that bad." I'm clutching at straws, hoping against hope that this is some kind of sibling joke.

"No," Bree replies, shaking her head again. "Chase is terrible with women. Even he admits he treats them like they're disposable."

"He always has done," Colt says in the background. "And he always will do. Guys like Chase don't change."

I feel like I'm going to faint. It all makes sense now. He didn't use me, not specifically. He just did what he always does. Evidently. He slept with me and abandoned me. That's exactly how it's felt, ever since I woke up alone this morning.

But… *disposable?*

Oh my God… what have I done?

Chase

It's eight-thirty by the time we arrive at the hotel in Denver, and although both Eli and I do a lot of traveling, we're both exhausted. We're also hungry, but we agree to order room service in our own bedrooms, and call it a night. We've spent the last thirteen hours sitting together in cars, planes and cabs, and we could do with some downtime. And a shower.

I dump my bags at the end of the bed and fall backwards onto it, staring up at the ceiling, and I can't deny, I feel kinda weird. I've been like this all day, although I haven't been able to put my finger on what's wrong. But now I'm here, in another hotel, by myself, I realize what I think it might be…

I'm lonely.

I know that's odd, because I'm often in hotel rooms by myself. But then I'm often in hotel rooms with other women too. Only now, I don't want to be with anyone else. I just want to be with Eva. And she's not here.

I left her behind.

And I didn't even say goodbye to her.

And I know now that I was wrong to do that.

I shouldn't have left her like I did, because she probably woke up, found the bed empty and that I was gone, without even so much as a kiss goodbye, and wondered whether the last few days had meant anything at all to me. Obviously, I don't know whether they meant anything to her, but I guess it's possible. And that means I should've at least been honest with her, and told her how I feel. And rather than pretending to myself that it was all about getting her into bed, I should have admitted that it meant so much more than that. I shouldn't have worried about whether I had the right to say something, I should have taken my chance while it was staring me in the face. I should have explained to her that I don't want whatever we had on the island to end and that I want to see her again, when we get back home. I owed her that much, at least.

And now it's too late…

Or is it?

Just because I screwed up and walked away, doesn't mean I can't say sorry.

I might have hurt her, but I can explain. And I can make it up to her. We just need to talk, and that means I need to call her.

I sit up and pull my phone from my pocket, going to my contacts, and I even start scrolling through them before I realize I don't have her number. Why would I? I've never needed it.

My head falls into my hands. What the hell am I going to do? I can't just leave things as they are. Eva's probably already decided I'm the worst kind of loser there is, and I need to at least say sorry for walking out on her.

My finger is hovering over the letter 'B', and I realize that I do have an option; I can call my sister. She'll have Eva's number, and although

I've got no intention of explaining my reasons to Bree, I can make up something.

I connect a call to her and wait… and wait. And eventually she answers, sounding a little out of breath.

"Chase? What the hell do you want at this time of night?"

"What do you mean? It's only eight forty-five."

"Not in Boston, it's not."

She has a point. In Boston it'll be nearly eleven, and from the sound of things, she might well have been occupied. "Did I interrupt something?"

"Yes, you did."

I can't help smiling. "Sorry, Sis."

"You will be," I hear Colt growl in the background.

"Have you got me on speaker?" I ask.

"No. But Colt is holding the phone for me. I'm kinda tied up." I know she's probably talking literally, not figuratively. Colt is a Dominant, after all.

"He doesn't need to know that, Bree," Colt says, sounding disgruntled. I can't say I blame him. I've never had a problem in the past with talking about my own sexual exploits, but there's no way I'd want to discuss the things I've done with Eva. Not with anyone else.

"He's right. You're my little sister."

"Oh, stop going all big brother on me. I get enough of that from Max. And besides, Colt and I are engaged now, so…"

"You're engaged?" I can't believe it. The last I heard, Colt had just moved into Bree's apartment. "When the fuck did that happen?"

"About a week ago," she replies. "On the same day that he bought us a house…" Her voice fades.

"He's bought you a house?"

"Yeah."

"And I'm only hearing about this now, because…?"

"Because you're never here," she says, reasonably.

"You could've called." I don't know why I feel so put out, but I do.

"Sorry," she mutters. "I should've told you." I feel kinda guilty now.

"I'm sure you've had better things to do with your time."

"Yeah, she has," Colt says. "Did you call for a reason?"

I wanna tell him to butt out, but I don't. He's gonna be Bree's husband, so I have to try and get along with him, even if that's never worked for either of us in the past.

"Yeah. I just need Eva's number. I remembered something on the flight, which I should have told her about, and I need to send her a message."

That sounds like a reasonable, work-related excuse. At least it does to me, and it clearly does to Bree as well.

"Oh, no problem. I was only talking to her a couple of hours ago, and she was saying that everything is going really well. But I can text you her number, if you need it."

"Yeah, if you could, that'd be great." I don't comment on their conversation. I can't afford to slip up. "I'll let you get back to whatever you were doing," I say instead, and Bree chuckles as we end our call.

I only have to wait a minute before my phone beeps, letting me know I've got a message, and sure enough, it's from Bree, although I imagine Colt had to send it for her, if she's as tied up as she seems to have been. Either way, I don't care, because I've got Eva's number, and I save it to my contacts list, and then debate whether to call her or send a message. It'll be gone eleven by now in St Thomas, and I don't want to wake her, so maybe a text message would be best. For now.

—Hi, I hope you're okay. I hope your day was good. We've just arrived in Denver and I know it's late, but maybe when you pick this up, you could call me? In the meantime, sleep well. Chase.

My finger hovers over the 'x' for ages, and I wonder whether to add a kiss or two, but think better of it, and press 'send' instead.

I know I haven't said any of the things I wanted to say, but I don't think a text message is really the place for that. And just sending something to her actually makes me feel better. I've opened the lines of communication; I've made a start. Now all I need is for her to call me.

I haven't slept very well, but that's because I missed having Eva beside me. I missed having her in my arms.

That's kinda strange, considering I only slept with her in my arms for such a brief time. But she felt so at home there, I'm lost without her and it took me hours to get to sleep, even though I was bone tired by the time I'd eaten, showered and finally hit the bed.

I'm spending today looking around the hotel we're staying in, which is open as usual in spite of the fact that it needs major work. Which is why I've been sent here, to scope out the requirements, which were originally to enlarge the public areas, and add new and larger kitchens. I hadn't expected Max to say that he wanted to increase the number of bedrooms here as well, but he did, and emailed me his instructions, saying he wants me to look at constructing an extra floor on top of the two existing ones. This is one of the first hotels our father purchased, back in the 1980s. Nothing much has been done to it since, and if I'm being honest, it shows. The design is kinda dull, comprising a U-shaped building set around a central swimming pool, a car park out front and a garden area to one side, that never gets used, with tennis courts on the other, which I believe are quite popular. It's a little dated and unloved, and I'm quite looking forward to giving it a face-lift.

I meet with the manager over breakfast. He's a guy called Bill Dawson, who's been with the company for years, and is really enthusiastic at the prospect of the changes we've got in mind. That's totally understandable. Any improvements on this place will be good for business.

"I don't suppose you've got a set of blue-prints, have you?" I ask him as we finish eating. "My brother's got some specific details he's asked me to look at, which I wasn't expecting, so I didn't bring the office copy with me." It's the truth. Max throwing this additional work in at the last minute has caught me out. I hadn't anticipated needing the plans, and therefore, I don't have them.

"Sure," he says, smiling at me through his steel-rimmed glasses, and nodding his blond head at the same time. "I'll have to go back to my office and look them out, but we've got a set. We have to, in case of emergencies."

I already knew that, but I find it pays to be polite, rather than make assumptions, and I thank him anyway. "Is it okay if I just wander around?" I ask, as another courtesy.

"Of course. You own the place," he replies, smiling.

"Thanks. I'll come find those prints later on. I won't be needing them this morning."

He nods and we get up from the table in the restaurant. I can't help thinking that Eva could make this place look so much better, and she probably will do, when I've finished my end of the deal. In the meantime, I've got work to do, although as I'm leaving the restaurant, with Eli in tow, I check my phone and can't hide my disappointment that I don't have any messages, or any missed calls either, and I turn the sound back up, being as I'm not in a meeting any longer.

I spend the day going through the public rooms in the hotel, studying the original notes Max gave me before I left Boston, which feels like a lifetime ago. I need to assess the level of work that's gonna be required to bring this place up to scratch. It's actually more than I expected, and I'm wondering if I should have allowed myself a bit more time here. I could stay longer if I had to, because I'm only heading home for some R&R. But that's not gonna happen, because I need to get back to Boston, preferably before Eva does. So, after I've collected the plans from Bill Dawson's office, I spend a couple of hours in my room, jotting down notes and making a start on some preliminary drawings, while the ideas I've had are still fresh in my mind. I'm gonna need to spend a lot longer looking at the kitchen, because I can't believe how small it is, and how much work is gonna be involved in enlarging it. And I'll have to study the plans to see what I can do about Max's new idea too, which has added to my workload when I least needed it. It's gonna be a busy two weeks, that's for sure.

But at least it'll take my mind off of Eva, and the fact that it's now evening, and I'm getting ready to go down to dinner with Eli, and she still hasn't answered my message.

"That steak was incredible," Eli says, putting down his fork as he finishes his meal and taking a sip of the red wine I ordered for us both.

"I know. The chef here is a genius. That's why Max wanted to have the kitchen and restaurant enlarged. We get really glowing reviews about the food, and the last thing he wants is for the chef to walk because he's gotta cook in a closet."

"That kitchen was really small, wasn't it?" he says, leaning back in his seat. He's been following me around all day, as usual, so he knows what I've been doing.

"Yeah. I've just gotta work out how to make it bigger, without losing too much space anywhere else…"

"So, you've gotta work a miracle?"

"Something like that."

"Well, at least the manager here seems a lot more on the ball than whoever the fuck was running the hotel at Point Knoll."

"Yeah, although that wouldn't be hard, would it?" He's just reminded me that I need to speak to Max about the situation down there. I'd kinda forgotten, what with everything that's been going on with Eva.

He smiles. "No, I guess not. And at least neither of us is having to share a room this time." His eyes sparkle mischievously.

"No, we're not," I reply, refusing to rise to his bait.

"Although I think you could, if you wanted to," he says, his smile broadening.

"Excuse me?"

"Haven't you noticed?"

"Noticed what?" I've got no idea what he's talking about.

He shakes his head, letting out a sigh as he leans in a little. "Your left, two women; one blonde, one redhead. They haven't stopped looking at you since we sat down." I turn my head and my eyes immediately lock onto the table in question, where two very beautiful women are staring right at me. The blonde has shoulder-length, straight hair and a light tan, while the redhead, who's currently biting her bottom lip, has a tangle of wild curls falling down her back. They whisper something to each other, and stand, picking up their purses, before they start walking straight toward us. They're both tall, and wearing very short dresses, which show off long, slender legs and slim figures, and I'm surprised by the fact that my body doesn't respond at all. Not in the slightest. In fact, I find it quite easy to turn away and look across the table at Eli.

"I'm just going to the men's room," he says, getting to his feet.

"Don't you dare leave me," I hiss at him, but he's already gone, striding off toward the entrance, and the bathrooms, which are in the lobby, and for a moment, I contemplate following him. Except the two women are already standing beside me, smiling down in my direction.

"Hi," says the redhead. "I'm glad your friend decided to leave."

"He is just a friend, isn't he?" the blonde asks, shuffling closer. "You're not… involved?"

"No, we're not." It's not the first time I've been asked that, and I doubt it'll be the last.

"Well, that's good to know." The blonde sits down in Eli's chair without waiting to be asked, while the redhead grabs another from a nearby table and settles it beside me.

"We've been watching you all evening, and we wondered if you wanna come up to our room?"

That was certainly to the point, and I look from her to her friend, and contemplate their suggestion. I mean, I've got no obligation to Eva. Let's face it, she still hasn't replied to my message, so she obviously doesn't care, even though I thought she might. In which case, why should I? I know that if I said 'yes' to these two women, I could have an entire night filled with mindless, no-strings sex. Hell, I could be buried deep inside one of them within the next five minutes if I really wanted to. And I wouldn't have to wake up and wonder about anything. Except probably which one of them to fuck first, before they went on their way again.

"What do you say?" the blonde asks, reaching across the table and running her hand down my arm.

The touch startles me, and I pull back.

"I—I'm sorry… I can't." I stand and look down at them.

"You can't?" The redhead is incredulous, and I don't blame her. I'm more than a little surprised myself. "What does that mean?"

"It means that, while I may not be involved with my friend, I am involved… with someone else." I hesitate over those last few words, because I know they're not strictly true. I'm not involved with Eva. Not in the normal sense of the word. But she's in my head, and until I can either talk to her and work out what's going on between us, or get her the hell out of there, there's no way I can think about even looking at another woman.

"Well, that's a damn shame," says the blonde, pouting slightly, although the redhead is already glancing around the room, presumably looking for someone else to proposition. It dawns on me then that all the women I've ever slept with have been like this: hungry, predatory, and mercenary about it. And while that's never bothered me in the past, I find it really unattractive now.

I make my excuses and leave them sitting there, walking over to the lobby, where Eli's waiting for me. I knew he would be. It's his job, after all.

"You're alone," he says, sounding puzzled.

"Of course I'm fucking alone." I look at him and frown. "And thanks for that."

"What do you mean?"

"I mean, thanks for abandoning me."

"Abandoning you? Since when have you wanted me sitting right on your shoulder in a situation like that?"

"Since now, okay?" I head for the elevators, and he follows, catching up with me.

"What's wrong?" he asks as I press the 'up' button.

"Nothing."

"Then why do you keep biting my head off, and more importantly, why don't you have two beautiful women hanging off of your arms?"

I ignore his first question, and just murmur, "Because I turned them down."

"Really? And might I ask why?"

"Why do you think?"

"How the hell do I know?" he says, biting my head off now.

I let out a long sigh, pushing my fingers back through my hair, and when I answer him, my voice is much quieter and more considered. "It's because of Eva."

He seems shocked, judging by his expression. "Wait a second... are you saying you're actually serious about her?"

"Yes, I am." There. I've admitted it. Out loud.

"Oh."

Oh? Is that the best response he can muster? "Why? Is that a problem?"

"No. It's just that I didn't think you were."

"Why not? You're the one who talked me into dating her. You're the one who convinced me I could be different for her."

"I know. But you kept talking like it was just about the island. You put so much emphasis on everything having to happen before we left St. Thomas, I assumed you weren't looking for anything permanent. And besides, you only had a couple of days together. I didn't think you'd have time to..."

"To what?"

"To fall for her."

I'm not willing to confirm that to him, not before I've said it to Eva. So I just shrug my shoulders. "What does it matter to you?" I ask, switching the attention onto him.

He looks a little sheepish. "Because I wouldn't have left her such a matter-of-fact note, if I'd known you were in this for the long haul, for once in your life."

"What do you mean 'matter-of-fact'? What did you say to her?" Fear creeps up my spine, but then I realize whatever he said, it can't have been any worse than me saying nothing.

"Just that we'd maybe try and catch up with her sometime. It was kinda offhand."

"Don't sweat it," I murmur. "It doesn't matter now."

"Why not?"

The elevator arrives, and we step inside, waiting for the doors to close.

"Because I sent her a text message when we got here last night, and she still hasn't replied."

"She could be busy," he reasons.

"It's ten o'clock at night there. She'd better not be fucking busy."

He holds up his hands. "Don't over-react. Remember what happened to me. She might just be catching up on her sleep. You kept her awake a helluva lot over those last couple of nights."

I can't deny that. "I know. But how long does it take to type out a text message?"

He tilts his head to one side and I know he's run out of answers. Just like I have.

"Try calling her," he suggests.

"At this time of night?"

"Why not? You're never gonna get to sleep if you don't."

I suck in a breath and nod my head. Because I know he's right. I need to call her. I need to hear her voice. And I need to know where I stand.

I get into my room, having said goodnight to Eli, and I sit on the edge of the bed, holding my phone in my hands. I feel nervous all of a sudden, but I can't really afford to just sit here prevaricating. If I delay for much longer, it'll be too late to make the call. So, I take a breath and find her name in my contacts list, pressing the green button and holding the phone to my ear. It rings five times, and then her voicemail cuts in. That means her phone is on, and it rang, but she didn't answer. Is she maybe in the shower? Or is she choosing to ignore me? I'm kinda hoping it's the former, but I've got this feeling deep in the pit of my stomach that I'm allowing the last vestiges of hope to get in the way of reality. What annoys me, more than anything, is that, if she doesn't wanna talk to me, or – worse still – she doesn't wanna see me ever again, why can't she just say so? A simple text message would do it. It would hurt like hell, but at least I'd know.

I go back to my contacts, only this time, I tap on the 'message' icon, and I type…

—Hi. Sorry to bother you. Something's come up to do with the Mermaid's Chair site and I need to talk to you urgently. Can you call me when you get this message. Thanks, Chase.

I know it's sneaky. But if she's not gonna talk to me any other way, then I'm not sure I care. I wish it could be different, but…

My phone rings and I struggle to hide my disappointment as I connect the call. As much as I want to hear Eva's voice, I wish she was calling because she wanted to hear mine.

"Hi," I say, before she can get a word in.

"Hello." God, she sounds distant. Really aloof, and sad. "What's wrong?" she asks.

"I don't know, Eva. You tell me."

There's a moment's hushed silence before she says, "What are you talking about? You said you had something to tell me about the hotel site."

"Yeah. I lied. You weren't taking my calls, or answering my messages."

There's a slightly longer pause this time, and then I hear, "I'm tired, Chase," and, just hearing the emotion in her voice, it feels like someone cut a hole in my chest and ripped my heart out.

"Is that why you haven't called me? Are you okay? You're not sick, are you? Are you having problems at the site? Are your team giving you trouble again?"

"Can you stop firing questions at me?" she cuts in, sounding desperate.

"Sorry. I didn't mean to. I just need to talk to you." There… I've said it.

"So now you want to talk?" She sounds angry, presumably about my silent departure.

"Yes."

I hear her suck in a breath. "Well, I'm sorry, but I'm not in the mood. Like I said, I'm tired. And I'm confused, and…"

"Angry?" I guess, giving words to my thoughts.

"Yes."

"Anything else?"

"Yes. But I don't want to talk about all this over the phone."

Neither do I. "I get that," I murmur. "And I get that you're angry with me. You have every right to be. But we still need to talk. So, can

173

we at least agree to meet up when we're both back in Boston?" She doesn't reply for a second or two, so I add, "Please, Eva," because I don't mind begging.

"Okay…" She sighs.

She doesn't sound very enthusiastic. But that doesn't surprise me. I've hurt her.

"Thanks," I say, even though I know I ought to say 'sorry' as well. I'd rather do that to her face though, so she knows how much I mean it.

"I really should get to bed." She does sound tired, and as much as I'd rather talk for the next hour or so, I don't argue with her. "Trent's coming round a bit earlier tomorrow, so I need…"

"Trent?" Something flicks in my head, like a light switch, and I can't hold back. "What the fuck is Trent doing coming around there?"

"He's driving me into work, remember? Eli organized it."

I feel like an idiot. A jealous, stupid idiot. "Oh, yeah. Of course. I forgot."

"You're good at forgetting things, aren't you, Chase?" she murmurs.

"What does that mean?"

"Nothing…" There's a brief silence and then I hear a sob, right before the line cuts out and I know she's hung up on me.

I redial her number, but after five rings, it goes to voicemail.

So, I return to my message app, and start typing…

— I'm an idiot. Forgive me. Please? I'll call you when you get back to Boston. C

I let my finger hover over that 'x' again, only this time I press it, and then hit 'send'.

Three days have passed, and Eva hasn't replied to my message. And I've surprised myself by being okay with that. Because at least she didn't come back and tell me not to bother ever contacting her again. And that's gotta be a good thing. It means I've got something to look forward to when I get home. I've got something to hope for.

And in the meantime, I'm keeping myself busy.

I've already established that Max's idea isn't gonna fly. The structure of the building won't withstand another story being added, not without major underpinning, and I don't think he'll wanna get into that. However, I have come up with another idea, which I'm working on, and which I hope he might go for, even though it's not quite what he had in mind. It won't mean closing the hotel while the work is being carried out, and it might just solve the kitchen problem too. If I can get it right.

Eli asked about my call with Eva the next morning over breakfast, and I told him what had happened. He said he thought I was crazy, and that I should have been up front about how I feel.

"Call her back," he urged. "Tell her the truth."

I shook my head. "No. I can't tell her that over the phone, and besides, we've agreed we're gonna talk when we get home."

"And you think it's a good idea to wait that long?"

"I don't have any choice. She made it clear she doesn't wanna talk to me right now, so this is my best shot. And I'm gonna take it. Even if I do have to wait."

"Why doesn't she wanna talk to you now?" He frowned at me.

I didn't feel like explaining to him that I'd left her, without saying goodbye, or that she was understandably mad with me for that. Her accusation that I was good at forgetting things would have made that obvious, even if she hadn't already admitted it. So I just said, "It's complicated. But if she needs some time, then she can have it. I owe her that much." *And more.*

Now all I've gotta do is get through the next couple of weeks, and then I'll be able to see Eva again. And when I do, I'm gonna tell her the truth. And that means I'm gonna tell her I'm in love with her. Because I am. Completely. So, I'm gonna put my heart out there… and hope to God she doesn't break it.

Chapter Ten

Eva

That has got to be the longest three weeks of my life.

By the time I got on the plane to come home from St. Thomas, I was so tired, I was starting to feel ill, and I've got to admit I'm so relieved to be back here in Boston, that I've done nothing but sleep since Friday night, when I walked through the door and dumped my suitcase, checked my post and fell into bed. I mean, I've woken in fits and starts, and eaten occasionally, but the dominant feature of the last two days has been sleep.

Now it's Sunday morning, and although I still feel ludicrously tired, I am at least out of bed on what feels like a more permanent basis. That's mainly because my brother is due to arrive this afternoon, and I need to do some laundry and make up the spare bed. And try not to think too much about how nervous I feel at the prospect of seeing Chase tomorrow.

I can't deny I was surprised when he contacted me. That didn't seem like the behaviour of the kind of man Bree and Colt had described. So I was stunned when he kept trying. It was a little below the belt for him to use the hotel as an excuse to get me to return his calls, but I suppose I could see his point, being as I had no intention of doing so otherwise. I was angry with him because it felt like he'd treated me as though I was disposable; like I'd become another notch on his overused bedpost. And although I didn't actually say that out loud, I obviously made it clear I wasn't happy with him because he guessed about my anger. He even guessed there was more to it than that. But I told him I didn't want to talk about it over the phone. Which I didn't. That said, I'm not sure I want to talk about it face to face either. Not that I've got much choice now, because of course, he had to confuse me even further, by asking to see me when we're both back in Boston again. Which is why I'm so anxious. Because he'll have been back for over a week now, so that meeting is imminent.

Except, I got back here two days ago and I haven't heard a word from him. Not a single word.

In between my snatches of sleep, I've been telling myself that I don't care. Why should I? Why should I care about a man who took me to bed, took my virginity, and abandoned me? Why should I care that he blew up in my face, just because his co-worker was giving me a ride to work? Or that he made me feel forgotten in so many ways, and that he has a reputation with women, which is beyond my comprehension? Why should I care that he asked – well, practically begged – to see me, but hasn't been in touch? Because I can't stop loving him, I guess. I can't just switch off my emotions, or my memories of how good he made me feel, any more than I can't stop Bree's words from echoing around my head. And knowing that he sleeps with 'anything that moves', not only do I feel somewhat belittled, I also can't help wondering how many women he's managed to squeeze into his bed in the three-week gap since we were last together.

And I can't stop crying.

I finish my coffee, clear away the tissues from the table, and take a shower. It's surprisingly exhausting, and afterwards, I have to rest for half an hour on the sofa, before I can even think about putting on the laundry.

I've got no idea why I'm so tired, but it's been like this for the last week or so. Which, thinking about it, is probably because there was a hurricane alert on the island.

I'd never been through anything like that before, and neither had any of my team, or Trent, who had a panic attack and walked off the site when the announcement was made. I had to rely on the local workers to tell me what to do and how to secure the site in readiness for the storm, which we were told would hit thirty-six hours later.

I decided that, even though we were almost finished, we needed to put the interior work to one side and focus on safety first. And the best part about that was that everyone took the situation really seriously and got on with the jobs they were allocated. Even Alyssa, who'd been a complete nightmare ever since Chase's departure. It was hard to put my finger on what was different about her, but she was behaving very strangely towards me, and recalling the way she'd flirted with Chase on his last day, I wondered if that had something to do with it. Either way, I wasn't going to get into any of her games, and ignored her as best as I could.

Obviously, the hurricane warning put all thoughts of personal problems to one side, and we worked as a team to make sure we got everything done.

After his initial breakdown, Trent returned and joined in, but didn't seem to want to take charge. Which meant I had to. And although I found it very stressful, and we all had a sleepless night during the preparations, we got there in the end. And then, despite our hard work in securing the site, the hurricane by-passed the island, and hit the coast of Florida instead. It wasn't as bad as they'd originally feared. There was no loss of life, and although there was some structural damage, it was minor compared to what might have happened. Evidently. For myself, I was just relieved that everyone on the island was safe, and after another few days we were able to complete our work and fly back to Boston. And at least all the members of my team are either on holiday or allocated to other projects for the next couple of weeks, so I won't have to work with them anytime soon. And I'm glad about that.

I smile to myself and let my head rest against the back of the sofa. It's no surprise I'm so tired when I think about everything that's happened to me over the last month.

Between meeting Chase, falling in love, discovering how incredible sex can be, and then finding out that he's not the man I thought he was. Plus going through the hurricane warning and having to take over the management of the hotel site in Trent's absence, I'm surprised I'm still standing.

Although I'm not. I'm sitting. And I need to be standing.

I need to be doing my laundry, and putting clean sheets on Ronan's bed. Because my brother will be arriving in a couple of hours, and I haven't done anything yet. I'm just grateful that he's making his own way here, and I don't have to meet him at the airport. I'm not sure I'm capable.

"Eva!"

I hold open the door and Ronan steps inside, giving me a hug.

He's tanned, and his blond hair seems even lighter and more dishevelled than usual, although that's not the biggest change, being as he's now sporting a beard.

"What's this?" I say, reaching up and running my fingers over the short hairs.

"I couldn't be bothered to shave it off when I got back from Greece at the end of the summer," he says. "And I've got used to it now."

"It makes you look..." I struggle for the right word.

"Distinguished?" he suggests.

"No. I was going to say older."

He grins and pulls me into a hug and as I reach up and put my arms around him, I relish that feeling of being safe, which has always come from my big brother. And from Chase. Before he left me, that is.

Ronan leans back and holds me at arm's length.

"You look tired," he says, frowning.

"I feel tired. But then I only got back from the Caribbean a couple of days ago."

"The Caribbean?" His frown deepens. "Wasn't there a hurricane down there?"

"Nearly. It hit Florida in the end, but they thought it was going to hit St. Thomas, where I was, and it was pretty scary, I can tell you."

"But you're okay?"

"Yes. I'm fine. I'm just tired, what with all the extra work, and the flight…"

He rolls his eyes. "Don't talk to me about flights. The direct ones were all booked, which was okay. It just meant a two-hour stopover in Paris. Except for some reason that became a five-hour stopover in Frankfurt."

"Why were you diverted?"

"I've got no idea."

I feel guilty for not noticing that he's late. But then Ronan's often late, because he's been held up by a student, or worse still, because he's flying in from somewhere remote, and is dependent on airlines and taxis, and other people.

"Do you want to come inside, rather than standing in the doorway?" I suggest and he smiles, picking up his rucksack, which he dumped on the floor to hug me, and stepping into my apartment.

I close the door and stand beside him as he looks around.

"Nice place." He turns and smiles at me.

"It's not mine; it comes with the job."

He leans into me. "It's still a nice place. And your bosses must think a lot of you, if they let you have a flat like this."

I shrug my shoulders, because I'm not sure what my bosses think of me. At least, I'm not sure what Chase thinks of me. And he's the only one of my bosses whose opinion matters at the moment.

"Shall I show you to your room? And you can take a shower, if you want."

"I don't know about 'want'. I think 'need' might be a better way of putting it."

I smile up at him and lead him to the guest bedroom, which is at the other end of the huge living area.

"This is the main bathroom," I explain as we pass a door to our left. "And my bedroom's through there." I indicate the door, which is slightly ajar, before standing aside and letting him enter his own room. "The shower isn't the biggest, I'm afraid." I go over to the ensuite and open the door.

He comes up behind me and peeks inside.

"No. I've seen bigger. But who cares?" He puts his arm around my shoulder. "You landed on your feet here, Eva."

I smile up at him. "I know."

I mean it too. Because it's true. I'm very lucky to have this place. And a job I love.

I just hope I haven't screwed it all up by sleeping with my boss.

Ronan has showered and I've ordered in a Chinese take-away, which we're eating on the sofa, because there's no dining table here, just a breakfast bar, which I rarely use.

"What are your plans?" I ask him, tucking into my special fried rice.

"Well, I was thinking about staying until after Thanksgiving, if you'll have me?"

I can't help grinning. "That long? Wow… that would be amazing."

I'd half expected him to say he could only stay for a few days. But the prospect of having him here for a couple of weeks is just fantastic.

"Don't you have to get back to the university?" I ask, because as Chase pointed out, it is November; Ronan ought to be teaching.

"Not this time." He smiles, like a kid with a new toy, and the says, "I won't be going back until next year."

"Next year?"

He nods his head with boyish enthusiasm. "The college has put some money into that major dig I mentioned in Peru, via a donation from some wealthy philanthropist, whose name I'm not allowed to know. And they wanted to have someone present."

"But why you? Surely, Colin is the senior lecturer."

"Colin is the head of faculty," he corrects me. "And that means he's far too important to tag along on a dig like this."

"But you just said it was major."

"And it is. Except we're not the main sponsors, and I don't think Colin wanted to play second fiddle to the guy the Americans are sending down there. I think there's some history between them."

"Oh, I see."

I know from past experience – or from Ronan's past experience – that rivalry between archaeologists can sometimes get completely out of proportion.

"We're due to start at the beginning of December," he says. "And I've got to have a couple of meetings with this guy called Professor McLean, who's heading up the dig. He's at Boston University, so I thought I'd use that as an excuse to come over here a bit early, to see my little sister and spend Thanksgiving with her."

"Hmm… whatever Thanksgiving actually is." I smile across at him, and he smiles back.

"Well, you are living here now, so you might as well get into the swing of things. Unfortunately, the timing of all that means I won't be able to see you at Christmas…" He lets his voice fade, and the reality of that prospect hits me.

"Oh." It'll be the first time we've spent Christmas apart, being as in the past, he's always made it home.

"I'm sorry," he whispers, putting his plate down on the table and leaning closer to me. "But this is a big opportunity for me, and I can't turn it down. The university have granted me a whole year's sabbatical, to undertake the dig, on their behalf. I wouldn't normally be entitled to that yet. I haven't been there long enough."

"I see. So that's why you're able to stay here for so long, rather than just coming over for your meetings, and flying back again for lectures?" I decide not to make a fuss about Christmas, but to let him have his moment. He deserves it. He works really hard. And as much as I don't like the idea of spending the festive season by myself in a strange country, I can't begrudge him this.

"Yes." He smiles. "It's also why I was able to spend my entire summer in Greece. Because I didn't have to do any prep work for this semester. It's not normally something I'd be able to consider, but I had a great time."

I'm not sure I want to know about that. Although Ronan takes his career really seriously, I have a feeling his idea of 'a great time' might not always revolve around the antiquities, and might have more to do with his female companions.

"So, you're going to be in Peru until next autumn?" I change the subject, the meaning of everything he's said finally adding up inside my head.

"No. Only until May. It's a six-month dig, but by the time I'm finished down there, the academic year will be almost over, so I'm being allowed some time off… for good behaviour."

"Six months?" I murmur. It's better than a year. Obviously. But it still sounds like such a long time. It's certainly the longest we've ever been apart, and I can't help feeling nervous. He obviously notices, because he takes my hand in his and gives it a gentle squeeze.

"Look on the bright side," he says, "At least with you being here, I'm only three thousand miles away, instead of six. And, with that in mind, once the dig is up and running and everything is more settled, I should be able to get a few days off here and there, so I can come and visit. If you'll have me."

"Of course I'll have you."

I smile at him, and he picks up his plate again and continues eating. "When are you going back to work?" he asks.

"Tomorrow, unfortunately."

"Why 'unfortunately'? Don't you like your job?" He turns to me, looking concerned.

"Yes." I don't mention my nerves over seeing Chase again. I'm not ready to explain that to him. "But it's been a busy few months. I could do with some time off."

"And you can't take any?"

"Not at the moment, no. The company's in the middle of a huge refurbishment project."

"And I'm guessing you're a big part of that?"

"Well, I don't know about 'big', but I'm a part of it, yes."

He shakes his head. "Don't put yourself down, Eva. They must trust you, or they'd never have sent you down to the Caribbean by yourself."

"I know. But I wish I could spend some more time with you." I change the subject because I hate talking about myself. "It seems such a shame that you've come all this way, and I'll hardly get to see you."

He nudges into me. "Don't worry about that. I'm sure I'll find plenty of things to keep me busy. And I can cook for you in the evenings."

I lean back, staring at him. "Are you serious? You want to poison me?"

He chuckles. "I've improved… a little. I can make a half decent bolognese sauce, and my chilli isn't too bad."

"I'll take your word for that. I still haven't recovered from your attempt at goulash."

He laughs out loud. "No. I'm not sure I have, now you come to mention it."

"Well, it was disgusting."

"No, it was worse than disgusting. It was inedible."

"I don't even know how you got it so wrong."

"Neither do I. I followed the recipe and everything…"

"Yes, but was it a recipe for goulash?" I ask, and he laughs, shaking his head.

It's raining this morning, but I'm not going to let that put me off walking to work, and I put on my jacket as Ronan finishes eating his breakfast.

"I thought I might take you out for dinner tonight," he says, looking up from his bowl of cereal.

"What happened to bolognese and chilli?" I ask from the door.

"Nothing. I just feel like taking my little sister out, that's all."

I smile over at him, and nod my head, because that sounds really nice, and then I let myself out, and make my way to the lift, checking my phone as I walk, and hoping that Chase might have sent a message.

He hasn't. He hasn't been in touch at all. And that feels strange, and even as I re-read his earlier text, and recall how he begged me to agree to meet him, I can't help feeling as though I've been dismissed; as though maybe he's found someone better to spend his time with.

I bite back my tears, refusing to cry over a man who doesn't even understand the word 'commitment', let alone know how to live by it, and I hurry through the light shower to work, arriving right on time.

After a month away, my office feels strange, and I hang my jacket behind the door, fetching myself a coffee from the kitchen, before I settle behind my desk and switch on my computer, discovering that I've already got an e-mail waiting for me from Bree, saying that she wants to see me as soon as I get in. I swallow hard, wondering what this can be about. I doubt Chase will have told her about us; I'm not important enough to him. But it seems possible that one of the team might have complained about something. That wouldn't surprise me in the slightest. So, taking my coffee with me, I make my way along the corridor to the elevators, and up one floor to where all the management offices are situated.

There's a reception area with three large sofas, where Bree's bodyguard Dana normally sits during the day, but she's not there as I exit the lift, and I turn to my right, walking along the hallway to Bree's office, knocking on her door.

"Come in," she calls and I enter as Bree looks up from behind her wide, light wood desk, her dark hair falling in ringlets over her shoulders.

"Hello, stranger." She smiles.

"Hello." At least if she's smiling, this can't be all bad.

"I hear things went really well down in St. Thomas," she says, nodding to the chair in front of her desk, which I sit down on, looking at her.

"You do?"

"Yes. I've had a report from Trent." She glances at her computer. "He says you saved the day."

"I—I wouldn't go that far." I can feel myself blushing.

"That's not what he says, and I'm really proud of you, Eva."

I take a sip of coffee to cover my embarrassment, and then mumble, "Thank you," because it feels appropriate.

"How did you get along with him?" she asks, and I startle, staring up at her.

"Who?" Has she heard a rumour about Chase? God knows how, if she has. We were really careful.

"Trent," she replies, and I sigh out my relief, and then try to breathe normally again, hoping she won't have noticed.

"Um… fine," I reply. "Why?"

"Chase was having a few issues with him. I just wondered what you thought… how you found him."

I wonder if I should say anything. I know Trent asked me not to, but it hardly seems right that the people he works for think he's being inefficient and unhelpful, when in reality, he's ill.

"He's not well." I blurt out the words on the spur of the moment.

Bree stares at me. "What do you mean, 'he's not well'?"

I shake my head and put my coffee down on her desk. "I'm sorry, but I can't go into details. He told me in confidence, and I can't break that, but he's having some health problems and they're affecting his work."

A frown settles on Bree's face. "Is Chase aware of this?"

"No. And I wouldn't have told you about it, except that I'm wondering if maybe there's something you can do to help him. You, or Max… or Chase?"

She nods her head. "It's kinda hard, when we don't know what's wrong. But I'm not gonna ask you to break a confidence." She thinks for a moment. "Trent might be more willing to talk to Max. They're closer in age, and it was Max who hired him in the first place. I'll ask Max, and see if he can find a way to speak to him."

"That would be good." I feel relieved at having told someone, and hopefully put Trent on the path towards getting some help. "He knows he's got a problem," I add, "but he's just being…"

"A man?" Bree suggests, and we both laugh.

"Yes. A man." I nod my head and pick up my coffee again, taking a sip. "So, what's next for me?" I may be exhausted, but I still have a job to do, and it's best if I look keen and interested, rather than giving the impression that I'd rather still be in bed. Which I would.

"It was gonna be Denver," she says, shifting some papers on her desk, and I feel my heart flip over in my chest, because I know Denver is where Chase was going, when he left St. Thomas.

"Was?" I query.

"Yes. Was. But that's all changed. There's gonna be a delay in starting that project."

"Oh?"

"Yeah. Chase had a few problems with something Max had asked him to do in Denver, which he said he'd resolved, and he sent Max a message telling him he'd talk it over with him when he got back. Except he hasn't been back yet. He's had to divert to Miami instead."

"Miami? Why?" I sit forward, but then think twice about it and try to look more relaxed, although my whole body is on edge.

"That hurricane... the one that was due to strike land in St. Thomas... it caught the coast of Florida and did some damage to our hotel in Miami. Chase has had to go there and assess the situation. He wasn't happy about it. In fact, he was livid, according to Max, but it had to be done."

"So, when will he be back?" I ask, trying to sound disinterested, as though my question is purely work related.

"He contacted Max at home yesterday and said he'll be another week." She looks up and rolls her eyes. "To be honest, that's worked out quite well."

Not for me it hasn't. "It has?"

"Yes. For one thing, it means he'll be back in time for Thanksgiving. But more importantly, he can fly back with our mom. She's been down there for a couple of months, visiting our aunt, and she hates flying. So he'll be able to hold her hand, and stop her drinking the airline's entire supply of scotch."

I manage a smile, as Bree explains that, in Chase's absence, she wants me to start work on the designs for the hotel in Richmond.

"I—I won't need to go there, will I?"

"No. We've got the plans and up-to-date images of all the rooms that Max wants upgraded, and besides, I think you've done enough travelling for now."

I can't disagree with her, and besides, the last thing I want to have to do is to leave again. Especially not when Ronan's staying, and I can barely keep my eyes open.

She tells me she'll e-mail over the pictures I need, and that we'll have another meeting on Friday, so she can see where I'm at with my ideas.

That schedule feels okay to me. It means I won't have to rush anything. And that's just as well, because I'm too tired.

As I walk back to my office, clutching my coffee cup, I feel slightly relieved. At least Chase's silence wasn't a rejection. It felt like it, but it wasn't. Because he's not even here. Of course, that could mean he's been sleeping with 'anything that moves' in Miami, as well as in Denver. It could mean he's been having romantic dinners, and picnics, and looking into someone else's eyes, while he makes love to them.

But I suppose I'll just have to wait another week to find that out. Won't I?

I still can't shake this tiredness. I'm even wondering now whether I'm unwell. And I think Ronan is too. In fact, I know he is, because he said to me last night, while we ate his bolognese sauce with some spaghetti – which was actually really good – that if I don't start to feel better in the next few days, he's going to take me to see a doctor. I didn't even have the strength to argue with him, and my only solace at the moment is that at least it's the weekend again. Although all that has meant is a return of my nerves. That's because Bree told me during our meeting on Friday that Chase is due to return home today – Sunday – and that means I'll see him tomorrow. I suppose my anxiety about seeing him again could explain why I keep feeling so sick, on top of my tiredness. Although I haven't dared to tell Ronan about that, because I know he'd be even more worried than he already is.

"You really are looking ever so pale, Eva," he says, coming out of his bedroom and sitting down on the couch beside me. "Are you sure you don't want me to take you to the hospital?"

"The hospital? No. I'll be fine. I've just been overworking."

"You told me that last weekend, and your week hasn't been that bad. But you keep getting worse, not better. Do you think you might have picked something up in the Caribbean?"

I shrug my shoulders, because to be honest, I was too busy working, and spending time with Chase. But I'm not about to tell Ronan that, and I'd rather just change the subject. "I don't know, but while we're discussing travelling," which we weren't, "when did you say you were going to be leaving?"

He smiles. "Are you trying to get rid of me?"

"No, of course not. But I can't remember now. Did you give me an actual date?"

"I didn't. But I'm booked on the evening flight next Sunday. Although how it can be nearly December already, I don't know…"

"Oh, my God… no." The words fall out of my mouth, as I realise what he's saying, and think about the date, and the tiredness, and how sick I've been feeling, and suddenly put two and two together.

Ronan sits forward, staring at me. "Eva, you've gone as white as snow. What's wrong?" he asks, his voice filled with concern.

I don't answer him, but pick up my phone from the coffee table in front of me and go to my calendar, double checking the date, and then looking at Ronan.

"It is the twenty-second today, right?"

"Yes. And? Is me staying until next Sunday a problem?" I drop my phone, unable to speak, and let my head fall into my hands, feeling even more sick than I did before. "Eva? Talk to me. Tell me what's wrong?" I feel him move closer, the sofa dipping beneath his weight and his arm coming around me, as I turn to look up into his worried eyes.

"I'm late," I whisper.

"What for?" He frowns.

"Don't be stupid, Ronan. I'm *late*, late."

His frown clears, but only slightly, and he swallows hard before speaking. "I—I didn't even know you were seeing someone."

"I'm not sure that I am. I mean, I was. At least, I think I was. Sort of. But now, I don't know what's going on."

"Eva, that doesn't make the slightest bit of sense."

I look up at him and murmur, "I know it doesn't," and then I burst into tears.

He puts both arms around me now, hugging me. "Hey," he says softly. "Don't cry. And don't panic either. You don't know for sure that you've got anything to panic over…"

"You don't think the tiredness, and the fact that I've started to feel sick might be fairly big clues?"

"You've started feeling sick?" he says, his eyes widening slightly.

"Yes. Today."

"Okay… well, I suppose that is fairly indicative. But it's possible you might be feeling tired and sick because you're unwell. We need to find a pharmacy, so we can get you a pregnancy test. And then at least you'll know for sure."

"And then can I panic?"

"Then we can start working out what we're going to do," he reasons, and I love him more than ever for including himself in my predicament, and not making me feel quite so alone. Even though I am. And I will be, considering he's going to be in Peru for the next six months. "Come on," he says, getting to his feet and pulling me up with him. "There's no time like the present…"

"How long do we have to wait?" Ronan asks, turning to face me as I come out of the bathroom, clutching the little plastic stick in my hand.

"Three minutes."

He looks down at his watch, and then back at me again, nodding his head. "So," he says, putting his hands in his pockets, "how likely is this? I mean, the guy you were with, who you're not sure you were with… did he use protection?"

I stare up at him. "I'm not sure I want to discuss this with my big brother," I reply, but he narrows his eyes and folds his arms across his chest, and I know from experience that he's not about to back down.

"You're my little sister, Eva, and it looks to me like some guy might have been careless with you. So, tell me, is it possible?"

I nod my head, and he lets out a long sigh, just as I turn over the stick and read the word 'Pregnant' in the small screen, and burst into tears again.

Chase

The flight from Miami doesn't land until seven-thirty, and my only saving grace is that at least I don't have to take my mom home. I've had to hold her hand during the entire journey though, because she hates flying, which has made me wonder why she takes these trips to see Aunt Celia. Obviously, I know how she manages the flight in the normal course of events; she gets drunk. Not ugly drunk; funny drunk. As only my mom can. But on this occasion, she just held my hand and talked, for hours. There were several times during the flight when I thought about asking Mom's bodyguard, Alexis, if she'd swap places with me. But I figured Mom would listen to me, about turning down the scotch, and she probably wouldn't listen to Alexis. And besides, Alexis has had to put up with her for the last two months; the poor woman deserved a break.

Even so, by the time we've said goodbye and Alexis has helped Mom into a cab, and they've driven away, I'm beyond fed up. Eli goes to rescue my car from the long-term parking lot, where he left it weeks and weeks ago, before we went to Atlanta, and left to myself, all I can think about is how badly things have turned out.

I should have been back here days ago. That was all part of the plan. In fact, that *was* the plan; to get back here before Eva. Except like all plans, it didn't quite work out. Eva will have been home for over a week now, and I haven't even had time to call her. Not that I wanted to call her, or text her. I wanted to see her, like we agreed, so I could tell her I'm in love with her, and I could ask her – or beg her, if necessary – to give us a chance. And I haven't been able to. Because I've been stuck in Miami.

I recognize the sleek lines of my dark blue BMW and step forward as Eli pulls up. He gets out and loads our bags into the trunk while I get into the passenger seat. I'm not in the mood for sitting in back by myself, and he doesn't seem surprised when he gets in, to find me right alongside him.

"Take me to the office?" I say, without looking at him, even though I'm aware that he's turned to face me.

"Now?"

"Yes."

"At this time, on a Sunday night?"

"Yeah… at this time on a Sunday night. There's something I need to do."

He doesn't comment, but puts the car into 'drive', and pulls out, heading into the city.

There's almost no traffic, so our journey is fairly short, and silent, which is just as well, because I don't feel like talking. Not to Eli, anyway. There's only one person I need to talk to, but before I can do that, I need to go to work. Because there's something I need to find out.

Eli parks up in my usual spot in the underground parking garage, and we both get out, and although I think about asking him to wait here for me, I know there's no point. At this time of night, with the offices being deserted, he's never gonna agree to that.

Instead, we walk together to the elevators, and I use my key to activate them, being as they're shut down for the weekend. Once the doors have opened, I press the button for the eighth floor, and we stand together, while we're carried upwards, until the doors open again.

Eli exits ahead of me, which doesn't surprise me in the slightest, and I follow, making my way to my office, where I flick on the lights and sit at my desk, leaving Eli standing over by the door, watching me.

"What are we doing here?" he asks at last, once his curiosity has finally gotten the better of him.

"I need to look something up," I reply, without giving anything away.

"And you couldn't do that from home? Or on your phone?"

"No. Some of our files are only available if you log in through specific computers."

He raises his eyebrows. "What kind of files are they, for Christ's sake?"

"Personnel files."

He nods his head slowly. "This is about Eva, isn't it?"

"Yeah, it is."

"Are you accessing her personal file?"

"Yeah, I am."

He frowns. "Are you sure you should be doing that?"

"I'm only getting her home address, that's all."

Once I've input my password, I click on the folder marked 'Personnel', which I know only Max, Bree, myself and Colt Nelson have access to, and when it opens, I scroll through to the letter 'S', where I find Eva's file. I click on that, and wait a moment, drumming my fingers on the desktop, and eventually the file comes up, showing the address of the apartment that Bree arranged for her. I pull out my phone and enter it into my contacts, under her name, before quickly shutting down my computer again.

As I stand, I glance up at Eli. "Okay?" he says calmly.

"Yeah... except I need to ask a favor."

He shrugs his shoulders, and I lock my office before we make our way back to the elevators.

"What's the favor?" he asks, being as I haven't said anything.

"I need you to take a cab back to my place, collect your car, and go home. And then I'll call you in the morning and tell you where to pick me up from."

"Excuse me?"

"I need you to..."

He holds up his hand as the elevator doors open and we both get inside. "I heard you the first time," he says, punching the button for the parking garage. "But I'm not sure you completely understand how this bodyguard thing works."

"Yeah, I do. But on this occasion, I'm asking you to let me do something by myself."

"I can't do that, Chase."

"Please, man. I haven't seen her for a month. And we've got a lot to talk about. I've got a lot of things I need to tell her... to explain to her. And I can't do it with you there."

"I'm not suggesting I'd be in the room with you," he reasons. "But I can't let you go by yourself."

"Yeah, you can. She only lives ten minutes from my place. If there are any problems, I'll call you. But I can't do this if I know you're sitting downstairs in the car, waiting for me."

"Because you're hoping she'll let you stay the night?" he says.

"Maybe. But also because I need to be completely alone with her. You've been in my shoes, Eli. You know what this feels like."

He looks at me for what feels like a long time. "Colt will go batshit crazy."

"Then don't tell him."

He lets out a sigh. "Okay. But if you're even slightly concerned, you call me. And then you call 911. Got it?"

"Got it." He holds out the car keys, and I take them from him. "And thanks."

I find Eva's apartment easily, and as I park on the street outside, I have to say, my sister did good. The exterior is red brick, and older than a lot of apartment blocks in the area, but inside the finish is sleek and modern, and as I wait for the elevator to take me up to the third floor, I nod my head in silent appreciation.

I'm feeling nervous, but kinda excited at the same time. It's been so long since I've seen Eva, and there's a part of me that can't wait to hold her in my arms, and kiss her, and tell her how I feel. But at the same time, I know she was mad with me, and I don't blame her. And I know I've gotta overcome those uncertainties and explain why I left her the way I did, before I can do any of the things I really want to do. Before I can tell her I'm in love with her, and that I always will be.

The elevator doors open and I hesitate as I walk out, unsure whether to go to my right or my left. I choose left, and make my way along the hallway, until I reach the first door, startling slightly, as I read the number 310, which is Eva's apartment.

I hadn't expected that, and I feel my palms start to sweat.

Pull it together, man. This is what you want.

I take a deep breath and ring her doorbell, stepping back slightly and waiting.

It takes a few moments, but then the door opens, and my heart literally splinters in my chest as I take in the sight of the tall blond man standing before me. It's bad enough that he's incredibly handsome, with a square, bearded jaw and pale blue eyes, but what makes this so much worse, what hurts more than anything, is that he's standing in front of me, wearing pajamas, and looking kinda sleepy; like he just got out of bed. And considering it's only just nine o'clock in the evening, that's not very inspiring.

"Can I help?" he asks, tipping his head to one side and pushing his fingers back through his hair. "Were you looking for Eva?"

"No!" I bark, and he jumps. "Sorry. No. I've got the wrong apartment."

I turn and quickly make my way back to the elevator, hearing the door close softly behind me.

How can she have another guy already? I get that she was angry with me, but…

The elevator doors open and I step inside as something else dawns on me. The guy looked very settled, like he was someone Eva had known for a while, not just a few days. Which means he must have already been in the picture, even when she was with me on the island.

"Fuck it!" I yell, and punch the elevator wall as I hit the button for the first floor.

She had someone else the whole time? Someone who was waiting here for her?

I shake my head. No. That doesn't make sense. I'm being stupid. She was a virgin. And a very innocent virgin at that.

This has to be someone she's met since. Someone who obviously moved quickly. Too quickly for me.

Why did I ever leave her? Why didn't I make sure she understood how I felt before I left? Why didn't I stay in touch? Why…?

"What's the fucking point?" I mutter to myself as the elevator doors open again, and I step out into the lobby, consumed with pain and regret.

None of it matters now.

It's too late.

I've lost her.

Dawn is breaking on the city skyline and I lean back into my leather couch, wishing I could sink into it completely and just disappear.

I've been sitting here all night, trying to work out where I went wrong. Because I know I did. My broken heart is enough evidence of that.

Leaving Eva without saying goodbye was a huge mistake. I know that. I knew it then. But I know it even more now. And not working things out with her while I was in Denver – regardless of her anger and hurt – wasn't very smart either. Because while neither of us wanted to talk about our feelings over the phone, I should still have let her know I was there for her, and that I wasn't giving up on us. The thing is, I thought doing what she wanted was the way to go. I thought giving her space was the wise move. How was I to know she'd take advantage of the distance between us, and my silence, to find someone else? It's not like I've ever done any of this before. I've never been in love. I've never even wanted to be. But I am now, and the woman I love is currently in bed, in the arms of another man. And that thought is so painful, I'm not sure I can take it.

I can't help remembering how hurt she was with me when I suggested she might fall into bed with the next man she met. I never meant to hurt her. But she didn't understand I only said that out of fear. A deep-seated fear that she'd find someone else, and break my heart.

And that's exactly what she's done.

Chapter Eleven

Eva

I stop crying eventually.

It takes a while, but Ronan gets me to calm down.

"Do you wanna talk?" he says, and I know that what he really means is that he wants to talk. He wants to know what happened, and with whom. But I can't explain it. Not yet. Because I can't even think straight.

"Not right now," I murmur, and he smiles.

"Why don't you get an early night?" he suggests, and I agree without needing too much persuasion. He says he's going to get ready for bed, but that he might sit up in his PJs and watch a movie or something. At least I think that's what he's saying. To be honest, my brain doesn't feel like it's working properly anymore. Because, as I walk through to my room and close the door behind me, all I can think about is Chase's words…

"I decided on the day my dad died that I don't wanna have children."

We might have talked about the fact that Chase isn't his father and shouldn't let him have that much control over his life, but that doesn't alter the fact that he didn't at any point say he was prepared to reconsider the situation. And now I'm pregnant, with his child.

And, as if that wasn't enough of a problem, I don't even know where I stand with him, because I haven't heard from him in weeks.

All I do know is that he's got a reputation for treating women like they're 'disposable'.

But even if he was interested in talking to me, or meeting up with me when he got back here, I can't imagine he will be, once he finds out that I'm pregnant.

God, what a mess…

The doorbell rings and I jump at the shrill sound, and am about to clamber off of my bed to answer it, when I hear Ronan's voice and reason that he must've got there before me. I can't say I'm sorry, because I'm not in the mood for talking to anyone, and I settle back onto the bed, at the same time as my phone rings, and I check the screen, just in case it's Chase.

It isn't. It's Alyssa, which surprises me, given that as far as I'm aware, she's still on holiday.

I think about ignoring her call, but then I reason that, for her to telephone me on a Sunday evening, it's got to be something important. So, I connect the call.

"Hello?"

"Hi… it's Alyssa."

I want to say, 'I know,' but I've learned it doesn't pay to be smart with her. So instead I just say, "Oh, hello."

"I'm sorry to call so late, but I wondered if we could meet up, outside of the office?"

"Outside of the office?" I echo, because her request has thrown me somewhat. We're not friends. We never have been, and I've got no idea what she can possibly have to say to me that can't be said at work. "I —I guess so."

"Great. Are you free tomorrow morning, at about eight? We could have breakfast."

"I guess. But what's so important that it can't wait? Or that you can't tell me now, over the phone?"

"It's something that I'd just rather discuss away from the office, that's all," she says, with an air of secrecy, and I wonder for a moment, if she's found out about Trent's problem. Or maybe if she's got one of her own. Although the thought of Alyssa confiding in me is almost laughable. Or it would be, if I didn't have so many problems of my own to deal with at the moment.

"Where shall I meet you?" I ask her, and she names a coffee shop that's just around the corner from the office. "Okay, I'll be there at eight."

She thanks me. She actually *thanks* me, and then she hangs up, and I lie back on the bed, wondering what on earth that can have been about. I know, being as it concerns Alyssa, that it won't be good. But considering the fact that I've just found out I'm pregnant, it's not really my priority right now.

I wake feeling sick, but then that's not surprising. At least, it's not as surprising as it was yesterday, because I know the reason now.

I'm not ill. I'm pregnant.

That thought echoes through my head as I slowly climb out of bed and hold on to my stomach, trying to control the rolling nausea.

I don't think I actually want to be sick, but my stomach is churning around and around, and as much as I'd like to sit here and let it settle, I don't have time. I've got to be at the coffee shop by eight, and it's seven-fifteen already.

I shower quickly and braid my hair, and then, after I've dressed in a skirt and blouse, I exit my bedroom to find Ronan sitting at the breakfast bar.

"You need to eat," he says, narrowing his eyes at me.

"I'd love to, but I've got a meeting."

"You have?"

"Yes. I got a call last night, from one of my team and they asked if we could have breakfast together this morning to go over something."

"Okay. Well, make sure you eat."

I shake my head at him. "That's the whole point of breakfast, isn't it?"

"Yes, but I know what you're like for skipping meals, and you can't do that now."

"I know." I can feel tears pricking behind my eyes, and he gets up and comes over to me.

He puts his hands on my shoulders and looks down at me.

"Just get through the next three days," he says softly. "And then you'll have four days off."

"I will?"

"Yes. Thursday is Thanksgiving, and Friday is a holiday here. And then it's the weekend. So, as I was saying, get through the next three days… then we can talk."

"Do we have to?"

"Yes. You need to decide what you're going to do."

I lean back and stare up at him. "I'm not having an abortion, if that's what you're suggesting I may not…"

He puts his fingers across my lips. "I'm not suggesting anything of the kind. I'm just saying that you've got some hard thinking to do… starting with telling the father. He needs to take responsibility."

I reach up and pull his hand away from my mouth. "I'm not sure he's going to want to."

"I wasn't making it optional." He's frowning down at me, and for a moment I see red.

"You can be really bossy sometimes, Ronan. Did you know that?"

He looks offended, and I want to take back my words. But before I can he says, "Do you seriously think I'm going to let some idiot get you pregnant and just walk away?"

"No," I whisper, calming in an instant, and Ronan puts his arms around me.

"I know this guy meant something to you, Eva, because I know you wouldn't have slept with him if he didn't. But you don't have to protect him. You can give me his name and address, and I'll go and see him…"

"No!" I raise my voice, and Ronan steps back, releasing me. "Look, I'm sorry. I didn't mean to shout, but can you please do what you just said? Can you give me the next three days to get used to the idea in my own head? And then, if you insist, we can talk."

"Okay."

"And in the meantime, can we just drop the subject?"

He pauses, like he's thinking over my request, and then he says, "If that's what you want."

"It is. I just need some time."

He nods his head "Okay. But remember, I'm here if you need me."

I smile at him, and he smiles back. "I know, Ronan."

"In that case, consider the subject dropped… for now. I'm gonna spend some time at the library this morning, and then I've got a meeting with Professor McLean," he says as I gather up my things. "Do you want me to pick something up for dinner?"

"Why don't we order in?" I suggest.

"Is my cooking that bad?"

"No, but if we order in tonight, we could maybe go shopping afterwards."

"What for?"

"Well, I think Thursday is a bit of a celebration here, so we could start getting ready for that, couldn't we?"

He smiles and takes my hand. "Yeah, I guess we could."

"And also, it's going to be my first Christmas here, *and* my first Christmas without you…" I struggle not to cry as I say those words, but manage to control myself. "I was thinking I might look at getting some decorations, so I can put them up after you've gone. It'll cheer me up."

He smiles and nods his agreement, pulling me into a hug, and I think to myself that, with any luck, going out tonight will distract me for a while from the train wreck that my life seems to have become.

Alyssa is already sitting in a booth near the back of the coffee shop when I arrive, and as I approach, she stands.

"Can I get you a coffee?" she offers.

"I don't mind getting my own."

She smiles, which is unusual in itself, and sets my nerves on edge. "No, I insist."

And before I can object, she's disappeared in the direction of the counter, and I decide I might as well take a seat. I remove my jacket first and lay it across the bench before sitting down and looking around. The coffee shop is fairly quiet, in terms of people eating in, although there's quite a queue at the counter, and I take my time studying the photographs on the walls, which are Italian landscapes, shot in black and white. They're very atmospheric and I like them.

"Here we are." Alyssa puts down a tray on the table between us and I notice that, not only has she bought coffees for both of us, but there are also two pastries as well. *What's going on here?*

She sits opposite me, unloads the tray and pushes it to one side before turning to face me.

"I like this place, don't you?" she says, looking around.

"Yes. I was just admiring the photographs."

"I know. They're great, aren't they?"

She sips her drink, although I notice she doesn't touch the pastry in front of her. I don't either, but I copy her action and take a small sip of hot coffee, even though it makes me feel sick again.

Putting my cup down, I look up at her and feel my stomach churn. And this time it has nothing to do with coffee or pastries. It's the look in Alyssa's eyes, which is calculating and slightly menacing. And suddenly I wish I was anywhere but here.

"W—What can I do for you?" I ask, trying desperately to control my voice.

"I've got something I want to show you," she says, smiling again as she reaches into her handbag, which is on the seat beside her. She pulls out her phone and presses a couple of buttons before she turns it towards me. "If you swipe to the left," she says, "you'll see there are more like that."

I take the phone from her and gasp as I see the image before me, feeling my blood turn to ice even as my face flushes crimson.

I'm looking at a familiar scene; the decked area that was outside the cabin in St. Thomas, with its yellow corner sofa and low table, overlooking the beach. And there, on the longest part of the sofa, is a couple, lying bound in the throes of passion. I recognise the man as Chase, even though he's mostly hidden from sight. I'd know him anywhere though, especially as I also recognise the woman who's hiding him. Because she's me. My legs are parted wide, with one foot up on the back of the sofa, while the other is on the floor, and Chase is deep inside me. He has one arm wrapped around me, while his other hand is playing with me. Intimately.

"Oh, God," I mumble.

"Take a look at the rest," Alyssa says, leaning forward.

"I don't need to."

"Look anyway." Her voice is more commanding this time, and I glance back at the phone, swiping left, and seeing more images of myself and Chase, in various stages of undress, as well as other pictures of us together on the sofa, one of which looks like we're both at the point of climax. I've turned my head by this stage, so I'm facing Chase and he's gazing down at me. Not that I can see him very clearly in this picture, but I can still remember the look in his eyes, even now. And I'm almost sure I saw something of my own love reflected back at me. Didn't I? Or was that wishful thinking?

Alyssa coughs, breaking into my pointless thoughts, and I look up to see the snide smile on her lips.

"What do you want?"

She chuckles. "Well, at least you realised I'm not here just to shoot the breeze."

"No… I never thought that."

Her eyes narrow and she snatches back her phone, turning it off without even glancing at the screen. "I want you to hand in your resignation," she says, and I feel like the ground is shifting beneath me.

"You want me to what?"

"You heard me. I'll give you a week from today to resign."

"And if I don't?"

"Then these pictures are gonna find their way onto the Internet so the whole world can see exactly what you and Chase have been getting up to."

"We weren't doing anything wrong," I reason.

"Really? You think sleeping with your boss, and keeping it a secret is normal behaviour?" She smiles and almost preens herself. "Except it wasn't a secret, was it? Because you're not as clever as you think. I guessed something might be going on between the two of you, when you said you'd report me to Chase, rather than to Bree. I don't work for him, so what would be the point in reporting me to him?" She tilts her head, sneering. "After that, I watched you. I watched the way you looked at each other, and then I tried flirting with him, and I knew something was wrong."

"Why?"

"Because he didn't react."

That seems incredibly arrogant to me. "So you followed us?" I guess, and she nods her head with a smile. "That doesn't alter the fact that we've done nothing wrong, Alyssa. We've committed no crime."

Her smile widens, and then she says, "But do you really want pictures of the two of you fucking, all over the Internet? Do you think anyone's gonna believe you didn't sleep your way into your job, once they've seen them?"

"But I didn't. It was Bree…"

"No-one's gonna care about that. And Max takes the reputation of the company very seriously. He'll probably fire you, regardless. At least this way, you can get out, without being publicly humiliated."

I look down at the table, where our coffees are cooling, the pastries untouched.

"Y—You want me to resign?"

"Yes."

"And if I do, you'll destroy the photographs?"

"Yes."

"You realise, don't you, that even if I do as you say, there are no guarantees that you'll get my job." I wasn't around when Bree broke the news to the team that Joanna was the one who was going to oversee some of the remaining refits at the hotels instead of Alyssa, but I can't imagine her reaction was pretty.

She surprises me with a smile. "With the amount of work the Crawfords are doing at the moment, they won't have much choice. They're gonna need someone to fill your shoes, and they're gonna need them fast. And I'm available."

I'm not sure her optimism isn't misplaced. I've seen her work, and it's not that good. But I can't afford to call Alyssa's bluff. The idea of having those pictures in the public domain is terrifying. The idea of being humiliated and ridiculed is worse.

"A week from today?" I say quietly, getting to my feet.

"Yeah. The Monday after Thanksgiving. Oh, and don't think you can go running to Chase, hoping he'll come to your rescue. He's not that kind of guy."

"What do you mean?" I stare down at her, noting the slow smile that's forming on her lips.

"You didn't think you were special, did you?" she says, mocking me with a shake of her head. "You didn't think you actually meant something to him? Dear God…" She rolls her eyes and stands herself, so we're on the same level. "Chase will fuck anything he can. Anywhere and anytime."

"Well, he didn't want you, did he?" I retort, and I see the tension in her neck, anger flickering across her eyes.

"I didn't want him either," she replies. "Not really. I was just testing him. But I saw him myself, going into one of the apartments, with a couple of women."

"When?" I ask, and she stares at me for a moment. "When did you see him?" I'm desperate to know, and I don't really care if it shows.

"It would have been the night after we all got to St. Thomas," she replies, tilting her head. "Which I guess would have been the same day as you arrived. But then, from what I've heard, that's not at all unusual. So if you thought…" Her voice fades and my ears fill with a rushing noise, like a loud waterfall. Except I can still hear sounds coming out of her mouth. And I can remember Chase and Eli going out that evening, and how keen he seemed to leave. And I know why now…

I can't be here. I can't. I grab my jacket and bag and run from the coffee shop, straight out onto the street.

It's raining, but I don't care. I stumble away, making for the office, before I realise I can't go there. Chase came back yesterday, and he's bound to be at work today, and I can't face him.

I turn and make my way back home, pulling my phone from my handbag as I'm walking, and tapping out a text to Bree.

— I'm so sorry, but I'm not feeling very well. I don't think I'll be able to make it in today. Apologies again. Eva.

I press send, even though I know my message is quite abrupt. But then, I reason, if I was genuinely feeling ill, I'd hardly wax lyrical, would I?

I continue on my way, my head spinning, my heart aching, but feeling somehow grateful that at least Ronan won't be there when I get back, and I won't have to explain my unexpected return to the apartment. Not that I'm sure I could, because it's all so complicated. It's all so awful… so…

My phone beeps in my hand, and I raise it, expecting to see a reply from Bree. Instead, I see Alyssa's name and I stop walking, holding my breath as I click on the message. There's an attachment and I gasp at the sight of the photograph of Chase and me on the sofa. It's the one I noticed earlier, where we were both about to climax, and I feel a stabbing pain in my chest, knowing I'll never get to experience that again. It's strange… I've only just seen this image, but standing on the pavement, and seeing it again, while strangers rush by through the pouring rain, it all seems so much more real, so much more painful, and I struggle to focus on the message below…

— Don't forget. One week. Or else…

The words blur, raindrops falling onto my screen, and I start to cry, because it's just hit me that, no matter what I thought I saw in his eyes, Chase slept with two other women just a few days before he took my virginity; before he made me feel so special, even though I wasn't. I sob loudly and mutter his name, and while a few people stare, no-one stops, and I stumble on my way again, my hair soaked, my heart broken.

How can this be happening?

How can everything have gone so wrong?

Not only am I pregnant by a man who made it very clear he doesn't want children, but I've just found out what he's really like, and that it's so much worse than I thought. And on top of that, I'm being blackmailed, and it looks like the only way out of that situation is for me to give up my job. But if I do that, I'll have nowhere to live, and I'll have to go back to England. I'll be six thousand miles away from Ronan, not three, so I won't see him for months and months…

I feel like I've lost everything. My job, my brother, and Chase. I've lost my entire future. And all I did was fall in love…

∾

Chase

I park my BMW outside Max's very sleek, modern house, and look across at Eli, who's sitting beside me in the passenger seat, for once.

"Are we gonna go in, or just sit out here all afternoon?" he asks.

"Sitting out here feels like quite an attractive proposition."

He sighs. "If you didn't wanna come, why are we here?"

It's a reasonable question, especially considering I invited him. But then I felt the need to have someone here as backup today. Probably because this is the first time I'll have seen anyone since I got back from Miami. I called Max on Monday morning and made up an excuse not to go into the office. And I haven't been in for the last three days. I told my brother I felt unwell and overtired, and I gave Eli the same excuse when I told him I wouldn't be needing him for a few days. In reality, though, I was just scared about having to face Eva. And if that makes me a coward, I don't care. I needed some time by myself. Not that it helped. I still have this aching hole in my chest, where I'm fairly sure I once had a heart. And I still don't understand what went wrong.

Max accepted my excuse though, and then told me I had to make it to Thanksgiving at his place, or he'd send Colt to find me. And while I'm not scared of Colt, I didn't need the aggravation. Which is why we're here.

"They're my family," I explain eventually. "And it's Thanksgiving. And Max wasn't taking 'no' for an answer."

"In which case, we should probably go in, before someone comes out here and asks why we're sitting in your car."

He has a point, so with great reluctance, I get out of the car. Eli follows, and I lock it, pocketing the keys and leading the way up to the front door. I ring the bell, and we wait, then the door is opened by Colt, who smiles at Eli, and just kinda stares at me. The guy really doesn't like me, and while I know his reasons, I'm not sure I need his judgement today. Not given how bruised I'm already feeling.

I ignore him and pass inside, hearing light footsteps running from the rear of the house, and I crouch down in readiness, unable to help the smile that forms on my lips as Tia comes tearing around the corner from the dining room. She's wearing a bright yellow dress, with a matching ribbon in her long dark hair, and she looks utterly adorable.

"Unca Chase!" she hollers and throws herself at me, her tiny arms coming around my neck.

I clasp hold of her and stand, clutching her to me. "Hey, baby girl. How's things?"

She doesn't reply, because she really is only a baby still, not even being two years old yet. But she nods her head, and then nestles against me, and I carry her through the dining room, and into Max's kitchen, where everyone is gathered.

Mom and Bree are sitting at the round table at one end of the room, while Max is standing by the eight-ring stove, stirring something. He turns to me as we enter the room.

"Good to see you, at last."

I nod my greeting and then pull back from Tia, getting her attention. "Do you wanna go sit with Aunty Bree and Grandma?"

She shakes her head and snuggles back into me, as Max raises his eyebrows.

"Looks like you've got a new fan," he says, smiling, and I join him on his side of the island unit, vaguely aware of Colt, leaning up against the wall, and Eli, who's still over by the entrance.

"Yeah…" I let my voice fade as I remember the conversation I had with Eva, when she threw that curve-ball at me about children, and whether or not I liked them. I recall saying to her then that I've never wanted to have any of my own. And I wasn't lying. But I also remember her telling me not to let my feelings about my dad cloud my choices, or words to that effect. And now, holding Tia in my arms and feeling her little body pressed hard against mine, I have to admit, I'm starting to wonder. I've never seen the attraction of kids before, but I have to swallow down my emotions as I cling on to my little niece, realization dawning on me that it doesn't matter whether I might wanna rethink my opinion about having kids at some point. Because the only woman I'd ever want to have them with is no longer in my life. She's with another man. I close my eyes and struggle for a moment, not to let it all show.

"You okay?" Max's voice brings me back to reality.

"Yeah. I'm just tired."

"How did it go in Miami?" he asks.

"It wasn't as bad as it might have been," I explain. "I've left a team down there, working on the repairs. Hopefully, they'll have it all completed in a couple of weeks."

He smiles. "That's great news. And how was Denver?"

"I was gonna talk to you about then when I got back to work, but I guess now's as good a time as any." I shift Tia in my arms slightly, getting her more comfortable, and then continue, "Like I said in my message, that idea of yours to build another story of bedrooms, isn't gonna work out."

"The foundations aren't up to it?" he guesses.

"No, they're not. I didn't waste too much time on it once I'd worked that out."

"But you came up with another solution?"

"Of course. How familiar are you with the layout there?" I ask and he shrugs his shoulders, going back to stirring whatever's in the pan in front of him.

"Fairly. Why?"

"Because there's an area to one side of the hotel that's laid out as a garden right now?"

"Oh, yeah." He puts down his spoon and opens the oven door, bending to check on something and then standing again and looking at me. "What about it?"

"It's completely pointless. The manager there told me that no-one ever uses it. So, I came up with a plan for demolishing that, and constructing a separate block in its place, containing a new restaurant and kitchen on the ground floor, and bedrooms above, with a walkway that'll lead back to the main hotel building. And then converting the old kitchen and restaurant areas into additional ground floor bedrooms."

"You've planned this out already?"

"Yeah. I haven't finished the costings yet, because I was gonna do those when I got back to the office, and I ended up in Miami instead. But the initial plans themselves are all complete. I did them while I was in Denver." Because I had nothing else to do with my evenings, apart from missing Eva, who was evidently far too busy with someone else to miss me in the slightest.

He nods his head. "Sounds like a great idea. Do you think you'll be at work on Monday?"

I take a breath, knowing I can't avoid the office, or Eva, forever. "I guess… yeah."

"Good," he says quietly. "That'll give you a chance to explain what went on while you were in St. Thomas."

I choke and try to disguise it by coughing. "E—Excuse me?"

He turns and looks over toward the table. "Bree, tell Chase what Eva told you."

I feel my chest tighten and my throat close over at the mention of her name, but I try to hide my feelings, even as I notice my mother frowning at me.

Bree turns in her seat. "Eva said that she spoke to Trent," she begins, and I have to fight the urge to clench my fists, especially as I'm still holding on to Tia.

"And?" Even I can hear the annoyance in my voice, and now everyone turns to face me, and I see Eli shake his head, just slightly.

"And you missed something," Bree continues.

"What did I miss?"

"The fact that Trent isn't well."

"He's not?" I wasn't expecting that, and I think it shows, judging from the pitying look Bree's giving me right now.

"No."

"But he told Eva about this?" I'm surprised, and slightly worried by that.

"Yeah. Mainly because she bothered to ask, I think." She gets up and wanders over, standing on the other side of the island unit. "You told me you were having problems with him, Chase, but you never took the time to ask him what they were."

"I did." I shake my head at her, defending myself. "But he told me everything was fine."

"Well, that's not what he told Eva."

"What did he tell her then?"

"I don't know. Whatever it was, he told her in confidence, and she's not breaking that. But she says he needs us to help him."

"Then we'll help him," I say, without hesitation.

Max steps a little closer. "I was gonna ask him to come by the office one day next week. Do you think you could be there? I'll probably talk to him by myself to start off with, to make him feel a bit more at ease. I can't imagine he wants to talk in front of an audience. But I wanna be able to offer him some reassurance that, if he needs time away from work, we'll cover for him."

"By which you mean, I'll cover for him?" I suggest, and he nods his head. I let out a sigh, feeling slightly ashamed that I didn't pick up on whatever's wrong with Trent, and at the same time relieved that, although I don't relish the prospect of traveling any more than I do already, at least being away from home will mean I can avoid seeing Eva for the foreseeable future. And that's gotta be a blessing.

"What's wrong?" our mother says from the other side of the room, and we all turn as one, wondering which of us she's talking to, and I suck in a breath when I realize her eyes are settled on me.

"Nothing," I reply, when both Max and Bree turn their gaze on me too.

"Yeah, right… Chase Crawford, I know you far too well to fall for that. Max tells me you've been away from work for the last three days, and I've never heard you talk about your job with less enthusiasm in my life. So what's wrong?"

"Does it have anything to do with Eva?" Bree asks out of nowhere, and I flip my head around, staring at her.

"How did you know about Eva?"

I could kick myself, because I know that, with those few words, I've given myself away. But it's too late now. Max comes over and stands directly in front of me, taking Tia from my arms and turning away, without even making eye contact with me. He goes over to the table, handing Tia to our mother, after which he comes back to me and, this time, he glares into my eyes. But before he can say a word, Bree gets there first.

"Are you the reason Eva hasn't been at work for the last three days?" she asks.

"No." I don't wanna think about where she's been, or what she's been doing. I'm not strong enough yet.

Bree shakes her head. "Really? Because this is all very odd. She came back last week, and she seemed okay, but then she called in sick on Monday morning – the day after you got back from Miami – and I haven't seen her since."

"And we haven't seen you either," Max says, narrowing his eyes. "Bree's right. It's odd that you've both been absent at the same time. Is there something going on?"

"No. I've spent the last three days at my apartment."

"With Eva? Or with your latest victim?" Colt says sarcastically.

"Neither." I look around, staring into his dark eyes. "Look... I know you don't like me, and I only tolerate you because you're Max's best friend, and you're now engaged to Bree. But none of that gives you the right to judge me. You don't even know me."

"I know your type," he says, glaring at me, his features hardening.

"You think?"

"Can you two cut it out?" Bree says, raising her voice. "None of this is helping."

"What with?" I ask. "What exactly is it you guys think you're helping with?"

"We're trying to find out exactly what you've done." Max's voice rings out, and I turn to face him.

"Wow... thanks for the vote of confidence, man. Why do you assume that whatever happened between Eva and me, I must be the one at fault?"

"You've got history," Colt says, although I don't bother looking at him. I know exactly what expression he'll be wearing. I've seen it before. Too many times.

"Maybe I have, but..."

"So you're admitting something happened?" Max interrupts.

"Yes." I can feel his disappointment, and he's already shaking his head as he turns and looks at our mother.

"Sorry, Mom... could you take Tia into the living room?"

She smiles at him and gets to her feet, and then stares at me as she walks across the kitchen, her smile fading, and I feel the depth of her dismay, which just makes me even more mad, because I'm kinda sick of being judged by everyone. Including my own mother.

Once they're gone, Max and Bree both round on me. "What the fuck is wrong with you?" Max says.

"What the hell have you done?" Bree speaks at the same time.

"According to you guys, everything," I reply. "But I don't know why you're bothering to ask. You've already made your minds up about me. And about what happened."

I start toward the door, but Eli gets in my way, blocking my exit. "Tell them," he says firmly.

"Why the fuck should I?" I look up into his eyes and, unlike with everyone else in the room, I'm not met with disappointment or judgement; just with sadness. And understanding.

"Tell us what?" Max says from behind me, and I turn to face him again.

"That she was different." My voice is little more than a whisper, but I can tell from the shocked expression on his face that he heard me.

"In what way?" he asks.

"In every way. In ways I can't describe. She was... the one, I guess. We had so little time together, but what we did have was perfect. And even though I had to leave, I didn't want it to be over, so the night I got to Denver, I called her."

"Is that why you wanted her number?" Bree asks, her voice much softer than it was before.

"Yeah. I couldn't tell you at the time, but…"

"You mean, you actually followed through?" Max interrupts again, clearly surprised.

"Yeah. I did. Although it took me the best part of a day to get her to return my call, and I had to use work as an excuse in the end to get her to speak to me, which was kinda surprising, considering she'd cried herself to sleep in my arms the night I left the island. But I…"

"Oh, no." Bree clasps her hand across her mouth.

"What?" We all look at her, and she glances at Colt, who goes and stands beside her.

"What's wrong, baby?" he says, pulling her into his arms, showing a much more tender side to his personality.

"That Zoom call… do you remember?"

He hesitates for a second, and then nods his head before they both look over at me.

"What's going on?" I ask, and Bree lets out a sigh.

"I'm sorry," she says, biting her bottom lip.

"What for?"

"I—I think I might know why Eva was reluctant to talk to you. And I think it might be my fault."

"How do you work that out?"

"Because the day you left St. Thomas, I arranged a Zoom call with Eva, and after we'd gone through all the work-related things we needed to talk about, I asked her how she'd gotten along with you, considering the two of you had never met before."

"And?" I'm intrigued by what Eva might have said.

"And, she was singing your praises, telling me how hard you'd been working, and I—I think I might have told her you have a bit of a reputation… with women."

I feel my shoulders drop. "What exactly did you tell her?"

"Nothing that wasn't true," Colt says, and I glare at him before returning my gaze to Bree and raising my eyebrows.

"I—I just said that you have a tendency to sleep with anything that moves."

"Just?" I shake my head. "Thanks for that, Sis."

"And I might have mentioned that you treat women like they're disposable."

"For Christ's sake!" I raise my voice and Bree actually cowers. Colt releases her and puts himself between us.

"I was a part of that conversation," he says, keeping his voice calm and reasonable, like he's negotiating with me. "If you wanna take it out on anyone, take it out on me."

"Why? Is that gonna get me anywhere?" I turn away and stare at the wall for a moment before letting my head rock back and focusing on the ceiling.

"We didn't know you were serious about her," Bree says in a quiet voice from behind me, and I turn again and see that she's no longer hiding behind Colt. And as much as I want to keep blaming her, I can't.

"It's not your fault." She gives me a slight smile, although I can't return it. "Even if you hadn't said those things to her, she'd still have been mad at me."

"Why?" Max asks, tilting his head to one side.

"Because I left her."

"What do you mean, you left her?"

"Just that. I left her in St. Thomas."

He frowns. "Well, obviously. But you had no choice about that, did you? You had to go to Denver. Surely she understood that?"

"Yeah, she did. But, given everything we'd done together, I think she also had every right to expect me to say goodbye to her."

"What the hell are you talking about?" Eli asks, stepping forward.

"I'm talking about the fact that, on the morning we left, I didn't say goodbye."

His eyes widen and he frowns at me. "Are you serious?"

"Yeah." As I'm talking, I feel even more of a loser than I did then, and they all stare at me, feeling the same way, I think. "I left her sleeping."

"Then I'm not surprised she was mad with you," Colt says. "And maybe feeling a bit used too."

"I didn't use her," I reply, justifying myself. "It wasn't like that."

"Maybe not from your perspective," he says. "But looking at it from her point of view, I'd be amazed if she didn't feel used by you."

That's hard to hear, and I take a step toward him. "I didn't use her," I repeat. "I just didn't know how to say goodbye. It's not something I've ever had to do before. Not to someone who actually matters."

Colt nods his head slowly, his expression changing to something a little more sympathetic, and I wonder if maybe he's starting to understand. Not that I really care.

"But you've spoken to her since then," Max says, his brow furrowed in confusion. "You said you spoke to her when you were in Denver. So why didn't you straighten things out with her then? You could've explained… apologized."

"No, I couldn't."

"Why not?" He shakes his head.

"Because she was mad at me."

"Chase, that's pathetic," he says, not giving me a chance to finish. "She was entitled to be mad at you, and you can't run away from your mistakes."

"I'm not. But you didn't let me finish what I was trying to say. When we spoke, she said she didn't wanna talk over the phone. And to be honest, neither did I. I wanted to explain in person. Because… because when you realize you're in love with someone, you wanna tell them that to their face." I stop talking and they all stare at me. "I probably shouldn't have said that," I murmur, letting out a long sigh.

Max comes over, putting his hand on my shoulder. "Your secret's safe," he says. "But I don't understand why you haven't been to see her. You could've cleared the air by now, surely? You've been back here since Sunday, and…"

"I have been to see her," I say, shaking my head. "I went straight there from the airport… well, after I'd been into the office to get her home address."

"Then I don't get it. Why isn't she here with you? You know you could have brought her along."

I let out a long sigh, because I know I'm gonna have to tell them, even though saying the words is going to hurt like hell. Just thinking about them makes my heart ache. "There was another man at her apartment," I murmur, moving slightly and leaning back against the wall for support.

"Another man?" Max says.

"Yeah. He looked really comfortable there too."

"So, what did you do?"

I look up at him. "Nothing. I told him I had the wrong apartment, and I left."

He frowns. "You mean, you didn't even bother to find out who the guy was?"

"No. I didn't wanna be there anymore. I had to get out."

He shakes his head, narrowing his eyes. "Please tell me you haven't spent the last three days getting laid… to get even."

"No, I fucking well haven't." I push myself off the wall and step closer to him. "I just told you, I'm in love with her. What the hell do you think I am? I used the excuse of being tired so I could stay away from the office, because I assumed Eva would be at work, and I didn't wanna face her yet. I didn't think I could. And, if I'm being honest, I still don't. But I'd just like to explain here, while you're all still judging me, that I've resisted temptation for the last month, ever since I left St. Thomas. And there have been plenty of temptations, plenty of offers, believe me."

"There have," Eli puts in, stepping forward and backing me up.

"I'm sorry," Max says. "I didn't mean to…"

"It doesn't matter," I interrupt, floundering. "None of it matters."

"Yes, it does." His voice is firm. "It hurts."

I think back to Eden, and her affair, and I know he understands how this feels, not that I can say that here.

"You're right. It does. What can I do though?" I murmur, feeling despondent. Hopeless.

"Well, for a start, you could stop jumping to conclusions," Colt says from the other side of the island unit.

Max and I both turn to look at him. "Excuse me?" I say, barely reining in the flare of anger that's just hit me.

"From what you've said, you never actually told her how you felt," he says. "Did you?"

"No. But this is coming from a guy who kept his feelings to himself for more than a decade, so…"

"We're not talking about me," he growls. "We're talking about you, and the fact that it sounds like you didn't give Eva much of a clue that you're remotely serious about her; not if you didn't even take the time to say goodbye to her. As far as she's concerned, she spent a few days with you, and that was it. You made no commitments, so she's a free agent. She can do what she likes. With whoever she likes."

"Well, I suppose." He has a point, although I'm reluctant to admit it. Mainly because it still hurts. And because it's Colt who's making the point, I guess.

He nods his head. "But the thing is, how do you know there was anything going on between her and this other guy?"

I can feel the tension between us rising again. "Do you need me to draw you a fucking diagram?"

He laughs, and I'm so tempted to hit him, even though I know I'll come off worse than he will. "Tell me what you saw," he says at last.

"I already did," I huff, but he just stares at me, so I carry on, "I saw a guy at the door, in his pajamas, who looked like he was ready for bed, or like he'd just climbed out of it. Is that enough 'evidence' for you?"

"No," he says simply. "Her apartment has two bedrooms, doesn't it?" He looks down at Bree, who nods her head, and Colt returns his gaze to me, continuing, "So, how do you know she hasn't got someone staying with her? You've got no idea who this guy was, because you didn't bother to ask. You've just jumped to conclusions, like I said. But I checked her out for Max before she started working with Bree, and I'm pretty sure there was something about a brother…"

A brother? I remember Eva telling me that her brother was coming to stay, and how excited she looked. And how adorable that was.

"Oh, shit."

I look at Eli, and then back at Colt. And then I run.

"Chase… get back here!" Colt's voice rings out, but I ignore him and head for the front door, pulling it open and sprinting to my car.

I'm inside, my foot on the gas, the wheels spinning and gravel kicking up behind me, before they've even made it to the front door, and I watch them in my rear-view mirror, standing at the top of the steps, gesticulating, as I speed down the driveway, hoping Max won't lock the security gates. He doesn't, and they open inward as I slow, right before I floor the gas again, and take off toward the city, grateful that Eli took pity on me and let me drive here today. Otherwise I'd have had to ask him for the keys, and he'd never have agreed to let me drive myself. Not with Colt there to talk him out of it. Which means I'd have had to take Eli with me. And that's the last thing I need, when I'm about to face Eva, and beg her forgiveness for being such a complete and utter idiot. Again.

Chapter Twelve

Eva

Ronan's been as good as his word.

He's given me the three days he promised, to get used to the idea of being pregnant. I haven't, of course. Because not only is it impossible to get my head round that fact, but I'm also trying to come to terms with everything Alyssa told me; with knowing the kind of man that Chase really is, with having to resign, with being blackmailed. And with losing everything.

Even so, we've made it to Thanksgiving.

I know how hard Ronan has found it not to sit me down and make me talk. I've seen him holding himself back, especially when I've burst into tears for seemingly no reason, when in reality the thought of going back to England – to nothing – has become too overwhelming for me.

I know I have no choice, but that doesn't make it any easier.

We didn't go shopping together on Monday evening. Ronan went by himself, because I wasn't up to it. I persuaded him not to buy any Christmas decorations though, on the basis that I wasn't there to choose them. The truth, of course, is that I almost certainly won't be here by Christmas. So what's the point? But he bought a few things for Thanksgiving dinner and I almost cried when he got back, because he was so enthusiastic about the whole thing. And when Tuesday morning arrived, he insisted I should call in sick again. I wasn't actually unwell, but I wasn't up to working, either. The same thing happened yesterday, and I have to admit, it's been a relief to spend the last few days here, with Ronan, just being quiet by ourselves. At least I haven't had to face Chase yet. Although I know I will, probably on Monday, either before, or after, I hand in my resignation.

Ronan finishes preparing the vegetables for tonight's meal. We've managed to establish that Thanksgiving dinner usually consists of turkey and is eaten most often in the middle of the afternoon. And while we're prepared to go along with some traditions, neither of us can face eating that early, and the thought of a turkey between the two of us his too much. So, we're having chicken, and we're planning on eating it sometime around seven.

"Thank you for looking after me," I whisper, giving him a smile as he dries his hands and then comes and sits down at the other end of the sofa, and I move my legs slightly to make room for him.

"That's what big brothers are for," he says, resting his hand on my calf.

"Is it?"

"Yes. That and asking pertinent questions." His voice drops and I know my time's up. He wants answers.

"What questions?" I'm stalling, buying time, and he knows it.

"Are you going to tell the father?" he asks, getting straight to the point.

"I don't know." It's the truth. I know I'll have to face Chase, but I still haven't decided what to do. Part of me says he has a right to know, but then I keep remembering what Alyssa said about him going into that hotel room with two women. What kind of man does that? Not one who's going to respond well to being told he's about to become a father, that's for sure. But then, he made it very clear to me, before we even slept together, that he didn't want children. So I can hardly cry 'foul', or pretend I didn't know the score. And besides all of that, I'll have to go back to England soon, so there seems little point in burdening him with the knowledge of a child he doesn't even want. He may as well get back to living his life the way he used to; the way he wants to.

"Who is he?" Ronan asks, surprising me out of my thoughts.

"My boss." I blurt the words out and regret it straight away, especially when I see the look of shock on his face.

"You slept with your boss?" he says, shaking his head.

"Yes."

"But I thought you worked for a woman."

"I do. But the company is owned by her, and her brothers."

"So it's one of the brothers?"

"Obviously. Chase and I were working together down in St. Thomas, and because there was a muddle with the accommodation, we ended up having to share a cabin, along with his bodyguard."

"Why the hell does the guy need a bodyguard?" he asks, raising his eyebrows and leaning forward.

"It's to do with the other brother, Max. His wife was kidnapped and killed. Since then he's insisted that the family have bodyguards."

He nods his head. "So, you ended up sharing a cabin with him?"

"With Chase, yes."

"And?"

"And he was very romantic. He took me out to dinner, and we had a picnic on the beach at sunset, and…"

"And he did everything he could to get into your knickers," he says, his voice laced with cynicism.

"Don't talk about him like that, Ronan. You don't know him." I'm not sure why I'm defending Chase anymore. Except that I still love him. I can't help it. I'm going to love him for a long time yet… maybe forever.

"And did you know him?" he asks.

"Evidently not," I whisper, although he obviously hears me.

"What does that mean?"

"Nothing." I'm reluctant to reveal the truth now, given his already jaded view of Chase, especially as I know the reality is so much worse than anything Ronan's probably thinking.

He moves closer, making me curl up, tucking my legs beneath me. "Talk to me, Eva. Tell me what you mean."

I sigh deeply, because I know him well enough to understand he's not going to relent. I've seen that look in his eyes far too often before.

"I mean that, since I left the island, I've discovered a few things about Chase."

"Like what?"

"Like the fact that he treats women as though they're disposable. His sister told me, and he even admits it himself, evidently."

I'm not sure I can tell him about the two women that Alyssa saw with Chase. Thinking about that is bad enough and I'm not up to saying it out loud.

"And you didn't notice this?" he says, sounding incredulous now. "You'd been working for this guy – albeit indirectly – for over four months, and you'd never seen any signs that he might be a bit of a player?"

I glare at him. "Don't say that." It makes everything sound so cheap and I can feel a lump rising in my throat, although I do my best to swallow it down. "And before you judge me too, can I point out that I'd never actually met him until I arrived in St. Thomas. He's rarely at the office."

"No, he's probably too busy with his many women," he says, shaking his head.

"Just stop it!" I shout and get to my feet. "You're not helping, Ronan. Don't you think I feel stupid enough already? I mean, as if it wasn't bad enough that I fell for my womanising boss, and that I fell into bed with him within a few days of meeting him, I had to forget to use any protection, and get myself pregnant as well, which is just fabulous when I know he doesn't actually want children. It just…" My voice cracks, and a tear hits my cheek as Ronan stands and pulls me into his arms.

"I'm sorry, Eva," he says softly. "I didn't mean to upset you." He strokes my hair and I lean into his chest. "And, by the way," he adds, "you didn't get yourself pregnant. It wasn't your responsibility to use protection, it was his."

I lean back and look up at him. "It was ours," I say firmly. "I was there too."

He pulls me close again, and as we stand for a moment, I let myself feel safe with him, just fleetingly, before he leans back again, frowning down at me.

"How do you know he doesn't want to have children?" he asks, seemingly confused.

"Because he told me."

"You… you mean the two of you talked about having kids?"

"Yes."

His frown deepens. "And you're sure this guy is a player?"

"Please, can you not call him that?"

"Okay. But are you sure that's what he's like?"

"Yes. Why?"

"Because men like that don't generally discuss things like having children."

"How would you know?" I snap.

"Because I'm no angel either. I wouldn't call myself a player, and I've never treated anyone like they're disposable, but I've never been in a serious relationship either, and I promise you, I've never talked about children with anyone. It just doesn't come up in conversation. Not unless you're thinking about a future with the other person."

"It does if you're as naïve as I am, and you blurt out the question over dinner," I whisper.

"You asked him?" Ronan says, his eyes widening.

"Yes, but it was a mistake, and I told him he didn't have to reply."

"And yet he did?"

"Yes."

"He didn't bat your question aside, or change the subject, or nip to the gents?"

"No. Why? Is that what you'd do?"

"God, yes." He smiles and then shakes his head. "Has it occurred to you that perhaps your boss was a bit more serious about you than you thought he was?"

"If he was serious, why didn't he say goodbye to me?"

"What does that mean?"

"It means that on his last day, I woke up to an empty bed, and an empty cabin. He left me sleeping and just walked away, without so much as a note, let alone a kiss goodbye."

Ronan tips his head to the right, and then back again, before he shrugs his shoulders. "I don't know why he did that," he says.

"No, neither do I. I just know that it hurt."

He pulls me in close again. "I'm sorry, Sis," he whispers and I can't help myself, I burst into tears. "I know it might not have been what it seemed," he says, and I feel him shaking his head. "He might not have been playing you. And maybe I'm doing him an injustice, but your boss needs to face up to his responsibilities. If he didn't want to have children, he should have taken steps to ensure it couldn't happen. And he didn't."

I know what he's saying is right. And in the general course of things, I'd even agree with him. But my situation is different. I'm being blackmailed, and as a result, I'm going to have to leave the country. So it doesn't matter whether I tell Chase. It doesn't matter whether we can sort out our differences. Either way, it's all over.

I pull away eventually and Ronan sits me back down, handing me a tissue from the box on the table. I wipe my nose and eyes and lean back, just as the doorbell rings.

"Who on earth can that be?" he says, and as I go to get up, he holds out his hands. "You stay right where you are. You need to rest."

"I'm pregnant, not sick."

He smiles as he walks backwards towards the door. "You still need to rest," he says, smiling, and I have to smile back, because he's my big brother and I love him.

He turns away and pulls the door open.

"You again?" I hear him say and immediately feel confused. As far as I'm aware, Ronan doesn't know anyone here, so his words make no sense, and I get to my feet, walking up behind him.

"Who is it?" I ask, and he steps aside... and my skin tingles, my heart beating fast in my chest, as I see Chase standing on the doorstep, staring at me. I've got no idea what he's doing here, or how he even found out where I live, but for now, I've got a more pressing question, given my current predicament and Ronan's greeting. "Have you two met?" I ask nervously.

Ronan turns to me. "No," he says. "But this guy knocked on the door the other night. Sunday, I think it was, after…" He falls silent and I struggle not to let out a sigh of relief, because I'm fairly sure he was about to say 'after we found out you're pregnant', or words to that effect. But he doesn't. Instead he coughs, and then says, "Do you remember? You were tired and decided to get an early night, and I sat up and watched that Tom Hanks movie."

"Yes, I remember."

"Anyway, this guy rang the doorbell, and I answered it, and he said he'd got the wrong apartment."

He turns back to Chase, tipping his head to one side, although Chase is staring at me, his eyes filled with concern, and something I can't identify. And I'm not sure I want to. He used to look at me like that when we were on the island, and I can't go there again. Not now.

"I—I'm sorry," I stutter. "I should have introduced you."

"You mean, you know him?" Ronan says.

"Yes. This is my boss, Chase Crawford."

Almost as soon as I've said his name, I regret it, because Ronan squares his shoulders and stands up straight, turning towards Chase, his face like thunder.

"So you're the guy?" he says, raising his voice.

Chase drags his eyes away from me and focuses on my brother. "What guy?" he says, and the sound of his voice tingles over my skin, making my body hum with need for him. Still.

Ronan steps forward, getting a little too close to Chase, who looks him straight in the eye – being as they're the same height. "You're the guy who doesn't know how to use a fucking condom," Ronan says.

Chase shakes his head. "What the hell are you talking about?"

"I'm talking about contraception," Ronan replies. "It's a simple concept, that requires you putting something on the end of it, so my sister doesn't end up pregnant…" His voice fades and I let out a sharp cry, because I can't believe he's said that. He had no right.

Chase startles and then turns to me, his eyes filled with sorrow and pain now, and I want to run and hide somewhere. Anywhere.

"You're pregnant?" he whispers.

I can't reply, because this isn't how I wanted to tell him; if I wanted to tell him at all. Which I'm not sure I did. But if I did, it wouldn't have been like this.

I turn to Ronan, my anger rising. "How could you?" I yell. "How could you tell him like that? It was my right to decide, not yours. You're my brother, not my keeper."

He holds up his hands. "I'm sor—"

"I don't want to hear it," I interrupt, my blood boiling now. "Just… just get out. Both of you."

"Eva… wait a second," Chase says, shaking his head. "Let me…"

"No. I don't want to talk to either of you. Not right now. Just go. Get out."

I push Ronan out of the door and he lets me, and then I slam it shut and let out a loud sob as tears hit my cheeks.

For God's sake… how much more?

Chase

I stare at the closed door for a second or two, and then turn to look at the man standing beside me. Eva's brother. Evidently.

He's staring at me too, but neither of us says a word, and then we both turn back to the door, as we hear crying coming from inside.

"No, baby… no," I whisper and raise my hand toward the doorbell again.

Eva's brother grabs my wrist, stopping me, and I glare at him. "Leave her," he says, shaking his head.

"Like that?" I nod towards the door. "She's sobbing her heart out."

"I noticed. She's been doing quite a lot of that, since she found out."

"About the pregnancy?" I suggest when he doesn't elaborate, and he nods his head. "How long has she known?"

"She did the test on Sunday, not long before you showed up."

I close my eyes and let my head rock back. "If only I hadn't jumped to conclusions," I mutter to myself.

"What conclusions?" he asks, and I open my eyes, looking at his furrowed brow.

"I—I assumed that you and she were…" I leave my sentence hanging and, after a second or two, his frown shifts and his face clears.

"Oh," he says, shaking his head.

"You looked kinda comfortable in your pajamas."

"And you concluded that Eva would have jumped into bed with the next man that came along?" he says, narrowing his eyes.

"Yeah. And before you say anything, I know that was wrong of me. She's not like that."

"No, she's not." He turns away, pushing his fingers back through his hair, before he looks at me again. "But you are, aren't you?"

"I am what?"

"The kind of man who jumps into bed with different women all the time," he says. "And before you try to deny it, don't bother. Eva told me she heard about it from your sister, and…"

I hold up my hand, and he stops talking. "I know about that conversation. And I'm not gonna deny anything. The man you're describing is exactly who I used to be, before I met your sister. But I've changed. In more ways that I can ever explain…" I let my voice fade as he sighs, shaking his head slowly from side to side.

"You're going to have your work cut out, convincing Eva of that," he says.

"I don't care. I'll do whatever it takes."

He raises his eyebrows, evidently surprised. "Well, the first thing you're going to have to do is to persuade her you didn't mean it, when you said you didn't want to have children."

"Except I did mean it," I say, and he takes a half step back.

"Oh," he says quietly. "In that case…"

"I meant it at the time," I interrupt, qualifying my comment. "But that doesn't mean I can't change my mind."

"I don't think it works like that," he says, with a shake of his head. "If you don't want kids, you don't want them, and Eva's not going to fall for you pretending you do."

"But I wouldn't be pretending," I explain. "It's kinda hard to put this into words, but when we talked about children, and how I felt about them – and why – Eva made me see things differently. She made me understand I can make my own choices now."

He frowns. "I'm guessing that's something that makes sense between the two of you?"

"Yeah. It does. I just need the chance to tell her she was right."

I move toward the door again, but he gets there first and blocks my path. "Not tonight," he says firmly.

"Why the fuck not?"

"Because she's tired, and she's upset and she won't listen to reason, not when she's like this." His face softens and he smiles. "I know her better than anyone," he says, "and she can be fairly insecure and introverted at the best of times. But she's pregnant as well now, and you need to allow for that. Come back tomorrow. Explain it to her then."

"You think she'll hear me out?"

He shrugs again. "You said you'd do whatever it takes, so it's gotta be worth a try, hasn't it?"

I step back from him. "Why are you doing this?" I ask, because I've gotta admit, his attitude is confusing me now. I doubt I'd be this generous if it was Bree on the other side of that door.

"Doing what?"

"Helping me out."

He pauses for a moment and then says, "I won't pretend I understand relationships, because I don't, but Eva's hurting. Badly." I didn't think my heart could ache any more. But it does. "I don't like seeing her like this," he adds. "And although I don't know you, I do know her. Just from the few things she's told me, I get the feeling that you made her happy, and that she felt comfortable, when she was with you, which isn't something she finds easy. And that being the case, I think it's best if the two of you can spend some time together, to try and work things out, because something tells me you're the solution, and not the problem."

"I hope so," I murmur, and he smiles as he holds out his hand to me.

"Eva didn't get the chance to complete the introductions earlier," he says, "but I'm Ronan."

"I know. She told me about you."

He raises his eyebrows as we shake hands. "She did?"

"Yeah. She mentioned that you're an archaeology lecturer. And she told me you always look after her, and that you make her feel safe."

He smiles. "She doesn't remember our parents, so I guess she looks to me for support. And Eva's just one of those people who needs to feel safe."

"I think I worked that out already. I—I'm just not used to any of this. It's not like I've…" He holds up his hand and I fall silent.

"Tell her, not me," he says. "Come back tomorrow and explain it all to her."

I nod my head and step away. "Can you give her a message from me?"

He smiles. "I can. Assuming she ever lets me back in."

I manage a smile myself and then continue, "Can you tell her I'm sorry for everything I got wrong, and that I'm not gonna leave her again."

"I'll tell her, but only if you mean it."

"I mean it."

He tilts his head, assessing me, I think, and then says, "Okay. I'll let her know."

"And I'll see you tomorrow," I say, turning away.

"I'll be here." I wonder for a moment, if he's still doubtful about me. I wouldn't blame him if he was, but he has no need to be.

I'm not going anywhere.

Ever again.

I exit the building and cover my face with my hands, still trying to take in the events of the last half hour or so. *She's pregnant. Eva's pregnant. And there is no 'other man'. I've got a chance…*

"Hey!" The voice from across the street startles me and I look up to find Eli staring at me. He's leaning against my car and pushes himself off, crossing the road. "What's up?" he asks.

"What are you doing here?" I say at the same time.

"Colt brought me over."

"How did you even know where to come?" I ask.

"Bree had the address. She arranged for Eva to live here." He glances up at the building. "So, what happened? And why do you look like you've had the shock of a lifetime?"

"Because I have."

"Do you want me to take you home?" he offers, holding out his hand and I give him the car keys, without hesitation, because there's no way I can drive, and the two of us make our way across the street. Eli opens the passenger door and I get in, staring out through the windshield, while he climbs in beside me.

"What happened? Did you see her?"

"Yeah, I saw her. And her brother."

"So it was her brother?"

"Yeah, it was." I turn in my seat, looking at him. "Sh—She's pregnant," I mutter.

"Oh my God. How the fuck did that happen?"

"How do you think? I didn't use a condom." I would have thought that was fairly obvious.

"Which time?" he asks, starting the engine.

"I didn't use one at all."

He turns to look at me, like I've taken leave of my senses. "Are you fucking insane?"

"No. To be honest, the thought didn't even enter my head."

"And she didn't bring it up? Or raise the subject of birth control?"

"I don't think birth control had ever featured on her radar."

"Seriously?"

"Eva was… well, she is kinda innocent."

"Even I got that," he says. "But surely…"

"She was a virgin," I whisper, but he obviously hears me, because he pauses with his hand halfway toward the gear lever and stares.

"A virgin?" he repeats.

"Yeah, and if you ever tell anyone any part of this conversation, I'll…"

He holds up his hands. "I get it," he says, sitting back and shaking his head. "How do you feel?" he asks, eventually.

"About what?"

"The pregnancy… well, all of it, I guess."

"I'd feel a fuck sight better if Eva hadn't pushed her brother and me out of her apartment and we hadn't had to stand there in the hallway and listen to her crying."

"Oh, man." He shakes his head.

"I know."

"Why did she throw her brother out?" he asks, turning to face me with a furrowed brow.

"Because he blurted out about her being pregnant, by way of telling me what an irresponsible asshole I'd been. And I don't think she wanted me to hear that."

"Hmm… sounds reasonable," he muses.

"Which part? Her throwing us out? Or him telling me how dumb I'd been?"

"Both. And her probably wanting to tell you about being pregnant by herself."

"If she was gonna tell me at all," I say, without thinking, and he frowns.

"What does that mean?"

"Oh… nothing. It's just, right before she slammed the door on us, she yelled at her brother that it had been her right to decide, not his. And, of course, there's the minor matter that I'd told her I didn't wanna have kids. It's making me wonder if she was thinking of… of getting a termination, and not telling me."

"You think she'd do that?"

"I hope not."

"You mean, you wanna go ahead with it?"

I turn and look at him. "Yeah… yeah, I do."

He pauses for a second, like he's struggling to take that in, and then he says, "When did you tell her you don't wanna have kids?"

"It was something we talked about when we were in St. Thomas."

"You mean you guys had the children talk already?"

"Yeah. It wasn't intentional. It just came up by accident, and although Eva said I didn't have to answer her, I thought I should be honest. So I told her, ever since my dad died, I've never wanted children of my own."

"And yet you do now?" He sounds surprised.

"Yeah."

"Because your girlfriend's pregnant?" Now he sounds skeptical.

"No. Because Eva said something at the time, when I told her how I felt. She said I shouldn't let my feelings about my dad dictate my choices. She said I shouldn't give him that much control over my future."

He sucks in a breath and nods his head. "I see." He turns to me. "So what are you gonna do now?" he asks.

"I'm gonna come back here tomorrow, and I'm gonna talk it through with her. All of it. Not just the baby, but everything. And I'm gonna get her back, if it's the last thing I do. And you're gonna let me."

He thinks for a moment and then nods his head, before he selects 'drive' and pulls out onto the street.

I can't believe how nervous I feel as I stand outside Eva's apartment. I want to see her again, and hold her, and kiss her. But I'm scared of what she's gonna say, and whether she'll reject me. Because I'm not sure my heart could handle it.

I ring the doorbell, being as there's no point in standing here any longer letting myself get more and more anxious, and after just a few seconds, the door opens and I face Ronan again. I half expect him to say that Eva won't see me, but he doesn't. He smiles and steps aside, letting me enter.

"Hello," he says as I cross the threshold.

"Hi."

I look over and see Eva sitting on the couch, staring at me, and I can't help smiling, simply because she looks so damn beautiful.

"Come on in," Ronan says, leading the way over, as Eva gets to her feet, and I take in her skin-tight jeans and fitted pale pink blouse, and her braided hair. Not to mention her perfect face. And then I see the wary look in her eyes, which is kinda worrying.

I stand in front of her, feeling like a high school kid on his first date, rather than the man she made love to so fiercely, just a few weeks ago, and the father of the child she's now carrying.

"I—I'm going to go for a walk," Ronan says, when the silence between us has stretched just a little too far. "I think you two have some things you need to talk about."

Neither of us disagrees with him, and he wanders over to the door, grabbing a set of keys and a coat from the hook, before he turns back, his eyes fixed on Eva.

"Call me, if you need me," he says, and then he's gone, and a stony silence fills the room, as I turn back to her.

"D—Do you want to sit down?" Eva asks eventually, and I nod my head, sitting at the opposite end of the couch to her, and watching her closely while she settles down again, looking at her fingernails.

"I'm sorry," I say, because I can't sit here in an awkward silence with the woman I love. I know I have to start somewhere, and an apology seems like the best place.

She looks up at me. "What for?" she says, only now there's a new harshness to her voice. One I haven't heard before. "For lying to me? For sleeping with other women? For leaving me? For getting me pregnant?"

I hold up my hands in surrender. "Whoa... wait a second." She snaps her mouth closed and a blush creeps up her cheeks, even as I move closer, letting my arm rest along the back of the couch. "I've never lied to you," I say, defending myself, which seems to have become a habit of late.

"Oh? Really?" She shakes her head, lowering it slightly, like she doesn't believe me.

"Okay, I lied once... no twice."

She frowns. "Twice?"

"Yeah. The first time was on the island, that first morning, when we had breakfast together, and I told you Eli had gone to help the hotel management with a security problem. That wasn't true. I'd actually asked him to go and have breakfast up in the main building, so we could be alone. I know I shouldn't have done that, but I just wanted to be with you, without Eli listening to every word we said."

She looks up and her face softens just a little, but then she says, "And the second time?"

"That was when I sent you that text message, telling you I needed to talk to you about work. That was a lie. But it was the only way I was gonna get you to return my calls. Other than those two instances, I can honestly say, hand on heart, I've never lied to you."

"You didn't tell me you'd slept around," she says. I can hear the hurt in her voice, and it cuts through me, like a knife.

"No, I didn't," I allow. "But that wasn't a lie. And, in fairness, why would I have told you that? No-one in their right mind would admit to having a past like mine. Not if he wanted to have a chance at some kind of future…" I let my voice fade and she stares at me.

"What about the other women?" she mumbles.

"What other women?"

Her brow furrows. "The ones you slept with."

"That was before I met you, Eva."

"No, it wasn't." She glares at me, rage filling her eyes, even though they're brimming over with tears. "I know about the two women you slept with at the hotel, in St. Thomas."

"What two women? I didn't sleep with anyone in St. Thomas, apart from you."

"Yes, you did!" she yells. "Don't lie to me."

I move a little closer, making a conscious and difficult effort to stay calm, because I really want to yell myself. "What are you talking about?"

She narrows her eyes. "I'm talking about the two women that Alyssa saw you taking into one of the apartments on my first night in St. Thomas. I know we weren't together then, but you still lied just now when you said they were all before you met me. You'd met me then, and…"

"I didn't sleep with them," I say, interrupting her.

She shakes her head. "Yeah, right. What did you do? Play Scrabble for a couple of hours?"

"No." I let out a long sigh and look down for a second before raising my eyes to hers again. I can see her hurt reflected back at me, and I know I have to tell her everything. "I didn't know what to make of you," I say, because I can't think where else to begin.

"What does that mean?"

"It means, you walked out of your bedroom that evening, wearing nothing but a towel, and you… you blew my mind. I'd never seen anyone quite like you, and I'd never reacted to anyone in the way I reacted to you, and I didn't know what to do. I'm used to being in control, at least where my sex life is concerned. My dad had taken control of everything else, but when it came to my sex life, I never went along with what he wanted. He wanted me to settle down, like Max, but I vowed I never would. I vowed to stay single, and to live my life the way I wanted… sleeping around, never getting attached."

"Go on then," she says, harshly. "Don't let me stop you. The door's over there." She nods over my shoulder, but I shake my head.

"No. That's not what I want anymore. You need to let me finish. I need to explain that, when I first met you, I was confused. Like I say, I'd never reacted like that before. You see, it wasn't just a physical reaction, it was an emotional one, and I'll admit, I was scared. I had to get out of the cabin that night, so I dragged Eli to the bar for a drink, with the express intention of sleeping with someone… anyone." She gasps and lets out a slight sob, and I move closer. "Please, don't cry. Just let me tell you what happened." She stares at me and then nods her head. "I—I went to the bar, and there were these two women. I went over to them, and after a while, we agreed to go to their room. They were leaving St. Thomas the next morning, so it seemed – at least in my head – like the perfect chance for some no strings sex."

"You went to their room?" she echoes.

"Yes."

"And you met Alyssa?"

"Yes, by accident. She was coming out of her room and we bumped into each other. I've never liked her, but I didn't worry about seeing her then. What I do with my own personal time is none of her business, and after we'd exchanged a few pleasantries, I moved on with…"

She shakes her head suddenly, and I stop talking. "I don't want details about what you did," she mumbles.

"There aren't any details," I say, and she frowns.

"What do you mean?"

"I mean that, when I got into their room, nothing happened. I—I couldn't get an erection. There were two women in front of me, willing to do whatever it took to please me, and nothing was happening. Because the only thing in my head, was you."

"So what did you do?" she asks, sounding intrigued.

"I told them I felt unwell, and I left. And then I found Eli sitting by the pool, and I talked to him."

"About what had happened?"

"Yes. But I also talked about you. I might have only spent a couple of hours with you, and mostly in his presence, but even then, I'd already worked out there was something different about you; something pure and innocent. And I knew I was the polar opposite of that. I didn't think there was any way we could ever be together. Not when I thought I was all wrong for you. But he convinced me *I* could try and be different. So, although I didn't have a clue what I was doing, I decided to give it a shot, and… well, you know the rest."

"Y—You didn't sleep with them?" she says, wistfully.

"No. I didn't."

She nods her head and sighs before she looks up at me again, a quizzical expression on her face. "Why would you want to?" she asks.

"Why would I want to what?"

"Why would you want to do that? I mean, what made you go over to two women and then agree to go to their room… together? Why not just pick one of them?"

Oh, God. I feel my stomach lurch, knowing this could end really badly. And yet I can't lie. "I—I've done it before," I whisper and, after a second's pause, she pulls away from me. I can see the shock and disappointment on her face, so I move closer. "Don't overreact," I say, although I think it might be too late for that.

"Excuse me?" She shakes her head. "Are you seriously saying that you're in the habit of sleeping with more than one woman at a time?"

"No. I'm not saying that at all. Because it's not something that's ever going to happen again, for one thing. But also, it wasn't a habit, even when I slept around. It was just something that happened... very occasionally."

"How often is 'very occasionally'?" she asks, narrowing her eyes again.

"Three times."

"With different women each time?"

"Yes."

"And yet you say it won't happen again?"

"Yes."

She shakes her head at me, like she doesn't believe me. Again. "Oh, and I suppose you're also going to sit there now and tell me you haven't slept with anyone in the weeks that we've been apart, are you?" Her cynicism isn't lost on me, but I stay calm and take a breath.

"Yeah, I am. Because it's the truth. You can ask Eli, if you don't believe me. He knows where I am every minute of the day, and who I'm with. So, if you feel the need to check up on me, then call him. I'll give you his number..." I pause for a minute, but she doesn't say a word, or move a muscle. "I'd rather you didn't though," I add, "because I've just told you I don't lie, and I'd kinda like you to trust me. Because you can, you know?"

She stares at me, and we sit in silence for a few seconds until I shift a little further along the couch, so my hand is right by her shoulder, close to her neck.

"I will admit that I left you," I say softly, returning to her original accusations, and she looks up at me.

"Why?" she says. "Why did you do that? Do you have any idea how that felt?"

"No."

"It hurt, Chase. I felt abandoned by you. And that was amplified when I spoke to Bree that evening and she told me about your… your reputation with women."

"I know what she said to you," I say, feeling ashamed. "She's told me about that conversation."

"Do you know how it feels to be treated like you're disposable?"

"I didn't treat you like that."

"Really?" She glares at me.

"Okay… it might have felt that way to you, after I left. But I used to have sex with women, without even knowing their names, so…"

"You expect me to feel grateful that you knew my name, when you couldn't even be bothered to wake me up to say goodbye to me, after everything we'd done?"

"No, I don't. I expect you to be just as mad at me as you are. I deserve it."

She takes a deep breath, calming slightly, and I copy her.

"Why did you do it?" she asks, eventually.

"Because I was still confused by you. I wasn't sure how you felt about me or what you wanted from me. And I didn't know what to say to you. I had no idea how to say goodbye, that's for sure. So… so I took the coward's way out and said nothing. I'm sorry for doing that, and for hurting you. And I'm truly sorry if I made you feel abandoned. I promise you, that was the last thing I wanted to do."

I move my hand slightly and let it rest against her neck, brushing her skin with the side of my thumb. She closes her eyes and shudders at my touch.

"And obviously, I got you pregnant," I whisper, and she opens her eyes again.

"Well… you don't need to apologize for that. I already know you regret it," she mumbles, hurt lacing her voice.

"No, I don't. Not in the way I think you mean. I should've taken more care of you, and I should've been more responsible, and considerate. But I'm not sorry it's happened. So, no. I'm not going to apologize."

Her eyes glisten, tears brimming. "But… but you said you didn't want…" Her voice falters.

"I know. I know what I said. But, if you remember, you said I didn't have to be like my dad; that I could try to be different – or better – and that I shouldn't let him control me anymore. I'll admit, none of that sank in immediately, but that was before we made love…" I let my voice fade and she stares at me.

"Did making love change things that much?"

"Of course it did. Again, I'm not gonna say it was an instant effect. At the time, I think I was just too busy being blown away by how incredible everything was with you. But once I'd left the island and was alone again, and missing you like crazy, then yeah… it changed everything. It changed me. It made me wanna be better. For you."

She stares at me and bites her bottom lip, and although I find that really tempting, there's something I have to know.

"Can I ask you a question?"

She nods her head, just once.

"Would you have told me about the baby, if Ronan hadn't?" Her shoulders drop and I know instinctively that I've hit upon a truth. "You weren't going to, were you?"

"I—I hadn't decided," she says.

"Why not? Were you gonna have a termination, and just pretend like it never happened?" The words have left my lips before I've even thought about it, and she frowns and pulls away from me, leaning right back into the corner of the couch.

"Of course I wasn't."

"Then why weren't you gonna tell me?"

"Because of what you said, about not wanting to have children. I didn't want you to feel obliged to… to…"

"Obliged?" I can't disguise the disbelief in my voice. "You think I'm here out of obligation?"

"I don't know."

"Okay. Let me explain something. I came back here on Sunday night, before I knew anything about the baby, because I wanted to see you. I wanted to say sorry for all the times I screwed up; for not saying goodbye to you, for getting angry about Trent driving you to work, for not being the man I knew I ought to have been… the man you deserve."

"Then why didn't you?" she asks accusingly. "Why didn't you say all of that?"

"Because it wasn't you that opened the door. It was a man, wearing pajamas, and looking very cozy in your home."

"Yes. My brother."

"I know. At least, I know that now. But at the time…"

She shakes her head and gets to her feet, putting some proper distance between us as she glares down at me. "You… you thought I had another man here?"

"Yes."

"After everything we said on the island? You actually thought I could do that?"

"Yes. And I'm sorry about that too. I've never been in a relationship before. I don't have a clue what I'm doing. And it seems I'm not great with jealousy."

"You've got nothing to be jealous of," she says, shaking her head and I stand too, closing the gap again, facing her.

"I know. I've been behaving like a child… like an idiot. For the last few days, I've shut myself away in my apartment, refusing to see anyone, or talk to anyone, nursing my wounds and convincing myself that you were cheating on me, even though I'd never given you any reason to believe that we're a couple, other than taking you to bed."

She looks up at me and I'm so tempted to kiss her, but just as I move closer, she lets out a sob and covers her face with her hands.

"Hey, baby." I reach out and pull her into my arms, and she lets me hold her, stroking her hair. "Don't cry."

"Why not?" she mumbles. "You just said…"

"Said what?"

She pulls back and looks up at me, her cheeks stained with tears, her eyes filled with more. "You just said we're not a couple, and we're not, are we?"

"We can be."

"How? We spent a few days together on a paradise island, locked in a bubble, just the two of us. This is the real world. There are too many other things in the way. It can't work."

I keep hold of her, even as she tries to move away. "Why not? Hell, it was more real with you on that so-called paradise island than it's ever been with anyone else."

"But all we did was have a few dinners…"

"And talk, and laugh, and make love. I've never taken the time to do any of that before."

"Yes, you have," she says, sounding confused. "You've made love to lots of women in the past."

"I've had sex with lots of women. I made love with you. You were different. You've always been different… right from the moment I first saw you. That's what I've been trying to explain."

"Different or not, what chance do I have?" she says, sounding desperate. "How can I ever hope to be enough for you, when you're used to sleeping with two women at the same time? And even if that wasn't the case, we'd still have to contend with the very simple, but very basic fact that we don't really know each other."

"Whoa… slow down."

"Why? This can't work."

"Yeah, it can. To start off with, you're completely wrong about one thing."

"What's that?"

"You are enough for me." I pull her closer and look into her eyes. "You're more than enough." She opens her mouth to speak, but I raise my hand and place my fingertips across her lips, silencing her. "I don't care about what I've done in the past," I say. "That's not what matters here. This is about the future, Eva. Our future. All three of us. And as for not knowing each other… we can work on it. I mean, we were doing okay with that on the island, weren't we?"

I lower my hand so she can speak. "I guess. But it's not that simple."

"Yeah, it is. It's as simple as we decide to make it." I cup her cheek, looking into her eyes. "I'm not giving up. Not this time. You might not be ready to trust me yet, or even to give me a chance, but I'm gonna wait until you are."

"I didn't think you were very good at waiting," she says, and although I think she's still harboring doubts about me, I notice a slight sparkle in her eyes, which reminds me of our first time together, when I pulled her out of the shower, after she told me not to wait anymore.

"I'll work it out. I know I screwed up, Eva. I know I hurt you. And if you need for us to go back to the beginning, then we can. We can talk, and spend time together, getting to know each other. We can even date, if you want. It's not something I've ever done before, but I'm sure I'll manage. The point is, we don't have to do anything you're not ready for."

She stares at me like she can't believe what she's hearing.

"But I'm already carrying your child."

I smile at her. "I know… and I guess that is kinda unconventional. But if this is what you need, then I'm okay with that." I look into her eyes. "I just don't wanna lose you." She sucks in a breath and looks like she's about to cry again. I'm not sure what to make of that, but then she yawns, which I guess is a bit of a clue. "Are you tired?"

"Yes. Being pregnant is evidently exhausting."

"Shall I leave and let you get some rest?"

She hesitates for a moment, and then nods her head, and although I feel a little disappointed, I take heart from the hesitation.

"Can I see you tomorrow?" I ask her, taking a step back.

She sucks in a deep breath and lowers her eyes. "Would you mind if I said 'no'?"

"Eva?" I can't help the hurt in my voice and she looks up again. "What did I do…?"

"Nothing," she says, shaking her head. "It's just that Ronan's leaving on Sunday, and this is the only chance we're going to have to be together… for the next six months." Her voice cracks and she looks like she's going to cry again. "Sorry," she says. "I don't seem to have any control of my emotions at the moment."

"I guess that's a pregnancy thing too," I whisper, moving closer to her again, and she gazes up at me and nods her head. "Look… you enjoy the weekend with your brother, and I'll see you on Monday. And maybe I can take you out to dinner?"

She hesitates again, for longer this time, and then whispers, "Yes."

I'll be honest, this time the hesitation is kinda worrying, but at least she said 'yes'.

And right now, I'll take that.

I won't say it's been an easy weekend, because it hasn't.

I've missed seeing Eva, and my worries over her hesitations, and the fact that she wasn't gonna tell me about the pregnancy have only been heightened by being apart. But I couldn't deny her these last two days with her brother. I know how much he means to her, and he's been there for her in my absence. Which is something that's not gonna happen in the future. Because I've got no intention of being absent. Ever again.

I know I've gotta slow things down and give her time to adjust to my past, but like I said to her on Friday, I'm not giving up.

Sunday night television is beyond boring and I'm wandering around my apartment, trying to decide whether to order in something to eat, or cook for myself, when my phone rings. I can't help hoping it might be Eva, and that maybe now her brother's gone, she might need someone to talk to, and she's turned to me. So the disappointment when I see Max's name on the screen is a little overwhelming.

"Hi," I say, connecting the call, and trying not to sound too downhearted.

"Can I assume Thursday didn't go well?" he says, and I realize that, not only did I fail to disguise my feelings, but I also haven't told him – or anyone, other than Eli – the outcome of my original visit to Eva's place, after I ran out on Thanksgiving dinner. I've been holed up here, keeping myself to myself, waiting for tomorrow, when I'm gonna get to see her again.

"Um… well, Thursday itself didn't go great, no."

"Why? What happened?"

"I found out that Eva's pregnant."

"Holy fucking shit," he whispers. There's a moment's silence and then he adds, "You guys have been apart for quite a few weeks now. Is it… is it yours?"

"Yes, it is." I growl out the words.

"Sorry," he says quickly. "Can I take it, from the fact that you said things didn't go well, that you're not pleased?"

"No. I am pleased. Well, I'm kinda pleased, anyway."

"You're not making sense, Chase." He sounds exasperated.

"Yeah, I am. But I guess you had to be there. She threw us out. That's why it didn't go well."

"She threw who out?"

"Both of us… her brother and me."

"Why the hell did she throw her brother out?"

"Because he was the one who told me about the baby. I don't think he meant to, but he was mad with me for getting her pregnant, and it all just came out."

"Oh, I see. And she wanted to be the one to tell you herself?" he says, making the natural assumption.

"No. I'm not sure she was gonna tell me at all."

"Seriously?"

"That's what she said when I asked her. She said she hadn't decided."

"How do you know that? How did you get to ask her, if she threw you out?"

"Because I went back there on Friday. Her brother and I had a long talk outside her apartment, and he suggested I give her some time to calm down, and go back again… and talk."

"And you did?"

"Of course I did."

"And?"

"She's mad at me, and she's hesitant about getting into anything. But I don't blame her for that."

"What are you gonna do?" he asks.

"Well, I'm not giving up, if that's what you're wondering."

"Glad to hear it." I can hear the smile in his voice. "Have you seen anything more of her over the weekend?"

"No. She wanted to spend some time with her brother. He was due to leave today, and they're not gonna see each other for a while. But she's agreed to have dinner with me tomorrow."

"Well, that's a start."

"I'm gonna have to take it slow with her, which isn't gonna be easy for me."

"You've gotta put her first," he says, like he's about to embark on a lecture.

"I get that. Even is she wasn't pregnant, I'd still get it. I'm just saying I'm not great at going slow. I was really crap at it when we were on the island. When I tried it, I ended up ignoring her."

He huffs out a laugh. "Somehow that doesn't surprise me, but you're gonna have to work it out."

"I know. She's worth it…" I let my voice fade, thinking about Eva's face on Friday, and how confused and tired, and vulnerable she looked. And how much I wanna make her smile again.

"Can I assume you didn't tell her you're in love with her?" Max says, taking me by surprise.

"N—No, I didn't. It didn't seem like the right time. She wasn't just mad with me for leaving her and not saying goodbye, or for the things Bree had said, but thanks to Alyssa, she's got even more doubts about me, and my past."

"Alyssa?" Max queries. "What's she got to do with anything? You haven't been screwing around with her too, have you?"

"Jesus, no. But, unfortunately she saw me going into one of the apartments with a couple of women on the night that Eva arrived in St. Thomas, and she obviously told her for some reason, although I'm not sure why, because no-one knew that Eva and I were seeing each other. Not that we were seeing each other at the time, you understand. I didn't cheat on her. I'd only known her for a couple of hours and… well, I was just feeling really confused by her then. But, either way, Eva didn't like the idea of me having had a three-way."

"Are you surprised?"

"No. Look… I know I've been an idiot, so you don't need to rub it in. The point is, that when it came down to it, nothing happened. I was standing in a bedroom, with two beautiful, half-naked women, and for the first time in my life, my dick didn't wanna know."

"What did you do?"

"I made up a dumb excuse and got out of there."

"So it was just the *idea* of it that Eva didn't like?" he asks.

"Yeah. And the fact that I've done it before."

"You told her that?" He's incredulous.

"I had to. She asked me, and I couldn't lie to her."

"No," he says. "No, you couldn't."

"And that's why I couldn't tell her I'm in love with her. I was already falling fairly low in her estimation after Bree's conversation with her. And Alyssa's revelations didn't exactly go in my favor either. I need to help her come to terms with all of that, and let her know she can trust me, and then maybe I can put my feelings out there."

"Because you feel the need to protect yourself?" he asks, sounding suspicious.

"No…" I let out a sigh, hating the fact that I'm having to justify myself to him, even though I understand why. My past gets in the way. All the time. "This isn't about me. Not really. Just because I haven't said anything out loud, doesn't make my feelings any less strong, and if she walks away from me, it's gonna hurt like hell. I know that. I've had a taste of it already. But she needs time, and me telling her I'm in love with her at this stage would probably only confuse her even more than she is already."

There's a moment's silence and then I hear him sigh, before he says, "I'm proud of you, Chase."

"S—Sorry?" I can't have heard that right.

"I said I'm proud of you."

My hearing wasn't playing tricks, but no-one's ever been proud of me before. Ever. I've never given them cause. And hearing that from Max, who's probably the most honorable guy I've ever known… it brings a lump to my throat.

"I—I don't think I've done very much to be proud of," I say, after a quick cough, because I'm not great with compliments – especially about my behavior. "Let's face it, if I'd been a reliable kinda guy, I'd never have gotten Eva pregnant. I'd know what to do in a relationship, and I wouldn't have the reputation that I've got, which is what's causing a lot of the problems between us."

"There's not much you can do about your reputation," he replies, and I can almost see him shaking his head at me. "None of us can change the past, no matter how much we want to." There a sadness in his voice which I can feel from here. "The point is," he continues, before I can comment, "you're working at it and you're putting her first. And no-one can ask for any more than that."

"And getting her pregnant?"

"These things happen," he muses.

"I half expected you to say, 'We all make mistakes,'."

"Do you regard it as a mistake?" he asks.

"No, I don't. I just wish I could be with her. It feels wrong, being apart."

"I understand," he says, his voice softening. "Believe me, I do understand."

I'm tempted to tell him I understand him too, a lot better than he thinks; that I know about Eden and her affair. But I'm not sure how he'd react to that, and being as this is the most 'brotherly' conversation I think we've ever had, I don't wanna screw that up. It's a secret I've kept for a while now. And I can go on keeping it.

"Thanks for listening," I say eventually.

"Hey... anytime. We should do this more often, you know?"

"Yeah, we should."

Neither of us says what I'm fairly sure we're both thinking, which is that, if it hadn't been for the fact that our father drove wedges between all of us, in his efforts to control us, to make us strive harder and compete at every level, we'd probably have been able to do this years ago.

I hear Max take a breath, and then he says, "How are you fixed tomorrow morning?"

"I don't have anything scheduled. Why?"

"Because I've had Trent on the phone this afternoon, and he's asked if we can meet him tomorrow morning, at his place. He says he wants you there."

"He does?"

"Yeah."

That's a surprise. "Do you know what's wrong with him?"

"No. He wouldn't say over the phone. The only thing he'd say was that he's got some things he needs to talk through with us, and he feels he owes you an apology."

"Well, he doesn't. If anything, it's the other way around."

"Maybe it is, maybe it isn't. But I think we should let him do this his way, don't you?"

"Of course. You... you didn't reveal Eva's role in any of this, did you?"

"No. He called up out of the blue and asked for the meeting. I didn't need to mention Eva, or even tell him we're aware of anything being wrong."

"I wonder what changed his mind? Why he's suddenly decided to talk. According to Bree, he seemed fairly adamant with Eva that he didn't want us informed."

"I don't know. But I guess we'll find out tomorrow."

"What time does he want to meet?" I ask.

"Ten o'clock."

"Okay... well, I'll come into the office, and we can go from there."

"I'll get Colt to drive us," Max says, and I feel my heart sink.

"Can't we use Eli instead?"

"Why?"

"Because Colt hates me, and I don't need the hassle right now."

Max laughs. "He doesn't hate you; he just didn't always approve of you. But I don't think he'll be giving you a hard time from now on."

"Why?"

"Because Eli laid into him after you ran out on Thursday."

"He did?" I'm stunned.

"Yeah. I don't know whether you noticed, in your haste to depart, but they both followed you outside to try and stop you."

"Yeah, I noticed. I just wasn't in the mood for stopping."

"I gathered that. And once you'd sped off, Colt came back inside, calling you all the names under the sun, to lock the security gates. Except I wouldn't let him."

"Why not?"

"Because I'd never seen you react like that to anyone, and I thought you deserved the chance to put things right with Eva, without having a bodyguard getting in your way."

"And Colt took that from you?"

"I'm about the only person Colt will take anything from. Except maybe Bree. And Eli, it seems, because once he'd agreed to let you go, and that he and Eli would follow you to Eva's place, Eli gave him a piece of his mind."

"What did he say?"

"Just that you're serious about Eva, and that Colt should maybe cut you some slack and stop judging you, because people can change. And he reminded Colt that he'd changed too, when he got together with Bree."

"Jesus… I'm surprised you weren't picking up body parts."

"I thought I might be, but I guess that's the thing with us all having served together. We can say things to each other that no-one else can. Colt knew Eli was right, because even though Eli doesn't know everything about Colt's lifestyle, anyone who served with him can see how different he is now he's with Bree, to how he was before."

"I'll take your word for that," I say, because to me, he's still the same asshole he always was.

Max chuckles. "You'll see," he says, and we end our call.

I sit back, marveling at that conversation, because it really is the first time I can remember either of us opening up to each other. And it felt good. I wish we'd been able to do it before, but hopefully, now we've broken down that barrier, we'll be able to do it again.

I'm feeling a little more relaxed, and decide to order in some Thai food, and while I'm waiting for it to arrive, my thoughts turn back to Eva, which isn't surprising. I am in love with her, after all. It's a strange feeling, and not one I'm used to, but I like it. At least, I do now that I've got a chance with her. And I do have a chance, because we're having dinner tomorrow night… unless…

I pick up my phone again, and go to my message app, but then change my mind and go to my contacts instead, looking up Eli's number and connecting a call to him. A message is too impersonal.

He answers on the third ring.

"Sorry if I've interrupted your evening," I say.

"You haven't. I was just watching a really crap movie, so you've saved me from myself. What can I do for you?"

"I was calling to let you know that we're gonna have an early start tomorrow. Can you call for me at six-thirty?"

"Sure. No problem."

"Thanks. And while I've got you, I wanted to say thanks."

"What for?"

"For what you said to Colt, on Thursday, after I ran out of Max's place."

"How did you know about that?"

"Max told me. You didn't have to do that. I know what Colt's like. He could've buried you. Or fired you."

"Yeah, I know. But he was being particularly mean at the time. And I've never liked injustice, in any form. It needed to be said."

I nod my head, smiling, even though he can't see me. "Well, thanks for being the one to say it."

"Anytime."

"Now, will you do something else for me?"

"Sure."

"Will you stop beating yourself up over Sienna?"

The phone falls silent before I hear him say, "I don't."

"Yeah, you do. You screwed up. Badly. But so did she. And I don't care what you say, you're still in love with her, so don't bother trying to deny it."

"I—I wasn't going to."

"Then why have you given up?"

"Because she asked me to leave, remember?"

"Yeah. But I also remember that she said she still loved you."

"That was years ago."

"So? You think there's a time limit on love? You think you're ever gonna stop loving her?"

"No," he mumbles.

"Then how do you know she doesn't feel the same?"

"What are you saying?"

"I'm saying I think you should find her. It wouldn't be that hard for you. Colt traces people all the time."

"I know, but…"

"But what?"

"What if she's married, or with someone? What if she's got kids? What if she's happy, and settled?"

"Then it'll hurt like fuck. But at least you'll know."

I hear him breathing in and out. "Who are you?" he says all of a sudden. "You're sure as hell not the Chase Crawford I know. He'd be telling me to forget Sienna ever existed."

"No, he'd be telling you what a dumb fucker you were to give your heart to a woman in the first place, and that you should be out there, living your life. And he'd be wrong. Because, without her, you can't, can you?"

"No. Not really."

"Exactly. I had no idea what love felt like until it happened to me. And I've had a very brief taste of losing it. And it hurts."

"Yeah, it does."

"But I've got a chance to put that right, and I'm gonna take it. Because the women we love are always worth it, aren't they?"

There's another brief silence and then he says, "Yeah… yeah, they are," with much more conviction.

"Okay then. I'll see you in the morning."

He doesn't reply, because he doesn't have to, and we both hang up.

Eli texts me to let me know he's downstairs, and I grab my phone and jacket, and leave my apartment, going down in the elevator, to find him leaning against my car, waiting for me.

He opens it and holds the door for me.

"Thanks for last night," he murmurs, not making eye contact.

"One good turn deserves another," I reply, and I get into the car.

That's all we need to say, and he goes around to the driver's side and gets in beside me.

"I didn't realize you had an early meeting," he says, starting the engine and reversing out of the parking bay.

"I don't. We're not going to the office yet."

"Oh?" He turns to face me, his foot on the brake now. "Where are we going?"

"Eva's place."

"At this time of the morning?"

"Yeah."

He stares for a moment and then shrugs his shoulders. "Man, you really have got it bad."

"You can talk."

We both chuckle and he exits the parking garage, turning to the right.

It's only a short journey, and neither of us says anything, which I'm grateful for, because I'm feeling nervous now. This is one of my more impulsive gestures, and I just hope it isn't going to backfire.

Chapter Thirteen

Eva

I wake up, and almost instantly, it feels like a dark cloud descends over me.

Not only is Ronan not here – because he left last night at around seven to catch his flight – but also, today is the day I'm going to have to resign, which means this is the beginning of the end.

I'll have to work out a month's notice, so by Christmas, I'll be back in England by myself, six thousand miles away from my brother, and three thousand miles away from Chase… from the man I love. And I do still love him. I can't get away from that.

I also can't get away from the fact that what was already a horrible situation has become so much more complicated since Friday, when he came over here and we talked. Ronan had told me he was coming, and persuaded me to listen to what he had to say, so his appearance wasn't a surprise. But I never expected him to be so apologetic, or so kind. Or so keen to work things out with me. I never expected to hear all of that about his past, either. But that's the past. I know that. And while I might have been angry with him, I still love him. And I'm not a fool. I know everything he told me is about who he was, who he used to be. It's not about who he is now. And the man he is now said he wanted another chance with me, that he was willing to take it slow, to wait, to regain my trust. Of course, he doesn't know about the pictures and Alyssa. He has no idea that we can't do any of that. Not now. But no matter how many excuses I threw at him, he never gave up. He kept telling me he'd work it out. He can't. Obviously. Because whatever he wants, and whatever I want, I still have to resign, and without a job, I'll still have to leave the country.

What made it even worse – if that were possible – was the fact that he was actually happy about the baby. I hadn't seen that coming. And it just makes everything so much more difficult.

But there's nothing either of us can do about it, so I've decided there's no point in telling him.

It is what it is. We were stupid, and we got caught. And now we're going to have to pay the penalty. Both of us…

But me especially.

I sit up on the edge of the bed and a wave of nausea crashes over me.

"Oh, God." I clamp my hand over my mouth and rush to the bathroom, raising the toilet seat and throwing up, before I collapse to the floor, reaching for some toilet paper to wipe my mouth. This is just what I need today, of all days.

It takes me a few minutes to stand, and when I do, the nausea returns, but somehow I know I won't be sick again. At least not yet. So I grab a quick shower and dry my hair, and it's only when I'm putting away my hairdryer that I begin to feel sick again, and have to rush back to the bathroom. This time around, it's worse, and I retch over the toilet for a good ten minutes before it feels safe to get up. My face is pale, but I splash some water over it and go back into the bedroom, finding a dress in the wardrobe and laying it on the bed. I'm rooting around for some underwear when my doorbell rings.

"What the…" I suck in a breath and pull my robe around myself a little tighter, heading out into the living room and making my way to the front door, my legs a little unsteady.

"Yes?" I pull open the door, and gasp, as I take in the perfect sight of Chase, in jeans and a white shirt, topped with a leather jacket, his eyes fixed on mine and dark with concern.

"Are you okay?" he asks.

"No. I've just been sick. Twice."

"Is this morning sickness?" he says, stepping closer, so he's almost inside my apartment.

"I assume so. It's the first time it's happened."

"Tell me what I can do. Tell me what you need."

"Orange juice?" I say, because it's about the only thing I can face, and I'm really thirsty.

"Okay."

He steps inside and closes the door, not giving me any choice in the matter, and guides me over to the sofa, sitting me down.

"Is it in the refrigerator?" he asks, moving towards the kitchen.

"Yes. But you don't have to…"

"Yeah, I do," he replies, interrupting me. "Where do you keep your glasses?"

"In the cupboard above the microwave."

He finds them and pours me a glass of orange juice, bringing it back and setting it down on the table before sitting beside me.

"Is there anything else I can do?" he asks.

"No. I'll just have a sip of this, and I'll get dressed." I lift the glass, but then hesitate with it halfway to my lips. "Why are you here? It's not even seven o'clock yet."

"I know. I thought I could drive you to work."

"Why?"

"Do I need a reason?" He tilts his head to one side.

"Well, no, but…"

"This may be the real world, and not that paradise island bubble we were talking about the other day, but it wouldn't hurt to ride to work with me, would it?"

That's so sweet, and he's trying so hard. But it's just another complication. And if he's going to keep doing things like this, it's going to make the next month even harder. And I'm not sure I can cope with that.

Chase waits for me while I dress, and although he offers to make me breakfast, or take me somewhere to buy it, I decline, persuading him

I'll have something later, once the nausea wears off. He isn't happy with my answer, but he accepts it, and helps me gather my things together, ready to take to work, before escorting me to the lifts, and riding down with me, where we meet Eli, who's sitting in the front of a dark blue BMW.

He greets me warmly, which just reminds me I'm going to have to leave him behind too, and then Chase tells him to drive slowly and carefully, because I've just been sick.

"As in morning sickness?" he replies.

"Yeah." Chase looks up at him.

"He knows?" I breathe, leaning a little closer to Chase, so he'll hear me.

"Yes, he knows." Chase turns to face me. "I'm sorry... wasn't I supposed to tell anyone?"

I shrug my shoulders. "I don't suppose it matters."

He frowns and shakes his head, and then turns to face the front again. And I want to tell him I'm the one who's sorry... I'm sorry it has to be like this.

We ride to the office in silence, but as Eli pulls the car into the underground car park, Chase turns to me again.

"I've got a meeting this morning," he says. "I'll be leaving at around nine-thirty, and I don't know what time I'll be back, but are we still okay for this evening? If you like, I can book us somewhere."

"Um... okay."

He shakes his head again. "Eva," he whispers. "Give me a chance. Please."

"I'm sorry," I murmur, because I am.

"Don't be sorry. Just let me prove to you that I'm not the man you think I am. Come out with me tonight. We can talk. We can make it a new beginning."

I can't tell him that this is the end, and not the beginning, so I nod my head and he smiles, and just that simple gesture breaks my heart.

By the time it gets to ten o'clock, I've completed my plans, and knowing Chase will be out of the building, I take my resignation letter to Bree's office, my hand shaking as I knock on her door.

I'd thought about just e-mailing it to her, but she's been so kind to me, I decided I couldn't do that to her. I owe her a face-to-face explanation. Even if I won't be able to tell her the truth.

"Come in," she calls, and I open the door, closing it again behind me and walking over to her desk.

"I—I need to give you this," I say, stammering as I hand over the letter.

She takes it from me, looking up at my face and frowning, before she opens the envelope and reads the words I typed, just a few minutes ago.

"Eva?" she says, shaking her head, her gaze returning to me again. "What's going on?"

"I'm really sorry, Bree. I wouldn't do this to you, if I didn't absolutely have to."

"Is this something to do with Chase?" she asks, and I feel myself blush.

"H—How did you know about Chase?"

"Because he was with us… with the whole family, at Max's house on Thursday afternoon, when he realised he'd made a mistake about the man who's been staying at your apartment. And then he ran out on us."

"Oh, I see."

"He thought you had another man staying with you, and was moping around, but Colt worked out that it was probably your brother?"

She phrases her statement like a question, and I realize Chase hasn't enlightened them as to the facts of the matter.

"He was my brother," I explain. "He'd been staying with me for a couple of weeks, but he's gone now, to Peru, for six months."

"Is that why you're leaving?" she says, glancing down at the letter again.

"No."

"Then why? I can't… I mean… you're not giving me any notice here, Eva. You wanna leave today, but you're not giving me a reason."

"It's complicated." That's the understatement of the century.

"And does it involve my brother? Because I know what an asshole he can be sometimes."

I shake my head. "It does involve him… sort of. But it's not his fault. He's been more than kind. Especially about the baby." I clamp my mouth shut, wishing my hormones weren't completely messing with my brain.

"What baby?" She stands, staring at me. "Are you… are you pregnant?"

I nod my head. "Yes."

"And Chase knows about this?"

"Yes. He found out on Thursday, when he came around and my stupid brother blurted it out at him."

"And Chase is okay with it? You said he was being kind?"

"Yes. He says he's okay with it."

"Well, despite his past, I've never known him to lie. If he says he's okay with it, then he is."

"I know. I don't doubt that."

"Then I don't understand why you need to leave, especially in such a hurry. Are you worried that we'll object to you working here when you're in a relationship with Chase? Because surely you've noticed that Colt and I are together, and we work in the same building…" Her voice fades as my eyes start to prickle with tears. "Hey, don't get upset," she says, coming around the desk and sitting me down in one of the two chairs, taking the other for herself.

"I—I'm really sorry, Bree," I say, turning to face her. "I can't tell you my reason. You don't have to pay me; I don't expect that, and I know I've let you down. I—I just need to do this."

"But, you do realise, don't you, that without a job, you can't stay in the States. Do you have something else lined up?" She seems genuinely concerned, and that's just making this even harder.

"No."

"You're gonna go back home?"

"I'm going back to England, yes."

I can't call it home, when I've got nothing there to go back to. Everything I want is here. But I can't have him.

I get to my feet and she watches me, confusion etched on her face.

"I know I'm asking a lot of you already, but can I ask another favour?"

"Of course," she whispers.

"Can you let me go now?"

Her eyes widen. "As in, right now? This minute?"

"Yes. And can you promise me you won't tell Chase until later this evening? Anytime after five would be fine."

"You're gonna fly out of here today, aren't you?" she says, getting up and looking me in the eye. And while I don't confirm or deny her statement, she knows she's right. "That's not fair, Eva. You can't do that to him."

"I have no choice." I raise my voice slightly, and she startles. "Please, will you just let me go?"

"If that's what you really want, then yes." She shakes her head. "I don't think it is, but I'll let you go"

"Thank you."

She pulls me into a hug, which is most unexpected, and then she releases me. We're both trying not to cry, although she's having more success with that than I am.

"Look after yourself, Eva. And my little niece or nephew." Her voice cracks, but she adds, "I'm gonna miss you."

"I'm gonna miss you too."

"Whatever it is – whatever's driving you away – I hope you work it out. And I hope you find your way back here again."

I can't say anything to that, because as much as I want that too, I know it's not going to happen. So instead I just nod my head, and taking a deep breath, I leave the room.

Once I'm outside, I lean against the wall, and pull out my phone, going to my messages, and finding the one that Alyssa sent me the other day; the one where she reminded me of the time constraints of her threat, and I type…

— *I've resigned. Your path is clear.*

And then, my legs unsteady, I make my way back down to my office, where I gather up my things and head for home, wondering how something that started so beautifully could end in such an ugly mess.

Chase

It's one-thirty in the afternoon by the time Max and I leave Trent's apartment, and I'll admit to feeling a little shocked.

"Didn't you see any of that coming?" he whispers to me as we get into the back of his Range Rover and Colt starts the engine.

"No."

"So, you had a guy working with you for months on end, you knew there was something wrong, because he wasn't pulling his weight like he normally does, but you never suspected anything?"

"Nothing like this, no."

"How could you have missed it?"

I'm feeling bad enough already. I'm not sure I need Max laying into me as well.

"I guess because guys tend not to talk about things like that. And in my defense, even he said he'd done his best to hide it."

"What's wrong with him?" Colt asks from the front seat, which breaks the tension for a moment.

"He's having anxiety attacks," Max says. "They sound pretty bad. That's why he's told us. They're so bad he's been to see a doctor, and he's gonna need to take some time away from work; quite a lot of time."

"And you're blaming your brother for that?" Colt says, surprising me by coming to my defense.

"No. I'm blaming him for not spotting the anxiety attacks in the first place."

"Right… because things like that are really easy to spot, aren't they?" Colt's voice is laced with sarcasm. "How many guys did we know in the army who had major melt-downs that we didn't see coming?" he asks, lowering his voice slightly. "How many times did we say afterwards that it came right out of the blue?"

Max falls silent and then turns to face me. "He's right," he says quietly. "It happened all the time."

"And this is no different. If this guy didn't want you to see it, he wouldn't have let you," Colt adds to reinforce his argument, even though it's already been made.

"Point taken," Max says, holding up his hands, although Colt can't see him, because he's concentrating on driving through the city. "I shouldn't have taken it out on you. It's just that Trent's almost one of us." I know what he means by that and I feel the same. "We need to help him."

"I know. And ordinarily, I'd step in myself, but I've got a few problems of my own to deal with."

"Problems? I wouldn't let Eva hear you say that. Women – especially pregnant women – don't like to be referred to as a problem."

"I wasn't meaning Eva. Not as such. I was meaning the fact that I went round to her place this morning to drive her to work, and she was being sick."

"Ahh… morning sickness," he says, smiling. "In case you haven't already guessed, it's from here on in that you give thanks you're a guy."

"That's not the problem though. It's that she went kinda quiet on me."

"When?"

"On the drive to work, when she found out that Eli knew about the baby, and when I checked with her that we were still okay for dinner."

He smiles. "Well, the dinner thing could be because you'd mentioned food, and she still felt nauseous. I know… I know with Eden, it went on for most of the day at the beginning, and just the word 'coffee' was enough to set her off." His voice cracks and it's obvious he still has trouble talking about her. Even now.

"You think that's all it was?"

"Probably." He clears his throat.

"And why was she worried about Eli knowing about the baby?"

"Maybe because she'd rather keep it quiet for a while?" Colt says from in front of us.

"Why?" I wasn't aware that he knew. But he does now, I guess.

He shakes his head. "Don't you know anything?"

"Clearly not. Enlighten me."

"Most women don't like anyone knowing for the first three months, because that's when the risk of miscarriage reduces."

"Miscarriage?" I whisper, feeling a shiver down my spine.

"Hey," Max says from beside me. "Don't worry. I'm sure she'll be fine. I'm sure they'll both be fine. You just need some time together."

"I know. And that's why I'm not gonna be able to take on any more work. I know I said I'd cover for Trent, but things have changed."

He shakes his head. "I kinda got that for myself. I'll have to look at getting in a replacement, while Trent has some time out to get treatment."

"We'll have to make sure he knows this is just temporary, and that his job is waiting for him whenever he's ready to come back."

"Yeah. I'll make that very clear to him."

I nod my head and let out a sigh of relief, wondering if Eva's eaten yet, and whether I might be able to persuade her to join me for lunch. We need that talk. We need that new beginning. And it needs to start now.

Colt parks the car under the office building and we all get out, making our way to the elevators.

As we're waiting for the doors to open, Colt turns to me.

"Congratulations, by the way," he says, a smile touching his lips.

"Thanks. Although I've still gotta persuade Eva that I'm worth taking a chance on. So I think you might be a little premature."

He pauses for a moment. "Have a little faith in yourself, man," he says, shocking the hell out of me.

"You do realize which brother you're talking to, don't you?"

I look up at him, and that smile fills out as he grins at me. "Yeah, but I've known Eli for a long time, and if he says you've changed, then I believe him. And besides, you're different around this girl. Even I can see that."

I don't know what to say to him, but I'm saved the trouble by the opening of the elevator doors, and we all enter, waiting for them to close again, as Max presses the button for the eighth floor; the management floor, where Max, Bree and I have our offices.

When the doors open onto the reception area, we're greeted by the sight of Eli and Dana, both sitting on one of the couches, as they usually do when their services are not required. I give Eli a nod and we start toward the double doors, just as they crash open and Bree comes through.

"Whoa…" Colt darts forward, holding out his arms to her. "What's wrong, baby?"

He sounds almost scared and although I've never heard that from him before, I can sympathize. I know that's how I'd feel if this were Eva. As it is, Bree's my sister and both Max and I step forward too, concerned by the look on her face, which is a mixture of fear, confusion and anger.

"Why the hell don't you ever answer your phone?" she says, turning to me.

"Me? Who's been trying to call me? I—Is everything okay with Eva? With the baby?"

My first thought is of her, but I guess that's because I'm in love with her.

"No, it's not."

Fear crashes through me, and I notice Max getting closer, and Eli suddenly appearing by my side.

"What's happened?" Max says, because my voice won't work, even though I've opened my mouth to speak.

"She's gone."

"She's what?" I say, out of sheer shock.

"Gone."

"What do you mean, she's gone?" Colt asks, letting Bree go and staring down at her.

"Just that," she answers him, but then she turns to me. "She came to see me this morning, and handed in her resignation, and asked if I'd let her go straight away. And then begged me not to tell you until after five o'clock this evening."

"Why after five?" I shake my head, trying to take it all in.

"Because she's gonna leave the country," Colt says.

"How do you know that?"

"I don't, but if you think about it, it's the only thing that makes sense. She's obviously got a flight booked, and she wants to be on it, on her way back to the UK, before you're any the wiser."

She's leaving me? *Over my dead body.* I turn to Eli. "Take me to her place... now."

He nods his head and we run, both getting to the elevator at the same time, although he presses the 'down' button, because his hands aren't shaking.

"Did she say five?" he calls over his shoulder.

"Yes," Bree replies, and Eli looks at his watch.

"We're gonna be better off going to the airport," he says. "If her flight is sometime before five, she'll probably be on her way there already."

"You think?" I stare at him, struggling for control, and he nods his head. "Okay. Take me to the airport then."

I've gotta hand it to Eli, I think he's broken the record getting me to the airport. He broke just about every traffic law in the book, anyway, and he pulls up outside the terminal building less than twenty minutes after we left the office.

"You go start looking," he says as I climb out of the car. "I'll park up and join you."

I don't even wait to thank him, but run in through the main entrance, feeling my heart sink to my boots. The place is heaving with people, and I realize I might never find Eva. As I step forward, and make my way toward the check-in desks, because that seems the most logical place to look, I even start to think about what I'm gonna do, if

I can't find her. I know the answer; I'll catch the next available flight to London, of course. I'll have to send Eli back to my place for my passport, or maybe see if Max can get Colt to bring it here. And I guess I'll have to find a way to get in touch with Ronan, because I've got no idea of how to contact Eva in London. Unless Bree has her address, maybe.

Before I get carried away with plans, I scour the rows of heads, lining up to check in their bags. But I don't know which airline she's booked in with, so I'm kinda lost. I'm wondering whether I should maybe go to the information desk and ask them to put out an announcement for her. Although what I'll get them to say, I don't know, and I'm just thinking that through, when my phone rings. I pull it from my back pocket and see Eli's name on the screen.

"What's happening?" I say.

"I've found her."

"You've what?"

"She's here."

I turn, looking around me.

"Where?"

"In one of the coffee shops."

"Which one?"

"Where are you?" he asks.

"I'm by the check-in desks."

"Okay. Make your way back past the main entrance, and you'll see a coffee shop on your right. She's there. And it looks like she's got all her bags with her still, so I don't think she's checked in yet."

"I'm making my way to you now."

"I'm standing by a pillar. I'll text you if she makes a move."

He hangs up before I get the chance to reply, and I start to walk more quickly, and then run, dodging past passengers and their luggage, until I spot Eli, leaning up against a pillar, just like he said. He sees me and nods his head to his left, and I turn and see her straight away. She's sitting at a circular table, on the edge of about twenty or thirty similar tables, all occupied with other passengers, sited outside a small coffee shop. She's clutching a glass of orange juice, her head bowed, and I stop and take a deep breath before I walk over and stand opposite her.

"Going somewhere?" I say, and she startles at the sound of my voice, looking up.

God, she looks pale. Even more so than she did this morning. And although her eyes are filled with fear, I know there's no way on earth I'm ever gonna let her go again. Not even for a moment.

"What's going on, Eva?" I ask, when she doesn't answer.

She lowers her head again and mumbles, "Nothing."

"Seriously? You expect me to believe that?"

"No. But I'd like you to leave." She looks up at me again.

"Hell, no. I'm not going anywhere. Not until you tell me why you're leaving me." I'm not going anywhere at all, regardless of what she says. But I need to get her to talk, and this seems like a good place to start.

"I'm not leaving you. I'm leaving America."

I pull out the chair in front of me and sit down, facing her. "Okay. Why are you leaving America?"

She sucks in a breath, looking down at her clasped hands. "Because I have no choice."

"There's always a choice."

Tears well in her eyes, but she doesn't say anything. She just continues to stare and nibble at her bottom lip.

"Tell me what's happened. Something clearly has. Tell me what it is, and I'll make it right."

"You can't," she says, looking up and raising her voice slightly, before she remembers where we are, and that we're surrounded by people. She blushes and lowers her voice before saying, "You can't make it right. I have to do this. And you have to let me. For both our sakes."

Is she serious? "If you're gonna try and tell me that this is for my benefit, then think again. I don't want you to leave, Eva. I want you to stay. Here. With me. I know things aren't ideal. I know we didn't plan for you to get pregnant. And I know you're scared and insecure. But you don't need to be. I'll look after you. Both of you. Whatever you think is wrong between us, we'll work it out. I promise."

She blinks twice, and then two tears fall onto her cheeks. "I—It's not that simple," she says.

"Okay. Simplify it. Because you're not going anywhere and neither am I. Not until you explain why you think it's okay to leave me, and to take our unborn child three thousand miles away, without damn well telling me. You got mad with me for walking out on you in St. Thomas, but this is so much worse. Can't you see that?"

"Of course I can." She's struggling to talk. "But I don't have any choice."

"You already said that. And you do have a choice. Let me help you. Whatever it is, I can…"

"No, you can't." Her voice cracks and she stands up, the chair scraping on the floor as she grabs her case, pulling up the handle and dragging it behind her, walking away from me.

I let her take a few steps before I stand myself and call out, "I love you, Eva. And if you leave me, I'm gonna follow you, no matter where you go. Because you're my life, and I'm damned if I'm gonna lose you, when I don't even understand why."

She stops walking and turns around, gazing at me. But then everyone else around us is staring too, clearly stunned by my outburst. Not that I care.

There's only one thing I care about. She's standing just a few feet away from me, and as I look at her, she kinda crumples. Then she bursts into tears, and I step forward and grab a hold of her, just as her legs give way beneath her.

"I've got you, baby," I whisper, pulling her close to me. "I've got you, and I'm never gonna let you go."

"You have to. Don't you see? That's what this has all been about. It's Alyssa. She's…" She stops talking, stumbling over her words.

"Is this to do with her seeing me with those two women? Because I thought we'd already…"

Eva shakes her head quickly from side to side. "No. It's nothing to do with that. She just told me about that to… to score points."

"I don't understand. How could she hope to score points? How did she even know about us?"

"Because she's got the photographs," she says through her tears.

"What photographs?" I've got no idea what she's talking about.

"Of us," she murmurs, lowering her voice, so I struggle to hear her.

"Did you say 'of us'?" She nods her head. "I still don't understand, baby. How can she have photographs of us? And why does that mean you have to leave?"

She sighs deeply, and turns her head away, looking defeated, and then she reaches down into her purse, pulling out her phone. She taps on the screen a couple of times before she turns it to me, and I feel my stomach lurch and my skin tingle as I look down at an image of Eva and me on the terrace outside the cabin in St. Thomas. I remember this moment well. I remember how good she felt in my arms, how wide I spread her legs and how much she enjoyed being that exposed. And how tight she felt on my cock as I buried myself so deep inside her, my fingers strumming against her clit and making her come. That's exactly what it looks like she's doing in this picture. And so am I, if my memory of the timing is correct, because I'm pretty damn sure we came together.

I also remember reassuring her how safe we were, and that no-one could see us.

How wrong was I?

"What the fuck?" The words leave my lips on a breath.

"Sh—She told me, if I didn't resign by today, she'd put the photographs of us up on the Internet for everyone to see. I—I couldn't let her do that. I—I couldn't."

"Hey… come here." I pull her close again, gripping her phone tight as I hold on to her. "Does she have more of these?" I whisper.

She nods her head. "She showed me her phone and there must've been about twenty pictures on there."

"Just of us on the terrace? Nowhere else?"

"No. Just on the terrace. She followed us home on that last night and took them."

"But how did she know to follow us home?" I ask her, leaning back and looking down at her.

"She said she thought something might be going on between us, after I told her I'd report her to you, if she kept being so horrible to me. I should have said I'd report her to Bree, not you. But your name was the first one that came into my head. And after that, she said she watched us."

"And noticed something going on?"

"Obviously. Enough to make her suspicious, anyway. She said that was why she flirted with you on your last day, to prove the point. And it worked." She sighs.

"How?"

"Because you didn't react."

"And that proved we were together, did it? Not just that I wasn't interested in her?"

"In her head, yes."

"She's nothing if not arrogant," I murmur, shaking my head. "And she said you had to resign, or she'd make these pictures public?"

"Yes. She said Max would fire me, if he found out what we'd been doing."

"I doubt that." I give her what I hope is a reassuring smile. "Max already knows what we've been doing."

"How?" She pulls back, her cheeks reddening.

"Because he knows about the baby. I think he's capable of working the rest out for himself."

"He knows about the baby?"

"Yeah. Look, I'm sorry. I didn't know you'd wanna keep it quiet for a while. I didn't understand about that."

"Chase, I think that's the least of my problems right now."

"I guess. But why didn't you come and tell me about Alyssa? Why did you go through with her demands, when you could've just spoken to me?"

"Because she told me about seeing you with those two women. She said I wasn't special, and I needn't think you'd help me."

I breathe deeply, feeling my anger rise, although I do my best to control it, because it's not aimed at Eva. Not in the slightest. And I cup her face in my hands and look deep into her eyes. "You know that's not true, don't you? About you being special, I mean?"

She shrugs her shoulders. "I guess I know that now."

She still sounds doubtful, and given everything that's gone on and what she's been through, that's not surprising. "Come home with me, Eva? Please?"

She pulls back and looks up into my eyes. "Home?"

"Yes. My place. Come back there with me now…"

"But I can't." She looks around, panic glistening in her eyes. "I have to—"

"You don't have to do anything. Except come with me. I can make this right again."

"How?"

"Honestly? I've got no idea. But I'll do whatever it takes to make it okay. I promise."

She doesn't say a word, but I see something change in her eyes; something that gives me hope, and I release her carefully and then take her hand in mine, looking over her shoulder to Eli, who's been watching us the whole time. He acknowledges my glance and steps forward.

"Can you take Eva's bag?" I ask as he approaches.

"Sure," he says, bending to pick it up, and giving her a friendly smile before he turns and starts towards the exit.

I look down at Eva, and she stares up at me.

"Shall we go?" I say, tilting my head to one side.

And without taking her eyes from mine, she nods her head.

Chapter Fourteen

Eva

We've been at Chase's apartment for nearly an hour now.

He kept hold of both me and my phone for the whole journey back here, and since then, it's been on his breakfast bar, which separates the kitchen from the expansive living area, where I've been sitting with my feet up on the leather corner sofa. Eli disappeared almost straight away, after he and Chase had a whispered conversation and then Chase went into what I assume is a bedroom, and returned with a really soft, dark grey throw, which he put over my legs, and then he fetched me a glass of orange juice, and phoned his brother.

I know it's Max he's talking to, because of some of the things he says, but I think Colt might also be involved with their conversation, too. I'm not entirely sure and I'm so tired, I'm having trouble keeping up, especially as Chase is wandering around the flat while he's talking, going in and out of rooms, like he's restless, impatient for something.

"Okay... once you've gotten hold of her, you know what to do," he says, coming into the living room from the bedroom he went into earlier and looking down at me. "No, she's fine. She's tired and resting, but she's fine." He falls silent and smiles. "Yeah... I will. And thanks."

He hangs up and throws his phone down onto the sofa by my feet before sitting right alongside me and pulling me into his arms. I let him, because it feels good to be held, and then I lean back a little and look into his eyes, asking him the question that's been plaguing me.

"Did you mean what you said, when we were at the airport?"

He smiles even more widely. "I said quite a lot at the airport, but I'm assuming you're talking about the part where I said I love you."

"Yes. Did you mean that? Or was it just a way to stop me from leaving… because of the baby?"

He shakes his head. "I told you, I don't lie. I'm in love with you, Eva. And although I may not be great at showing it, that's only because we're not together enough. If at all. And it's also because I've never been in love before, and this is all really new to me. But I promise you, I'm gonna make more of an effort to get it right. I'm gonna spend more time with you, and I'm gonna make up for all the times I've let you down."

I lean into him, because his words are soothing, and I want his body to soothe me too, and he holds me closer. "You haven't let me down," I murmur into his chest.

"Yeah I have," he says, and I feel his hands skim across my back.

I tilt my head and look up at him. "That's not true. Ever since I've known you, you've been everything I could've wanted. Except maybe when you left me without saying goodbye. But I did that to you too. And I guess, when all's said and done, we all do stupid things when we're in love, don't we?"

He stares at me, and then frowns. "A—Are you saying you're in love with me too?" he asks, eventually, although I can hear the edge of doubt in his voice.

"Yes. I am. I have been for ages, and ages. I—I think I first started to wonder when you took me to that restaurant at the harbour. And I knew for sure after the picnic on the beach."

"So, the very next evening?" he says.

"Yes."

He nods his head. "I think I knew when you walked out of your bedroom wearing nothing but a towel."

I chuckle and shake my head. "That wasn't love, that was lust. You can't possibly have loved me then; you didn't know me."

"I loved you," he says slowly, with utter sincerity. And while that ought to be a joy to hear, it doesn't quite ring true,

"Is that why you went out that evening and tried to sleep with two other women?" I tilt my head to one side and he copies me.

"Partly. Falling in love with you scared the hell out of me. And while I know now what was going on, at the time, I was just confused. I know it sounds ludicrous, but I think I even felt angry with you, for messing with my head so much; for being so perfect, and sexy, and innocent, and bewildering. I thought if I could just get away from you, if I could just be myself, then everything would be fine." He shakes his head and sighs. "Except I didn't want to get away from you. And being myself turned out to be very overrated. Because I didn't wanna be that guy anymore. And I sure as hell didn't wanna be with those two women. I wanted to be with you."

"I'm glad you didn't sleep with them," I whisper, and he smiles.

"So am I." He leans forward slightly. "The next day, when I took you to the hotel site for the first time, and was showing you around, I remember thinking how relieved I was that I hadn't gone through with anything the night before. I loved just holding your hand, and being close to you, and none of it would have been the same if... if I'd betrayed you."

Betrayed me? "We weren't together, Chase. I know I got upset and accused you of all kinds of things, when we talked the other day, but you wouldn't have been betraying me."

"Yeah, I would. Because my heart was already yours." He closes the gap between us and brushes his lips against mine. And then he groans deeply, our tongues clashing in an instant as he pulls me close to him and our breathing quickens.

"Move in with me," he whispers, breaking the kiss.

"Sorry?"

"I said, move in with me. I know I've screwed up in so many ways since we first met, but letting you go was the biggest mistake of my life, and I don't wanna let you go, ever again. Not even for a night. Not even for a second."

"But we don't know each other." I may be in love with him, and he may be in love with me, but it's still not as straightforward as all that.

I feel like one of us needs to be the voice of reason in this, even if I am tempted by the idea… and by him. Especially after that kiss.

"We went through this before, and I told you then, we'll get to know each other. We got along okay in St. Thomas, didn't we?"

"You mean on a romantic island, in our own little bubble?" I repeat my words to him, because they still stand. "Yes, we did. But as I've already explained, this is the real world, Chase."

"Yes, it is. And I'm still capable of being romantic in the real world, in case you haven't noticed."

He leans in and kisses me again.

"It's not just about romance." I try to stick to the point, even though his kisses make it hard to think straight.

"I know," he says, looking down at me. "There's also the not insignificant detail that you're growing our baby." He rests his hand on my flat stomach. "And I wanna be around for that. For all of it. I wanna help you when you're sick, and look after you when you're tired. I'm not going anywhere, Eva. I promise. If you're worried about my past, then you don't need to be. I can't change it. I can't change any of the things I did before I met you. But I've changed me. And I'm not gonna change back."

I believe him. I honestly do, and I reach out and touch his cheek with my fingertips.

"I know," I whisper. "And I am tempted. I really am. But I don't even have a job anymore. I can't legally stay here." I can feel tears welling in my eyes at that thought.

"You do have a job. Bree was with Max just now, when I spoke to him. She's torn up your resignation letter…"

"She can't do that!" I sit up, fear rising inside me. "Alyssa will publish the photographs. That was the deal. I had to resign by today, so she could have my job, and if I didn't…"

"Calm down," he says, shaking his head and cupping my face with his hand. "It's not gonna come to that."

"How do you know?"

"Do you trust me?" he asks, a little unexpectedly.

"Yes."

He smiles. "Okay. Then stop worrying. And believe me… it'll be okay."

I stare up at him, and let him pull me in for a hug, relishing the strength of his arms and wishing I could believe him. And that I didn't still feel like my life is about to disintegrate all around me.

Chase

I wish Eva had said 'yes' to moving in. But I guess there's still too much uncertainty in her life at the moment. And that's never going to sit well with her. Not when she needs, more than anything, to feel safe. I knew that was a requirement of hers even before Ronan explained it to me. So I guess I'll have to wait a while. At least until I've dealt with Alyssa, anyway.

I keep hold of Eva, hoping I'm giving her some reassurance at least, and that she feels secure in my arms. Because she is. Nothing's gonna touch her or hurt her while I'm around. And I'm gonna be around for a very long time.

My doorbell rings, making Eva jump, and I release her. She looks up at me, and lets out a sigh, which sounds like disappointment, and I smile to myself as I get to my feet, going over to the door and opening it to find Bree standing there, which is exactly who I'd expected to see.

"Hey, Sis."

"Hey yourself."

She comes in and looks over at Eva, her face softening.

"How are you?" she says, walking over, ignoring me now.

"I—I'm fine." Eva goes to stand up, blushing and looking embarrassed. That's hardly surprising, being as I imagine the last time the two of them were together was probably quite different. And very awkward.

"No, sit down." Bree joins her on the couch, putting her purse down on the table. "I'm sorry I broke my promise and told Chase you were leaving," my sister says, in a rush of words.

"It's okay," Eva replies with a smile. "I don't blame you."

I feel relieved they've got that out of the way. I know from my conversation with Max that Bree was worried about Eva's reaction. Obviously, I'd rather Eva had said it had worked out for the best this way, but maybe that'll come later.

They both look up at me, Bree looking kinda expectant, and Eva with confusion written all over her face.

I go and kneel beside her, taking her hands in mine. "I've gotta go out, baby," I say softly, noting the fear in her eyes. "But I won't be gone for long, and Bree's gonna stay with you."

"Where are you going?" she asks, blinking rapidly.

"The office."

"Why?"

I think she already knows the answer to that, but I tell her anyway. "To see Alyssa." I sigh and lean into her. "Eli's been over to her place and picked her up."

"What are you going to do?" she asks.

"I don't know yet." That's not entirely true. There is a plan, of sorts. I just don't want Eva to know about it until it's all over and done with. She'll only worry even more.

"You will be careful, won't you? She's… she's toxic."

"I know. But you need to relax. I've got this. Okay?"

She hesitates and then nods her head and I lean in and kiss her, just briefly, unable to stop the slight moan that escapes my lips.

"I'm gonna miss you," I whisper, even though my sister is sitting just a couple of feet away.

"You are?" Eva seems surprised, although God knows why.

"Yeah. I am. I don't think time, or distance, or anything else will ever diminish the way I feel about you. No matter where I am, or who I'm with, or what I'm doing, you're all I ever think about."

Eva blushes, staring up at me. "Wow," she whispers.

"Wow, what?"

"You really meant it when you said you could still be romantic, didn't you?"

I kiss the tip of her nose and then get to my feet. "Hell, yeah," I say softly and she giggles, and I smile, like I don't think I've ever smiled before, because that sound is like heaven here on earth.

I grab my keys and Eva's phone from the breakfast bar and give my girl a wink, and Bree a wave, before leaving and making my way down in the elevator.

Now I'm alone, I allow my anger to surface for the first time since Eva showed me that damn image on her phone, bracing my arms against the wall of the elevator, and breathing deeply. I've got no idea how I'm gonna control myself with Alyssa, but I guess I'm gonna have to try. Somehow.

Downstairs, Dana is waiting by Bree's car.

"I'm supposed to take you back to the office," she says, getting behind the wheel, while I climb into the passenger seat.

"Thanks," I murmur, as she selects reverse, and I stare out the window. I want to think about Eva, and about the fact that she wouldn't agree to move in with me, and what I might be able to do to change her mind. But my head is too full of what's coming; of this meeting with Alyssa. And I can't think straight. I just know I can't let Eva go again. And I'll do whatever it takes to get her to stay.

Luckily, Dana's obviously picked up that I'm not in a talkative mood and just drives me the short distance to our office building, letting me out on the street, before going to park the car, and I ride up in the elevator, where Eli meets me.

"She's in Max's office," he says, holding open the double doors and letting me pass through into the hallway. "Colt's in there too."

I nod my head. "Good."

"How's Eva?" he asks.

"She's good, thanks… considering."

"She's gonna stay?"

"I don't think she's gonna leave the States, if that's what you're asking."

"It wasn't," he says.

"In that case, I don't know. I asked her to move in with me, and she threw up some roadblocks. But I'm thinking I might have handled it wrong. I…" I stop talking as we pass through the frosted glass doors into Max's outer office. "Where's Valerie?" I ask, nodding to the vacant desk his secretary usually occupies.

"Max sent her home early," Eli replies. "He and Colt decided it was better that way. The fewer people who know about this, the better."

"Good idea." I glance at Max's door and take a breath.

"Try to stay calm," Eli says, patting me on the shoulder.

"Easier said than done," I murmur, and push the door open.

Inside, Max is seated behind his desk, with Colt leaning against the wall to his right, his arms folded across his chest.

Alyssa is sitting in one of the two chairs facing Max and she turns upon hearing the door open. She smiles and flutters her dark eyes at me as I walk over, taking my place beside Max, and I narrow mine at her, although she doesn't seem to notice and simpers, settling back in her seat with the air of someone who feels safe in their position.

"Is anyone going to tell me why I've been brought here?" she says, crossing her legs, so her skirt rides up, revealing just a little too much thigh.

"Blackmail," I say simply, and she blinks a couple of times.

"Blackmail? What are you talking about?"

"This."

I pull Eva's phone from my pocket and turn it around, being careful not to show anyone else the picture on the screen, while revealing it to Alyssa, whose eyes widen.

"I—I don't see what that's got to do with me. It's a photograph of you and Eva."

"Yeah, sent by you to Miss Schofield, with the message…" I scroll back up the page. "'Don't forget. One week. Or else…'" I look up again. "You'd already told Miss Schofield to her face, at the meeting you had with her last Monday, that if she didn't resign by today, you were gonna put this photograph, and all the others in your possession, on the Internet, so I don't really know why you're bothering to deny it."

She tilts her head slightly. "Why are you bothering to call her 'Miss Schofield', when you're fucking her?"

I take a half step forward, but Max holds up his hand. "What my brother does in his own time, is his own business. He and Miss Schofield are both over twenty-one. They can do as they please, and should be allowed to, without being threatened, or blackmailed, by someone like you."

Alyssa blanches slightly.

"You don't know I was blackmailing her. You've only got her word for that."

"Yeah," Colt says, stepping forward and pulling himself up to his full, intimidating height as he stalks around the desk. "And the CCTV footage that shows Eva Schofield leaving the coffee shop around the corner at just before eight-thirty last Monday morning. And you leaving two minutes later."

"That doesn't mean a thing," she blusters, looking up at him.

"Then you won't mind me taking a look at your phone," he says, holding out his hand.

"Of course I will." She sits back in her chair, trying to move as far away as possible from him.

"Why? If you've got nothing to hide, you can't have any objections." His voice is menacing, even though he's not touching her. He's not even close enough to touch her, but he's scaring her. That much is obvious.

"It's private," she reasons, raising her voice.

"Okay. I'll call the cops, and we'll see what they've got to say about it." He takes his phone from his inside jacket pocket and presses on the screen a few times.

"You wouldn't dare," Alyssa says, and he stops.

"Why wouldn't I?"

"Because you wouldn't want to have the Crawford family name dragged through the press. I know things about you." She looks at me, smirking. "I've seen you, and your women."

"Do you think we care about that?" Max thunders, standing himself now.

"None of us care about that," I add. "My past is yesterday's news and as far as I'm concerned, it's irrelevant. You're hurting the woman I love, and I'm not just gonna sit back and let that happen."

I never thought I'd say anything like that, but the words sound good. They sound right, and Colt looks at me, smiling.

"There's no need to worry about the press," he says, shaking his head. "I've got enough friends on the force to ensure this won't come to light." He turns back to Alyssa. "And you, young lady... you'll be behind bars before your feet touch the ground."

She suddenly leaps to her feet, darting forward, and reaches out, trying to grab his phone, but he holds her off with one hand.

"Stop it." His voice is unbelievably quiet, but really fierce at the same time, and she backs down. "Now, quit fooling around and give me your phone. Or I'm gonna fuck up your life so bad, you won't even know what day of the week it is."

She glares at him, but he just glares back, and eventually, she steps over to the chair and reaches into her purse, retrieving her phone, which she holds out to Colt.

"Unlock it," he says, and she does, handing it over to him.

"I hate you," she murmurs at the same time.

"Don't sweat it, sweetheart," he replies, looking down at the screen in his hand. "I've been hated by a lot better people than you."

He moves away, focusing on the phone, and we all stand in silence, watching him as he presses on the screen every so often, before he turns back, offering the device to Alyssa, waiting until she's taken it before he looks over at me.

"I've deleted all the pictures of you and Eva," he says.

"What about copies?" I ask, and we all turn to Alyssa again.

"There aren't any," she mumbles.

"Sure about that?" Colt says, moving closer to her again.

"Yes," she hisses at him. "I wish there were, but there aren't."

Colt stands his ground, and Alyssa turns to leave.

"Wait." Max's voice is commanding, and she stops in her tracks. "We're not done yet," he adds, and she turns back to face him. "Come over here," he says, indicating the seats in front of his desk as he sits down himself.

She hesitates and then steps forward, sitting again.

"You've worked for Crawford Hotels for how long?" he asks, although I'm pretty damn sure he knows the answer to that question already.

"Nearly three years," she replies.

Max nods his head and opens the top drawer of his desk. "That's quite a while," he muses, almost to himself, as he pulls out an envelope and removes a single sheet of paper from inside, placing it on the desk and pushing it over to her. "You need to sign this," he says, offering her a pen. She doesn't take it, but stares at him. "It just says that you agree not to discuss anything that's taken place here today, or that took place on St. Thomas… with anyone. And it clarifies that, if you fail to adhere to that agreement, Crawford Hotels has the right to sue you." He leans forward. "In which instance, you'll lose everything. I'll make sure of it. Personally."

She snatches the pen out of his hand and scrawls her signature on the line at the bottom, throwing both the paper and pen back across the desk at him.

"Thanks," he says, picking them both up. "And now, get out. You're fired."

"I'm what?"

I can't believe she's surprised by that. But she is.

"You're fired. Did you honestly think I was gonna let you keep your job, when you've been blackmailing my brother?"

"I wasn't blackmailing your brother. I was blackmailing his latest fling."

"Don't talk about Eva like that," I growl, but she just shakes her head, smiling.

"Eli is gonna accompany you to your desk," Max continues, like neither Alyssa nor I have spoken. "You're gonna pack up your things, and then he's gonna escort you from the building. I'll give you three months' severance pay, which is more than you deserve, and I never want to see you near any of our properties again. Not even as a guest.

Is that clear?" She nods her head, dumbfounded. "And, if you so much as approach Miss Schofield, I'll make sure you never work in this profession again. Anywhere. Do you understand?"

"Yes," she mutters, and picking up her purse, she makes for the door, with Eli behind her.

"Eli?" Colt says, and they both stop, looking back. "Don't take any shit from her."

"No, boss."

He holds the door open, letting her pass, and then looks at me, giving me a smile, before he goes out, letting the door close behind him.

We all heave a collective sigh before I sit down in the chair Alyssa just vacated, and Colt sits beside me. I've got to admit, I'm feeling dumbstruck at the moment. I knew vaguely what the plan was when we set this up earlier on this afternoon, but I had no idea Max and Colt would have my back in the way they did.

"Thanks, guys," I mutter, leaning back in my seat.

"What for?" Colt turns to me.

"All of it. Everything. You're really quite scary when you wanna be. Did you know that?"

"Yeah." He shakes his head, like he's surprised I've never noticed that trait in his character before. "The good thing is, I don't very often wanna be."

I twist in my seat and turn to face him. "Did you... did you look at the photographs?" I ask him. "I've only seen one, but I know what we did. I know what they'll have contained."

He smiles. "Yeah. But it's okay. I've got a really bad memory." He's trying to make light of the situation, but it's not helping.

"Even so, I feel kinda uncomfortable, knowing you've seen Eva like that. I mean, how would you feel if that had been me looking at pictures of Bree?"

"Being as she's your sister, it would be beyond weird," he says, and even I have to smile, because he has a point. But before I can comment, he leans over, looking right at me. "You've gotta remember, Chase, with my lifestyle, I'm impossible to shock. Those pictures meant something to you, because they were of Eva, but to me, they're just part of the job. They didn't even register. Honestly."

I'm not sure I'm convinced by that, but I can't keep arguing the point. And in any case, I appreciate his candor. It's the first time he's really spoken to me at any great length. And it's definitely the only time he's ever mentioned his lifestyle, which I know he's very guarded about. And I appreciate that, as well as his help.

"Okay. Thanks."

I turn and look at Max, who's smiling at me. "If you don't mind me saying so, what the fuck are you still doing here? Don't you have somewhere better to be?"

I stand. "Yeah, I do. Thanks again… for everything."

I turn away and head for the door. "Dana will take you back to your place," Colt says over his shoulder, and I pause with my hand on the door handle, looking back at him. "And if you could ask her to hurry back here with my fiancée, I'd appreciate it. I wanna take her home and try something on our couch. I'm feeling kinda inspired."

He wiggles his eyebrows and I shake my head, even though I can't help smiling.

"Asshole," I whisper, knowing he'll have heard me, and both he and Max laugh as I open the door and pass through, closing it behind me.

I let myself into my apartment, and Bree and Eva look up at me from the couch, their expressions giving away their relief, coupled with what looks like fear. On both of their faces.

"Is it done?" Bree asks, because she has some idea of what the plan was.

"Yeah. It's done." I walk over to them, my eyes never leaving Eva's.

"Is what done?" Eva looks from me to my sister and back again.

Bree stands. "I'll let Chase explain it all to you," she says, and then glances up at me as I toss my keys and phone onto the coffee table. "Is Dana downstairs?"

"Yeah. She's waiting for you. And so is Colt. Back at the office."

I give her a smile, which she returns, before grabbing her purse and heading out the door, with a wave.

"What's happened?" Eva asks impatiently, as I sit down right beside her, and taking her hands in mine, I explain the events of the last hour or so. She listens intently, not saying a word, until I've finished my story.

"D—Did Max really fire her?" she asks eventually.

"Yeah."

"So I'm never going to have to see her again?"

"Never."

"And the photographs? Colt destroyed them?"

"Yes." She doesn't seem to have realized that, in doing so, he's also seen them. And I'm not about to enlighten her.

"But what if there are copies?" she asks, her eyes widening as that thought dawns on her.

"Alyssa said there weren't any."

"And you believed her?"

"Colt was kinda intimidating when he asked, so yeah, I did."

"But what if she was lying? What if she puts them out there?" I can hear the panic rising in her voice, and I pull her into my arms.

"Then I won't be very happy, because you're mine, and I don't want anyone else to see you like that… except me. But at the end of the day, there's nothing more we can do, and I'm not gonna spoil what we have now by worrying about something that might never happen." She leans back slightly and looks up at me. "We've done all we can, Eva. And I honestly don't think we'll hear from Alyssa again. But if we do, I'll deal with it, and I'll protect you. I promise. And I'll also make damn sure we never do anything to get caught out again." I brush my fingertips down her cheek, and she shivers. "I'm gonna take much better care of you from here on in."

I slide off of the couch onto the floor, settling on one knee, and she gasps, clearly reading my intentions, especially when I twist her around, lowering her feet to the floor, so she's facing me.

"Chase?" she whispers, but I reach out and place my fingers over her lips, silencing her.

"Let me say what I need to say, baby. And then you can talk." She nods her head and I remove my fingers, holding her hands in mine, clasped tight between us. "I—I was wrong to ask you to move in with me earlier on." She frowns. "Moving in together isn't enough for you. It isn't enough for me, either. I know we need to be a couple, but I need that to be forever, not just for now. So, will you marry me?"

"Y—You want to marry me?" she whispers, as though there could be any doubt about that.

"Yeah." I smile at her. "I want to marry you. I want you to be my wife. And I want to be your husband. I wanna keep you safe, Eva. And before you say we don't know each other, I want to spend the rest of my life getting to know you, because I never wanna stop learning. Not when it comes to you." I edge a little closer, leaning into her, our breath mingling between us. "Say yes, baby. Please."

She nods her head, swallowing hard and letting out a strangled, "Yes," as I release her hands and push her legs apart, settling between them before cupping her face and kissing her. As our tongues clash, she moans, and I let go of her face with one hand, moving it around behind her and pulling her closer still, so her ass is right on the edge of the couch, our bodies fused, my hard-on pressed against her, which makes her groan even louder, her breasts heaving into my chest.

"I—I want you," I breathe, leaning back and looking into her eyes, as I caress her swollen lips with the side of my thumb. "But it was always like that with you." She smiles and lowers her eyes, like she's embarrassed. "Hey… look at me." She does, our eyes locking. "It's okay," I whisper. "I get that you're not ready yet, and that's okay. I'll wait. You agreeing to marry me doesn't change the fact that I need to earn your trust again, or that there are things you wanna talk about, and that you need to work out about me, and about my past." I look down at the narrow gap between us, before I admit, "I—I need you to know I'm not proud of a lot of the things I've done, but I suppose I never really thought that what I was doing might have a bearing on my future. Hell, I never even thought I had a future. Not with someone like you." I raise my eyes again and look at her. "I'll tell you whatever you wanna know. There can't be any secrets between us."

"Were there a lot of women?" she asks, surprising me by getting right down to it.

"Yes."

She nods. "And apart from having sex with two women at the same time, and making love to me on the terrace at the cabin, in full view of anyone who happened to be walking by – evidently – are there any other shocking skeletons in your closet?"

"No, I don't think so. But I love the fact that you understand I had sex with all the others, but I made love with you."

"Well, you told me there was a difference," she whispers, and lowers her head, but I raise it again, my finger beneath her chin, and I hold her gaze.

"The difference is you, Eva."

"It's us," she says.

"Yeah, it is."

"In which case, can we agree to leave the past in the past?"

"Sure. If that's what you want."

She nods her head. "It is. I don't need to know any more. And I don't want to. Like you said, we can't change any of it, and it's not what's important now. I trust you, Chase… completely." I smile at her as she moves her hand around to stroke my cheek. "We came too close to losing the future to waste time dwelling in the past…" She leaves her words hanging, but the look in her eyes tells me everything I need to know, as does the smile twitching at her lips, and without thinking about it, I flex my hips forward and she gasps at the contact of my arousal, right against her core.

"Sorry," I mutter. "I guess I'm just really crap at waiting for you."

She puts her arms around me and I brush my lips against hers, as she sighs deeply and murmurs, "Then don't."

Epilogue

Eva

I'm about as pregnant as it's possible to be. Ideally, I'd like to be lying down in an air-conditioned room, with Chase bringing me iced water and rubbing my feet. But that's not to be, because today is Bree and Colt's wedding, and there's no getting out of it.

That said, Chase is being incredibly attentive, just as he has been throughout the entire pregnancy. He's still had to go away on business, but he's kept it to a minimum, and quite often, I've been able to tie my work in with his, so we've travelled together. That's been fun. Or at least it's been more fun than being apart.

He's been to every doctor's appointment with me too, even the ones where his presence wasn't really required. In the early days of morning sickness and all-day nausea, he didn't leave my side. When the tiredness became overwhelming, he let me sleep on him. All the time. He's cooked, run hot baths, rubbed my feet and tolerated my hormones. He's even been out at one o'clock in the morning to buy me strawberry ice cream and cake, because I simply had to have them.

Not only that, but he's bought us a house; a truly beautiful house. It's five minutes away from where Max lives, which also means we're close to Bree and Colt. And that's a good thing, because they're having their wedding at their home, so the drive wasn't too far.

Our home isn't modern, like Max's. It's more like Bree and Colt's, with wood cladding all over the outside. Although, where theirs is grey, ours is a dark cream colour. Inside, we've got five bedrooms, and four receptions, and a kitchen that's so big, you could lose yourself in it. If Chase would ever let me.

Best of all, there's a studio apartment above the double garage, which the previous owners had put in for their teenage daughter. It's small, but has everything you could need. And when we saw it, Chase turned to me and said it would be perfect for Ronan, when he comes to stay. I think I fell even more in love with him then, for understanding how much my brother means to me, and that I still need him in my life, even though I have Chase.

When we moved in, most of the house was already decorated in fairly neutral colours, and we were quite happy with that. But Chase immediately set about decorating the nursery in shades of blue and white, because we'd discovered we're having a boy. We're both overjoyed about that. Although I can still remember Chase's reaction, the night after the sonogram, when we found out. We were lying in bed together, and he turned to me, placing his hand on the bump, and said he hoped our son would be a better man than him when he grew up. I found that very moving, and put my arms around him, holding him close to me.

"There is no better man than you," I said, and Chase looked at me, shaking his head. I wouldn't let him speak though, and continued, "And our son is going to be just as good, because you're his father."

I noticed his eyes glistening then, and he rolled me over onto my back. "I don't deserve you," he whispered, leaning down and kissing me, his arousal pressing into me.

I smiled up at him. "Yes, you do. And I think I'd quite like you to prove it. If that's alright with you."

He smiled back at me, and raised himself up, entering me gently, but loving me hard. As only Chase can.

"You're not too hot, are you?" Chase comes and sits beside me, having been talking to Max inside the house for the last ten minutes. "We can move, if you want to. There's more shade at the back."

"Stop worrying, Chase. I'm just relieved we decided not to get married until after the baby's born. Between the morning sickness, the aches and pains, and the swollen ankles, I don't think I could've handled it... or found the time."

He turns to me, smiling. "Is this your way of telling me you don't wanna have any more kids?" he says, tipping his head to one side.

"No." I look up into his eyes and see the shining love there.

"Good," he whispers, leaning in to me.

"Do you want to have more then?"

"Hell, yeah," he says and I have to giggle. "What's funny?"

"You. You've changed so much. You sat in that restaurant last autumn and told me you never wanted to have children of your own. And now, look at you? You're about to become a father for the first time, *and* you're saying you want more."

"I know."

"So you don't doubt yourself anymore then?"

"Yes. All the time."

"Then, I don't understand. If you're not sure..."

He reaches out and caresses my cheek with his fingertips. "I am sure. When I'm with you."

"Then stay with me," I whisper.

"Always." He leans over and kisses me, his lips grazing over mine, and as he pulls back, everyone falls silent and we both glance around to see Colt and Max step out from the house and walk down the aisle together, signalling the beginning of the ceremony. They make their way to the front of the rows of seats and stand there expectantly. They're both giants, but they're very elegant in black tuxes, and they bend their heads close together, whispering something, just as some music starts to play.

"It's Tia's turn now," Chase says, holding my hand, and everyone turns to see Max's daughter walk down the aisle. She's carrying a little basket of cream rose petals, which she scatters onto the ground. She looks absolutely adorable in an off-white dress, and every so often, she glances up at her father, and bites her lip. I turn back to him, to see that he's smiling at her, the look on his face a mixture of pride and love, which makes my throat tighten.

She reaches her destination, and Chase's mother takes her hand, sitting her down on the chair in front of us, turning around and giving us a smile. I first met Kathleen, as she insists I call her, when Chase invited the whole family out to dinner so he could announce our engagement. I hadn't expected him to do that, but he reasoned it was easier to tell them all in one go. He also said that having Max and Bree there would curtail his mother's excesses. Personally, I don't find Kathleen excessive, but then, I suppose, she's not my mother.

Telling Ronan about the engagement had to be done more remotely, by phone. He was thrilled, and didn't seem that surprised. Which surprised me. He fitted in a brief visit to us in February and then again, just for a few days, when he finished in Peru, full of stories about the 'great find' they'd made down there. But he's back in Oxford now, and although he's ruing the fact that the Americans are getting to do most of the follow-up work on the dig, he's got a pile of things to catch up on. So I'm not sure when we're going to see him again.

"You've gone really pale, baby," Chase whispers, as attentive as ever, and I turn to look at him. "Are you sure you're okay?"

"Yes. I was just thinking about Ronan, that's all."

"You miss him, don't you?"

"Yes." I put my hand on his thigh. "But I'm okay. Honestly."

He puts his hand over mine and we turn together, and I suck in a breath, just as Chase whispers, "Jesus…" and we watch Bree walk down the aisle.

She's wearing an off-white dress made entirely of lace, and although her skin is clearly visible through it, it's not indecent. It's just very sexy, and I turn and look at Colt, whose eyes are fixed on his bride. Dark and very intense.

As she comes up to him, they face each other, both taking a breath, as the celebrant starts to speak, going through the formalities, and I lean into Chase, as he puts his arm around me, offering his support… as usual.

When it comes to the part where Bree and Colt have to say their vows, Chase seems to tense, although I don't know why, and I sit up slightly, paying a little more attention, and trying to ignore the niggling pain in my side.

Bree goes first, looking up at her groom, and saying, "My darling Colt, I enter into this life with you, without reservation, fear or confusion, but with a clear and trusting heart, knowing that our love will bind us together through all time." Chase huffs out a half laugh, which he struggles to disguise, and Bree smiles up at Colt. He shakes his head, narrowing his eyes even though he's smiling, and waits for her to continue, which she does, "You are my rock, my light, my best friend and my love. And now, you are my husband, and together we will walk through life, side by side. Equal, and one."

Colt hesitates for a second and then leans down, whispering something to Bree, who giggles and nods her head, before he stands upright.

"What was that about?" I whisper to Chase, and he looks down at me.

"I'll tell you later," he says and looks back at Colt, seemingly even more nervous now.

Colt takes Bree's hand in his, looking down at it, and then focuses on her face again.

"Bree," he begins, before taking a deep breath, like he's finding this hard, "I've been in love with you for so long, I can't remember how it feels not to be in love with you. You're the first thing I think about in the morning, and the last thing I think about at night. And every moment in between is filled with you. Just you. Because without you, I am nothing. I am a shell of a man. You put flesh to my bones. You give voice to my thoughts. You put blood in my veins and love in my heart. I am proud to walk by your side, and I will do so, protecting you, keeping you, and loving you, until my dying breath." He releases her hand and moves in closer, their bodies touching. And then he captures her face with his hands. "You're mine, baby," he says, his voice dropping, and Bree nods her head, although even from here, I can see the tears in her eyes and it's hard not to shed a tear myself, simply because that was so beautiful. And so unexpected.

The celebrant completes the service, declaring Colt and Bree to be husband and wife, and giving him permission to kiss her, which I don't think he really needs, and as he takes her in his arms, I turn to Chase.

"Why were you so anxious just now?" I ask, my whisper barely audible above the crescendo of applause.

"Because I wasn't sure what Colt was gonna say," he murmurs back. "The guy isn't exactly renowned for being romantic, and I guess I was just worried he might not be up to the task."

"Well, it looks like he proved you wrong." I smile up at him.

"Hmm… doesn't it?" He shakes his head in wonder and smiles. "And now, it looks like I've got a lot to live up to."

"Absolutely," I tease, leaning into him. "I fully expect you to top that."

His smile becomes a grin. "For you, baby… anything."

I let my head rest on his shoulder and he puts his arm around me again, and I know I'm where I belong. Even without having said our vows yet, I'm his. For life. And he's mine too.

Chase

I'm relieved the ceremony is finally over.

Not only is Bree now married to Colt, but I can get Eva out of the sun. I'm worried about her. The baby's due in just over a week, and although she's been sitting down for most of the day, I'd rather she was sitting down inside.

"C'mon, baby… let's get you into the house." Keeping my arm around her, I stand, bringing her with me, and we make our way indoors. She looks up at me and I smile down at her, supporting her. "God, I love you," I whisper, leaning down and kissing her cheek.

"I love you too," she murmurs, and I can see the truth of that in her eyes.

I never knew it could be like this. Love, I mean. I always thought that life with just one woman would be dull. Hell, I'd even gone out of my way to prove that point. But now, I know without a doubt that there is no other woman in the world who will ever be right for me. Eva makes me so happy, and so whole, and I tell her that all the time, because I know it needs to be said. I also show her too. Because words are no substitute for actions.

I've had to find different ways of showing her over the last couple of weeks, because Eva's found sex too uncomfortable. And there's no way I'm gonna do anything that hurts her. But just being with her, holding her, kissing her, talking to her, looking at her… it's all I need. She's all I need.

I know Eva's about done with being pregnant now. The weather's not helping, obviously, but she's struggling to get about, and sleeping is proving tricky too. Neither of us can wait. I'm desperate to meet our son, even though I'm kinda nervous about becoming a dad too. I told Eva how I felt, when we found out we're having a boy, and I think she was a little surprised by my admission. She seemed to be, anyway. I've spoken to Max about it too, and he's done his best to reassure me that I just need to be myself. It felt weird hearing him say that, because I would've thought that was the last thing our little boy needed. Being me has never been such a great idea in the past. But then Eva reminded me that the past doesn't matter, that I don't have to repeat the mistakes our father made, and it was then that I realized what she and Max were trying to tell me. I need to be the man I am now; the man Eva's made me. The better man.

I find Eva a seat on the couch in Bree and Colt's living room, which is nice and cool, and I sit down beside her.

"Is this okay?" I ask her, and she smiles and nods her head. "Sure?"

"I'm sure," she replies. "And now, I want you to explain to me why you found Bree's vows so amusing."

I chuckle to myself and lean in closer. "Because of Colt."

"That doesn't make sense. Her vows were directed at Colt."

"I know, and that's the whole point." I shift even closer still, so I can whisper, "You heard what she said, about their love binding them together?"

"Yes."

"Well, what you don't know, and you can't repeat to anyone, is that Colt is a Dominant."

She frowns. "A what?"

I let out a sigh and smile, shaking my head. "God... I love your innocence, baby." I put my arm around her. "A Dominant is someone who likes control. In fact, he – or she – is someone who *takes* control. In Colt's case, it's just a sexual thing, but with some Doms, it can be much more than that. It can seep into every aspect of their lives."

"I—Is he faithful to Bree?" she asks, her eyes wide with shock.

"Yeah, of course he is." I smile at her. "He's devoted to her."

"But he likes to control her?"

"Well, dominate her... sexually. Yes."

"And she's okay with that?"

I smile and nod my head. "She told me once that she finds it very liberating."

"Seriously?"

"Yeah. And while she might be his submissive, that's her choice. I think that's why she made a point of calling them equals."

She nods her head. "Whatever he said to her after that, it made her giggle," she says, remembering Colt's reaction.

"Yeah, but I'm not sure I wanna know about that. She's still my sister."

"Are there lots of people who do... that kind of thing?" she asks.

"Yeah. Quite a few."

She tips her head. "Is it something you've done?"

I smile, remembering how she said she wanted to leave the past behind us, and that she didn't need – or want – to know anything more about my previous life. And for the best part, she's stuck to that. Except every so often, she'll ask a question like this one. And I'll always tell her the truth.

"No, baby. It's not my scene. Never has been. Obviously, if you wanted to…" I leave my sentence hanging, and she shakes her head.

"I don't think so," she whispers. "I think I like things just as they are. Or rather, as they were." She leans into me. "And I'd rather like them to be that way again, assuming our son ever puts in an appearance. Speaking of which, he seems to have decided that my bladder is a football. Again."

"Do you need the bathroom?"

"I always need the bathroom." She sighs, and I get up, offering her my hands and pulling her to her feet.

I keep a hold of her, and accompany her to the bathroom by the stairs, waiting in the foyer. I've gotta admit I like Bree and Colt's house. Not as much as ours. But I like it. I especially like the paintings they've chosen to hang, and I make a decision with myself to try and source some original art for our own home…

"Chase?"

I turn and see Eva exiting the bathroom, looking a little worried, and I stride over to her.

"What's wrong, baby?"

"I—I don't know how to put this, but my waters just broke."

"What?" She can't be serious. "You're sure?"

"I'm positive."

"But we didn't bring your bag. We're not ready for this."

She smiles and reaches up, caressing my cheek. "I don't think it's optional, Chase. The baby's coming, whether we like it, or not."

I take her hand, feeling like an idiot, and sit her down on the bottom of the stairs. "Stay here. I'll be two minutes."

She nods her head and then winces, clutching the bump, hissing in a breath between gritted teeth.

"Was that a contraction?" I ask and she nods again, and I'm torn between staying and going.

"Go and do whatever you need to do," she says, answering my problem, and I lean over and kiss her forehead before turning and running back into the living room. I can't see Max or Colt, so I head outside into the garden, where they're both standing with Bree, and I run over to them.

"What's up?" Max says, seeing me approach.

"It's the baby…"

"Now?" he says, understanding at once without me having to explain.

"Yeah. Now. Eva's waters just broke. But we didn't bring her bag or anything."

Max rolls his eyes. "Okay." He turns to Colt. "Can you find Eli?"

Colt nods and disappears, and I turn back to Max. "How's Eli gonna be able to help?"

"He's gonna drive you to the hospital, and you're gonna give me your keys, so I can go back to your place and pick up Eva's bag."

I nod my head. "It's upstairs in our bedroom."

"Okay."

I hand him my keys just as Eli approaches, followed by Colt.

"I'll find you," Max says. "Now go."

I don't wait to be told twice, and with Eli a step behind me, I go back into the house, where I find Eva pacing the hallway.

"I thought I left you sitting down," I say, putting my arm around her and helping her to the door, which Eli's holding open.

"I know, but it got too uncomfortable."

"Tell me you're not gonna give birth in my car," Eli says as we pass him.

"I'll do my best," Eva replies, giving him a smile, right before the next contraction hits.

"It's been five hours," Eva says, relaxing slightly and letting her head rest on the pillow, as the latest contraction releases her, just temporarily.

"I know, baby." I lean over and kiss her forehead, and then her cheek, and she glares up at me.

"If you think you're ever coming near me again, Chase Crawford, then you can think again." That's the third time she's threatened me with a life of celibacy, and while I'm pretty damn sure she means it at the moment, I know she won't. Not in the long term. I know Eva far too well.

The midwife looks up at me from her position near the end of the bed and gives me a knowing smile. I guess she's heard it all before. And far worse, probably.

"You couldn't get me some more ice, could you?" Eva says, her voice a little more forgiving now.

"Sure, baby."

Eva's been sipping on water, but has found that sucking on ice chips is far more thirst quenching, especially when she's breathing so hard. Luckily, they have a machine down the hall, just for the purpose, and I take her cup, giving her a quick kiss before I exit the room.

Outside, I draw in a deep breath and quickly make my way down the corridor, past the waiting area to my right.

"Hey."

I turn on hearing the familiar voice of my brother, and see Max standing by the window. Like me, he's taken off his jacket, and has rolled up his shirt sleeves, and he steps forward, holding Tia in his arms. I smile at him and then glance over his shoulder and notice he's not alone. Sitting on the chairs are my mom, Bree, Colt, and Eli. And while everyone else is still wearing wedding attire, Bree has changed out of that jaw-dropping dress of hers, into a white sundress.

"What are you guys doing here?" I can't disguise my surprise.

"Where the hell else would we be?" Colt says.

"At your own wedding, maybe?" I suggest.

He shrugs. "Some things in life are more important," he says, putting his arm around Bree. "And anyway, we've done the part that matters. We've said our vows."

"Yeah. And given the rest of us a helluva lot to live up to," I reply, and everyone chuckles.

"What's going on?" Max says, nodding toward Eva's room.

"It's horrendous," I say quietly, because it is. "Why does no-one tell you it's this bad? Seeing Eva in this much pain. It's…" I suddenly can't talk, and Max turns and hands Tia over to Bree, before walking right up to me.

"It's hard, but it's so much worse for her. And she's gonna need you to be strong. Because, believe me, it's gonna get harder yet."

"Harder?" I find that difficult to believe.

"Yeah."

"Then how is she gonna get through it?"

Our mom gets up now and comes to join us. "Because that's what women do," she replies. "And even though she's probably cursing you right now, I can guarantee you that after your baby's born, she'll forget the pain. She'll love your son like nothing else on earth. And she'll love you more than ever too. Don't ask me how that works. Just know that it does."

"And maybe get back in there?" Max suggests, and I nod my head, giving him a smile, before I run down to the ice machine and fill up Eva's cup.

My own is already running over.

Another hour and a half, a few more curses, and a possible fractured hand later, our son is born, and I see the instant burst of love in Eva's eyes, as he's placed on her chest and she gazes down at him.

"He's here. He's finally here. And he's ours," she says, looking up at me. "Oh my God… Chase."

Tears fall from her eyes and I lean over, letting my own mingle with hers as I kiss her.

"You're so brave," I whisper. "And I love you so, so much."

"I love you too."

"Can I just say something now, while I've got you to myself still?" I'm ignoring the midwife, because she's busy and seems to be ignoring us too.

"Of course." Eva looks up at me, tearing her eyes away from our son, just for a moment.

"I know we said we both wanted to have more children, but I had no idea what you were gonna have to go through to give birth. Not really. I do now though. And if you wanna change your mind, then I'm not gonna complain."

She smiles. "Well, I'm not sure I want to go through that pain again. At least, not any time soon. But I'd sell my soul for this feeling." She looks down at our son, still lying on her chest, his blue eyes wide in wonder as he gazes at his beautiful mother. "This is something else. And it's worth it. Having him... having you. It's worth every single second."

"You've always got me, babe."

"I know." She blinks a few times.

"So, you are gonna let me come near you again then?" I ask, teasing her a little.

"What do you think?" she teases me right back, but then says, "I—I didn't think it was possible to love you any more than I did, but I do."

I nod my head, all teasing forgotten. "Nowhere near as much as I love you."

It takes a lot longer than I would have thought to get Eva and our son cleaned up and looking presentable, and by the time they are, it's dark outside and although I'm not even sure if my family is still here, I ask if they can be allowed to come in. The midwife says yes, but not all at once, and she goes outside to tell them.

A few minutes later, Mom pokes her head around the door, and I smile, knowing she'll probably have insisted on meeting her first grandson before everyone else. Which I guess is only fair.

She comes across to the bed, where Eva's sitting up, and leans over, kissing the baby's forehead.

"Oh my goodness, he's perfect," she whispers.

"Yeah, he is."

She turns to me. "He looks just like you."

It's true. He does have dark hair, rather than blond, like Eva's, and there's a definite squareness to his chin, which I recognize from photographs of both Max and myself as babies.

"I think that too," Eva replies, smiling up at my mother.

"How are you?" Mom says to her.

"I'm better than I was a few hours ago," Eva replies, nodding her head, and I bend down, taking the baby from Eva, so she and my mom can talk, which they do, while I wander over to the window, looking out across the city, showing our baby the lights blinking in the darkness, and all the while, feeling somehow like I don't belong... like this can't really be happening to me. Even though I know it is.

"I'm gonna go," Mom says eventually, and I turn, stepping back into the real world. "Everyone else is desperate to see you all, and the midwife said we couldn't take up too much time. Eva needs to rest."

"Yeah, she does."

I smile over at the most beautiful woman in the world, who smiles back at me, right before her eyes drop to our son, who's cradled in my arms.

"We'll be home tomorrow, Mom," I say as my mother comes over to kiss the baby's head again. "You can come and see us then, if you like."

"I'd love to." She reaches out, touching my arm, and nods her head, even though she doesn't say anything, and then she leaves the room.

"Are you okay?" Eva asks once we're alone again for a moment.

"I'm fine. I—I'm just getting used to how this feels."

"It's surreal, isn't it?" she says, and I heave out a sigh of relief.

"So it's not just me then?"

"No. I keep thinking he can't be ours. Except I know he is."

I smile at her, grateful that she understands; that she feels the same, just as the door opens again, and this time Bree and Colt step into the room.

"Oh, my God, he's beautiful," Bree says, coming straight over to me, while Colt hangs back slightly. "C—Can I hold him?"

"Of course."

I carefully hand my son over to my sister, being sure to support his head, and she looks down into his face. "Oh, Colt..." She turns to look at her husband, and I notice tears forming in her eyes as he crosses the room to where we're standing, putting his arm around her and gazing at her, and then at our baby, cradled in her arms. "I know we said there was no rush, but do you think…?" She looks up at him, a kind of uncertain, yet pleading expression on her face, which I remember well from when she was younger and was desperate to get something she wasn't sure she'd earned, in our father's eyes.

"You know how I feel about this. I told you. There's nothing I want more."

She looks up at Colt again. "So does that make it a good thing that, in between work and planning the wedding, I forgot to book the appointment with my gynaecologist to get my next shot? It's due this coming week, but we're gonna be away on our honeymoon, and I've been going crazy trying to work out how to tell you."

"You didn't need to worry," he murmurs. "In fact, your timing is immaculate. Although I'm not sure your brother wanted to hear any of that."

"No, he didn't," I reply, and we all laugh.

"I suppose we should give you back to your daddy," Bree says, clearly talking to my son now, and I stare at her for a moment, her words taking a while to register. That's the first time anyone has called me 'daddy', and it hits home that I'm someone's father. And that the role comes with responsibilities.

I snap back to reality though as Bree holds my son out and I take him from her, before she leans up and gives me a kiss on my cheek, and then goes over to Eva.

"Congratulations," Colt says, patting me on the arm, because I can't shake hands at the moment.

"Thanks." I give him a smile, and he smiles back.

"Stop looking so worried. You wear fatherhood well, you know?"

"It's scary," I admit. "But it looks like you'll be finding that out for yourself before too long."

"Yeah." He glances over at Bree, who's laughing with Eva. "C'mon, babe," he calls out. "Let's leave these guys in peace. They've got a son they wanna get to know."

Bree moves back over to us, and they stand together.

"I'm sorry if we screwed up your wedding," I say as Bree rests her head on Colt's shoulder.

"It's not a day we're gonna forget in a hurry," she replies.

"I'm never gonna forget the day you became mine," Colt says, turning to her, and on that surprisingly romantic note, they leave the room.

"Well, I think we can guess what they'll be doing tonight," Eva says, chuckling and then regretting it as she winces slightly and then repositions herself on the bed.

"I think they would have been doing that anyway, given that it's their wedding night," I point out, and she shrugs, nodding her head, although I can tell she's getting tired now and I wander over, putting our sleeping son in his crib, before leaning down and kissing Eva gently. "Are you okay?" I ask her.

"Yes, I'm fine."

"Do you want me to tell the others to leave it for tonight?"

"No. I'll be okay."

I nod my head and decide we'll keep it brief, as Max opens the door, bringing a sleepy Tia in with him, held in his arms. Despite her exhaustion though, she wants to get down, and he lets her, holding her hand as she wanders over to the crib and stares at the baby.

"What's his name?" she whispers, and I gaze at Eva, smiling.

"Thomas," she says, turning to Tia, and Max smiles too now.

"That wouldn't have anything to do with where he was conceived, would it?" he murmurs, coming closer to me.

"It might."

He holds out his hand, and I take it. "Congratulations," he says, with feeling.

"Thanks. Although I doubt you'll be thanking me when I haven't been into work for a few weeks."

He shrugs. "Take as long as you need. I don't know why I have to keep reminding you and Bree, but you own the company too, you know?"

"Yeah. And speaking of that, I was gonna talk to you next week about whether we can sit down sometime and try to work out a way for me to do less traveling. I appreciate that you've not asked me to go away so much in the last few months, and that Eva's been able to come with me, but she wants to stay at home with Thomas, and while I know I have to work, I don't wanna be away from them too much."

He smiles and pats me on the shoulder. "I do get it," he says, looking over at Tia, with so much love in his eyes, it takes my breath away. "And we'll work it out. I promise. I'm interviewing for nannies on Monday morning, but you can call me anytime."

"You're interviewing for a new nanny? Don't the agency usually do that?"

He shakes his head. "After the last few disasters, I decided to do it myself."

I can't say I blame him. He's had so much trouble finding a nanny for Tia, it's ludicrous. They either want to rule her life with a rod of iron, or get Max into bed, with nothing in between.

"Well, hopefully, if you meet them yourself, you'll get more of an idea what they're like."

"That's the plan," he replies, moving away, toward Tia and taking her hand in his. "Come on," he says. "We need to get you home to bed. I'm sure Uncle Chase and Aunty Eva will let you go round to play with Thomas sometime soon. But in the meantime, we need to let Eva have her surprise, don't we?"

He looks down at Tia while I stare at him and then at Eva.

"What surprise?" she asks and he shrugs.

"It's just something I organized earlier. Eli picked it up for me, and he's waiting outside with it now. And I think it's high time we let him bring it in, so you can get some rest. You've earned it."

"She certainly has," I say, although looking at the light in Eva's eyes, I know she's not even remotely tired now. She's intrigued and kinda excited, and I've gotta admit to feeling a little curious myself.

Max leans over the bed and gives Eva a very gentle kiss on her cheek, whispering, "Congratulations, Mom," to her, and then he lifts Tia into his arms again and leaves the room.

"What's going on?" Eva asks.

"I've got no idea."

I go across to her, checking on Thomas at the same time. He's sleeping soundly, and I feel my heart swell in my chest.

"He's perfect," I whisper, and turn to face Eva. "Just like you."

She smiles and parts her lips to speak, just as the door opens and we turn to see Eli come in. He doesn't say a word, but steps aside, and Eva gasps as her brother is revealed in the doorway, a huge grin on his face.

"Hey, beautiful," he says, coming into the room and straight over to the bed.

"Ronan?" She sounds like she can't believe he's here, and to be honest, I'm struggling with it myself. "How did you get here?"

"I got a phone call," he says, letting his bag drop to the floor. "From Max…" He looks over at me. "Your brother?"

"Yes."

Ronan nods his head. "He told me that Eva had gone into labor, and that I should get myself to Heathrow Airport, where a ticket would be waiting for me at the check-in, and that someone would collect me from Logan, when I arrived, and would bring me here. It was all really rushed, and slightly crazy, but that's exactly what happened."

"But how did Max even know your number?" Eva asks.

"That would have been me," Eli says from his place by the door, where he's still standing.

"You?" I turn to look at him.

"Yeah. Max asked me to track down Eva's brother." He looks over at Ronan. "Didn't take long. Your details are all over the Internet, after that find of yours down in Peru."

Ronan smiles. "Yeah. I expect they are. Although it's not officially my find. The credit has to go to Professor McLean. Not that any of that matters right now."

He turns back to Eva, smiling, and I move away, giving them some time together and going over to Eli.

"Thanks," I whisper.

"What for? It was Max who arranged it all."

"I wasn't thanking you for that."

"Then what were you thanking me for?"

"Convincing me not to give up, back in St. Thomas; making me see reason, making me realize that love's worth fighting for. I don't wanna think about how much I could've lost."

He looks down at the floor for a moment and then nods his head. "Speaking of not giving up, I've been meaning to tell you... I managed to find Sienna."

I turn to face him. "Wow." I hadn't expected that. "And?"

He smiles. "And I called her. She was kinda surprised to hear from me after all this time, but we talked, and then she agreed to meet me."

"So she's still single?" I ask.

"Yeah. God knows how, but she is. She's been with a few other guys since we broke up, but I guess it's fair to say that I've been with a few other women too." He looks at me and we both smile.

"And you've seen her again since then?"

"Yeah. We've been taking it slow." He smiles at me. "I'm considerably better at that than you are, by the way."

"I think everyone on the planet is better than me at that."

He chuckles, and then says, "We've talked a lot about what happened and we've agreed that it's in the past, and we wanna leave it there."

"That sounds hopeful."

"It is hopeful. We're going away together next weekend, if that's okay with you?"

"Of course it is. I'm gonna be otherwise occupied." I smile. "So, you're not that great at taking it slow after all?"

"We've been dating for nearly four months. I seem to remember you struggled with four days, when we were on the island."

"Yeah, I did."

He coughs and looks down at his feet before raising his face to mine again. "I'm sorry I haven't told you. I—I just wanted to work things out for myself."

"You don't need to apologize."

He smiles. "I wanted to thank you too."

"What for?"

"For telling me to go find her. You were right. I should never have given up on what we had."

I look over at Eva, who's talking to Ronan and gazing at our son, and then I turn back to Eli.

"No. You should never give up. No matter what."

The End

Thank you for reading *Chasing the Dream*. I hope you enjoyed it, and if you did I hope you'll take the time to leave a short review.

And if you want to find out more about me and my books, including forthcoming releases, please visit my website at www.suziepeters.com, where you can also sign up to become a member of Suzie's Circle, giving you access to **exclusive free stories**.

In the meantime, if you want to find out what happens next in this series, keep reading for an excerpt from book three...
Looking for Love.

Looking for Love

Never Give Up: Book Three

by

Suzie Peters

Chapter One

Cara

I cover my nose and mouth with my hand, trying to blot out the smell of damp and the mold that's growing up the walls. I'd probably bury my head under the pillow, but that's just as damp, and the musty smell coming off of the graying cover is enough to make me want to vomit. At least my hand smells clean and fresh, because I just showered, in a desperate attempt to wash off the filth of my life. Not that I ever can, because the memories are always there, no matter how hard I scrub at my skin. Even when it's raw and red, I can still remember… everything.

I turn over and stare out the window, although I can't see very much because of the built up grime and dirt, both inside and out. I know there's a moon out there. Somewhere. And stars to wish on. Although I don't bother wishing that much these days. I've got nothing left to wish for.

Jared's seen to that.

I swallow down my tears and sit up, shaking my head.

"Why?" I whisper out loud. "Why am I still here?"

Because you're scared, the voice in my head replies.

And that's true. I'm scared of Jared. In fact, I'm terrified of him. I've left him before, more often than I can remember. And he's found me. Every single time. He doesn't come after me because he loves me, though. He comes after me because I'm his meal ticket, and when he brings me back to this one-room hovel, he pretends is our home, he makes my life a living hell. So much worse than anything I thought I'd left behind me, I've stopped thinking about leaving. It's not worth it.

Except…

I let my head drop into my hands, tears gathering in my eyes.

I know Jared's gone to see Ivan tonight. And I know what that means.

Ivan is a giant of a man, an Eastern European, who I don't even think is called Ivan. I think that's just what everyone calls him, because he talks with an accent that sounds a little like Russian. And, in all probability, with the things Ivan is into, he doesn't want anyone knowing what his real name is anyway.

Not that I know exactly what Ivan does. I just know that he hurts me. And Jared lets him. In fact, Jared actively encourages him, and anyone else he owes money to, while he sits in the corner, watching and smirking, letting them do whatever they want. Because that way they seem to forget about his debts, and just use me instead.

I can still remember the pain from last time though, and how Ivan laughed when I begged him to stop, when I told him I'd do anything else but that. How I pleaded with him not to hurt me, and how he pulled my hair and made it so much worse.

And I know I can't do that again. Ever.

Even living with my mom and Ray was better than this.

At least I had hope then.

But Jared's robbed me of that, as well as my self-respect and whatever innocence I had left.

I jump as the sound of a key turning in the lock brings me back to reality. Jared's back early. Normally when he goes to see Ivan, he's gone for a couple of hours at least. I quickly lie down again and pull the covers over me, pretending to be asleep, hoping he won't notice how much I'm shaking.

The door slams and I struggle not to react, not to show my fear, but to lie completely still, as I hear him throw his keys onto the shelf by the door, and imagine him dumping his wallet beside them, just like he always does.

"I know you're awake," he says, his voice laced with an unspoken threat.

I still don't respond, but I hear his footsteps on the hardwood floor, getting closer and closer, and then the covers are pulled from me and I realize the pretense is pointless and turn over. Even in the dim moonlight, I can see the bright glare in Jared's eyes.

"You're early," I say, to make conversation.

"Ivan didn't show," he replies, and I struggle not to let him see my relief. But he smiles anyway, in a wicked, knowing way, as he chews on his nails, a nerve twitching at the side of his eye, and I recognize the signs. He's getting strung out, and needs a fix. And because Ivan didn't make it, he's going to have to wait. And waiting isn't something Jared does very well. "Don't look so happy," he says, shaking his head. "I'll still find a use for you."

He fumbles with the buckle of his belt and I sit up, pushing him away, knowing that, in this state, he won't be strong enough to fight back.

"If you think I'm gonna let you…"

He raises his hand and I wonder if I've read the situation all wrong, whether maybe he has scored and I'm gonna get a beating, and I shift back as fast as I can.

"You don't have a fucking choice," he yells, and although he lowers his hand, without striking me, he knows he's got me scared enough to do what he wants, and that's all he needs.

He goes back to fiddling with his belt and this time he has more success, undoing it, and pulling it from its loops, wrapping one end around his hand.

"Mess with me," he says, leaning over and hissing in my face, "and I'll show you how mean I can really be."

"I'm not gonna mess with you." The fight has gone out of me, and as much as I hate myself for being so weak, I feel hemmed in my him. It feels like the lesser of two evils to just let him do what he wants, rather than fight him, and come off even worse than usual.

He smiles and then leans in closer, kissing me, his breath tasting of cigarettes and something sweet and rancid that I don't want to think about.

"I'm gonna warm you up for Ivan," he whispers, clutching my chin in his hand and squeezing until it hurts. Tears form in my eyes, but he ignores them and unbuttons his jeans. "You'll have to be my fix for now." His voice wavers slightly, and he coughs in my face, but then continues, lowering his jeans and underwear. He's not aroused, but then he rarely is these days, unless he's watching me with one of his friends, of course. "Now, sit forward," he barks, and after a moment's hesitation, I do as he says, shuffling to the edge of the bed. "Open your mouth," he says and I look up at him, wondering how it came to this; how I let things go this far.

"Please, Jared," I beg, trying to get through to him. "I don't want to…"

He ignores my pleas and takes advantage of the fact that I've opened my mouth to insert his flaccid penis.

"Now… suck," he says, holding the back of my head.

He tastes repulsive – musty and unwashed – and to stop myself from gagging, I shake my head. He pulls out of me and leans over, his face barely an inch or more from mine.

"Do as you're fucking told," he shouts, slapping my cheek with the palm of his hand. "Or I'll use my belt on you."

He stands up again and shifts closer, just as his phone rings.

"Fuck it," he bellows, and bends down to find it in the pocket of his jeans. I take my chance and shimmy backwards, but he holds up a finger at me. "Stay exactly where you are," he warns, and then he glances down at his phone, a smile settles on his lips, and he holds his cell to his ear. "What the fuck happened to you, man?"

He falls silent for a moment or two and then steps away, almost tripping over his jeans, which are still bunched around his ankles.

"Shit… did they catch up with you?" He waits. "No… no, I guess not."

He seems preoccupied now, so I take advantage of the situation and move further back onto the bed.

"I can come and meet you now, if you like," he says into the phone. "And then, when you've finished your other business, I can bring you back here." He pauses, listening, and then turns and looks over at me, grinning. "Yeah. Cara's here. And she's really looking forward to seeing you again."

I feel like being sick, and my stomach churns as my mouth dries and my hands shake, but then I realize Jared is standing right beside me again, buttoning up his jeans.

"I'm going out," he says, as though I haven't just overheard his conversation. "Ivan got held up earlier. The cops paid a visit to the house he lives in, but luckily he escaped out the back as they were coming in the front. He had to lie low for a while, which was why he couldn't make our meeting." He makes it sound like they'd have been in a boardroom, with briefcases and a full agenda to get through, rather than gathering on a street corner or in a back alley. And if I didn't feel so scared, I'd laugh. He leans over and runs his finger down my jaw line before grabbing my chin again. "I'm gonna go see him now. He says he's got a few other guys to catch up with, and then I'm gonna bring him back here. That's the deal I've made with him, and he says he likes it that way." Jared grins and releases me, with another slap to the cheek. "If you want my advice, I'd lose the pajamas. Ivan's not a patient man. He won't wanna waste time getting you out of them. So you may as well get naked first and save him the trouble."

I swallow down the bile that's rising in my throat and watch as Jared gathers his keys and wallet and heads out the door again, without another word.

No sooner has he gone than I feel my heart start to thump in my chest, and my hands sweat and tremble, and I know I have to get out of here, before he comes back with Ivan. Because there's no way I'm going to let him touch me again. There's no way I'm going to submit to that man's vile demands. I'd rather die first.

Except I'm not going to die. I'm going to leave. And this time, I've got to make a better job of it. Because if Jared finds me again, I'm not sure I'll survive. I might be scared of him, but I'm so much more scared of what's going to happen to me if I stay.

I let the tears fall, knowing what that means, knowing what I'm giving up by leaving, but trying to ignore it as I get up and fumble with putting my hair up into a ponytail and pull on my jeans over the top of my pajamas, before zipping up my blue hoodie. It might be warm outside, but there's a limit to what I can carry.

I grab my rucksack and empty my books onto the floor, wiping away my tears as I realize that I'm not gonna be needing them again. Because this is my sacrifice for escaping. This is what I'm giving up for the hope of a new life, somewhere else. I'm abandoning my education, and the future I've spent the last few years trying to create for myself.

But what choice do I have?

None.

I fill my bag with as many clothes as I can fit in, adding some underwear and toiletries; just the basics, nothing extravagant. I don't own anything extravagant anyway, so it's easy to pack.

And then I find my purse and take out the cash I've got stashed in there, hidden in the tear I made inside the lining; the secret place that Jared's never thought to look. It's not much, but it's enough and I put it in my pocket, leaving my purse behind, along with all its other contents, including my phone, my bank card, my keys and my contraceptive pills. I certainly won't be needing those again. And if I leave it all here, it might lull Jared into thinking I haven't actually gone for good. At least for a while, anyway. And that 'while' might just buy me enough time to put some distance between us. It might just buy me my freedom.

Then I head out the door, pulling it closed behind me.

I don't look back. There's nothing to regret.

I've got no idea where I'm going to go.

I just know that, wherever it is, it's got to be better than here.

Max

That was a much more eventful weekend than any of us ever thought it would be.

It was always gonna be busy, because my sister Bree was getting married to my bodyguard and oldest friend, Colt. It was a beautiful wedding, which they held at their house, not far from my own home, just outside of Boston, and everything was going smoothly. In fact, it was going better than that. Colt was so thrilled to be marrying my sister, and although I jokingly questioned his sanity a couple of times before the ceremony, it was really easy to see how in love he is. Bree looked amazing; maybe a little sexier than I'd expected, but I could tell from Colt's reaction that he didn't mind one bit. Her dress was decent, hiding everything that needed to be hidden, but suggesting a fair bit. And I know from my own experience how tantalizing that can be, when the woman you love shows off just enough to make you want more. They'd said their vows, with Colt blowing everyone away by revealing a truly romantic side to his nature. One that not even I'd seen before. And then everyone was just standing around talking, having a good time, and enjoying themselves. That is, until the proceedings were interrupted by my brother Chase's fiancée going into labor.

I guess that wasn't entirely surprising, being as babies have a habit of arriving when you least expect them, but in this case, the timing was interesting. To put it mildly. They hadn't brought Eva's bag with them, so while Chase's bodyguard, Eli, drove him and Eva to the hospital, I went back to their place to fetch her things, and took them over there. I didn't actually get to see Chase, but just handed over Eva's bag at the reception, and was about to leave again, when everyone else arrived. And by everyone, I mean my mom, Bree, and Colt, who was carrying my daughter, Tia. I asked what they were all doing there, and Bree explained that, once we'd gone, they'd all decided they felt a little flat, not to mention worried, and that they'd rather be there than at home, so Bree had gone to change into something a little more practical, and they'd left their guests to entertain themselves. We set up camp in the waiting room, which was where we found Eli, who hadn't wanted to leave either, and he and I set about trying to track down Eva's brother who, like her, is English, but unlike her, still lives there. Between us we arranged for him to get from London to Boston, and he arrived not long after my nephew Thomas was born. He's a really cute baby, which I guess isn't that surprising, being as his mom is beautiful. And my brother isn't exactly ugly either.

It seems odd to think of Chase as a father. It's not something I ever thought would happen. Actually, I don't think it's something he ever thought would happen either, not when you consider the kind of life he used to live; moving from one woman to the next, without batting an eyelid about commitment or responsibility.

Until Eva came along, that is.

And he discovered what love is all about.

And that's why he spoke to me on Saturday evening, at the hospital, and asked me to find a way for him to spend less of his time away from home in the future. He's used to traveling around, all over the US and the Caribbean, updating and remodeling the hotels we own, as well as designing new ones, and only returning here to our offices in Boston once every few months. But he's got a family now, and he wants to be with them. And I get that.

And I will work it out for him.

Somehow.

He's so happy, I could almost feel jealous. Because happiness is something I've forgotten how to feel. That said, I don't envy him. I'm pleased for him. I'm pleased he's found someone special. Because I know how that feels. I had it myself. With Eden.

Before it all went wrong…

We were high school sweethearts, and I can still remember the first time I saw her. She was walking down the hallway, her dark brown hair falling around her shoulders, clutching her books to her chest, and looking nervous, because it was her first day and she didn't know her way around. Just at the sight of her, my heart flipped over in my chest, my stomach felt like it was filled with butterflies, and my mouth dried. And when she looked at me, our eyes met, and I knew... I knew she was the one.

She knew it too, evidently, although I didn't find that out for a while.

It took me a couple of weeks to pluck up the courage to ask her to go out with me, and two dates before I kissed her. But once I'd kissed her, there was no holding back. We might have been young, but we were in love. And we told each other that beautiful fact on a balmy summer night, right before we made love for the first time. And it really was the first time. For both of us.

It was perfect too. Because she was perfect.

And I knew then that there would never be another woman for me.

Of course, it wasn't all plain sailing. We'd been together for just over a year, when I decided I didn't wanna toe the line and do my father's bidding. I didn't wanna follow the path he'd laid down for me since before I was even born, by joining our family business. And in a crazy act of rebellion – which I've gotta say was fairly typical of me back then – I joined the army instead.

My best friend Colt came with me, more out of boredom than anything, and when we got home again, and I told my parents, I honestly thought my father was gonna have a heart attack. He didn't. That came later. Much later. At the time, he yelled and paced, and pointed his finger, accusing me of betrayal. He actually called me Judas, which just made me laugh. Especially as I knew there was nothing he could do. I'd enlisted. It was a done deal.

Telling Eden about my decision was a whole other story, and I feared it far more than informing my father. I loved her, and I wasn't sure she'd understand my reasoning. She surprised me, despite my misgivings, and when I told her what I'd done, she simply threw her arms around me. It wasn't that long after 9/11, and I think she thought I was being heroic, taking a stand, righting a wrong. And although she was scared, she was also proud. She told me that herself. But then, it was easy to be proud to start with. Colt and I had to go through training before we could do anything else, and that meant we were still around – at least some of the time. And while Eden and I weren't able to have

319

that long summer we'd looked forward to sharing, at least I was there. Vaguely. I could still be with her, from time to time. The problem came when I got my orders to ship out to Afghanistan. That's when it all got real. Too real for Eden, anyway.

We fought then. Man, did we fight. I only had a couple of days before I had to leave, and while I'd looked forward to spending that time making love and holding her, and telling her how much I loved her, in reality, we spent almost all of it fighting. She'd changed her mind, she said. Being a hero and righting wrongs suddenly seemed a lot less important to her. She pleaded with me to stay, even though she must've known that was impossible. She cried and struck out at me, begging me to reconsider. And I reasoned with her that I couldn't. I'd made my decision.

That was when she called me selfish. It was the day before I was due to ship out and we'd been arguing inside her house, and getting nowhere. Again. And I'd decided to leave and try writing to her instead. Except she wasn't giving up, and she continued the argument, even as I opened the front door and stepped outside.

"You're a selfish asshole, Max," she yelled, and I turned to face her. "I didn't sign up for this."

"I know, but I need to do it."

"Why? So you can get even with your dad? Why do you have to defy him?"

I moved closer to her then, but she stepped back, so I still had to raise my voice, to explain, "It's not just about my dad. There's something I need to prove."

She stared at me for a moment and then burst into tears, her legs giving way as she collapsed to the floor in front of me. "You don't have to prove a damn thing to me," she sobbed, and I rushed forward, kneeling before her and holding her in my arms.

"I know. But I need to prove a few things to myself, Eden."

She leaned back then and stared at me, our eyes locked. "I'm so scared of losing you," she whispered.

"Don't be. I'm coming back." I grabbed her behind the neck and pulled her close, kissing her so hard it almost hurt. Her tongue clashed with mine and her breasts heaved against my chest, and for a moment, I thought about staying, about going AWOL, and just lying in her arms, forever.

But then she broke the kiss and turned to Colt, who was sitting in his car out on the street.

"Colt?" she called, and he looked around. She said his name a second time then, and he cocked his head, as though he didn't understand why she was repeating herself.

"Yeah?" he said.

"Don't you dare let him die, you hear?"

Colt nodded and gave her a fake salute. "No ma'am," he called back, and then Eden stood and held out her hand, and I took it and let her lead me back into the house.

Her parents were out at work, and we went straight up to her room, where we undressed each other and then lay on her bed and made love, with a hunger I don't think either of us had ever felt before. I watched her intently, taking in her perfect, slender body, her swollen lips, her hardened nipples. I felt her soft fingers caressing my skin, her hands around my stiff cock, her tongue licking over me, her mouth surrounding me, and her tight, wet pussy clamping down as she came… over and over. And I listened too, to every moan and sigh, to every cry of ecstasy and every time my name crossed her lips. I wanted to absorb it all, to carry it with me, to keep me sane through all the insanity I knew I was about to face.

Eventually, I had to leave, of course.

And I did.

But I came back.

And Eden was always there, waiting for me.

And the few months I had at home between each tour were like heaven here on earth. Because I could spend at least some of that time with Eden. And, for me, just a moment with her was worth a lifetime's waiting.

It was on my third tour that I was injured. Not that I have any memory of what happened that day, other than Colt's voice yelling for a medic, and telling me to hang on, as I drifted between life and death.

I saw Eden's face then, telling me not to leave her, begging me to stay. And I did. Somehow I made it out, thanks to Colt. And I got home again, to face several difficult surgeries. Eden was there, at my bedside, crying most of the time, and making me wish I could hold her and tell her it would all be okay. Because it was. With sheer determination and the help of a truly amazing doctor, I got back to her. Permanently. And then, once I'd gone through months of painful therapy, sufficient to regain the strength in my leg, and I could get down on one knee, knowing I'd be able to get back up again, I asked her to marry me. I wasn't gonna take a chance on losing her again. She threw herself into my arms then, and whispered, "Yes," in my ear, and I thought my heart was gonna burst in my chest. Because I was so damn happy.

That happiness continued for years and years. Endless... or so it seemed.

I'd had my taste of freedom, and it had nearly killed me. So, I went into the family business, following in my father's footsteps and becoming his understudy, knowing that one day, I would be the CEO of Crawford Hotels.

I'm not gonna say that working with my dad was easy, because it wasn't. We rarely agreed about anything. But that's hardly surprising, when you consider that I'd always resented him. From the moment I'd understood his intentions, I'd despised him for them. I loathed the fact that he'd chosen my life path without consulting me, and that he'd done the same for Chase and Bree, too. But in their case, while he was planning and controlling their lives, he wasn't including them in his business plans. I knew that right back then, even if they didn't. And I hated him for it. As they grew up, he dictated what he wanted them to do, where he wanted them to study, and what jobs he wanted them to undertake. Right down to the point of finding them employment, when the time eventually came. But no matter how hard they worked, or how deep their loyalty, there was never any question of them actually working for the company, or even having a share in it. Chase and Bree didn't know that all their hard work and diligence would eventually lead to nothing by way of reward. Or that our father was playing with them like they were his own personal puppets, in an inexcusable theater of his own making.

I knew, though. I've always known. But when he died – of that predictable heart attack – I ensured that Chase and Bree never discovered his true intentions. He'd bequeathed the three of us, and our mother, a share of his personal fortune, but he'd left the company – our family's future – entirely to me. I didn't like how that felt. So I signed over a third of the business to each of them and told them it had been our father's wish. I took on the role of CEO, just like he wanted, but I brought my brother and sister in-house, where they belonged, and we've been working together ever since.

I've never told them that their inheritance was really my gift, and not our father's. I've never told anyone. Not even Eden. Or Colt. It was my final act of rebellion against the old man, and just like joining the army, I've never regretted it.

I worked hard, but so did Eden. She loved her job, which back then was as a marketing assistant for a publishing company, and while we'd talked about having kids one day, we'd agreed when we got married that there was no rush. We were happy. We were the happiest people we knew…

Or at least I thought we were, up until that night, a little over three years ago, when I got home from work and found Eden sitting at the island unit in the kitchen of our house in Lexington. She wasn't cooking, or even studying our usual takeout menus. She was just staring into space.

She turned when she heard me come in and to start with, I wondered if she was gonna raise the subject of kids with me again. It wouldn't have surprised me. I'd had my thirty-fourth birthday just a couple of weeks beforehand, and even though Eden was a few months younger, we both knew time was moving on, and having a baby was something we'd talked about quite a lot, although not recently. We'd planned on starting a family a few years earlier, when we'd hit thirty. That had felt like a milestone – for both of us – and we'd sat down and talked everything through. Eden had surprised me then, deciding she wanted to wait just a little longer. There was a lot going on at work for her, and she asked if I'd mind waiting another year or so.

"I'm gonna take a career break," she'd reasoned. "But I need to time it right."

I'd wanted to tell her she didn't need to worry. That one advantage of being married to a multi-millionaire was that she didn't need to fret over things like career breaks. But I knew how much she loved her job, and how much it meant to her, so I agreed. What was one more year, after all?

But then, as with a lot of plans, it went wrong.

That year was almost up when my dad died, and I had to take over the business. It took me a while to get things organized, to bring Chase and Bree on board, and start running the place my way. And then, by the time things were a little more settled for me, and I'd established what I was doing, Eden got this great promotion at work, which meant much longer hours and a lot more responsibility. She was thrilled though, and I was so proud of her. And, I guess, between one thing and another, we'd never gotten around to it.

"Hey, what's wrong?" I asked her, going straight over to her side.

She looked up at me, tears welling in her eyes. "I need to talk to you," she whispered.

I felt an icy shiver of fear run through me, but I wasn't sure why. "Okay, talk," I said, sitting down next to her. I reached out to take her hand then, but she pulled it away and let it rest on her lap, and I think that's when I knew I wasn't gonna like whatever it was she had to say. And that it probably didn't have anything to do with babies.

She sighed deeply. "There's no easy way to say this," she murmured. "So I'm just gonna say it." She raised her head then, and looked me in the eye. "I'm having an affair."

I suppose I'd half expected something like that, just from her demeanor. But even so, her words hit me like bullets, piercing my heart.

"An affair?" I repeated, although I knew I'd heard her right.

"Yes."

"Who with?"

"Does it matter?"

I got up then, standing over her. "Of course it fucking matters." She startled, cowering back slightly. But I didn't care. I didn't care if she was scared. She'd broken us. "Who is he?" I thundered.

"Patrick. My boss." The words fell out of her mouth on a breath.

"Your boss? The guy you've been going to all the book fairs and functions with?" She nodded her head, blushing slightly, and suddenly things started to fit into place. The promotion she'd gotten at work had meant she'd not only had to work longer hours, but she'd had to travel more, to exhibitions and book festivals, all over the country. I wasn't happy about it, because I missed her when she wasn't with me, but I could see she loved what she did, and I didn't say anything. Looking back, knowing what she'd been doing in my absence and remembering how happy she'd been, I felt sick. Right to my core. "How long has it been going on for, Eden?"

She lowered her eyes again and mumbled, "A year. Give or take."

"So, since about six months after you got your promotion?"

"Give or take," she repeated, and I wondered about her vagueness.

"Did you sleep your way into that too?" I asked, bitterness lacing my voice.

"No." She sounded offended by my inference. But what right did she have to be offended by anything I said or did?

"So, you've been fucking your boss for a year?" I didn't want to think about the 'give or take'. "How often?" She blinked a few times, and I wondered if she was going to cry, and how I might react to that. Half an hour earlier, my instinct would have been to hold her. But now? I didn't want to touch her. I didn't want to be anywhere near her. "Forget I asked that," I said, stepping away. "I don't care how often you fucked him. I don't care about any of it."

And with those lies echoing in my ears, I turned away and went through the dining area and back out into the lobby, climbing the stairs to our bedroom, where I packed a bag. It didn't take me long, but then in the back of my mind, I was thinking I'd come back in a couple of days and collect everything else, when I knew she wasn't there. At the time, I just wanted out.

Downstairs, Eden was waiting for me in the lobby, leaning against the wall near the entrance to the dining room.

"You're leaving?" She sounded surprised and pushed herself off the wall, walking over to me.

"Of course I'm leaving. What do you expect me to do?"

"I don't know. Stay and talk? Work things out? I thought... I thought you loved me."

I laughed, although I have no idea how. "Are you serious?"

Looking at her face, tears streaming down her cheeks, it seemed she was.

But then, so was I.

I checked into one of our hotels and stayed hidden away from the world for a few days. Eden called so many times, I lost count, and after the first couple of hours, I turned off my phone. I wasn't in the mood for talking, or listening to her pleading to my voicemail, crying, and begging me to come home. I wanted to think. Although that wasn't such a great idea either, because all I could think about was Eden with her lover. Patrick. I'd met him a couple of times. He was tall, but not as tall as me, with an athletic build and a mop of dark blond hair. He wore glasses, but he wasn't bookish or geeky, and I couldn't deny he was handsome. Very handsome. Because of those images, I didn't sleep much. But that left me with a lot of time to consider my future, which looked bleak. Not to mention very sad and lonely, without her. Because as hard as it was living with the knowledge that she'd cheated, living without her was so much harder. She was a part of me, and when she wasn't there, I felt incomplete. I felt empty.

So, I called her.

I didn't ask where she was or if she was with him. I just asked if we could meet. She sounded pleased, enthusiastic even, and we chose a bar and set a date. Except it wasn't a date. It was nothing like a date. It was more like a negotiation. Or should that be interrogation?

I saw her straight away, the moment I walked in, and I'm not gonna deny, she looked good. She always looked good. She had on a dress that I liked. It was black, low cut, and very sexy, and I knew she must have worn it specially for me. Her makeup was subtle, but immaculate, and she'd put her hair up too, leaving just a few strands framing her face. And walking toward her, my eyes fixed on hers, that was the moment I realized I'd never stop loving her, no matter what. She looked nervous too, though, and as much as I wanted to take pity on her, I couldn't. She'd hurt me. Badly. And when I reached her table, and she stood and stepped forward to kiss me, I instinctively pulled back.

"I—I thought…" she whispered as we sat.

"You thought what?"

"I thought you wanted to get back together."

"I wanna talk, and then we'll see."

I'd missed her, and I needed her, but I needed answers first.

I waited until we'd ordered our drinks, although I don't think either of us was thirsty, and then I started. "Before we got married, when I was away in Afghanistan, and you promised you'd wait for me… did you? Did you wait for me? Or did you fuck around then too?"

"I haven't fucked around," she murmured a little sulkily, trying to sound insulted. "And yes, I waited for you."

"So, is Patrick the first?"

"Yes, he is."

I nodded my head. "Why did you do it?"

She sighed. "It's not personal, Max. It's not about you."

"Of course it's fucking personal. And who else is it about, if it's not about me?"

"What I mean is, it's not a reflection on you. I'm not… dissatisfied."

"Then why? I don't understand."

She hesitated, and then said, "Curiosity, I suppose. I've never been with anyone else."

"Neither have I."

"I know." She fell silent then, as the waitress brought over our drinks, setting them down on the table between us, before she drifted away again. "Patrick and I were at a book fair in New York," Eden said, in a quiet whisper. "He came onto me on our second night there. He told me he'd always liked me, always wanted me."

"And you forgot about us?" I couldn't believe what I was hearing. "Do you honestly think I've never been approached, or propositioned in all the years we've been together?" She stared at me but didn't reply. "I've never once been tempted," I told her firmly. "Not once." I paused and took a sip of wine before putting my glass down again. "Was there something I wasn't doing for you? Is it that I wasn't romantic enough? Was I not paying you enough attention? Is that what this is about?"

She shook her head. "You were always romantic, and attentive. That's what I've missed most over the last few days."

I didn't want to talk about how much I'd missed her, so instead I said, "Was it just about sex then? Was there something I wasn't giving you that he could? Because to my knowledge, there isn't anywhere I haven't fucked you. So whatever it was you were looking for, please tell me. I'd love to know."

She shook her head. "I've already said, I wasn't unhappy with you, and I wasn't 'looking' for anything. He made the suggestion. He asked me to go to bed with him. And I guess I just wanted to know what it would be like with someone else."

"And what? Once you'd found that out, you decided you'd keep on trying? Just in case it was different the second time around, or the third, or the fourth?" I leaned forward. "You've been screwing the guy for a year, or more. That's a helluva long time to work out your curiosity. Or did curiosity become something else?" I sat back again, my fear threatening to choke me. "A—Are you in love with him?" I asked the dreaded question.

"No," she said. "I'm in love with you."

"Really? You expect me to believe that?"

"Yes. It's the truth."

I wanted to tell her that her version of 'the truth' didn't really count for much anymore. But I didn't, because I'd asked to see her, and I did wanna try to work things out. And fighting wasn't gonna achieve that.

So I took a much larger sip of wine and looked up at her again.

"Are you still seeing him?" I asked.

"No. I broke it off with him, the other night. The night I told you." She reached across the table, but I didn't react and eventually she pulled her hand away again. "I want you back, Max," she said. "Please."

"How much do you want me back?" I asked her and she tipped her head to one side because she didn't understand me.

"What does that mean? Are you trying to blackmail me, or something?"

"No. I'm just asking what you'd be willing to do to get me back."

"Are we talking about sex?" she said, a smile twitching at her lips, and I leaned forward again.

"No, we're not. I've got a condition attached to me coming back, and to us trying again. But before I tell you what that is, being as you've raised the subject, you've gotta understand one thing…"

"What's that?"

"If we do get back together, it's probably gonna be a while before I wanna have sex with you again."

She gulped then, but nodded her head. "I—I guess I can understand that," she whispered. "So, what's your condition?"

"It's non-negotiable, Eden, and if you say 'no', I'll walk away now, and you'll never see me again."

She sucked in a breath, looking scared. "Tell me," she whispered.

"I want you to give up your job." Her face paled, and she swallowed hard. "You love what you do, and I get that, but I need you to prove you love me more. That's the only way this is gonna work. I know you say you've broken things off with him…"

"I have," she interrupted.

I didn't answer her. Not directly. Instead, I just said, "I can't bear the thought of you going into work every day and seeing him, or him seeing you. You shared your body with him. You gave him something that you vowed was mine, and mine alone. So if you want me back, it's all, or nothing, I'm afraid."

"I'll do it," she said, without hesitation, and I actually let out a sigh of relief. Right before I stood up. "Wait… where are you going?" she asked.

"Back to the hotel."

"But… but… I thought…"

"You thought I was gonna come home tonight?" I guessed.

"Well, yes. I've agreed—"

I shook my head, and she stopped talking. "I'll come home when you're not working anywhere near that guy. And not before. Call me when you've resigned."

"Will your phone be turned on?" she asked, with more than a hint of sarcasm.

"Yes. I only turned it off because I needed time to think." That wasn't a lie.

"And because you didn't wanna talk to me," she added.

"No, I didn't." That wasn't a lie either. "Let me know when he's not a part of your life anymore, Eden."

"He's not," she said, getting up and looking into my eyes. She reached out to touch me, her fingertips almost making it to my arm, but I backed off just in time. "Please, Max… please." She sighed, withdrawing her hand. "I've broken it off with him already. I promise. And I'll resign tomorrow. But… but I've gotta work out my notice."

"And how long is that?"

"Three months. They increased it after I was promoted. But, Max, I can't…"

"I'll come home in three months, then." I didn't let her finish. Nothing she said was gonna change my mind. "I won't live under the same roof as you while you're still seeing him… in any capacity. Is that clear?"

She nodded her head, and without saying another word, I turned and left.

I'll admit, I spent a sleepless night contemplating three months without her, because while I was adamant I wasn't going back until she was free of him, I didn't relish that prospect. By two-thirty in the morning, I'd convinced myself that, when she handed in her resignation, he'd beg her to stay, and that she'd allow herself to be persuaded; that he had some hold over her that I didn't. And then, tortured by what he might offer her that I couldn't, I got up and paced the floor, wondering if she'd ended it with him at all. I imagined her leaving the bar and going straight to his place, and I pictured them together, driving myself half mad with images of him pleasuring her.

It was because of that sleepless night that I ended up showering late, and therefore didn't pick up the phone, when Eden called the next morning. She left a message though…

"It's me. You asked me to call when I'd resigned, and I have. I did it first thing this morning as soon as I got to the office. I don't expect you to like this, but I had to give the letter to Patrick. Personally. Because he's still my boss. Or he was, anyway. I—I told him I needed to leave right away, with no notice, because I don't want to wait three months, Max. I want you back now. And, although he wasn't happy – about any of it – he agreed. I'm at home now. I've done what you wanted. So, please can you come back to me?"

I could hear the crack in her voice as she hung up, and although I really ought to have gone to work, I decided not to. Because we had a deal.

I let myself in and dropped my bag on the floor just as Eden came running through from the dining room, stopping short in the lobby and staring at me. She was dressed for work still, in a fitted white blouse and dark gray skirt that ended just above her knee and clung to her hips like it was glued to her. And I remembered then that she'd dressed like this every day since just after she won that damned promotion, and I knew it had all been for him.

"You came." She looked surprised.

"I said I would. I keep my promises, Eden."

She clearly felt the intended jibe, but she ignored it and stepped forward, and I felt something like static electricity pass between us. She must've felt it too, because her eyes sparkled, and as much as I tried to fight it, I couldn't. I moved toward her and grabbed her, holding her against me and kissing her… hard. Moaning into my mouth, she pulled her blouse from the waistband of her skirt, undoing the buttons, then huffed impatiently, and broke our kiss to yank it over her head, throwing it to the floor. She gazed up at me, her lips swollen. But suddenly kissing felt too intimate, so I reached out, pulling down the cups of her bra, exposing her breasts and I leaned in close, biting on her nipples, as I undid her skirt, pushing it over her hips and letting it fall to the floor for her to step out of, before I stood again and walked her backwards until she hit the wall that led into the dining room, my body hard against hers.

I'd told her it would be a while before I'd be ready to have sex with her again, and I knew I was about to prove myself wrong. I think I even knew that what I was about to do was a mistake. But I didn't care. I needed to stake my claim.

I tore her lace thong from her body, undoing my pants and lowering my zipper at the same time, and then, raising her left leg over my right arm, I entered her. And I fucked her. She came. Twice. Her screams echoed around the lobby, her hands clutched at me, her legs trembling and her breathing hard and ragged, as I hammered into her, eventually exploding silent and deep inside her.

She flopped into my arms, but I couldn't hold her. I couldn't bring myself to put my arms around her. So instead, I let her go, lowering her leg to the floor and pulling out of her. My cock was still hard, and she looked downwards before raising her eyes to mine, the fire glowing within them.

"You want more?" she said, and I nodded my head, because I wanted everything. I wanted all of her. She was mine. And I needed to prove it, to myself, as much as anything.

She turned away from me and bent slightly, her hands resting on the wall for support, her ass framed by her black garter belt, and I knew what she had in mind, reaching out, and letting my hands wander over her perfect skin. She parted her legs a little, and I moved between them, the head of my cock resting against her tightest hole… that once forbidden place I'd first claimed so many years before, with my fingers and then, finally, with my cock.

I pushed inside her and she let out a hiss of satisfaction, just like she always did, nudging back into me to get my whole length, and I obliged, pounding into her, harder than ever, until she came a third time, begging me not to stop… never to stop.

She felt so good, so tight, so mine. And then, as that thought crossed my mind, another, more horrible one took shape, and I stopped moving.

"Tell me you didn't let him fuck you here." My voice sounded strained, but horrible thoughts can do that, I've found.

She twisted her head around, looking back at me over her shoulder. "No," she said, sounding offended again. "I'd never have brought him to our house."

She'd misunderstood me, and while I wasn't sure if that was intentional or not, I was at least relieved that she hadn't brought her sordid affair into our home.

She'd just brought it into our marriage.

Even so, I couldn't let it go. I had to know.

"I wasn't talking about the house, Eden. I was talking about you. Here." I flexed my hips just slightly, to make my point more obvious, and then I held still. So still, I could hear her sigh. "You did, didn't you? You let him fuck your ass."

I pulled out of her, and she stood upright, turning around to face me.

"I'm sorry," she whispered, and I staggered backwards. I might have come back to her, but as I thought about the reality of her with another man, and the intimacy that entailed, it all suddenly became too raw, like a wave of pain and sorrow, and hurt and anger, hitting me all at once. And I knew, if I didn't get out of there, I was going to lose control. "Are you okay?" Her voice came at me through the foggy haze of emotions. But it was the last thing I wanted to hear.

"Of course I'm not okay." She stepped toward me, but I held up my hands, stopping her. "This was a mistake."

"What? Coming back here?" I could hear the fear in her voice, and although it touched something deep inside me – that hard-wired element of me that was built to protect her – I turned away. "Max?" she said, after a very long silence. "Are you gonna leave me again?"

"No," I said, taking a breath and regaining my composure, although I'll admit, I glanced at the front door, feeling tempted to use it. "I told you I'd come back if you left your job, and you did. But I shouldn't have done what we just did. I'm not ready."

I pulled up my pants, tucking myself in, and walked over toward the door.

"Where are you going?" She came after me, clutching at my arm, her panic rising.

I shook myself free of her. "I'm gonna go upstairs and unpack," I said, grabbing my bag and trudging up the stairs.

I didn't look back.

And, wisely, she didn't follow me.

It was only after we'd spent the day in separate parts of the house, and then eaten a silent, awkward dinner, that we decided to go to bed, and that's when Eden realized I'd set myself up in the guest room, rather than our own.

"I told you, I'm not ready," I explained, when she queried what was going on, standing in the hallway outside our bedroom door.

"You seemed ready enough earlier." She sounded bitter. Hurt. Used. And I wanted to laugh at the irony of that.

"Yeah. But like I said, I shouldn't have done that."

"Then why did you?" she asked, raising her voice.

I wasn't sure what right she felt she had to be angry with me, but I stayed calm, not rising to the bait.

"To stake a claim; to prove you're mine. But I was wrong."

"No, you weren't. I am yours."

"Not in my head, you're not." I moved closer to her. "These clothes," I said, touching the soft fabric of her blouse. "You wore them for him, didn't you?" She didn't answer, and I stared into her clouded eyes. "You used to dress differently," I continued. "Before... before him, your clothes were much less fitted, less revealing. Did he like you to wear things like this?" She cleared her throat nervously and then nodded her head. "And you did it?"

"Yes."

"Even though I've never asked you to do anything like that for me? Even though I've never once asked you to change a single thing about yourself for my benefit?"

"You asked me to leave my job," she countered.

"For the sake of our marriage. Not for my sexual gratification." She bowed her head. "Why, Eden? Why did you change for him?"

She looked up at me and sighed. "Because he made it so... exciting."

That hurt. A lot.

"Was I that boring?" The words fell from my mouth and she reached out for me, even as I stepped away, protecting myself.

"No." Her voice rang out. "You were never boring. I—I just wanted to try something new. Something different."

"And you couldn't do that with me? I would've done anything for you. You know that."

She took a breath and shook her head. "I'm sorry, Max," she whispered.

"You think 'sorry' makes it okay? You think it's gonna help me forget you were his, and not mine, for all those months? You think 'sorry' is gonna stop me remembering that when you went away on those business trips with him, while I was sitting here, missing you, it was his lips that were kissing you, his fingers that were touching you... his cock that was inside you?"

"If you feel like that, why did you come back?" she asked, tears brimming in her eyes, and I let out a long sigh, pushing my fingers back through my hair, and trying to remember the reasons myself.

"Because I want you to be mine again," I said eventually. And it was true. Despite everything, deep down, I wanted her back. "But we can't click our fingers and pretend your affair never happened. I need time, Eden. You only told me about this guy a few days ago. You can't expect me to act like everything's okay, just because you want it to be."

She turned away then and opened our bedroom door. "Is it ever gonna be okay?" she said, the sadness in her voice touching my frozen heart.

"I hope so," I replied. Because I did. I really did.

I lay in bed that night, knowing she was just down the hall, wanting her so much, but realizing that if we were gonna make it work, we had to take things slow. I'd been wrong to take her like I had. That was just papering over the cracks. And I didn't wanna do that.

So, I took some time off work, using my home office when I had to, but devoting as much of each day as I could to us, and our relationship. I needed to find a way back. I needed to rediscover the woman I'd fallen in love with. Because while my love for her was never in doubt, I felt like

I didn't know her anymore. And if we were gonna stand a chance, then I needed to take the time and make the effort to get to know her again.

It was beyond awkward for those first few days, because neither of us knew what to say to the other, and Eden's sentences almost always began with the word 'Sorry', which didn't seem like a great way to move forward. It was hard not to notice that she'd gone back to wearing less formal clothes; the things she always wore at home, on the weekends, when she wasn't with him. And initially, I really struggled with comparisons, even though I tried not to think like that. It was hard though, not to wonder why she'd let him dictate what she should wear, why she'd called him 'exciting', whether he was better in bed than me.

But then, one evening, about ten days after my return, we watched a movie together, and because it was a comedy, Eden laughed, and hearing that sound flicked a switch deep inside me. A memory, I guess. And I turned off the television and moved closer to her.

"We used to laugh more, didn't we?" I said, and she looked up at me.

"What do you mean?"

"Before your affair, we used to laugh more."

She lowered her eyes, because we hadn't mentioned the 'A' word since the day I'd come back. But we couldn't keep avoiding it. We needed to talk, without recriminations. So I reached over and placed my finger beneath her chin, raising her face to mine. She gasped at my touch, and although I withdrew my finger again, she maintained eye contact now. And I knew the time had come.

"Yes," she whispered.

"So, did we stop laughing because you were having an affair? Or was it the other way around? Did you have an affair because we stopped laughing?"

She sighed. "I don't know, Max. And I'm not sure it matters."

"It matters to me. If you were unhappy…"

"I wasn't," she interrupted, moving closer to me on the couch. "Please believe me, I was never unhappy with you. I know it's hard for you to understand, but that's the truth, Max."

I looked into her eyes, seeing a sad desperation, and the distant echo of a woman I'd loved for as long as I could remember, and I think I knew then that there was only one way forward for both of us. And looking back had no part in it.

"We need to laugh again," I said, and she tipped her head to one side, surprise etched on her face.

"We haven't had much to laugh about lately. Thanks to me."

"That's true." I didn't see the point in denying it, especially as another vital ingredient in moving forward was going to have to be honesty. In everything. "But we can look to the future, can't we? Instead of looking backwards?"

"How?"

I shrugged my shoulders. "To be honest, I don't know. But there's gotta be a way. I refuse to believe there isn't. I very much doubt it's gonna be easy. And I fully expect that things will be a little different between us."

"In what way?" she asked.

"I've got no idea. But it wouldn't surprise me if I didn't sometimes get suspicious, or jealous, even though I was never either of those things before. I haven't forgotten what happened, and I haven't forgiven you. Not yet. But I want to. I wanna work this out. I wanna be us again. It might be a different version of us. It might be a better version of us. Who knows?" I reached out and cupped her cheek with my hand, and she gasped again, closing her eyes for a second. "You're the only woman I've ever loved, Eden," I said, when she opened them again, and I saw they were glistening. "What you did... it broke my heart. It damn near broke me." She blinked, a tear fell onto her cheek, and I wiped it away with my thumb. "But I don't wanna be broken any more. I wanna start mending... mending us."

"Then sleep with me," she said in a quiet whisper. "Make love to me. Please. I need you, Max. Y—You say you've always loved me, then show it. Show me your love."

She looked up at me, the emotion in her eyes too painful for me to interpret. And that instinct to protect her kicked in. I had to heal us. I had to take the first step toward forgiveness and a new beginning. It had to come from me. So I leaned in and brushed my lips across hers, every nerve in my body sparking at the contact.

And then I stood and carried her up the stairs to our room, where I made love to her. I didn't fuck her. I made love to her. I gazed into her eyes the whole time, kissing her, touching her, joining our bodies, and yes… making her mine. It was hard not to picture her with him, and while I was tempted to ask her whether he'd been better than me, I didn't. Because this was about love, not pride. It was about us, not him. When we came – together – she cried. And so did I. And when she noticed my tears and started to say sorry, on a whispered sob, I stopped her, and I held her, and I told her I loved her.

And then I wrapped her in my arms until sleep claimed us.

I moved back into our room the very next morning, and we spent a couple of days in bed, rediscovering each other, before I had to go back to work. My professional responsibilities were calling out for my attention, and I had to answer. And while I still had moments when I thought about what had happened, I tried not to let them dominate. I tried to focus on the future, not the past.

And the future took on a whole new light when, about a week later, I got back from work, and Eden met me in the lobby, looking a little weird… kinda worried and edgy, but kinda excited at the same time.

"I need to talk to you," she said, and I felt afraid, because I could still remember very vividly the last time she'd said those words to me.

"W—Why?" I asked, unable to stop myself from stuttering.

She smiled then. "Don't look so scared. It's nothing bad. At least, I don't think it is."

"Can you just tell me? Whatever it is?"

"I'm pregnant."

I hadn't expected that. I don't know what I'd expected. But it wasn't that.

"You're… you're pregnant?"

"Yes." She nodded her head. "And before you ask the inevitable question… it's yours."

"I—I wasn't gonna ask that." She looked at me, tilting her head to one side. "Okay, so maybe I would've done… eventually. But can you blame me, in the circumstances?"

"No. But I know it's yours because the timing is right. I've checked the dates and the day you came back here was exactly halfway through my cycle. And besides, I—I always made him use condoms."

I liked the fact that she hadn't used his name, especially at a time like that. "You always made *me* use condoms," I reasoned.

I looked down at her and she smiled. "I know. But if you remember, you didn't use one that first time, did you? When you were staking your claim." I winced slightly at the memory, but she didn't seem to notice, and added, "And I've never really *made* you. It was more of a mutual agreement. And it wasn't my fault that I couldn't tolerate the hormones in contraceptives." That much was true. She'd tried taking the pill early on in our relationship and hadn't gotten along with it at all. I'd appreciated her trying, though. And she was right. I hadn't used a condom when I'd come back here that day. It hadn't been intentionally done, but then none of that was intentional. Or maybe some of it was. Maybe I wanted to get her pregnant... to really stake my claim. I've never been able to work it out.

"So, we're gonna have a baby?" I said at last, and she nodded her head.

"Are you happy?" she asked.

"Yeah, I am."

I was too. It felt like a new beginning.

Tia was born the following February, and watching Eden go through labor gave me a new respect for her. And for all women, I guess. I've been shot. I've come close to death, and I've known real pain, both physical and emotional, but I'd never really understood love until that day. Seeing what Eden had to go through to bring our daughter into the world, and then witnessing the love between the two of them at the moment Tia was born... it was miraculous. And it brought this man to tears.

It also brought Eden and me so much closer together. It was as though we renewed our love for each other through Tia, and between us all, we created a new bond; a much stronger one. I was still sometimes haunted by nightmares and memories, and I'm not gonna claim things were perfect. But they were getting there. We were working at it. Together.

Tia would have been a couple of months old when Eden announced over breakfast one morning that she'd joined a gym, and that she had an appointment that morning to meet her new fitness instructor.

"What's her name?" I asked, taking an interest, because I knew Eden was bothered about the weight she'd gained during the pregnancy, and which she was having trouble losing. It didn't matter to me. I loved her, regardless of what size she was. But I knew it mattered to her.

"*His* name is Darius."

"Your trainer is a man?" I felt a chill run down my spine.

"Yes. He's giving me a two-hour session today, and hopefully, if it works out, then I can go a couple of times a week."

"And who's gonna look after Tia?" I was putting up roadblocks – or at least trying to – and I knew it.

"Your mom. I spoke to her yesterday afternoon, after Darius called to confirm the appointment. She's gonna come over here and babysit, while I'm gone." Eden reached out, touching my arm with her hand. "She's really looking forward to it."

"I'm sure she is."

"Max, what's wrong?" She looked at me, frowning. "Don't you want me to go?"

"Honest answer… no, I don't. Look, if you wanna get fit, I can have a gym installed here, in the pool complex."

"I know. But I wanna get out of the house. I miss going to work. And I miss seeing other people."

"Any people in particular?" The words left my lips before I could stop them, and she sat back, startled.

"No. But it's very clear you still don't trust me."

I sucked in a breath. "I'm trying to."

I saw the tears in her eyes. "I—I thought we were past all this."

"We are, for the most part. But sometimes, it comes back to me. I can't help it. I still picture you with him, and it's hard… it's hard to forget," I replied with absolute honesty.

"But surely, you know I'd never hurt you again," she said, almost pleading. "You have to believe that, at least."

"I never thought you'd hurt me in the first place, Eden."

My words hit her, and she broke down in front of me, her tears flowing as I stood and pulled her to her feet and into my arms.

"Forgive me," she whimpered into my chest. "Please, Max, please. You have to forgive me."

"I'm trying. I really am."

She leaned back then, looking up into my face. "If you don't want me to go, I'll cancel the appointment."

I shook my head, knowing that keeping her in the house wasn't gonna help, no matter how hard I was still finding it to let her go. She'd eventually hate me for imprisoning her, and we had to live a normal life, with all the freedoms that involved. Or it would all have been for nothing. "No. You don't have to do that."

"Then you do trust me?"

"I love you. Is that enough?"

She sighed, and I could feel her disappointment. "Why can't you take that last leap?" she asked. "Why can't you accept that I'm never gonna cheat again, and trust me?"

I pulled her close to me again. "I'm getting there. Honestly. I'm doing my best."

I spent the whole morning worrying, talking myself in and out of different scenarios, and then chastising myself for not trusting her, for even thinking that she'd cheat again, after everything we'd been through, right before the image of her with 'Darius', or whatever his name was, would spring into my head again.

She'd said she was gonna call when she got home, and when it got to midday and I hadn't heard anything, I started to worry.

I started to panic an hour later, when my mom called and said Eden still wasn't home, so I called her cell, and it went straight to voicemail, those images becoming all too real.

But then at just after two, my phone rang, and I saw her name appear on the screen. I heaved out my relief and answered, reminding myself not to question her, but to trust her…

"How did it go?" I asked as a greeting.

"Max Crawford?"

The man's voice on the end of the phone took me by surprise.

"Yes. Who's this?"

"It doesn't matter who I am. What does matter is that I've got your wife." My heart stopped beating.

"What do you want?"

"I want you to shut up and listen. Now, if you ever wanna see her pretty face again, you'll fill a sports bag with a million dollars in hundred-dollar bills, and you'll leave it by the Parkman Bandstand in Boston Common at six pm."

I stood up, even though my legs could barely support me. "What about Eden?"

"She'll be there, don't you worry."

"How do I know she's still alive?"

There was a moment's silence, and then I heard, "Max…?" It was Eden, and she sounded terrified.

"Eden? Are you okay?"

"No. Please, Max…"

They cut her off, and after a second or two the man came back on the phone. "Satisfied?" he said.

"No, of course I'm not fucking satisfied. Lay one finger on her and I'll…"

"You'll what? I don't think you're in a position to be making threats, do you?"

I took a deep breath. "I'll get your money. I'll do what you want. Just don't hurt her."

The man laughed. "Do what I ask, and I won't. I might play with her a little though."

The line went dead, and I dropped my phone, clenching my fists as I let out a roar that started in my stomach and filled the room, reverberating around and coming straight back to me, breaking my heart.

My secretary, Valerie, came crashing through the door. "Are you hurt, Mr. Crawford?" she asked, and I stared at her, trying to get my brain to work; trying not to fall apart, because I couldn't. I had to keep it together. I had to get Eden back.

"No, I'm fine," I said, surprised by the normality of my voice. "Can you get my bank on the phone? That's *my* bank, not the company's one. And then can you call the police?"

She stared and then departed, almost as quickly as she'd arrived, and I flopped into my seat, wondering if involving the cops was the right way to go. The man on the phone hadn't said not to, and I was guessing he'd assumed I would. So why not? I sure as hell didn't know what I was doing.

The next few hours are still a blur. A detective called Skinner arrived at my office within about fifteen minutes of me explaining the situation to him. He tried to talk me out of paying the ransom, but soon realized he was wasting his time, and spent the next hour on the phone making plans, while I arranged for the money to be delivered, and finally plucked up enough courage to call my mom and tell her what was going on, and ask her to stay with Tia. Not that she needed asking.

I'd never been more scared in my life. Not even when I'd been in Afghanistan. Not even when I'd faced death. But Detective Skinner made it sound like this kind of thing was all in a day's work. And I let myself believe him, as I placed the bag by the bandstand, and walked away, hoping and praying that Eden would be in my arms again soon.

What happened next is a confused mess of memories and nightmares. I remember a man, wearing torn jeans and a denim jacket, with a Yankees baseball cap on his dark head, walking up to the bandstand, opening the bag, and then making a phone call. And then I saw another guy approach, with Eden beside him, and I felt overwhelmed with a mixture of exhilaration and anger. She looked disheveled and terrified, her eyes darting around, searching for me, I guessed. I didn't wanna think about what they'd done to her and I went to move forward, but Skinner held me back, reassuring me he had men surrounding the area, and that the kidnappers wouldn't get away… and just as he said that, all hell broke loose. I don't know what happened, whether the kidnappers were spooked by something, or one of the cops got an itchy trigger finger, but someone fired a shot. And before I knew what was happening, we were in the middle of a gunfight. And, even though Skinner was screaming into his radio for his men to cease firing, it was too late. I saw Eden buckle and fall to the ground and I took off across the park, stray bullets still raining around me. But by the time I got to her, she was already dead, blood seeping from a wound in her chest, and another in her stomach. I fell to my knees beside her, holding her in my arms, and howled out my grief. Because despite everything she'd done, I still loved her. And I wanted more time to make things right again.

Eventually, Skinner pulled me free, and he took me home, where my mom burst into tears, thinking that the blood on my shirt was mine, and then crying again, when Skinner explained it was Eden's, and that she was dead. Mom offered to stay, to help out, but I declined. I wanted to be alone. And so she and Skinner left, and I sat for a while… numb, unable to take it in. And then it got too much for me, so I called the only person I could think of.

I called Colt.

He was there within fifteen minutes, and he's been with me ever since, because as well as helping me grieve, and cope, and keep it together, the one thing I needed him to do, more than anything, was to keep my family safe. To make sure that I never had to lose anyone else I love.

Colt had started a security business when we came out of the military, and he agreed to put bodyguards on my whole family, and that he would guard me himself. Personally. I was grateful for that, especially at the beginning, when just breathing in and out was such a struggle, because while I might have a brother and a sister, who I love dearly, no-one gets me quite like Colt.

He was with me when Detective Skinner called round a few days after Eden's death and told me that there hadn't been any sexual assault involved. I collapsed when I heard that. I'd been imagining all kinds of things ever since her death, and while nothing was going to bring her back, at least I knew she hadn't been raped. Skinner also informed me that, although both the kidnappers were dead, the police had pieced together some information from their phone records, and emails, and had reached the conclusion that the two guys had followed Eden from the house, rather than picking her up randomly at the gym. Knowing that she'd been deliberately targeted made me even more nervous, and with Colt's help I increased the security at my home, as well as making sure that Bree and Chase, and my mom were not only guarded, but were living in properties that had enough security to keep them safe.

Call me paranoid, but I never wanna go through anything like that again.

Ever.

I rarely talk about what happened. I hardly ever talk about Eden, and never about her affair. I can't bring myself to remember that our 'perfect' marriage wasn't what it seemed.

That said, I mentioned it to Colt last summer. But that was only because he was being a dick to my sister, blaming Bree for a situation that wasn't entirely her fault, and making them both suffer as a result. My revelations shocked the hell out of him, but I knew he'd always regarded Eden and I as the ideal couple. As had a lot of people, myself included. And I wanted him to understand that being in love with someone isn't always what it seems, and it sure as hell doesn't give you the right to hurt them. Even if they've hurt you. I think he probably knew that already. He just needed to have it reiterated to him, in words of one syllable, being as he'd forgotten when he was well off.

Other than that, though, no-one knows about Eden's affair.

And I prefer to keep it that way. I can hide my anger and my hurt, and let everyone else believe I had it perfect... even though I know I didn't. Even though I know my wife didn't love me enough to be faithful to me. Yeah, we were working things out, and trying to get back to something close to what we'd had before, but I'm never gonna be able to escape the fact that, for at least a year of our supposedly perfect marriage, my wife was sleeping with another man.

I haven't dated at all since her death, because I'm not sure I could trust anyone. I trusted Eden, and look where that got me. And anyway, I've got Tia to think about. She's my focus.

She was only two months old when her mom died, and she has no memory of her at all.

At the beginning, my mother helped with caring for Tia, although I wanted to do as much of it as I could myself. I wanted to feel the connection to Eden through our daughter. But I have to work. And my mom has a life of her own. So, about three months in, I started hiring nannies. And that's when my problems really began.

I've lost count of the number of nannies we've had, but we're well into double figures. It's not that I'm difficult to work for – at least I don't think I am – but for various reasons, none of them have lasted. They generally seem to fall into two categories; the older ones are really strict with Tia, who's not quite two and a half, even now, and doesn't need to grow up living by an inflexible set of rules. I was raised like that, and I don't want it for her. And the younger ones? Well, they have a horrendous habit of hitting on me, to the point of embarrassment.

I don't understand why it's so hard to find someone who'll just do their job, look after my daughter, with kindness and consideration, and leave me alone.

But, having had a couple of complete disasters over the last few months, I've decided not to trust the agency to make the selection for me, and I'm gonna carry out the interviews myself.

I've got four women coming to my office today, all supposedly hand-picked by the agency to my specifications.

I guess only time will tell if any of them prove to be what I'm looking for.

... to be continued

Printed in Great Britain
by Amazon

49559390R00196